THE CRIMSON SNOW

THE CRIMSON SNOW

A REALM OF CHAOS AND VOID

LAURA VEGA

The Crimson Snow

Cover design: Olivia Cazacu

Edited by Kate Popa

Formatted by: Daiana M.

E-book ASIN: B0D57V9SBC

Paperback ISBN: 9789695692493

Hardcover ISBN: 9789695692486

To all who have embarked on journeys sparked by heartbreak, wandering as ghosts through their own stories—this is only the beginning of your adventure. Remember, even tears can turn into butterflies.

Shadowmarket
OTHERWORLD REALM
Mystweave Library
Mirror Alley
Screams & Pierces
Shadow Center
The Veil
The Wailing Forest
The Weeping Forest
Wraithwood Household
Ashcroft Household
Shadowmere Row
Clock Tower
Haunted House
Iceveil Square Plaza
Coldhaven
HUMAN REALM

PART I

Tales of the Crimson Fox & the Hungry Wolf

In the realm of crimson and horror's embrace,
A clever white fox danced with grace.
Was she born to such blood and dread,
Or did a lonely wolf lead her instead?

What if the crimson's hue, so bright,
Hid secrets darker than the night?
Perhaps the fox, with cunning gleam,
Was truly the architect of the scheme.

Who bears the blame in this twisted game,
Destiny's hand or the wolf's untamed aim?
Or is it the cleverness of the fox's wile,
That weaves the threads of this haunting style.

Retrieved from *Golden Tales from the Otherworld*
by Galen Sorrowspring, Ch. 5, p. 78.

PRELUDE

A haunting tapestry of red and white draped the world. The girl's hands bore the stains of scarlet and snow—a chilling emblem of the carnage she had orchestrated. Crimson splattered the landscape, each droplet a silent witness to her deeds. Where she once might have recoiled from such gruesome sights, she now found herself captivated by their stark beauty and inherent chaos.

The almost innocent creature pondered regret, a shadowy presence just beyond her reach. Would it haunt her, this silent accomplice to her actions? She welcomed the thought, yearning for guilt to someday burden her soul. Yet, for now, she reveled in the comforting emptiness that defined her. Tears and screams echoed in the distance. "Such pitiful creatures," she mused, smirking.

"Didn't I tell you?" A voice, unmistakably sinister, slithered into her ear, dripping with dark allure. The girl recognized it instantly. "That you would become the most magnificent villain this world has ever seen?"

Then, the voice dissipated into the wind. With a flourish of malevolence, she allowed herself a wicked, full-bodied grin.

Her eyes, deep ruby red and devoid of remorse, danced with cruel delight. She wondered if everything had transpired for her to become the mastermind destined to bring down the realms once again. She was not just a villain but the architect of their downfall—and she laughed because no one else knew.

The girl heard the clock start again. It was a countdown for them, for him. For the first time, she relished the noise of time, the din of the void and chaos.

Chapter I

The White Fox

Once upon the snow, a lone white fox wandered—clever, yet solitary.
In a world cloaked in white, it hid, fearful of being seen,
craving company.
It roamed the wintry woods, finding solace in the quiet of the night,
Yearning for connection beneath the soft glow of cold starlight.

Retrieved from *The Great Love Story of The White Fox*
by Illyra Everdawn, Ch. 1, p. 5.

Five Days Before the Incident
Seraphine Ashcroft

Seraphine darted through Coldhaven's dark alleys, her crimson cloak torn, her heavy furred brown dress a vivid slash against shadow-drenched cobblestones and snow. The cold air brushed her cheeks with icy kisses. As she navigated the streets, she paused to glance at the welcome sign and rolled her crimson eyes. "Where fairness and judgment purport to rule," she read mockingly, aware that the city was far from fair. Perhaps she should scratch that out.

"*Where lies and deceit call the shots, watch out for the sneaky smiles around town*" seemed more fitting.

The town was a sad view. The stone buildings were cracking, the ground was gray and lifeless, and everything deteriorated year after year. There was also a certain smell. It wasn't bad but felt wrong, as if something were rotting from the inside out, and maybe it was. Perhaps they all were. Coldhaven had been cursed to endure an endless winter. While Seraphine adored the snow, people prayed to the Ancient Brannon, protector of all human realms—not that he had done anything for this town—for a spark of warmth. It was an ironic hope, given their prevailing coldness. The townsfolk were as harsh and unyielding as the frost gripping the streets, often cruel—sometimes to the world, but mostly to her.

Although Seraphine denied it to herself, she longed to belong, for them to appreciate and recognize her as one of them. However, they never did. *They never will.* Most saw an omen of bad luck and chaos in her, all because of some unfounded rumor about her "nature."

To her, this town felt more like a prison than a home, where unfounded lies and judgy eyes caged her.

tick-tock

tick-tock

tick-tock

tick-tock

Seraphine paused at the clock tower. Rising tall and imposing at the center of Coldhaven, it was the only building radiating beauty and life. "You, my dear clock, are quite the spectacle," she murmured, half-expecting the ancient tower to respond. *Maybe it will,* she noted. She had seen stranger things.

Yet, what truly made her pause was the certainty of being watched—perhaps by the moon or something more sinister. *Hopefully, the latter,* Seraphine mused with a sarcastic smile. "Shy, shy, shy, aren't you?" she taunted, addressing no one in particular as she left the clock behind.

Ding-dong

Ding-dong

Ding-dong

Ding-dong

The clock struck midnight. "For Brannon's sake!" Seraphine exclaimed, shocked by how incredibly late it had become.

Seraphine had lost track of time while working at Iceveil Square Plaza that evening. She typically handled simple tasks—clearing snow, filleting fish—tasks most people avoided. Although the owners were reluctant to hire her, she completed these jobs quickly. Today, however, was different. A conversation she had overheard in Mr. Eliah's tailor shop captured her attention.

"I must be cursed," a young woman in her twenties had declared to the tailor. She was draped in a tight cream dress, excessively adorned with fur on her wrists and skirts, making her look like a white bear. As she adjusted her glossy blonde hair and flaunted a necklace adorned with shiny pearls, she complained, "I was supposed to wear the most beautiful earrings with this at one of the Wraithwood balls."

With her hood up and face hidden, Seraphine blended in easily while organizing some new fabrics.

Lowering her voice and disregarding Seraphine's presence, she whispered conspiratorially to the tailor, "I think it was one of those creatures—brownies, or maybe something worse... perhaps a pooka."

Seraphine pulled her hood closer around her face and bit her tongue to stifle a laugh. *A brownie? That's utter nonsense.* Most humans hadn't been able to see creatures from the Otherworld like brownies, pookas, or merrows—not since the Great War and the veil's creation. Nemera, the Ancient of chaos and nature, now reigned over the Otherworld, a domain filled with both nightmarish and dreamlike beings. These creatures ranged from the ethereal beauty of the sea and clear sky to the grotesque repulsiveness of moldy bread and the terrifying force of storms, all spun into the stuff of fantastical tales—much like the woman's exaggerated story.

Really, the woman could benefit from some actual *reading.*

The ever-gracious Mr. Eliah smiled at the woman. "Oh, but why would someone dare to do such a thing to such a fine lady?" Eliah then made a face at Seraphine from the other side, eager to escape the conversation and trying not to laugh.

"Jealousy, maybe? Someone wants me to look bad at the ball. You know, Evren Wraithwood once mentioned how pretty my earrings were!" she exclaimed, placing her hand on her heart with feigned distress. "A fine lady such as myself—chased by creatures... Oh, this distress is going to make me age."

This time, Seraphine couldn't help but laugh at the absurdity. The woman stared at her, bewildered by her reaction. Clearing her throat, Seraphine explained, "Well, any *brownie* worth their salt wouldn't stoop to such trifling pranks. It's more likely the work of a lesser known, more cunning trickster, looking for trivial treasures like earrings."

"Trivial, you said?" the woman interrupted, approaching Seraphine.

"Yes, you see—" Before Seraphine could explain further, the woman clutched her cloak.

"If you are going to speak ill of my possessions, do it without a covered face," the woman snarled.

Seraphine just smiled as the woman pulled her hood off. *Ah, damn me.* Eliah closed his eyes, silently praying for an escape.

"Well, you would know better, wouldn't you? Aren't you a little monster just like them?" the woman spat out, her recognition flashing dangerously as she gazed at Seraphine. The glimmer of fear that darted across her face was quickly masked, but not before Seraphine caught it. A part of her relished that thrill—the fear she instilled. Deep down, she sometimes wondered if she was more akin to *them* than human.

As she stood surrounded by dresses and fabrics, under the woman's judgy gaze, the myth about Aurum, the Ancient of death, echoed in her mind. Ruler of the Underworld, this figure, marked by a crimson gaze akin to hers, was known only through whispered tales and the pages of forbidden books. Such lore suggested why a dark omen might've shrouded her since birth. Yet, despite these legends, she remained strikingly human, cursed by her unusual eyes and a tendency to speak inconvenient truths before intolerably irritating people.

"I do," Seraphine said, a wry smirk curling her lips as her eyes flicked to the woman's pearl-adorned neck. *Not so unlucky today, though.* As she looked up at the window and the darkening sky, shadows stretched across Iceveil Square Plaza like fingers of the night. Realizing she had lingered too long, she gathered her scant earnings and thanked the tailor. With a final, mischievous whisper of words toward the irritating woman, who nearly toppled backward, Seraphine turned away and left the shop.

Though she was late, at least she had the stolen pearl necklace secure against her wrist. Seraphine felt the weight of the cold gemstones mixed with a satisfying sense of reclamation. "A brownie? I am far more skilled than them," she whispered to the night, her words dispersing like mist.

After crossing the edge of town, Seraphine entered the Weeping Forest, where trees resembled gray skeletons adorned with frostbite. Hunters, including her father, Leander Ashcroft, spoke of hearing weeping banshees drift across these ancient trees. He had warned her against traversing the forest with a dark heart lest she fall into the arms of shadow walkers, soul eaters, and bone singers. Yet, Seraphine had never encountered one. *Perhaps my heart isn't fully tainted.*

Yet.

As a branch cracked under her foot, her heart quickened. Rolling her eyes, Seraphine realized she had succumbed to her father's childish stories. "Silly night tales to scare children," she whispered. Yet, she acknowledged that sometimes nightmares were indeed real—like the banshees' weeping.

Like her.

As she wove through the dense, sparkling snow, the scent of pine enveloped her. She breathed deeply, allowing her hood to fall back and the moonlight to caress her pale cheeks. Her eyes' crimson and the flutter of her hazelnut hair stood stark against the pristine snow. She marveled at the beauty of the stars and the moonlight, boundless as her yearning for freedom. *Someday, perhaps.*

Seraphine reveled in the peace of the night, savoring the chance to smile unobscured by her hood, free from wary glances or fear. Perhaps that was why she considered this forest her sanctuary. Few dared to venture here, but her father, understanding her deep connection to the forest, never barred her from its embrace and made sure she knew every path through it.

He also shouldered many burdens because of her. Feeling a pang of guilt, she dismissed her tender thoughts. Seraphine needed to keep moving to ensure she arrived on time.

Quickening her pace, she noted the snowflakes around her. "What a lovely dance," she whispered, appreciating the serene spectacle as she maneuvered through the forest's intertwining paths.

Her journey mirrored the precise turns of a ballroom dancer too—a scene she had only imagined. To the left, beneath the gnarled limbs of a scowling tree, she danced, and near brittle, frost-clad bushes, she twirled right. Skirting a path where frozen thorns lay scattered, she leaped left gracefully and as naturally as the swirling snowflakes.

Quietly, Seraphine moved to a darker, more secluded part of the forest, where a lone tree stood. To any passerby, it was just another weathered tree scarred by brutal winters. However, to Seraphine, it was a gateway.

"You're late, again," the tree—or more precisely, the Realmwood Sentinel—chided, its voice echoing from within its ancient bark. Sentinels, guardians of realms, doors and secrets, typically manifested as trees, indistinguishable from their surroundings. This one had a face intricately woven into its gnarled bark, both fascinating and unnerving.

"Not late enough to find you asleep," Seraphine retorted. "Wait, were you perhaps waiting for me? I'm touched." Her voice was dripping with sarcasm.

The tree, or what passed for its face in the aged wood, grimaced. "Ungrateful and petty thing, just enter already. I wish to sleep," the sentinel grumbled, its tone gruff, belying its normally stoic nature.

With a glance at the sentinel, Seraphine stepped forward, crossing the threshold beneath the arched branches.

Just like that, the world turned **upside down.**

Chapter 2

The Gray Fox

Beneath a veil of smoke and shadows, the slight fox crept,
Encircled by fangs, cruel beasts thirsting for its breath.
Cornered, with no path to flee, the fox tinged its coat
A deep, mournful gray—the hue of dusk and despair's depth.

Retrieved from *Golden Tales from the Otherworld* by Galen Sorrowspring, Ch. 15, p. 9.

Seraphine Ashcroft

As Seraphine crossed the threshold, the world transformed—a dizzying, surreal reversal that defied the ordinary laws she knew. She stepped into the Otherworld realm, a domain known in tales, where there was no snow but a dark land bathed in an eternal season, neither hot nor icy cold, surrounded by trees adorned with multicolored foliage.

Over time, she learned that the veil didn't just conceal this place. It physically inverted it relative to the human realm. Beneath her feet, the ground felt like clouds and water, while the sky seemed as hard as earth and pavement. The stars were static, and Seraphine felt as if she were floating. The air was thicker but richer, infused with the essence of nature, tangible enough that she sometimes considered wrapping the air around her fingers and bottling it.

In Coldhaven, she was a mere human and an ill omen, yet amidst the chaotic throng of creatures, she felt unique and fortunate to have been granted access to a place from folktales. On this side of the veil, Seraphine was free. *I am home.*

Seraphine drew a deep breath to steady herself before venturing farther into the *Shadowmarket,* a labyrinth of shadowed stalls and endless curiosities, a haven for creatures of the dark arts.

While Seraphine navigated through the Shadowmarket, iridescent wings of aos sí fairies flickered by dangerously. Above, eerie wails of sluagh mingled with the market's clamor, haunting the air. Hags and bogles haggled fiercely, their noses nearly touching. Sleek kelpies, with eyes gleaming with mischief, prowled for the unwary. The market, alive with entities bearing horns, multiple tails, or ethereal glow, was a vivid testament to the dark magic infusing every corner.

Shops overflowed with enchantments and oddities: vials of potent potions, ancient tomes in enigmatic hides, and bizarre objects defying explanation. With a sarcastic twist of her lips, Seraphine recalled a naive misadventure. A seemingly innocuous lamp shop had almost ensnared her, turning her into part of its inventory. That memory sharpened her caution. *I won't be falling for such tricks again.*

Trickery and mischief were as valuable here as gold, and she had become a master at the game, having earned a peculiar respect among the shadow dwellers. Perhaps it was the thrill of the game or mastering the art of deception, but she relished outsmarting those who thrived on beguiling others. "Another day, another dance in the dark," she said, her voice a whisper lost in the bustling market.

Seraphine halted before a shop in the darkest corner of the market. Its timeworn wooden facade flickered intermittently under the soft glow of candles, casting grotesque shadows over sinister wares: gnarled animal limbs, jars of preserved fangs, and murky vials of unidentifiable liquids.

"Someone could use an upholsterer," she sighed, eyeing the shop's sign, which was carved from wooden branches and labeled with what the owner claimed to be magic berry juice, *Screams & Pierces*. Knowing the owner, Seraphine suspected it was actually inscribed with blood, not "fairytales and magical" berries.

Standing behind the counter was Theodorah, a terrifying witch from the Hollowspring lineage—reputed to be older than the realms and wiser than the Ancients, or so the hag would brag. Her hair, a cascade of snow-white locks intertwined with withered roses and sharp thorns, blended into her deep green cloak against the dim background. To many who ventured into the Shadowmarket, Theodorah personified the terror that pervaded the place. Her smile, laden with sharpness and horror, was designed to incite fear and demonstrate power. However, it never affected Seraphine.

"Hey, Dorah," Seraphine called out, her voice carrying a light, easy grin as she stepped into the shop's familiar confines. Her eyes radiated and sparkled with something few humans had ever seen: genuine trust and care.

"I thought you weren't coming. What keeps those crimson eyes of yours lingering in that dreadful human realm?" Dorah rasped, her voice an ethereal echo filled with nightmares and tinged with an accent.

"Indeed, the human realm is nothing but a web of tears and deception, a purgatory of ennui," Seraphine said, dramatically placing a hand on her forehead.

Dorah smirked. Seraphine leaned against the shop front, inches from Dorah, who smelled like leaves and vanilla. Close to the hag's long, pointed ears, entangled in thorns and decayed roses, she whispered sardonically, "Babies, puppies, and oh, those horrendously brilliant, shiny dresses." Then, she lay on the floor, batting her eyes playfully.

"Impertinent child, have you no manners? You can't lie down on one's shop floor," Dorah muttered, the roses in her hair opening and closing—a display of her irritation. Yet, her tone betrayed a deep-seated fondness. "I should have left you to the arms of a pooka or a spriggan the day you found yourself lost in this place."

Seraphine stood again, brushing dirt from her dress, and smiled at Dorah. "Oh, you wouldn't have! I make your life miserably delightful," she retorted, moving closer to the hag and kissing one of the hair flowers. Dorah had indeed been the reason she had survived her first foray into the Otherworld.

Seraphine had been three or four years old when she found herself running through the forest, convinced she was chasing a white bunny with crimson eyes like hers. It appeared just outside the Weeping Forest, and she couldn't resist following it, as though it were a game. It was midnight, and despite her father's shouts echoing as he ran after her, she couldn't stop.

Moving between the arched branches of the sentinel tree, she stumbled through the veil and fell to her knees. Disoriented and frightened, Seraphine found herself amidst the bustling Shadowmarket. Initially, she thought it was all a nightmare, but the reality became undeniable, especially as the creatures around her began to take notice.

Creatures mocked her, pushed her aside, and some, like the kelpies, circled ominously, feigning attempts to devour her. Banshees screamed in her ear, turning her ordeal into the living embodiment of the frightening tales her father used to recount. Terrified, Seraphine ran, cried, and hid beneath the whispering leaves of talking trees. She dashed from one terror to the next throughout the night and into the dawn until a hag appeared. Among all the fearsome entities, Dorah was the most daunting, yet she sat quietly in front of Seraphine, simply waiting.

Minutes—or perhaps hours—passed without Dorah moving.

When Seraphine had calmed slightly, Dorah extended her hand, offering guidance back through the veil to the human realm. However, she first showed her more of the creatures of the Shadowmarket and plucked some talking flowers from the trees, magically transforming them into butterflies right before Seraphine's eyes. What had started as a harrowing nightmare subtly shifted, weaving itself into a dreamlike wonder.

After Dorah thrust Seraphine back through the tree portal, her father found her and scooped her in his arms. She was buzzing with excitement, eagerly recounting her ordeal. Naturally, Leander was skeptical. Seraphine attempted to show him the portal but to no avail. Her father simply laughed it off as a child's dream.

Undeterred, Seraphine knew it was no dream. Despite her young age, she returned night after night, discovering that the veil briefly opened for one hour after midnight. Eager to share this secret world, she tried to bring her best friend Max along, timing it perfectly. Yet, he, too, ended up face-planting in the snow just outside the portal. It seemed the veil would only admit her. As such, she continued her visits alone, each becoming less frightening.

Dorah would always be there to greet her, escorting her through the Shadowmarket, imparting arcane knowledge, and spinning tales of the Otherworld. Over time, Dorah had transformed from a figure of fear to a motherly presence, albeit in her own mysterious and gruff manner.

"Also, I have something that might interest you, something truly precious," Seraphine declared, cunningly hiding a pearl from the stolen necklace in her palm. It was of little value, but she knew the art of negotiation with the old hag.

"Precious? Looks more like trash to me. I know your tricks, Seren," Dorah retorted with a snarl.

"This item—" Seraphine continued, feigning seriousness. "Is imbued with such malevolence that you could trade it for an entire selkie."

"Lies and fabrications. I taught you better than to attempt such flimsy deceptions on me," Dorah scoffed, dismissing her. "Be gone. You're driving away my customers."

She stood her ground. "Well, it seems I may just take this to old Bauchan instead. He's desperate enough to trade his soul for far less," she taunted, knowing that Dorah detested losing a bargain.

"Oh, what a shame. I guess I'll just go then." Seraphine feigned a disappointed sigh and turned as if to leave.

"For Nemera's wings! How much?" The urgency in Dorah's voice betrayed her interest. Seraphine had her right where she wanted.

"Ten coins," Seraphine asserted boldly.

"*Ten* coins for an unseen item? Are you out of your mind?"

"Perhaps I am. But you know me. So, ten coins, or I'll see if that charming Fir Darrig over there might offer fifteen," Seraphine challenged, gesturing vaguely at the crowd.

"Eight coins. That's my final offer," Dorah growled, unwilling to let the deal slip through her fingers.

"Deal," Seraphine agreed promptly, satisfied with the outcome, though she'd have settled for less. Her commitment to avoid less reputable shops wasn't a real sacrifice. The Shadowmarket was teeming with opportunities.

As she handed over the pearl, Dorah examined it closely, her expression softening with surprise. With a reluctant nod, the witch conjured eight coins from magic leaves with a puff of her breath.

"There. It pains me to say I've overpaid, but you've learned well. Let that suffice for today's lesson," Dorah muttered, a mix of annoyance and pride coloring her gruff tone.

The girl placed the coins in a pocket of her dress and smiled.

"Seren," Dorah called out, her voice laden with seriousness.

Oh no, not this again, Seraphine thought, forcing a pained grin. She looked at the old hag, already anticipating the familiar lecture.

"You've burdened yourself enough here and in that dreadful realm of yours. You've worked enough for them... Why persist in laboring for those humans? It's not just for your family, is it? Your father would surely agree with me." Seraphine knew he would but stayed silent. Dorah pressed on. "You could live among us, work with me. You're far too skilled just to cut fish and admire pretty dresses. You could be much more here, Seren."

Seraphine had always dreamed of staying in the Otherworld. Yet, she required more time. Her father and sister still needed her care. "I... I'm but a mere human. While I may be accustomed here, what about the other parts and creatures of this realm? I don't belong." *But I want to. I yearn to stay and witness more leaves transform into butterflies, more monsters into wonders.*

"Are you?" she challenged, setting aside some dried animal parts and producing a bottle resembling liquor.

"Am I what?" Seraphine inquired, watching as Dorah downed the bottle effortlessly. *Well then.*

"Human," the witch countered, her gaze piercing, the roses in her hair seemingly watching too.

Seraphine rolled her eyes. "For Brannon and Nemera's sakes! Yes, I am. No horns, tails, or magic here. If not human, then what? A stone? A ghost?" she half-joked, though she often thought of herself as a ghost, a mere presence but nothing more.

With the tenderness that neither her family outside of the Otherworld nor any creature here could match, Dorah touched her cheek and looked at her. "Always praying to the wrong Ancient," she murmured. "You hold the world and an endless universe of keys and souls in your eyes yet remain unaware. A mere human couldn't reach this realm, but you know that. You're just too afraid to admit it, to see it, to see yourself as other than what you've been told all your life."

With that, the witch moved to the other side of the shop, fetched another bottle, and organized some curious items. Still, Seraphine caught what could have been sorrow in the old hag's eyes.

They shifted to lighter topics, like gossip about a notorious wanderer merrow and amusing stories Dorah had overheard from the old trees. All the while, Seraphine assisted Dorah with various clients searching for nameless items.

As Seraphine prepared to leave, a cat sith approached. Larger than the usual kind, almost the size of a puma, it had stark white eyes and a distinctive red mark under its ear—a symbol Seraphine vaguely recognized.

Dorah tensed at the cat sith's arrival. "What an unpleasant visit," she said, tension coloring her voice.

The cat sith smirked disturbingly and spat out a piece of paper.

Intrigued, Seraphine watched as ancient symbols materialized on the paper. She recognized the language but couldn't decipher the message.

Dorah read it, her face paling. Moving quickly, she retrieved a hidden box from the back of her shop.

Before Seraphine could get a clearer look, the paper burst into flames and disintegrated. "That's overly dramatic," Seraphine concluded.

Dorah produced a tiny vial containing a liquid that shimmered like captured starlight, its aura as sinister as a serpent's hiss. "This is all I have. No more requests like this," she told the cat sith, who swallowed the vial, likely hiding it beneath one of its formidable teeth.

"And tell your master he's not welcome here anymore," the witch declared, turning her sharp gaze on Seraphine. "What in the bean-nighe are you still doing here, Seren?" she snapped, her patience thinning.

Acknowledging the urgency of her schedule, especially with an important appointment pending, Seraphine exited the shop, but not before casting a final glance at the enigmatic cat sith. She made her way through the tenebrous labyrinth of the Shadowmarket, her mind teeming with questions about the cat sith, her earlier conversation with Dorah, and the unsettling cryptic message.

Chapter 3

The Crystal Fox

What is a broken mirror but a puzzle of its past?
Each shard, a whisper of shadow,
Like tiny diamonds that foretell the future—
Scattered fragments reflecting
Visions of what might have been or what must be.

Retrieved from *Otherworld Codex: The Hidden Portals*
by Malvrek W., Ch. 100, p. 1870.

Seraphine Ashcroft

After walking a few minutes through the market, Seraphine veered into a hidden alley. Here, amidst the dirt and debris, stood a large mirror. It wasn't shattered but appeared disassembled, a relic she had discovered years ago. Nothing in the Otherworld was ever as it seemed, and this mirror was more than a reflective surface—it was another gateway to her secret sanctuary, her preferred lair and hunting ground.

Thorny black roses, about fifty in total, ensnared the glass, weaving a dark embrace. "Hello, mirror," Seraphine purred, her voice echoing slightly, stirring the dormant roses.

Reacting to her voice, the fragmented pieces trembled and shifted, as if shards of ice skittering across a frozen lake, seeking to reform. The roses unfurled their petals, revealing sharp-toothed maws. "Bloody creature," one hissed, followed by the others chanting in chorus.

"Crimson drops to bind the gate,
Mirror shards reflect your fate.
Offer what the shadows seek,
Whisper secrets, soft and meek.

Blood to roses, thorns embrace,
Eyes that mirror back your face.
Sacrifice to cross the line,
Twined paths of wolf and vine."

This chant, a haunting refrain she'd learned to decipher over time, echoed each visit. Drawing nearer to a particular rose, it quivered in anticipation. Teasingly, Seraphine retreated just as it seemed she might allow it to bite her, chuckling at their snarled frustration.

Time was of the essence, and her fondness for these games had to be curtailed. She ceased her antics and offered a finger to one of the ravenous roses. It snapped at her, its bite sharp and precise, drawing blood.

As Seraphine withdrew her bloodied finger, the roses grinned wickedly, their thorns withdrawing from the mirror's edges. "Welcome again," they whispered collectively, their voices a harsh murmur as the mirror stilled, its pieces aligning perfectly.

Touching her clear reflection, Seraphine stepped through the mirror, passing into her hidden haven.

Seraphine entered the most magnificent place she had ever encountered in the Shadowmarket. Encased into a castle of mirrors and multicolored roses, the library stretched across more than fifteen sprawling floors, each overflowing with books. This made her ponder the magical prowess required to encase such an expansive domain into a mere mirror. Yet, this vast knowledge repository captivated her.

Here, ancient tomes from all realms adorned the walls: narratives of human exploits, chronicles of Otherworld creatures, and venerations of the mighty Ancient gods, particularly Brannon, the creator of humans, and Nemera. A section was dedicated to the Underworld, including some accounts of Aurum's deeds.

However, this section was part of the forbidden archives, locked away and shrouded in secrecy. Despite the relevance to her crimson eyes and their connection to Aurum and the Underworld, Seraphine never sought access. That realm, often excluded from casual discourse due to a political rift between the Otherworld and the Underworld, was a topic she preferred to avoid.

Sometimes, she wondered if her avoidance was driven by fear of discovering unsettling truths about the human whispers surrounding her. Shaking off these unnerving thoughts, she marveled at the library—a paradise nestled in a labyrinth dedicated not to deception but to the pursuit of knowledge.

Knowing the library's etiquette well, Seraphine approached a desk at the center of the room, flanked by unlit candles. At its heart lay a small silver plate accompanied by a note.

Welcome to the Mystweave Library
Dear trespasser of mirrors and doors, before you stands the hallowed vestibule of arcane bore. To pass these thresholds, surrender a fragment of your essence and behold the illumination that awaits.
Withhold and be engulfed by shadows where roses sink thorns into silence.
PS: Heed this whisper, no relic shall part from this place without its echo left in place. What is borrowed must be returned.

Seraphine carefully placed a slice of finely stolen cheese on the silver plate, a token of gratitude for the library's guardian. In moments, a single candle flickered to life, followed swiftly by the others, illuminating a path with their glow. The light danced across the room, reflecting off mirrors and creating a kaleidoscopic effect with the vibrant roses, filling the area with shimmering colors, like a crystal palace. From a distance, she caught a glimpse of movement. She thought it was the elusive Bogle, this enchanted library's guardian. While she occasionally spotted his hands darting among the shelves, he remained mostly concealed.

Today, Seraphine was intent on bringing a few books back home. Dorah had hinted at some intriguing tales tucked away on the second floor, perfect for delving into during her spare moments. Climbing the stairs, she turned left, then right, and left again, navigating to the secluded hallway leading to the library's tales section.

As she approached, Seraphine paused, struck by the corridor lined with paintings. She had explored this gallery before, spending hours trying to unravel the cryptic stories they depicted. Despite inquiring throughout the market and pressing Dorah—who had dismissively called her mad—no one seemed familiar with the tales.

However, something different caught her eye this time. "There it is," she murmured, her gaze intently scanning the sequence of artworks. Each painting captured scenes of a chase: a wolf and a fox locked in an eternal pursuit. One showed the wolf, bloodied and fierce. The subsequent images were murkier, with faces of both humans and Otherworld folk blurred or scratched out, as though someone wished to hide their identities.

Yet, one partially obscured figure stood out. It was a man, or something resembling one, with a regal semblance in the Otherworld, his features marred but with a distinctive symbol visible on his neck: a red ink mark, eerily similar to the one she had noted beneath the cat sith's ear.

She resolved to press Dorah for more information on her next visit.

As Seraphine traversed the hallway, she arrived at the tales section of the library, a place nothing short of magical. Each book was an enormous tome, adorned with the most exquisite drawings and covers, some seemingly crafted from the hair of mystical creatures. Amidst these, a small black book caught her eye. It vibrated slightly on the shelf, as if eager to be opened—a common occurrence in this enchanted realm, yet always a sign that the book was particularly keen for a reader's attention. Compelled, she picked it up, feeling its energy pulse as she placed it in her bag, hoping it would remain even once back in the human world. The book's title shifted and shimmered, much like the mirror she knew so well, with letters dancing across the cover.

Seraphine carefully placed a pearl from the stolen necklace in the now vacant spot on the shelf—a placeholder and a pledge to return the book. Without leaving something of equal or greater value, the library's vigilant guardian would never permit her to exit with one of their prized volumes. She recalled when colorful roses had ensnared her, scratching her arm and forcibly reclaiming the book because she hadn't made a proper exchange.

Another time, Seraphine had left a piece of bread, which had decayed by the time she returned the book. The library, or perhaps the librarian's displeasure, had manifested dramatically, hurling books at her in a furious whirlwind, leaving her with a bruise that lingered for three weeks.

These experiences had ingrained in her that the value of knowledge in this realm demanded a timeless and substantial tribute. A pearl should suffice for this transaction.

As Seraphine stepped back through the mirror, the thorny roses swiftly re-entwined, veiling the gateway once more. The mirror fragmented, scattering into a disjointed reflection of herself. The ever-changing whispers of the roses marked each exit.

"In the hushed veils of the night,
Bloody creature, shade of crimson light,
Do you truly grasp what you are?

A spectral being from a realm afar?
Have you glimpsed beneath your guise,
Or do you dwell still, bound by lies?

Did you know? Do you know? Wish to know?"

This time, the whisper seemed personal, prompting Seraphine to respond. "What ought I to know?"

The roses trembled, murmuring among themselves.

"She does not know."
"How would she know?"
"You do not know."

Then, in unison, they spoke again.

"You remain blind, so unaware,
Where mist and blood blend thin as air.
Just a fox from realms beneath, in stealth, you creep.
Beware the tongues you trust, the secrets they keep,
For worlds may tremble where the little jumper leaps."

"Fine, I will go. Just stop," Seraphine retorted, in no mood for riddles as she made her way back to the streets, heading toward the veil entrance to the human world.

Hastening her steps, she approached the part of the forest housing the sentinel's arched branches. Thankfully, her departure from the Otherworld wasn't bound by the time stringent rules that governed her entrance.

Just as she neared the path to safety, a wooden hand, gnarled and knotted like ancient tree roots, clasped her ankle, pulling her to the ashen ground. "What in the—" she started but cut herself off as she realized the nature of her assailant.

A banshee of the woods, a grotesque fusion of mourning and arboreal spirit, with bark-like skin and hollow eyes full of despair, stared at Seraphine. Trees screamed behind her, leaves swirling down as though sensing an ominous presence.

Regaining her footing, Seraphine confronted the banshee. "What do you want?" she demanded, her voice steady despite her inner turmoil.

"Crimson fox, beware," the creature whispered, her voice echoing like wind through dead leaves, her breath harsh and uneven with fear. "Avoid the one who stains the snow red, who hunts with eyes of frost."

Frustrated, the girl retorted, "You speak in riddles. I have no time for games."

"Then listen well, for the winter that gathers in his gaze is a harbinger of your doom," the banshee persisted. "Should it find you, crimson will paint the earth, and the veil that separates life from death, folk from human, will tear asunder."

With the forest now filled with the mournful howls of ghostly trees and the rustling whispers of hidden creatures echoing the banshee's words, Seraphine knew it was time to leave. *Such nonsense.* Moving away from the creature, she quickly stepped under the arched branches that led to the human realm.

Grim Wanderer

Enshrouded in his winter cloak, woven from snow and starlight, he lingered in the shadows as the girl with crimson eyes returned to the human world.

A smile curled his lips, as sharp as the bitterness engulfing his heart. The Grim Wanderer—a moniker he had adopted a few years ago—had taken on the task of molding her into a force that would untangle and correct what was destroyed before.

Fully aware that once the girl discovered the truth behind what he had done and made of her all these years, she would likely destroy him. *You better do it, Crimson Eyes. Otherwise, I may destroy this realm and myself once more.*

What tragic irony, the Grim Wanderer thought, raised to suppress all human emotions, as rigid as trees, as boundless as air, and as ancient as the hidden depths beneath the frost. Yet, here he stood, ready to be undone by her—the schemer and puppeteer of the only force that could vanquish him.

Her stumbling upon the Otherworld was nothing short of utter madness, spurred by his actions, when he had placed a crimson-eyed bunny, a hidden pooka, in her path. The Grim Wanderer hadn't foreseen that the creature would lead her to the veil nor that she would be permitted to cross it.

Yet, as daring and resilient as the girl with crimson eyes proved to be, she returned time and again, a wicked smile on her face he knew so well. At that thought, he realized it was already dawn. He withdrew a piece of paper from his pocket, watching as the magic ink shifted the number from five to four.

Four days.

He observed her disheveled hazelnut hair and torn dress, her face unhooded here in the forest. The Grim Wanderer marveled at how the crimson-eyed girl gracefully navigated the surrounding perils, her movements light and almost ethereal, as if dancing with the trees and snow. He was amused by the irony of it all. He was more than familiar with the Otherworld but barred from returning, at least for now. However, he wouldn't be coming alone next time.

The Grim Wanderer smiled at that thought.

Silently, he descended from his perch, his movements as stealthy as the night's shadows. This ritual had spanned decades, even centuries. He watched over her from the penumbra, ensuring she was always where she needed to be—or perhaps in the right place at the wrong time.

He swore to keep his distance this time, yet he yearned to be closer, captivated by her eyes, which he had seen in countless lives. Regardless of their color, they were always a kaleidoscope of starlight and dreams, now with a hint of glittering bloody roses.

Before the Grim Wanderer could continue his usual vigil on her, a cat sith appeared.

"By Nemera's wings! I thought you were lost," he exclaimed as Shadoweater approached.

Bound to him by a blood pact after being ensnared by magical traps, the creature served as his familiar. It displayed its sharp fangs before dropping a bottle into the snow and dissipating into thin air, reemerging as an inked silhouette on his arm.

He secured the bottle under his cloak and quickened his steps to follow the girl's path.

"Are you certain about this?" the sentinel tree's deep, ancient voice boomed.

"Why? Have you grown fond of her?" the Grim Wanderer retorted sharply, his tone as cold as frost. "Spare me the conversation. Trees like you should remain silent, not play protectors."

The tree sighed. "You remain as blind and naive as ever, Grim Wanderer… or whatever you call yourself now. You're walking right into the wolf's jaws."

Undeterred, he strode toward the city, the sentinel's warning dismissed. Deep down, he knew he was the wolf, orchestrating a resurgence for an old and clever fox, a game she might despise. Still, the girl needed to master it to finally win, regardless if it cost him everything.

Although she *is everything to me…*

Chapter 4

The Black Fox

In shadows lurk creatures with faces angelic,
Mouths of wolves, fangs gleaming with night's dark stain,
Their hunger for mischief mocks the moon's pale glow,
Venturing beyond where its silvery light dares tread.

Retrieved from *Otherworld Creatures Guide: Banshees & Other Terrors* by Ash Branchfall, Ch. 3, p. 35.

Four Days Before the Incident
Seraphine Ashcroft

The early morning air was brisk when Seraphine entered the town, and the sky still clung to the soft tones of night. Although she knew she should rush home to rest, something compelled her to linger.

Navigating the quiet, chilly streets, she reached the town center. She looked up, ostensibly examining the clock tower's sturdy stone structure adorned with roses and thorns frozen in time. Legend had it that this area had once been a vibrant spring haven, and these frozen flowers stood as a stark reminder of what once was—a marvel of preservation, silent witnesses to the passage of centuries.

However, Seraphine wasn't there just to admire the roses. She was hunting.

Closing her eyes, she focused, attuning herself to the ambient sounds—the wind's whisper, the ticking of the clock, and the tingling sensation on her neck increasing with each passing second. Then, as expected, she picked up the faint but distinct sound of steps behind her. *There you are.* She smirked, though she saw no one.

Seraphine first noticed this sensation a few years ago—a subtle warmth on her neck, a presence that followed her from the Weeping Forest back into Coldhaven. Recently, the feeling had intensified. It wasn't accompanied by fear but rather a soothing familiarity that sparked her curiosity.

Despite devising a routine to try and catch a glimpse of her unseen follower, Seraphine never managed to spot the elusive presence.

Yet, she was certain it was there—something observant and stealthy was watching her. It might even think she was unaware of it. Sometimes, she wondered if it was all just her imagination, a figment conjured up by her need for company. Nevertheless, she hoped it wasn't. *I will find you someday. You can bet on it.* She inhaled slowly to center herself and resumed her walk to the family cottage.

Her steps were deliberate, each a calculated move in her silent game of cat and mouse. She could almost feel the eyes on her. A part of her relished the thrill, the unknown dance between hunter and hunted. It made her heart race, a stark contrast to the cold morning air.

Seraphine would uncover this mystery, but for now, she played her part, feigning ignorance, biding her time.

The sun bathed her family cottage in the cold morning light. It was old and plain, yet her father had raised her there, making it the most special place in town. Leander engaged her in games of hide and seek, filling their home with laughter from his many tales. The walls, covered in scratches and fox drawings, showcased their painting sessions. The warm, woody interior created a cozy sanctuary.

Unlike for her, most folks deeply admired her father, praising his prowess as a hunter. Even so, Leander never spoke of her mother, unwilling to share a tale or a name, as if her memory was forbidden. No paintings or keepsakes hinted at her mother's existence. Sometimes, Seraphine wondered if her distinctive eyes were a legacy from her mother since Leander's were hazel and gold.

Warming her hands by the fireplace, Seraphine knelt and placed a piece of cheese in a corner. Nearby, Scarlet, the crimson-eyed bunny she had captured years ago, hopped toward the treat. She hoped her slight tardiness wouldn't unsettle the household routines.

Thalassa, Leander's new wife, was probably still asleep, as was her half-sister. Usually rough and indifferent, Thalassa disliked Seraphine, a fact Seraphine kept from Leander, who had enough burdens. With frequent, prolonged hunting trips due to game scarcity, her father was mostly away, sometimes for months. To help out financially, Seraphine had begun picking up odd jobs.

After setting down the cheese, she grabbed a piece of bread from the wooden kitchen table and peeked back at the fireplace. The cheese had disappeared—too fast to attribute to the bunny.

"I'm hungry too," she whispered to the nearly empty room, then moved to her bedroom. The room was plainly decorated but filled with wall drawings of flowers, roses, and foxes. In the center was her bed, surrounded by books scattered everywhere. Her large window offered a stunning view of snow-covered landscapes and distant mountains.

Too tired and with work looming in the afternoon, Seraphine quickly undressed and stepped into the small bath area. There, an old tub awaited her alongside a broken mirror. As she bathed and brushed her hair, she considered decorating the mirror with roses, imagining it as a doorway to her library in the Otherworld.

Looking at her reflection, Seraphine noted how pale and thin she had become. She told herself years ago that one should always be as cold and unfazed as winter, and she had been—most of the time. Still, she felt like she was slowly drowning in all the sorrows she could never express.

This time, she not only let some tears fall, but she also stepped into the old tub and dove as deep into its waters as she could, her tears mixing with the water and her screams silenced by its density. She could see her hazel hair moving in dazzling waves around her while she finally shut her eyes and the world outside her. She held her breath, preferring to see how much she could bear without air.

Ten seconds, not wanting to dwell on her best friend who had abandoned her. Twenty seconds, drowning her stepmother's disdain. Thirty seconds, biting hard at the wary glances of the townspeople or the rumors of her being a monstrous creature because of her eyes. Forty seconds, freezing all the unknown that would surely come after her. Fifty seconds, burying deep all the ungraceful things she had done. Sixty seconds, camouflaging how much she sometimes enjoyed those ungraceful things.

At that, she resurfaced and coughed violently, her gaze unfazed as droplets of water clung to her lashes. *One nightmare at a time*, she told herself. Stepping out of the tub, barely covering herself with an old towel, she laughed softly at her reflection in the broken mirror. Instead of feeling angry, she was amused by the ungraceful things she had done. She didn't feel bad for being considered evil incarnate. Sometimes, Seraphine liked it too much. *What is wrong with me?*

Her reflection suddenly spoke back to her with an ethereal, distorted voice. "There's nothing wrong with you."

Shocked, she heard the mirror crack again, splitting her reflection into three. *Maybe it was the wind, and the mirror was already partially cracked*, she thought.

As Seraphine moved away from her cracked reflection, she heard the voice again, clearer, nearer, right in her ear. "How much can your heart hold before it breaks completely?"

Instead of being shocked this time, she decided to answer, voicing a raw truth she had been afraid to consider. "I-I don't know."

"Are you taking enough gigs these days?" Thalassa asked. She was tall and elegant, her long, flowing raven hair and brown eyes speckled with green nothing short of enchanting. It was no wonder Leander had fallen so quickly for her, though Thalassa clearly loved him.

"I'm doing what I can, Thalassa," Seraphine replied dryly, petting Scarlet, who was licking the cut on her finger that the black rose had made. She watched as Thalassa counted the seven coins she had earned at the Shadowmarket. Seraphine always saved one extra for herself.

"This barely covers the needs of this house. Your father works hard enough, and this is the best you can do?" Thalassa scoffed. Seraphine bit her tongue so hard she was certain that if she opened her mouth, the blood would perfectly match the crimson fury in her eyes.

"Your poor sister is studying to become a proper lady while you go out and do what exactly?" Thalassa continued, glaring at Seraphine with disdain. She flicked her glossy hair back and cupped Seraphine's face, causing Scarlet to hop away. "Do your job, or you might as well be gone."

One nightmare at a time.

Thalassa was the night to the mare, so hard to avoid. She would wish for her to be just that, a bad dream where she could snap her fingers and Thalassa would disappear.

Seraphine would love to be gone. As soon as she could ensure her sister and father no longer needed her to work, Seraphine would leave—either to the Otherworld or perhaps to explore the world beyond Coldhaven. *One day, I will be so far and surrounded by warmth that all you'll have left to quarrel with is your own wicked reflection.*

Seraphine pulled her face from Thalassa's firm hold. "I'm working with the fisherman later today. You're welcome to join me so we can double the earnings," she said, knowing that Thalassa would never lift a finger. She sometimes wished she could push Thalassa into the Otherworld—maybe a kelpie would fancy her glossy hair.

How do I bring a kelpie here?

"I would be delighted to see that. Do it," the ethereal voice Seraphine had heard in the bathroom whispered in her ear, and she closed her eyes. She wasn't afraid, having long decided she was losing her mind and was fine with it. It might be her own thoughts manifesting, but something about the voice made her fingers curl.

"Just stop," Seraphine whispered to no one, to someone, to herself.

"What?" Thalassa stopped pacing in front of the fireplace, looking at her curiously.

She opened her eyes and faked a sweet smile. "Nothing."

Thalassa's smile broadened, confirming the assumption that whatever Seraphine had heard had been only for her ears. "Oh, my dear Seren, that is exactly what you are! Nothing. And you know I have more pressing matters to attend to than fish guts and dockside chatter. That's more your style, and what else can you do? It's not like you can study or get married. You have a... reputation," she quipped. "But perhaps a change of wardrobe could do you some good. You're far too comfortable in that ragged cloak of yours. One might think you're ashamed to be seen in anything else." Thalassa was fully aware the cloak had been a gift and that she could not afford new dresses either.

Seraphine clenched her jaw, resisting the urge to retort. She knew better than to get involved in such petty arguments or to seek Thalassa's approval. Brushing past her stepmother, she decided to check on her sister before leaving to work with the fishermen.

Aeliana's room was chaotic, strewn with books and dresses. She was nestled among a pile of cushions, clutching a book and studying its pages with furrowed brows. Aeliana was not a fan of reading, but Seraphine and Leander worked hard to pay for her tutors and proper education.

"What's got you looking so serious, Lia?" Seraphine teased, a faint smile tugging at her lips.

Aeliana eyed up from her book. Her eyes, reminiscent of Thalassa's, contrasted with her hazelnut hair and the soft smile she shared with Leander. "It's this blasted tome on *Eldorainian* history, something about the veil's creation and the Ancients. I can't make heads or tails of it. The language... it's like nothing I've ever encountered," she admitted, exasperation creeping into her voice.

Seraphine leaned over to inspect the book, her fingers tracing the intricate script on its pages. She had grown accustomed to deciphering such old languages, a skill honed through years of practice in the

Otherworld. The book did indeed talk about the veil's creation. *Why is Aeliana reading something like this?* That topic had been forbidden. Their continent of Eldorainian had suffered the most after the war. "Where did you get this book?"

"It was in a bag that one of the tutors gave me last week to read through. Why?" Aeliana asked, confused.

Maybe they didn't even notice they gave her this book, Seraphine mused.

"Nothing. It's all just tales and superstitions. Nothing worth losing sleep over," Seraphine reassured her, her smile wistful. "And why read about the Ancients? They seem to have forgotten all about Coldhaven. About us."

Aeliana's eyes widened, a flicker of fear crossing her features. "But, Seren, you can't say such things. What if they hear you? What if they curse us for our blasphemy?"

Seraphine chuckled softly, the sound bittersweet as it echoed through the room. "We're already cursed. Winter town, remember? What harm could a few more curses do? Look at me. I'm still on my feet despite my eyes."

Her sister hugged Seraphine tightly. As she looked up, Aeliana's eyes gleamed with mischief. "You know what I heard?"

"Indulge me." Aeliana was a couple of years younger than Seraphine and an image of innocence, so she could only imagine what she was about to say.

"I heard that Evren Wraithwood is some kind of god," she whispered, the sparks in her eyes seemingly brighter than the sunrise. "They say he's as mysterious as the night, as untamed as the wolf, and oh-so handsome, like a prince."

Seraphine snorted derisively, her cynical smile deepening. She had never met Evren Wraithwood, who was known for hosting lavish balls. "More like a dirty wolf lurking in the darkness, preying on the unsuspecting and probably reeking of filth."

Aeliana giggled at her sister's jest, and they stood there for some minutes, sharing jokes and dreams about escaping Coldhaven. Seraphine soon left for her room, but not before taking the forbidden book from Aeliana's delicate hands.

The ethereal voice returned, whispering in her ear, "Wouldn't you like to meet him? I bet you would."

She rolled her eyes, moving across the cottage. "Wouldn't you like to shut up? I bet *you* do."

Slash!

Since the crack of dawn, Seraphine had been laboring away, peeling and slicing through the icy flesh of freshly caught fish. Mr. Vale, the fisherman, had stepped out for "just a moment," but hours had passed. She hoped he would increase her payment to compensate for his prolonged absence. Unlike the tailor, who was fond of her, Mr. Vale gave her occasional gigs. Like many others, he could hardly look her in the eyes.

Aside from her rare ability to traverse the Otherworld, Seraphine saw nothing cursed or evil about herself. Her education was decent, albeit cut short by the need to support her family. Yes, her eyes were unusual and linked to the Underworld, but she was not a monster, creature, or omen of bad luck. She sighed, knowing there was no fixing any of that.

She took the head of another dead fish and cut again, enjoying the melody of the knife against the hard scales.

Slash, slash, slash.

Somehow, the raw smell of the fish she despised made her think of Evren. Had Seraphine been born appearing more ordinary, she would've probably joined her sister at the mysterious soirées hosted by Evren Wraithwood. Despite knowing little about him, Seraphine was convinced he was utterly insufferable, imagining him as a real-life abhartach—a legendary, dwarf-like creature, not particularly pleasant to behold. She couldn't suppress a laugh at the thought.

For years, her family had never received an invitation to the Wraithwood estate, causing Seraphine to wonder if she was somehow to blame. Whenever she passed the imposing, ostentatious Wraithwood castle on her way to the Iceveil Square market, she couldn't help but stare. Ancient and solid like the town's clock tower, its massive stone walls were adorned with symbolic carvings, surrounded by frozen flowers and vibrant red roses, eternally suspended in time.

Still, if an invitation were extended, Seraphine vowed she would never attend. *Or perhaps*, she pondered, *I may go just once*. She was curious to glimpse the life from which she was barred, to dance like the snowflakes she so loved.

Or at least I'll try. It's not like I know how to dance or how to be close to anyone, anyway.

Max, her former best friend, was invited, but she decided to pay no mind to that name. He left with millions of questions unanswered. *If I could see him again…* "No, no, no," she said, cutting her thoughts short and slicing more raw fish instead.

Slash, slash, slash.

The shop door chimed. Seraphine mustered a strained smile and looked downward, hoping to avoid making eye contact with the patron. "Hello, can I assist you—" Her voice trailed off, choked by the sudden lump in her throat when she recognized the pair of shoes she had seen countless times.

The knife she was holding fell to the floor.

Before her stood Maxwell Everhart.

Max.

Brannon truly hates me.

Chapter 5

The Wailing Fox

Born from earth, shadows deep,
Eyes of beauty, fur of fright.
A lone wolf wanders, bound to weep,
Loveless through the endless night.

Retrieved from *The Great Love Story of The White Fox*
by Illyra Everdawn, Ch. 5, p. 23.

Seraphine Ashcroft

Her heart raced, a swarm of black butterflies fluttering in her belly. Max had once been Seraphine's only friend. At one point, she had even envisioned a life together. He was like the sun, golden-eyed and radiant, the closest she'd come to feeling the spring's warmth. However, she wouldn't succumb to his presence. Max had left her, and Seraphine had chosen to forge her path alone. *Just breathe, Seraphine. Become the voided creature they all fear. Show no emotion. Be a ghost.*

He wasn't alone, though. A group of well-dressed but scornful men flanked him. Max's eyes briefly met hers, showing a glimmer of remorse before a cold indifference settled in. "Well, well, if it isn't Seren. It's been too long. A year? I had no idea you worked here," he commented, his tone stripped of any warmth that had once characterized their interactions.

Regaining her composure and forgetting about the knife on the floor, Seraphine replied hesitantly, "Y-yes, I'm just filling in. The owner, Mr. Vale, had to run some errands. You... I thought you'd left." He appeared unchanged, his blond hair and golden eyes as striking as ever, though his smile felt forced and unnatural.

Max's expression faltered as he caught sight of her eyes, his attempt at indifference momentarily slipping. "Left? No, I've been here all this time. I simply chose not to seek you out. I'd rather not mingle with your kind." His words sliced through the air.

The group's laughter echoed around them, deepening Seraphine's humiliation. The realization that he had intentionally avoided her was a painful betrayal.

One nightmare at a time.

"I see. So the rumors are true," Seraphine shot back, her voice trembling. However, she drowned it all—the humiliation, the hurt—filling her cup of sorrows once more. "I may be an outcast, but at least I am not a coward or a deceiver. Like you."

She held his gaze fiercely, daring him to avert his eyes first. Max had been Seraphine's best friend since they were children. In time, he had become her only companion, ending in her falling for him in their twenties. A year ago, she declared her love for him. He told her he felt the same. Then, a week later, he disappeared. A rumor started that he was to be engaged with a proper lady. Max never contacted her or sought her out. Seraphine sent letters for months—every day, but there was no response.

Max's eyes widened in surprise. He opened his mouth to speak, but Mr. Vale's abrupt entrance interrupted the standoff.

"What is the meaning of this?" he demanded, his tone sharp.

Seraphine's heart sank. *How many nightmares am I supposed to handle at once?*

One of Max's companions, a tall and strikingly handsome man with raven hair, gently placed a hand on Mr. Vale's shoulder. His smile, both captivating and faintly sinister, softened his approach. "My apologies, sir. We've come to procure a sizable quantity of fish for a ball I'm hosting tonight. However, it seems your employee harbors some... resentment and rudeness toward my friend. Oh, I guess it must be about Max's—"

Max cut off his words, looking at the extremely handsome male with painful pleading. "This is no place to discuss such matters."

"Is it not?" he remarked, his intense gaze settling on Seraphine this time.

It sent shivers down her spine. She felt he was pushing her to ask him, to confirm the rumor she ardently wanted to hear from Max's mouth. His eyes roamed around her face, and she noted that they were an unusual yet mesmerizing blend of gray and clear blue dotted with white specks reminiscent of snowflakes. Despite dismissing it as improbable, she felt an inexplicable familiarity about him.

How in the world had Max ended up with such company? Is this person from another town? She had wandered this town for years, and Seraphine was certain she had never seen him. *I don't think you could go unnoticed looking like that.*

Mr. Vale stepped back, his face etched with incredulity and indignation. "Young Wraithwood, my apologies. I should have recognized you immediately," he stammered.

Wraithwood?

This is worse than a nightmare... it's real torment, like a winter storm.

Seraphine shared Mr. Vale's astonishment, yet shamelessly, she couldn't stop her eyes from drifting back to him—the most admired and, to her, the most hated person in Coldhaven, a prince without a crown. Evren Wraithwood's presence was wholly unexpected, his appearance seemingly confirming her grimmest suspicions—an arrogant, entitled nobleman masquerading as a gentleman. His handsome features were undeniable, yet Seraphine knew too well that such beauty could be misleading. Her experiences in the Otherworld had taught her that outward allure often concealed deeper, darker truths.

However, she had to admit, she liked that darkness. Or was it his darkness? Or the contrasting darkness in those eyes, with those white flecks? She quickly dismissed the thought and reminded herself who this person was to begin with.

The owner's eyes blazed as he turned toward her. Already predisposed to dislike her, the infamous Evren Wraithwood's presence just intensified his anger. What a noisy wolf that man was, and somehow Seraphine found Evren's presence more maddening and unnerving than Max's. She pondered whether she should feel relieved or concerned, considering minutes ago, she was on the verge of feeling heartbroken once again.

"You. I showed mercy because of your father's reputation, but you've proven yourself a menace. Leave now, and do not return," Mr. Vale spat.

"Mr. Vale, listen—" Seraphine began, but he interrupted sharply.

"Do not come back here. Ever. You bring misfortune to this shop and to everyone in it. Leave now, and I might refrain from informing your father of this incident." With those final words, Seraphine walked to the door, throwing one last resentful look at Max.

While she walked away from her post, relieved that Mr. Vale had promised not to tell her father about the occurrence, she glanced at Evren *Muddy* Wraithwood again. He stood beside the entrance, blocking her path with a look of mingled anger and curiosity. *Is that a smirk on his face?* Seraphine moved toward the door, looking down to hide her face under the hood, ready to step into the deep winter of Iceveil's streets.

As she neared Evren, he whispered—or so she thought—"Interesting. Is your heart breaking enough? Or can you endure more?" Those words chillingly echoed others she had heard before in her mind. Perhaps she mixed Evren's voice with the whispers she had been hearing.

There's no way.

She suddenly stumbled and fell onto the hard cobblestones, scraping her cheek. As Seraphine attempted to rise, a warm trickle of blood stained the pavement. "In the name of Nemera," she cursed under her breath.

"Begging to someone different than Brannon? You deserve that, witch," Mr. Vale declared coldly. Seraphine lay there, fixated on the blood drops dotting the gray stones. "I won't pay you a dime. Consider yourself lucky to leave unharmed," he added scornfully.

Max, Evren, and their group exited the shop, but she remained on the ground, not daring to look up. Evren's voice carried back to her. "I'll return later to pick up the large order, sir. For now, my friend Max has a wedding to prepare for. Isn't that right, Max?"

Lifting her head, Seraphine met Max's eyes. There was a deep sadness there, but his tone was dismissively neutral. "Indeed, I am looking forward to the company of a refined and elegant lady."

Then, carelessly, Max stepped close, his foot catching and dragging Seraphine's beloved crimson hood. The one Max had given her years ago, the only remaining trace of their friendship.

"Stay down, Seren, where you belong, in the dirt, with your kind. And get yourself a new hood. This one's beyond repair and does little to hide those cursed eyes of yours." With a swift kick, Max tore the hood further, its fabric ripping apart easily. "See? It's worthless now," he said coldly before turning away.

At that moment, her tears mixed with the blood. Seraphine felt she might drown in her own grief.

Still, she slowly stood, leaving the ruined hood behind. A solitary snowflake landed on her face, marred by blood, tears, and the day's grime. With a heavy heart, she turned and fled the scene.

Seraphine ran swiftly, tears freezing on her cheeks and falling into the snow. Like the flowers, those frozen tears were destined to endure forever—cruel reminders of her sorrows. Drops of frozen blood now permanently marked the snow near the entrance to the Weeping Forest.

She couldn't think straight after the encounter with Max. Mr. Vale would likely spread rumors about what had happened, complicating her job search since most were eager to stay in the Wraithwoods' good graces. *And what did Evren say?*

Seraphine quickened her pace. Without Mr. Vale's payment, she needed to trade anything she could at the Shadowmarket—just one good deal was enough. Then, she remembered the pearls in her dress pockets. If she could reach the veil and speak with Dorah and perhaps some others, she might manage to earn some coins in time.

Bang, bang, bang.

The clock indicated one hour till midnight—plenty of time, yet Seraphine felt desperate to distance herself from the town. She needed a safe place to breathe.

Run faster, Seraphine! Faster!

As she entered the Weeping Forest, the atmosphere was unsettlingly strange. She attributed that to herself and her feelings. She followed her usual path, yet somehow, she kept finding herself walking in circles. Left, right, left—her usual markers were nowhere to be seen. It was as if the forest had shifted, the trees rearranging their ancient trunks to confound her. The entrance to the veil should have been clear, but now it was obscured by some unnatural trickery of the woods. *Something's definitely not right.*

Continuing her disoriented trek through the woods, Seraphine stumbled upon a warning sign. It resembled those typically seen at the forest's entrance, but this one appeared much older, weathered by time and elements. She had never seen it before, which seemed impossible. Seraphine knew every path, every forest nook like the back of her hand.

"Welcome to the Wailing Forest," the sign read.

Wailing? She hadn't heard of it before. Not to mention, this was supposed to be the Weeping Forest. Her teary eyes focused on the sign once more, noting there was more.

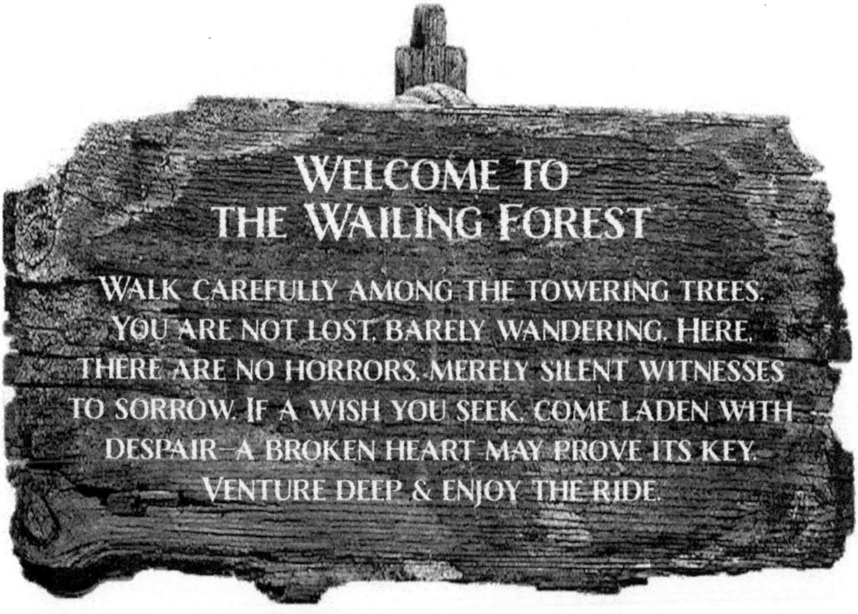

"What is all this?" Seraphine murmured, looking around and wondering if someone had placed this here as a joke. If that was the case, then it got her. Yet, deep down, she knew it wasn't a prank. Unease blossomed in her stomach.

Suddenly, the wind began to push her. She tried to hold onto the sign, but the wind was stronger, compelling her to move away from it.

She bent down, seeking shelter beneath an old tree. Perhaps she was just tired and had misunderstood the path. Maybe she had imagined the sign altogether. She had been hearing voices, so she might've started imagining things too.

Seraphine sighed deeply, the wind pushing her against the tree as she tried to figure out her location. It didn't matter if she was losing her mind or her heart or if everything seemed against her today. What mattered was that she needed to find a way back. Despite feeling damned for life, she wouldn't allow herself to get lost and frozen in the forest. Deep down, she knew that living was the greatest torment she could bestow upon those who had wronged her.

As the storm raged on, she wondered if it was also affecting all of Coldhaven. They had storms before, but this one seemed personal.

"Breathe, just breathe," she muttered to herself, holding on to the tree.

Seraphine still had time to reach the veil. She moved her frozen hands to cover her face but realized she had left her cloak behind. She almost laughed. *The Ancients must truly hate me.* She slowly focused her eyes, looking around for a clue, a path, but she had no idea where she was. Despite her weariness, never in her life had she been so disorientated to the point she lost her way.

Then, she felt that usual tingle in the back of her neck. Seraphine was not alone.

Grim Wanderer

The Grim Wanderer hovered nearby, shrouded in shadows, watching the crimson-eyed girl crumble before Maxwell. This heartbreak was no accident. It had been orchestrated, a cruel thread woven into the tapestry of manipulations he had designed around her. He had subtly nudged Maxwell toward a marriage of convenience, leveraging his considerable influence and dark connections. Yet, he wasn't devoid of flair for the dramatic—he believed Maxwell was unworthy of Seraphine, and in his twisted perception, he was doing her a favor.

However, the sight of her so defeated stirred an unexpected unease in him. Initially, the Grim Wanderer had planned to lead her astray in the Weeping Forest, to make her miss the veil or arrive hopelessly late. However, his plans had evolved, now leading her not just astray but to a place of his own making—a darker, deeper part of the forest.

The Wailing Forest, a hidden extension of the Weeping Forest, retained fragments of magic from the Otherworld and the Underworld. Now, it served as a secluded refuge for the Grim Wanderer.

Still, tonight, of all nights, he should have stayed away. Urgent matters awaited him, yet he found himself drawn to Seraphine's resolve as she stood in the snow. Her eyes were fierce with determination as she calculated her way out against the strong wind, probably seeking a path to the veil.

The Grim Wanderer watched her, captivated by her resilience. Her dress was torn, with no cloak to shield her from the cold. *How is she not freezing?* Like poisonous roses or ghostly kisses, like all the things forbidden in the most decadent way, her strikingly beautiful scarlet eyes were impossible to ignore.

"Who are you?" she called out suddenly, her voice cutting through the forest's silence. Although Seraphine couldn't see him, her instincts were sharp. "What are you then, if not a who?"

Amused and taken aback by her perceptiveness, the Grim Wanderer couldn't help but laugh—a sound that hadn't escaped his lips in centuries. He should have known better. She had always been clever, outsmarting him centuries ago during their first encounter. Now, she remained a cunning fox, ever so capable of seeing through veils that others could not.

As she stood scanning the shadows for any sign of him, he realized he was on the brink of making a monumental mistake. He looked at the dark sky as he released his hold on the magic. The storm stopped. The moon was clear now and high, and he could see some brilliant stars—not as shiny and beautiful as those in the eyes of the crimson-eyed creature but still a sweet companion.

The Grim Wanderer watched her breathe and close her eyes in relief. *How many times have we been under the same moon, the same sky? Had she ever wished for company besides the stars and old trees, just like me?*

"Answer me!" Seraphine said louder this time, undeterred.

He should've just moved away and let her follow his initial plan. However, her eyes were shining with so much emotion, so much fierceness, so much of her that, against his better judgment, the Grim Wanderer answered her.

Seraphine Ashcroft

"Hello there, Crimson Eyes," a rough, dark voice echoed through the woods.

Seraphine felt the trees arch as if drawing closer to the voice, almost purring at it, compelled by it. The wind was static once more, and this time, Seraphine was not looking for a way out.

One would normally be afraid of an unknown voice in such a dark place, but something about it felt just right, familiar even. Driven by curiosity, Seraphine paced from one tree to another, trying to pinpoint its source. *Let me catch you.*

"Are you just going to hide there like a scared cat?" she called out, a hint of irritation in her voice. "Look, I've had a terrible day. So, if you're here to play games, just leave me alone. I have places to be." Her frustration was palpable, but she hoped he would answer again. Perhaps he knew a way out of this place. Glancing up at the moon, she realized it was already midnight. The veil would close soon.

"Definitely not. I am not a scaredy-cat—that's a bit too offensive, Crimson Eyes," he retorted mockingly. His voice seemed to echo all around, or perhaps it was just her imagination playing tricks. It was a little distorted too, as if his voice was veiled somehow. Still, she couldn't see him.

Now that the storm was over, she noticed that the place was stunningly beautiful—the tall trees were adorned with sharp icicles and snow that glittered like diamonds, while the snow underfoot felt softer, like flour. Despite the chill in the air, she noticed snowflakes gently falling. She wondered if people realized that snow came in different shades of white.

What is this place? She knew now that this was not her forest.

"I think you are since you keep hiding. Anyway, whatever or whoever you are, what is this place?" Seraphine said, her eyes sharp, scanning every inch of her surroundings for any movement, anything that could reveal the source of that voice.

"Well, it seems like you keep avoiding the obvious and, as always, are looking in the wrong places," he said, just as she felt something brush her head—snow.

She looked up and saw it. Perched on a branch of one of those arched trees was a tall figure cloaked in the most stunning white fur she had ever seen. It appeared as though the cloak covering his body and face was woven from whiteness itself.

Seraphine had been a fool. All this time, she thought she was the hunter, but it seemed she had been the prey all along. Whoever this was, he wasn't an inoffensive creature or ghost from the Otherworld but a predator. Instead of fear, however, she felt something akin to interest.

He jumped down from the tree, landing right in front of her. Oddly enough, she couldn't see his face. A hood hid it, revealing only his mouth. He seemed human, but something was off about him. He was very tall—she was tall herself, yet he towered over her by a head.

"You talk like you know me. Are you the one who has been whispering to me?" Seraphine countered, keeping a good distance from him as the usual tingle at the back of her neck intensified.

He leaned against a tree, his furred cloak blending with the snow. "Maybe I am," he replied, catching a snowflake in his hand. Seraphine noticed his lips quirked up. Suddenly, the snowflakes froze in mid-air, the wind ceased, and time seemed to stop.

How ridiculous—winter and snow frozen in time. If this was a dream, she didn't want to wake up. She realized then he was different, unlike anyone she'd met. *What is he?* Her curiosity, mixed with an inexplicable pull, made her step closer to his overwhelming presence.

"Where are my manners?" he said, performing a mock bow. "You may call me the Grim Wanderer." He circled her slowly. "I was one of the unfortunate inhabitants of the Otherworld, ruled by Nemera, stuck here in the human realm after the creation of the veil," he said with a sly grin. "My job is to grant deals occasionally, like any Otherworld creature. Well, not *entirely* harmless, indeed, but neither are you."

"Grim Wanderer?" Seraphine laughed, feeling a strange thrill. "You must have a proper name."

"I do have a name, Crimson Eyes, but I won't share it with you," he said, stepping closer.

Seraphine bowed her head, trying to see more than his mouth. His face remained blurry, but he looked human.

The more human-like they appear, the more powerful or deadly they tend to be, or so the books I read in the Otherworld said. What unnerved her most was how he made her heart beat faster—not from fear, but from something she despised. Trying to ignore this, she decided his claim of being trapped here seemed genuine, and his chattiness was oddly comforting, which, again, uneased her.

"Well, that must be such a terrible thing, living among humans like us," she whispered, moving closer. "What a nightmare! Damn Nemera! What kind of ruler leaves behind such a scaredy-cat in this terrible place?"

He smiled, dimples gracing his cheeks.

Dimples. They were the cruelest trait since she found them mesmerizing.

"Aren't you a trickster? What is a nightmare but a mere misinterpreted possibility of a dream?" he purred.

Seraphine felt warmth filling her chest and cheeks at the realization that they were inches apart now.

"Now, to your question, you are in the Wailing Forest. How you got here, I'm not sure. This is the first time I've seen a human enter this place, unless..."

"Unless what?" Seraphine spat, her gaze sharp. He was alluring, but if he was from the Otherworld, he couldn't be trusted.

The Grim Wanderer waved his hand, and the world resumed its pace. Snowflakes began to fall again. He started to pace back and forth among the trees, feigning deep thought, hiding behind one tree and appearing between others.

"Unless you were desperate enough, broken-hearted perhaps, that the forest allowed you entry. This place was established centuries ago and can only be found by someone with a profound desire for a wish, someone so broken and sorrowful that the forest's single option is to offer a doorway to alleviate their pain. It's one of the few remnants from the Otherworld still present in the human realm."

"That sounds like a fairytale," she said, her voice skeptical.

He shifted slightly, stopping in front of a tree not far from her, his voice somber. "Fairytales aren't kind, Crimson Eyes. They are woven with lies and sorrow—you know that. Deals are designed to favor my kind. Tales are more than just stories. They are lessons meant to discourage repetition. There's nothing fairytale-like about them. Actually, let me tell you a story. I am feeling quite chatty tonight."

"And desperate for attention, Grim Wanderer. First climbing trees and now spinning tales," she remarked. Though she couldn't deny a spark of interest, Seraphine sat on the snow-covered ground. "Indulge me then," she continued, a mix of skepticism and intrigue in her tone. "Tell me a story, lie to me, trick me, do whatever since it's too late for me to get over what I had in my plans for tonight. Just one condition, and I will listen."

"What is it that you want?" His voice echoed around her like a dark melody.

She closed her eyes. "Make it interesting."

He laughed. "Deal."

Chapter 6

The Lonely Wolf

Born of agony,
Agony etched in veins,
None could discern the hue,
Whether crimson or something cruel,
Pale as ghostly clouds,
Blue as the abyss that devours.

Retrieved from *The Great Love Story of The White Fox*
by Illyra Everdawn, Ch. 8, p. 35.

Three Days Before the Incident
Seraphine Ashcroft

The Grim Wanderer nestled in the space next to her, the deep snow crunching beneath him, and began, "Before the realms were born—before humans, creatures of the Otherworld, and those of the Underworld emerged—the Eternals of chaos and voidness created three Ancients, magical, god-like entities, each charged with a crucial task to maintain the delicate balance of life. Among them is Brannon, whom you know as the guardian of the human realm. Interestingly, some legends claim he molded humans from crows. His fundamental responsibility was to oversee life."

Seraphine was enraptured. Although she knew the tale well, having read it in history books at Coldhaven and the Otherworld's library, hearing him recount it added a magical resonance to the familiar words. It was as if she were experiencing the magic herself, woven into the fabric of reality.

The Grim Wanderer continued, his voice tinged with nostalgia, "Then, there is Nemera, the Ancient of the Otherworld. She was tasked with overseeing life in the form of nature. That's why creatures of the Otherworld spring from animals or elements of the earth. Much like Nemera herself, they are prone to mischief, yet they invariably strive to maintain and protect life to a certain extent." Then, his voice turned distant, as if he were drawing from a well of personal memories. "And then there is Aurum, the lord and Ancient of the Underworld."

The Grim Wanderer sighed softly, the frosty air visible with each breath. "Aurum was tasked with overseeing death—not in a sinister way, but as a crucial element of balance. His creatures, much like those of the

Otherworld, are drawn to death, feeding off it to sustain the equilibrium of nature. It's a natural and necessary function." A mix of seriousness and intrigue surrounded him as he elaborated on his tale. "Thus, the three realms coexisted. The Otherworld and human realm lay side by side, interacting frequently. Humans would come to us seeking deals driven by their desires, and in turn, we'd offer protection and prosperity to their lands. Meanwhile, hidden portals connected the human realm to the Underworld, handling souls and the afterlife. Some interactions were harsher, of course. After all, the Underworld has quite the reputation."

His voice took on a somber note as he continued, "Everything seemed balanced, the world vibrant with colors. What they hadn't foreseen was the day a lonely creature from the Otherworld fell in love with a mere human. The real tragedy of the story was their belief that love conquered all. He even petitioned the arcane courts of the Otherworld, pleading for permission to age alongside her, to grow old and eventually pass into the Underworld as a normal soul. But, alas, even a creature of the Otherworld can be deceived."

The Grim Wanderer seemed to look at the sky, the weight of the tale heavy in his voice. "The arcane courts, perhaps driven by their own hidden agendas, presented him with a quest. They promised that if he succeeded, they would grant his wish. If he failed, he would face severe consequences. Unbeknownst to him, his task was to hunt a peculiar and very cunning animal. Reluctantly, he pursued the creature, despising the very idea of taking a life, even if it meant fulfilling his heart's desire."

He paused, and Seraphine followed his gaze toward the starry night sky. "In a cruel twist of fate, they had transformed his beloved into that very animal. So, in the end, he unknowingly killed his own love—the person for whom he was willing to challenge the very fabric of his existence. She was just a human, caught in a twisted game of rules and power."

"What happened after that?" she whispered, her heart aching with sorrow.

He shrugged slightly, his tone laced with irony. "It's said that the three Ancients, horrified by the cruelty of what had occurred, clashed with each other, each defending either the human or the Otherworld creature. To maintain peace, they decided to establish the veil, restricting movement between the realms. As you can see—" The Grim Wanderer gestured to the stark, wintry landscape around them. "The consequences were far-reaching. The imbalance led to the destruction of cities, eternal winters, and unfulfilled desires. Underworld creatures struggled to maintain the balance between life and death, sparking political turmoil with the Otherworld. The human realm was left isolated, eventually forgetting our existence entirely, which in turn wreaked havoc in the Otherworld, culminating in chaos. So, yes, it ended up 'greatly,' didn't it?" His sarcasm was palpable.

Seraphine couldn't help but wonder if he had been alive back then to have seen all that.

"But this tale isn't just about the veil or the realms. It's about him. The Otherworld silly creature. After he accidentally killed his beloved human, he was devastated. Heartbroken, he wandered into this very forest. He pleaded desperately for someone to revive her, but it was impossible. Then, he prayed for death, but killing a creature from the Otherworld requires more than mere magic. Finally, he begged for his heart to be frozen, to numb all his pain."

Seraphine watched him intently, absorbing every word of the story unknown to her.

"And so," he continued. "A creature from the court of Sorrowspring, which governs the water beings, heard his plea and granted it. He didn't understand the full consequences nor what would be demanded of him, but he asked for it. At first, he felt relief. There was silence in him, no pain, no tears. He thought perhaps he could move on."

"But then the water creature revealed that to maintain his frozen heart, he must continuously hunt and kill the same type of animal his beloved had been transformed into. Without pain or feeling, he pursued the creature. Yet, as he was about to deliver the fatal blow, memories of his beloved flooded his mind. Not even a frozen heart could shield him from the resurgence of such deep pain."

"He couldn't fulfill the hunt, so the deal was undone. After that, the poor creature chose to wander the realms in solitude."

Seraphine, moved by the story, pressed, "What happened to him?"

"He was a creature from the Otherworld, so his fate remains a mystery," he replied softly. "Some say he became a lone wolf, roaming indefinitely. Whether he lived or died is unknown. But remember, deals are perilous, and a broken heart cannot be mended by freezing it. And sometimes, love is a precursor to pain and grief." As he spoke, the Grim Wanderer gestured gracefully, causing snowflakes to swirl around the trees, each flake brushing against Seraphine before dissolving.

Seraphine laughed, the snowflakes tickling her nose, the cold air making her breath visible. "And is it all true?" she asked.

"Perhaps some parts are true, perhaps not. But it's a good tale, don't you think?" he concluded with a slight smile.

She marveled once again at his dimples and how human-like the Grim Wanderer seemed.

As Seraphine pondered the story, she understood that not all dreams were what they seemed, not all good tales had happy endings, and not all nightmares were purely terrifying. *Some are valuable lessons.* Wrapped in the wintry forest's embrace, she had never felt so warm, even as sleep began to envelop her.

Grim Wanderer

He watched Seraphine sleep, her chest rising and falling with each breath, peaceful yet unknowingly ensnared in a web of fate he had woven.

"What a pity," the Grim Wanderer murmured. His hand trembled as he held the countdown magic paper, now displaying just three days.

"Still as clever and cunning as ever," he mused, recalling her spirited defiance, unchanged despite the centuries. *Not that she can remember.* As he watched her, his heart ached with ancient sorrow. Leaning closer, his breath mingling with the cold air, he whispered, or more, he pleaded to her, "I am bound neither by creature nor human norms, yet you've always been the exception. I am truly sorry for the pain to come."

With practiced ease, he lifted the pearls from her pocket. Everything was unfolding as planned, yet nothing felt right.

I am a monster.

Seraphine had lost her job, her heart was shattered, and soon, her world would crumble entirely. The whispers of her bad luck, spurred by her unusual eyes—red eyes that he had falsely claimed mirrored those of Ancient Aurum—were nothing but a ruse to isolate her further.

Now, the whispering and playing with her head was something he did not plan. He just could not help himself. The Grim Wanderer wanted to be closer to her.

As the moon climbed higher, casting silver light through the trees, he knew time was slipping away. "Time. Time. Time," he whispered, each word a heartbeat, each heartbeat drawing closer to the inevitable.

He draped his white-furred cloak over Seraphine, shielding her from the chill. From his pocket, he produced a rare sea leaf, its edges shimmering. The leaf, a bargaining chip from the Shadowmarket, was meant for moments like these. He placed a small piece on her lips, ensuring her sleep would be deep and undisturbed for a couple of hours.

Releasing his cat sith, the creature's eyes briefly glowed as it materialized. "Guard her well. I must finish this before dawn," he instructed, his voice steady yet heavy with unspoken regret.

You are a monster. You are a monster. You are a monster.

With a final look at Seraphine, the Grim Wanderer turned and walked back toward the town, his steps rhythmical but silent on the forest floor.

Tick. Tock. Tick. Tock.

Seraphine Ashcroft

Seraphine awoke in a dense forest full of flowers, roses, and green. *How did I get here?* The Grim Wanderer was nowhere to be seen.

Spring.

That's impossible. Seraphine had been living in an eternal winter since birth. She was only familiar with the seasons from her books. The Otherworld seemed like a possibility, but she knew that whatever the weather was, it was not a regular spring.

Before she could dwell on that, a raspy, mournful, and terrifying howl echoed in her ears. Her heart pounded as the sound of pursuing paws thundered, getting closer and closer to her.

"Run," a voice whispered in her head, and for the first time, she decided to take the advice and took off.

Each step was desperate, fueled by a primal fear she could not understand, the ground beneath her feet a blur of roots and fallen leaves that were turning black and red.

The air was thick with an ominous chill, and with every breath, she felt a presence drawing closer, its howls a haunting melody of menace and despair. The forest seemed endless, a labyrinth of darkness and whispering trees that spoke of ancient curses and untold stories. She dared not look back. Even the flowers seemed to be crying and screaming for her to keep running.

Yet, in the depths of her terror, a strange sense of familiarity washed over her. This chase, this terror, they weren't the first of their kind. She had been here before, running from the same inevitable fate.

Just when her strength waned and her resolve crumbled, Seraphine turned and looked at the beast, a massive wolf, its presence overwhelming. There was no escape, no way out. When the wolf opened its sharp mouth, the nightmare fractured, sending her spiraling back to the beginning of the chase.

"A nightmare… This is a nightmare," she realized.

An ethereal voice brushed her ear. "This is not a nightmare, but you better run from it—like you always do. Run from your destiny, from what you are, what you were."

Then, it began again—the run, the chase, the fear, the same end. Seraphine tried to change it, but her body was in control. It was like a memory, unchanged, impossible to alter.

Trapped in this cyclical torment, Seraphine realized with chilling clarity that these weren't mere dreams. They were memories, fragments of a cursed existence replaying endlessly in the depths of her slumber.

This realization did not bring peace but a deeper, more profound terror. As the nightmare reset again and again, beginning anew with her running through the darkened woods, Seraphine understood the inescapable truth of her situation. She was not just fleeing a predator. She was confronting her own haunted past.

When the wolf opened its mouth for the fourth time, she swore she heard it speak, uttering the same words as it closed its jaws on her.

"I am sorry."

Chapter 7

The Hidden Wolf

And there, in the heart of the forest,
He stood, gazing upon what he believed to be a mere mortal,
Yet, knowing deep within, she was far more than flesh and bone.

Retrieved from the Grim Wanderer's journal.

Grim Wanderer

The Grim Wanderer walked across Coldhaven, just beyond the eerie whispers of the Weeping and Wailing Forests. Moving silently like a specter, he felt equally ethereal.

This place, however, he wished to traverse quickly. Despite knowing the girl was safe, asleep in the sheltering woods, urgency gnawed at him. A myriad of tasks lay unfinished, this one proving most formidable.

As he skirted the perimeter of Iceveil Square, the clock tower loomed in the distance, its hands frozen as if clasping the past. He had witnessed its unchanging face for centuries, echoing his own temporal stasis. Tonight, his path diverged, leading him toward a cottage on the town's outskirts—an abode now surrendered to decay, its fetor wafting across the cold night air.

Years ago, the crimson-eyed girl had cursed that house. He remembered watching her, but he hadn't stopped marveling at her. *Such a curious mind from such a young age.* At the front of the house no one dared approach, the Grim Wanderer knew it wasn't inhabited.

He wondered if she, too, sometimes delighted in the fact that she was able to create such a disaster from a young age. Still, he knew he had no time for that topic now.

Then, he brushed a finger under his arm, where another blood-inked tattoo lay on his skin, representing another of his familiars. The tattoo moved, and a creature appeared in front of him. Just like the cat, he had collected some interesting friends over the past decades.

This time, it was a barghest named Grimnight. It was large enough that most people would mistake it for a wolf, but it was a monstrous black dog that lived in the darkest corners of the Otherworld. He smirked. *My father had certainly loved them.* They were vicious, with large teeth and claws, yet very easy to command. Grimnight had been his for a long time, a reminder of his past and family.

They both ventured inside the cursed house. The house's exterior walls, once painted a cheerful hue, now bore the scars of neglect, with paint peeling away to reveal the rotting wood beneath. Vines crept up the sides like fingers seeking to choke the life from the bricks, their grip unyielding.

As he stepped inside, the air grew thick with the musk of mold and the sharp tang of mildew. Each footfall kicked up clouds of dust, the particles dancing in the slivers of moonlight that pierced through the cracks in the boarded-up windows. The floorboards groaned under his weight, the sound echoing off the walls of the narrow hallway that led deeper into the house's darkness.

A boggart waited at the end of the hall in what used to be the living room. The creature was perched atop what once might have been an ornate armchair, now nothing more than a frame covered in tattered fabric and festooned with cobwebs. The boggart's skin was leathery and wrinkled, mottled with patches of mold and fungus that seemed to pulse with a life of their own. Its eyes were too large for its face, bulbous and unblinking, glowing faintly red in the gloom.

Its mouth, twisted into a grotesque smile, revealed rows of sharp, jagged teeth, like shards of broken glass, ready to tear and rend. The boggart's hair was a tangled mess of knots and leaves, with insects crawling in and out of the dark tresses.

"Hello, little thing," the Grim Wanderer spoke, his voice a calm contrast to the unsettling hiss that perpetually seemed to emanate from the boggart.

The creature cocked its head, the movement jerky and unnatural, as if it were not used to being addressed so casually by something it couldn't dominate or terrify. The Grim Wanderer still could not believe that his crimson-eyed girl had turned this brownie into a living nightmare, a boggart. *Oh, what a funny way to trick humans.*

"I must apologize. I was a little late. I had some... unpredictable things come my way," he said smoothly, producing a folded letter from one leaf and extending it toward the creature.

The boggart's fingers, thin and bony, snatched the letter with surprising swiftness, its nails scraping against the paper. After reading the letter, the creature's smile widened.

"So, I can return home and be free of this house?" Its voice was a harsh whisper that seemed to scratch at the air.

"Only if you do as I said in the note. No mistakes."

"I will make sure to proceed with the most expected outcome, but there is something missing..."

The Grim Wanderer interrupted him. "Here."

He gave the boggart the bottle that his cat sith had retrieved from the Shadowmarket. The bottle was beautiful to the eye but as deadly as a beithir.

"Be careful with that. You shall return the remains of the bottle's liquid to me after the first part of the deal is finished."

"I won't fail you," the boggart said and then disappeared again, hiding in the wall of the rotten house.

"Good," he said more to himself before leaving the house.

It was still dark, and the Grim Wanderer still had some time before the girl would wake up. So, he headed to the last standing place for this checkmate move.

The Grim Wanderer threaded his way through the forest's darkness again. He took a detour near the edge of the woods that was shrouded, bordered by gnarled trees with thorny limbs that reached out like the fingers of the dead. Every step stirred the scent of decay, the undergrowth crunching underfoot. He moved with silent urgency, accompanied by Grimnight.

A frozen lake lay at the center, its surface a mirror to the starless sky above. The air was sharper here, each breath a razor slicing through the lungs. Most hunters avoided this place, and he was sure the crimson-eyed girl knew about the whispering tales of the frozen lake at the border to the Weeping Forest.

"Isn't this a pleasant surprise?" a raspy female voice said.

He looked around toward a blackened tree near the frozen lake and smirked. "I am pretty pleasant indeed. Why don't you come out and say hi, darling?"

The voice muffled a dark retort. "I hope Nemera plucks each limp of your body."

"Ah, my memory is quite dusty. I just recalled it!" the Grim Wanderer said, laughing, moving closer to the dark tree. "You cannot move, a beauty cuffed to a tree, caged between realms. What a twist of fate."

As he neared the tree, he saw a figure hidden behind the old tree, which was rotten to the core as the creature bound to it—a baobhan sith.

The creature was a horrifying tapestry of beauty and terror, draped in a gown of shimmering emerald that clung to her form like moss to a tombstone. Her skin was an unnatural shade of alabaster, luminescent under the moonlight, making her appear as a spectral apparition. When they met his, her eyes shone with a predatory gleam, reflecting a hunger not for sustenance but for suffering.

Long, tangled hair the color of raven feathers fell around her shoulders, moving as if alive with a serpentine life. The air around her was heavy with the scent of blood and the faint, almost imperceptible, whisper of decay. It was said that the baobhan sith could enchant with her gaze, luring her victims to a gruesome demise with the promise of her lips, which were as red as the blood she so craved.

Her lips curled into a smile of cold, calculating malevolence. As the Grim Wanderer approached, her chains rattled softly against the tree she was bound to, a chilling sound that seemed to echo across the frozen lake.

"Let's make a deal, shall we?" With a flourish, the Grim Wanderer produced a key using another one of his leaves, the metal glinting ominously in the moonlight.

Leaning close, he whispered into her ear. As the key turned in the lock, the shackles fell with a thud to the snow-dusted earth, liberating the baobhan sith from her bonds.

The Grim Wanderer handed her a piece of red cloth, the color vivid against the stark whiteness of the snow. Her smile widened, a grotesque display of cruel intentions as her long, sharp teeth gleamed ominously in the moonlight.

Freed, she moved with unholy grace toward the city, her every step an elegant menace.

Seraphine Ashcroft

Seraphine awoke with a throbbing headache, her thoughts foggy as if she had slept for an eternity. The strange dreams that haunted her sleep were already starting to fade, slipping through her fingers like wisps of smoke. She tried to grasp the threads of her nightmares, but the effort made her head pound even harder.

"You do sleep a lot. You know that, right?" The Grim Wanderer's voice broke through her haze.

So, it hadn't been a dream after all. Seraphine had no idea how long she had been lying there in the snow of the Wailing Forest. Then, she noticed a faint light rising, illuminating the surroundings.

She had lost the entrance to the veil. *Damn the Ancients!*

To her own surprise, she found herself smiling, feeling inexplicably lighter. Perhaps the Grim Wanderer was a good influence, or maybe she just needed the rest.

"I do not. I was just tired," she retorted, noticing a bizarre taste of pine in her mouth. "Do you ever take that hood off your face?"

"I do, but just in front of those who are worth it," he replied with a teasing lilt, his eyes gleaming beneath the hood.

Would I ever be worthy of it? She wanted to be, for some reason.

"And you snored. A lot."

Seraphine rolled her eyes at him but then remembered the tale he had told her before she had fallen asleep. The idea of having a heart frozen, free of everything—no pain, no remorse, no fear—intrigued her. She had pondered such a state many times, but now, with his story in mind, she couldn't help but wonder aloud, "If I were to ask for that deal you mentioned in your tale, would you do it? Do you have the power?"

The Grim Wanderer was silent for a moment, his mouth a straight line. "Freezing a heart requires someone from the line of Sorrowspring or a higher authority in the Otherworld. That being said, I would, and I can." His words were heavy with caution.

Seraphine wondered whether he was from the Sorrowspring line or if he held a more politically significant position he wished to conceal.

As he turned away, he continued, his furred cloak flowing like a dark river, "But I must implore you—never make that deal if you can avoid it. The horrors and sacrifices required to complete the deal carry a terrible cost. I won't deny you the choice, but if you can, please avoid it. You are destined for an amazing life regardless." At that, the Grim Wanderer knelt in front of her and held her hand, spreading it open.

Seraphine held her breath at the touch. His hand was warm like the sun but soft as snow. He cleared his throat. "You know what I see in your crimson eyes?"

She was afraid to know, but she shook her head gently. He placed a small snowflake, perfectly shaped, on her palm, his hand still holding hers. "You are like a rose in the middle of winter." The snowflake shifted, and from it, a stem started to grow, creating a rose made of ice and snow. "A red rose, unreachable but lasting, enduring. Something you would not expect to grow against adversities, but that beautifully does so. And more."

Then, the Grim Wanderer pulled his other hand away, never leaving hers, and bit his own finger. He moved his finger and let a drop of blood fall onto the frozen rose on her hand.

"A starlight of crimson that perseveres over the winter and heartbreaks. A touch of spring in an eternal winter," he whispered as the rose absorbed his blood and turned red, slowly melting and transforming into a real flower—unlike those she had seen in books.

Seraphine touched the rose, the petals softer than velvet. When she smelled it, she felt as if she were inhaling life.

"Beautiful," she muttered, as if in a daze. Not even in the Otherworld had she seen a real, common spring rose.

"That she is," the Grim Wanderer murmured.

While she could not see his face, she felt as if he were looking at her with a depth of feelings she longed to understand. He seemed as alluring as he was dangerous.

"Can I keep it?" she asked softly. The rose might die and freeze soon, but she just wanted to hold it a little longer.

He smiled, a gesture so subtle it felt like a secret shared between them. "You can keep everything."

She stood, holding the rose and missing the warmth from the Grim Wanderer's touch. It was time to go home. He knew the way out, so she walked with him, following a few steps behind. His presence was comforting, somehow familiar. She pondered whether he was the same presence she had repeatedly felt. As she walked, she realized she also needed to concoct an explanation for why she had been kicked out of the fishery and why she hadn't brought home any coins that day.

"Oh, Brannon, help me," Seraphine whispered.

Grim Wanderer

The Grim Wanderer was exhausted. He had barely made it to the Wailing Forest in time. Now, he trailed alongside the girl with the crimson eyes.

Not to mention, Seraphine was smiling. *One could die for a smile like that.*

As soon as they reached the edge to Coldhaven, she moved past him, her scent enveloping him. She turned to him, her crimson eyes shining with eagerness and a sentiment he dared not define, and waved in farewell. Her hair flowed smoothly in the chilly air, her eyes sparkled, and a pang of guilt washed over him. The Grim Wanderer knew all too well that her happiness might soon evaporate.

"Thanks for the rose," she shouted and then pointed a finger at him. "But stop messing with my head. I know you are the one whispering here and there!"

"So bossy. I was just messing around. I told you before, I am harmless." He wasn't, but he felt like enjoying himself with her chattiness and beauty at dawn.

Seraphine huffed, and he couldn't help but want to approach her again. He could go as far as draining his whole blood so she could have a million roses just to see her smile a million times more. All he had done to get to this point could reflect on how mad he was for wanting her, for seeing her, even if it meant losing her.

"Don't do it, especially if I am naked in my bathroom, you pervert." She sneered, but he sensed an undertone that implied she was joking.

"I promised, I saw nothing. I was far enough, and one could define me as a gentleman." This he was. He had been across the wall of her cottage, hiding in the shadows. Now, he was indeed tempted to see all of her. When it came to her, there was nothing but want. "Unless you wish me to, in that case…"

The Grim Wanderer saw her blush even from afar. He had to bite his lip to keep from saying something utterly inappropriate. Or something entirely cheesy, like how he could compare those rosy cheeks to the colors of the sunset on days when the light was at its peak and the moon rose at its brightest.

"You have a death wish. Now, I shall go. It wasn't unpleasant to cross paths with you… Grim Wanderer." Seraphine turned back again.

The way she pronounced that name sent a shiver to his core. *Little does she know.* Still, he would do anything for her to call him by his real name. For her to remember.

As she walked away, she seemed like she was dancing with lightness. He truly smiled, savoring what might be one of the last times he would see her like this—smiling, not yet despising him.

Before he could lose sight of her, he opened his palm. A tiny blue leaf began to swirl in the air, tracing her path before slipping discreetly into her dress's pocket.

CHAPTER 8

THE BLUE FOX & THE SHADOWED WOLF

How dreadful a life, to exist without another's embrace.
For centuries, I've witnessed time's relentless march,
yet the tragic fate of that cursed little fox haunts me still.
May she find herself once more in the labyrinth of time.

Retrieved from Theodorah's journal.

Seraphine Ashcroft

Seraphine reached her cottage, bathed in sunlight that seemed brighter than ever. She was able to hide the rose under her cloak. One might think she was a witch for having something that did not exist in these lands. Still, she wouldn't have regretted a thing. Before she could think more about that matter, the front door opened, and Leander Ashcroft appeared like the sun after a long night.

"Heya, Seren!" he shouted from afar, his voice woody and full of warmth.

Seraphine ran and jumped into his wide arms. Strong as he was, he still stumbled back slightly. He was sunlight and comfort personified, and she felt like she wasn't drowning anymore.

"I missed you," she muffled into his shoulder. She could smell white, pure winter and the forest in him.

"I missed you too," he replied, setting her down and holding her hand. Leander looked at her, and she worried at how tired he looked. He was very handsome, but she could see some lines around his eyes, his hair a little messier. She promised herself to work really hard so he could take a break from useless hunting. At this point, there was nothing to hunt. *Everything is dying around Coldhaven.*

"Seren, there's something I must tell you," he began, but before Leander could continue, her sister burst out of the house, a grin stretching across her face.

She waved four letters sealed with a crimson red seal. "We've been invited to the Wraithwood household for a ball!" Aeliana resembled a cheerful little seelie fairy, practically bouncing with excitement. "Not that I am not happy to see you here, Dad. But this is the event of the year—"

"Can't believe she is more enthused about a ball. She is growing too fast," her father muttered under his breath, and Seraphine laughed, silently agreeing with him.

"All of us are invited?" Leander said, his tone tinged with concern. Perhaps he wondered why now, just like her. After meeting Evren, Seraphine was sure there was no way in any of the three realms they would ever be invited. However, she felt a little daring after talking with the Grim Wanderer.

Seraphine took the invitation, smiling like a fox. *Payback time.* "Well, that's unexpected, but I guess it won't hurt to enjoy a night away. It says it's to be held two nights from now. We still have time to get—"

"You are not going, Seren," Leander interjected.

Seraphine looked at her father, her smile faltering.

"But we are all invited. It would be—"

"No, you are not going there. You are never to be near that household," Leander insisted, gripping her hand and looking into her eyes pleadingly.

She was bewildered by his intensity, feeling hurt.

"Look, I know we're short on some stuff. I don't mind using some of my old dresses," Seraphine pleaded, suddenly desperate to go, to see Max, to pain Evren, and to feel like part of the town.

"I don't want you there!" Leander shouted, the force of his voice cutting through the air.

Silence fell sharply around them. Even her sister stared at Leander as if he were a stranger.

"We will go, but you will stay here. I do not want you there with us."

Seraphine froze, unable to accept the words that came from her father. *What a twisted world.* Thalassa's laughter echoed from the background.

"Good. We don't have enough money for new dresses anyway, so it's better to keep you here, Seren dear," Thalassa said mockingly. "Also, it seems like you've been skimming some of our savings. I found some coins in your room. You know that's stealing, don't you?"

Seraphine was aghast. "I earn my money from my work, and I've never, ever stolen a coin. I provide whatever I can, you know that." Her face turned red, incredulous at the accusations. Then, she saw her father and sister avoiding her gaze.

Do they believe I am stealing? Perhaps that was what her father had wanted to talk about. *Does he think I might steal from the Wraithwood house?* Her father knew she was keeping savings for herself. He would never think bad about her like that.

I don't want you there.

Thalassa's smile widened, and Seraphine stormed to her room without another word.

She heard Thalassa in the background, "Leander, you need to get a hold of her. It's getting out of hand. I received a note that she disrespected the poor fisherman and Evren Wraithwood."

Wanting to hear no more, Seraphine slammed her door loudly. "Breathe, just breathe," she told herself, but there it was, the drowning feeling again.

This time, she felt like claws were dragging her to the bottom of her own pit. Seraphine took the rose out and placed it on the desk. It represented a momentary happiness spent alongside the Grim Wanderer. However, in truth, there was no happiness. There was just void and confusion and pain.

There must be some misunderstanding. Seraphine needed to calm down. Then, she would talk with her father. There was no way they thought of her as a thief. *Cursed? Fine. But a thief?* Well, she was, but never to her family. *That's not good either.*

Sitting on the edge of her bed, she felt something heavy in her skirt. Reaching into her pocket, she found five coins. It was too late for explanations now. At a different time, she would have screamed out of happiness. Now frustrated and defiant, Seraphine threw the coins out of her bedroom window.

Seraphine heard muffled sounds outside her bedroom and was sure Leander and her sister tried to speak to her, but Seraphine was still mad, so she kept her door locked. She had been staring at the same spot on her ceiling for hours, her mind a whirlwind of anger and confusion. *How had everything gone so wrong?*

Wanting to escape her swirling thoughts, Seraphine moved to the tiny desk by the window and opened the black book she had borrowed from the Mystweave Library. Some reading might help her escape her mind.

The truth was that she locked herself up not because she was angry but because she couldn't face her father. He was her hero, and yes, she hadn't been the most upright and perfect daughter, but she was too scared to acknowledge that perhaps her father thought the same as the rest—that she was a mistake, an omen of bad things, a thief, a trickster.

No, I won't consider it. Seraphine opened the book. The book seemed enchanted, which was normal coming from the Otherworld. Whenever she lifted her eyes from its pages, the letters shifted, rearranging themselves into a different story.

The first was titled *The Winter Haunt and the Prince*, but it quickly became *The Haunted Winter Prince*. It was bewildering.

Seraphine flipped through other pages, finding illustrations of animals, creatures, and items from the Otherworld. These images also transformed with each blink, morphing into new depictions, except for one. It was in the middle of the book, unchanging.

A wolf.

"Why so quiet?" The familiar voice broke her concentration.

She didn't need to look up, recognizing that tone by now. She had felt the tingle in her neck minutes ago, so she was just waiting for him to say something.

"What are you doing here?" Seraphine turned and saw the Grim Wanderer sitting on the edge of her bed, the picture of relaxation.

His lips quirked up. "Can't say. Seems like I cannot stay away from you," he purred, and Seraphine turned around. Such playfulness was strange for her, yet it felt like a sweet caress on her heart. *Do not even think about it.*

"Well, that is sad. Don't you have anything better to do? Like scaring people, perhaps?"

Grim Wanderer

The Grim Wanderer surveyed Seraphine's bedroom, noting its cozy simplicity. However, it was the walls that captured his attention, adorned with multiple paintings of flowers and foxes.

Foxes?

He disregarded the infuriating detail and focused on Seraphine. He knew she was on the verge of some painful family conflicts. Of course, he had a hand in all this. It was part of his plan—so was to offer comfort. He needed her to trust him, yet he also genuinely cared about her well-being, his mind and heart always cracking and twisted whenever it came to her.

His hooded gaze wandered to her. There she was, still in that old torn dress, her hair pulled up messily, showing a beautiful long neck he so much wanted to trace with his fingers. Seraphine had a black book in front of her, and somehow, she looked so humanly normal and fragile, her eyes slightly dim and worried.

No. Normal is a poor choice of words, he decided. She looked like a dream, too, something he would always yearn for and never truly be able to have.

How many times would the mere presence of her enchant me? It had been an endless loop of yearning and wanting without release. Some locks of hair fell, grazing her cheeks, and for a moment, the Grim Wanderer thought that even such mere movement of her shiny hazelnut hair could be considered pure delirium. *I am in so much trouble.*

Clearing his throat, he stood by the large window. "I might go and scare some people later, but in the meantime, I can be an invisible guest or friend. I think you would rather like that. You seem… torn."

She turned around, holding a letter. "What is this?"

He tried to take the paper from her grasp, but she snatched it away.

"A sentence of death," Seraphine mocked, stretching her legs and looking smitten. Such a complexity she was. One moment, her eyes could be a deep, sorrowful red, and then they could turn into devilish crimson.

The Grim Wanderer moved and slowly took her wrist—an excuse to touch her—pressing her palm until she was no longer holding the letter.

Opening the letter, he smirked. "Ah, an invitation to a ball! You humans fancy me with such theatrics," and it was true. *What a waste of wine to be held captive in a dress and pretend to smile while chatting with liars and deceivers.*

Balls were a mere mask to secure a position in society. However, he had never seen her at one, and this seemed like a good movement in his game.

"I think you should go and dance. Can't keep that talent hidden in the winter forests and trees."

"I'd rather be seen by them than by that smelly excuse of a man." Snatching the letter from his hand, she tore it in two. *Well then.*

"Wraithwood?" He eyed her carefully. Seraphine wasn't fond of that name—that, he was sure.

That, I made sure.

"Yes, quite sure you are familiar with that name. Everyone here knows it," she said, and based on her look, she did not find this situation as amusing as he. "He is a like a… wolf, not a good one, just a lonely and smelly one. He is a self-centered human, a pompous brat with no manners, and yet…"

"And yet?"

"I do wish to go, not because I want to fancy myself in dresses, just… I don't know. I am bluffing and blaming all this on someone I have seen just once because I am mad and not thinking straight."

The Grim Wanderer moved slightly closer to her. "I am sure he is all that. Perhaps he is even worse. But you do not need to mingle with him. You can just go and have fun. I am not a fan of balls, but if you go, I can keep you company, hidden in the shadows, perhaps scare that Wraithwood excuse of a wolf away for you. I can even hide your beautiful, graceful dancing from undeserving eyes. If I don't, perhaps…" He trailed off.

"What?" she said, curiosity filling her gaze.

"The trees and snowflakes that are always delighted with your moves might feel jealous, Crimson Eyes. Such a view is not for everyone. I am sure they want to keep that view to themselves. Who would have guessed that the trees and snowflakes could be so bitter and envious."

"Just the trees and the snowflakes are jealous? No one else I should be concerned about?" Her eyes flickered from crimson to almost dark, tasty wine.

The Grim Wanderer smiled, licking his lips slowly at the thought of delicious Otherworld wine. Still, those eyes of hers were making him drunk enough. "I can think of a very handsome-ish creature from the Otherworld that might want to join your little fan club alongside the trees and snowflakes. But this is neither here nor there. I doubt you get all worked up for a mere ball. What else is getting in that twisted mind of yours?"

Seraphine sighed loudly and looked at him pensively. "It's not the ball… I am… I don't know what I am, what I should feel. I feel mad and sad and torn, and happy and eager and guilty. Is that normal? To feel everything and nothing at all?"

If she only knew I feel just like that every single day of my miserable existence. "Let me listen to what pains you then. You can even pretend I am not here. Maybe that will help ease whatever is making those crimson eyes so sad and dim."

She smiled. "There is no way I can pretend you are not here."

"Good, I feel the same way about you. There is no way I can pretend you are not this extraordinary being." *I mean it.*

Seraphine moved up to open the window, her hair falling to her back in slow waves from her messy bun. She revealed a small ladder outside.

"That is what a trickster from the Otherworld would say. Try better next time." She then jumped outside the window and sat there.

"Yes, you are right. But right now, I am not a creature from the Otherworld. Not a trickster, not a whisper in your ear. I am your ghost," he said while sitting beside her on the outside ladder.

"I am so tired… Whatever I say and do is wrong, and I am hurting. I just don't know what I am supposed to do…" Seraphine closed her eyes.

All this was his fault, and he could use this time to push her more for his plan to succeed, but instead, he decided to take a break from his role as the Grim Wanderer. He wanted to be himself, too, so he gently nudged her shoulder. "As a creature that is probably older and wiser," he began, hearing her laugh softly.

"Weren't you a ghost? Aren't those silent?"

"You are ruining my moment, and there are hunting ghosts. I guess they speak once in a while."

"I am quite cursed, so that makes sense, I guess," she said quietly.

He moved closer. "There is one piece of advice I hope you take to heart. Which you have, if you were wondering." Laying down his covered head, he whispered in her ear, his lips and nose caressing her pale and delicate skin, "You are the most extraordinary being I have ever encountered." He saw her eyes drifting close, but she didn't pull away. "And you can be whatever you want to be. You want to be rich? Be it. You want to flee this town? Do it. You want to lie down and do what people expect you to do so you can be a hero? That is fine. But I hope you do whatever makes you feel like you are yourself—even if that makes you a villain in others' eyes."

At that, Seraphine turned, nose to nose. His face was hidden, but she felt his gaze on her deeply, profoundly, unworthy.

"And Seraphine," he added, realizing he had said her name aloud for the first time. "Trust me, with those eyes, you would make an extraordinary villain. The greatest and most dangerous one the world has ever seen." He paused, and longing came alive in her eyes—to be free to feel like herself. She was no villain, but in a world full of fake heroes, the real ones, the purest hearts different from others, would always be that. "Just do whatever you wish. The world is full of mystery and adventures. Do not let such human thoughts get to your head."

"I do not want to be a hero," Seraphine whispered so low he barely caught it. Surprising him, she inched closer, her eyes drifting lower momentarily, leaving to display a crown of dark lashes. "Nor a villain. Though the way you make it sound, it seems quite fitting for me. Still, I just want to be me, normal me—no hero, no villain. Merely ordinary."

"Ordinary is the most dangerous and brave thing one can be." With that, she had fallen again for his tricks. Seraphine had opened up to him. Her sorrows and concerns now belonged to him.

Now that it was done, he could leave. However, he couldn't move away from her. Not when she was so close. Seraphine was an addiction, one he did not ever plan to quit. Her eyes were now open again brilliant, stardust painted in wine and crimson, and her mouth was a prison he couldn't escape. He was a prisoner already, hers, even if she wasn't aware of it.

For a moment, he inched closer and saw her close her eyes, his breath mingling with hers. Waiting for him. *Just one kiss.*

"I must go," he said quietly, distancing himself from Seraphine.

Without waiting for a response, he walked away, disappearing among the snowflakes falling from the clear sky as he turned off his emotions once more. He didn't dare to look back. They would eventually see each other pretty soon, according to his plan.

It was better this way. He needed to focus now, or all his work would be for nothing. Not to mention, the stakes were high. It was either win or lose a life.

Her life.

Chapter 9

The Curious Wolf

In the Otherworld, roses bloomed,
Thorns screamed in a symphony of anguish,
And the people cowered in shadows,
For beauty thrived in the bloody, dark fear
That draped itself over the boundless black night.

Retrieved from *The Garden Poems: Madness & Rosses*, Ch. 1, p. 15.

Seraphine Ashcroft

Seraphine stood outside for a few more minutes, replaying the conversation with the Grim Wanderer in her mind. For a moment, she thought he would kiss her. She did not even know him, except that he was a deviant who enjoyed tormenting her by whispering odd things, which seemed like trouble.

However, she wanted to be kissed. To feel wanted and normal. *Was it because of how I am feeling or my feelings toward him?*

When the Grim Wanderer left her there, she felt lonely, but there was also relief. If she were to kiss anyone—to gift a piece of her heart—she needed to ensure it was because she wanted to, not because the circumstances influenced her to drown her sorrows by such theatrics as kisses and unfounded love. While it was improbable the Grim Wanderer had feelings, using him was wrong. That was not how she wanted to be.

Still, Seraphine missed him already. Whoever the Grim Wanderer was, a selkie in disguise or even a hag, it didn't matter. For her, he was not any other friend but a safe place. It felt like they had known each other for a lifetime. *Perhaps he will even show his face to me one day.*

Retreating indoors, Seraphine closed her window and retreated to her bed. Sleep had almost taken her when she jolted awake by the sound of her window abruptly opening.

"What the—"

Peering into the room, she saw nothing amiss at first. Then, her eyes caught sight of a small purple leaf fluttering through the window like a delicate snowflake. It drifted toward her, and as soon as the leaf landed on the bedside next to her hand, it morphed into a letter.

Crimson Eyes,
Thanks for your company. Or, well, you're welcome for my company, I should say. While I am out in the woods scaring countless folks with my handsomeness, I wanted to give you this leaf. It will lead you to me in case you want to hear more of my great advice.
P.S. I also found some pearls in the woods, which I am sure you stole. So, I took them, but I will return them to you. Seems like you may want them.

The letter morphed back into a little purple leaf. Seraphine almost laughed at the note's cheeky tone. *What a self-centered creature. As if—*

Her gaze returned to the leaf, breaking her thoughts. It was beautiful and shaped like a heart, purple with small glittering spots, unlike anything she had ever seen, even at the Shadowmarket. She carefully picked up the leaf and slipped it into her pocket. Perhaps she could gather some pearls and trade them at the Shadowmarket tonight. *Maybe Father would—*

Suddenly, screams pierced the air, jolting her from her train of thought.

Seraphine stepped out of her bedroom and saw her father at the entrance of their house. Her sister and Thalassa were hiding near the kitchen table. As soon as Seraphine appeared, her sister looked at her with terror and mouthed, "Run."

"This must be a mistake," her father said, probably to someone outside. "There is no way this involves her."

Seraphine moved closer to her father and was surprised to see a full crowd of townspeople outside, their faces contorted with anger, some crying. Coldhaven was a small town, so most faces were familiar.

Pushing Leander and trying to get hold of Seraphine, a woman she recognized shouted, "There, you little cursed thing! You, *you* killed him!" Her voice broke, and she began to sob uncontrollably.

Then, Seraphine realized the woman was Mr. Vale's wife. She used to visit him occasionally whenever she was at his shop.

But killed who?

Seraphine moved toward the entrance door. Although her father tried to hold her back, she pushed past and approached the lady since this was a misunderstanding. "Ma'am, I am sorry, I am not quite certain about what you are talking about, but if there is something I can help with—" Mr. Vale's wife slapped her across the face, sending Seraphine tumbling to the ground.

What on Nemera's wings?

Slender and short as the woman was, Seraphine felt the slap to her core, the woman's sorrow overwhelming. Looking up, she found herself in the snow, blurry faces all around her until she could locate two familiar and clear visages between the chaos of the situation: Max and Evren Waithwood.

Max looked concerned and almost as if he was restraining himself. He should know better when it came to Seraphine, but he seemed just a bystander and a coward. Meanwhile, Evren was missing his smirk and all-mighty presence. His eyes were darker, a winter storm in them.

As Seraphine tried to stand up, she felt a pain that made her stick to the hard ground. Her ankle was twisted, probably when she had landed on the snow.

Lifting her head, she looked at Mr. Vale's wife. "You have no right to do that! I have done nothing. How dare you come onto our land and do this? I don't even know—"

"I have no right?" the lady retorted, tears and fury in her eyes, her face contorting between pain and hatred. "M-my—" she stuttered, struggling to find her words. "My husband was killed just before dawn. He was found in the Weeping Forests."

No, that can't be. Seraphine had just seen him yesterday. She knew Mr. Vale had been angry with her, but to hear that he had been killed was terrifying. She had even planned to visit him today to apologize. "I am so, so sorry. I did not know. I—" Seraphine stuttered, unsure why all this was somehow connected to her.

Everyone was whispering, and multiple eyes in different shapes and colors looked at her. Yet, she focused again on Evren Wraithwood, who was whispering something to Mr. Vale's wife while someone threw a crimson cloak at Seraphine. It was the one she had left at the front of the fishery, the one Max had torn.

"This! The body was found drained and wounded in multiple places. Such a cruel and vengeful death. The only thing left was this cloak, which, if I recall correctly, belonged to you, Miss Ashcroft. I saw you yesterday using it and also getting kicked out of Mr. Vale's shop for your inappropriate behavior," Evren said loudly before crouching in front of her and looking into her eyes. His gaze was no longer a snowstorm but a tornado of dark and ice.

"I was kicked out thanks to you and left the cloak there. Max was there, too, and you know it. Perhaps someone took it!" she hissed at Evren and then turned to Max.

With a pained expression, Max said, "I saw the fight, and yes, you were wearing the cloak. I did tear it, but I didn't see you leave without it."

Shocked and unease clouded her gaze. "That is no argument nor reason to blame this on me," Seraphine shouted. "I have been out all night and day, I—"

"Where?" Evren interrupted.

"Where what?"

"Where have you been all night? I asked your father, and he told us you came home this morning," Evren stated, his voice devoid of all emotion, his eyes changing, enchanting in a way that reminded her of nightmares.

Seraphine could not answer. If she told them the story of her meeting with the Grim Wanderer, they would probably not only blame her but also be convinced she had completely lost her mind.

"Silence, it is then," Evren declared, standing up and moving just behind the crowd.

Lost in her thoughts, Seraphine touched the snow at her fingertips. Before she could muster any idea that might help her, she felt a throbbing ache in her face. Looking around, she saw a rock.

Someone must have thrown it at her. "Are you kidding me?" she bellowed.

In a flurry, the other townsfolk started to throw more things at her: rocks, fish, anything they could get their hands on.

The whispers and screams were harsh enough to make her stay on the ground. Her ankle hurt while dozens of painful strikes hit her, one after another—rougher, darker, aiming to kill.

Steadily, Seraphine realized that she might not get exiled. This would probably end her. However, even if she knew this was a misunderstanding, deep down, she was aware she would always be the villain of the story.

What a sad turn of events. For the first time, Seraphine gave up and closed her eyes as pain filled her body and mind. She tried to picture her forest and the Grim Wanderer, her hopes to chat with him again or see him without his hood dissolving into thin air.

Seraphine could feel tears and blood covering her face, her body, and her dress. She dared to open her eyes, and the snow around her was painted red by her own blood. She tried to cover her face, but as soon as she moved her hand, she noticed a dark substance coming from her fingers, like small black veins. She couldn't tell what it was, so she decided to lay her head down, not begging, just waiting, holding on as much as she could.

"Cursed child."

"Killer."

"Monster."

Another strike, a bigger rock, she guessed, cracked on the left side of her head, and her eyes closed, her body unbalancing and melting with the cold snow. While everything seemed red, she did the only thing she could.

Seraphine smiled, her lips stretching in the freezing snow.

They might call her anything they wanted and blame her for all the unfortunate things in their miserable lives, but they were the killers since that was what they intended to do with her. *Monsters. Worse than me.* Even if she died there, at least she knew that she was better than them. There were no winners there, just losers and monsters. Ultimately, Seraphine smiled because, this time, she wasn't one of them.

"Please, no, stop, please."

Seraphine heard Leander plead. She tried to focus her eyes, as weak as she was. Her father was running for her, tears in his eyes. She wanted to tell him that it was fine, that she could take this, but she was dizzy and couldn't muster a word. Between the cold chaos, she felt his arms covering her, protecting her, a sip of warmth crossing her bones and body.

No. Go away.

Seraphine wanted to push him aside. People were so erratic that there was no distinction between Leander and her, and Leander had now become the object of the crowd's attacks. *No, this is not right.* However, she couldn't move. Her father was covering her with everything he had.

Stop, please, stop. Seraphine wanted to scream, but nothing came out of her. She heard someone say from afar, "Please, let's calm down. This is not what this is about. Mr. Ashcroft here is—"

She couldn't catch that. She felt someone trying to hold and kick her, but Leander was there, moving her softly, caressing her while bearing the beating.

Seraphine managed to raise her head a little more and saw her sister hiding behind Thalassa, who seemed afraid for the first time and genuinely concerned. Then, she shifted her gaze to Max. Max was looking at her, seemingly unfazed and perhaps wearing a hint of a smile.

Somehow, she saw Evren Wraithwood again, confirming her suspicion that she wasn't seeing clearly. He seemed to be screaming and trying to keep people in line. Evren looked miserable, as if this was too much to handle even for him.

However, people were not listening to him, the one person they always wanted to impress. Seraphine sometimes thought the only reason why the town was cursed, rotting, and cold was because of the people. Not the other way around.

Then, Seraphine felt her father's embrace once more, tugging her in the cold snow. He was trying to move them both but failing.

Just leave me here.

"Beat me, kill me. My life for hers. Throw whatever you have at me. I will receive the punishment on her behalf," Leander declared firmly, holding her in his arms.

Alarms went off in Seraphine. This time, she fully opened her eyes, moved her hand, and tried to push him away. "No, Dad. Please, no," she whispered painfully, a taste of blood in her throat. She could not let the folks harm him.

Not him. Not because of me.

However, his only response was to hug her tighter, covering her more and caressing her hair like when she was younger. "You've done no wrong, and I will stand by your side until this is done. Until I am done. A world without you is one without stars—that's how special you are."

She heard his voice cracking as more tears fell from her eyes and his too, her pain slowly becoming an afterthought.

"I-I have so many things left to tell you, so much—" The onslaught of the crowd abruptly silenced his words, shouting and hurling objects at them. Yet Leander bore the brunt of it all.

Seraphine thought she heard a distant scream piercing the air until she realized with chilling clarity the scream was her own. She was imploring them to cease their cruelty, but the crowd was relentless.

No, no, no. Brannon, if you can hear me, let it be me, not him.

After some time, people stopped. Maybe they had run out of rocks, and she heard people starting to whisper. They had punished her and him for nothing, but it was done, and she was breathing. Before she could muster a word, she felt Leander's weight heavy on her body.

"Dad?" Seraphine asked, her voice torn, unnatural even to her own ears.

Evren hastily approached Seraphine and Leander. "Mr. Ashcroft, please. This is enough, stand—" His face paled, his eyes shutting closed, and a tear fell from those raven lashes.

Seraphine followed its path down to the snow. *Why is he crying?* Evren had started this mess. Seraphine wanted to stand up and go home with his father, but she couldn't move. Leander was still caging her. She opened her mouth to speak, but something stopped her as her gaze shifted, and she saw Thalassa crying in the snow, her sister sobbing uncontrollably.

Somehow, time seemed to slow. Everything was silent now, and people weren't looking at them. Some appeared paler than Evren and the snow, and others turned to run away. Max was nowhere to be seen, just as Mr. Vale's wife.

Suddenly, Evren appeared in front of her again. He slowly caged her arms and pulled her toward him, as if she was a mere rag doll. For a moment, she thought Evren was warm, too, like her dad, and she let him pull her away. Seraphine saw no indication that he was doing this for fun or as some kind of trick. He looked pained, his striking features now a torn canvas.

"What is it?" Seraphine asked Evren, feeling stiff as Leander's body still caged her. Then, she felt the lifelessness in her father's touch.

"Seraphine, just... I—" Evren looked to her side as if he were seeing a ghost.

Seraphine looked to her side and saw her father's face, his arms limp and unmoving. Leander wasn't breathing. His eyes were closed, and his face was bloody and bruised.

Seraphine pushed Evren away as she moved toward her father. She used her bruised hands to shake Leander's body. The lack of response from her father only worsened her fear as she desperately started to talk to him, her voice barely a whisper.

"Speak to me, please! Don't leave me… Dad, breathe!"

Just breathe, please.

Seraphine hugged her father's limp body. As she leaned her ear close to his chest, she asked the ancients for a sound.

However, there was no heartbeat.

Then, she truly screamed a shout that came from her soul, piercing the sky and the whole world. In the daze, she saw some remaining folks falling to the ground and holding their ears. Seraphine kept screaming until there was no air left in her lungs and no vigor in her body.

Impossible. This was not supposed to happen.

Her father, her entire world, was now dead.

Seraphine stayed there, holding Leander, until she felt two arms pulling her away from him again. She did not fight. In the distance, she could hear her sister and Thalassa screaming. There was so much horror, so much pain, that the world felt like it was turning black.

The last words Seraphine remembered being consumed by the darkness were distant but clear, "This was not supposed to happen."

Chapter 10

The Silent Fox

The veil was forged, and realms fell under its curse. Cities languished in perpetual cold, their inhabitants transformed into silent threats—darker, some whisper, than the denizens of the Otherworld or even the Underworld itself.

Retrieved from *Ancient History of The Realms*
by Malvrek W., Ch. 50, p. 672.

The world was just that, tears and screams.
The snowflakes no longer danced.
They cried.

Chapter II

The Lonely Fox & the Sad Wolf

And so, as the world donned its veil, she fell deeply
in love with a mortal man.
A love so vast, so profound, no anchors could rend it asunder.
Yet, when it shattered, each left with fragments of
their once-whole hearts,
Yearning for a reunion—perhaps in the afterlife,
like two delicate butterflies.

Retrieved from Leander Ashcroft's hidden letters to Seraphine.

Two Days Before the Incident

Grim Wanderer

The Grim Wanderer knelt in the snow, overwhelmed by regret. Tears carved cold paths down his cheeks. He had freed that monster to frame Seraphine but had not foreseen this tragic outcome. The deal was for the baobhan sith to hurt the fisherman, not to kill him.

The creature no longer existed. He had made sure of that after he realized what she had done.

Humans were cruel and weak. However, he was even worse, a facade, a ruse. Yet, for a moment, he thought they would let her go, that they just wanted her out, driven out from town. Still, this catastrophe had never been part of his design.

His hands stained in blood, the Grim Wanderer fell into the snow of the Wailing Forest and screamed into the bleak, white expanse. Seraphine did not deserve this fate.

The irony twisted in his gut—the catastrophe would likely ensure the success of his larger plan. He knew now that this turn of events was entirely beneficial. However, the cost was excruciating.

The Grim Wanderer hid again. He watched everything and saw when the crimson-eyed girl lost it, when the light in her eyes turned dark. The red rose turned black and venomous in front of his eyes.

The image of Leander Ashcroft, daring and brave, sacrificing himself for his daughter, haunted him. He had died a hero's death. Meanwhile, the Grim Wanderer had done nothing.

As the stark realization settled in, he understood the bitter truth: he was no different from the wrathful townspeople. He was a monster too.

Seraphine Ashcroft

Seraphine woke up, dizzy, clinging to the faint hope that everything had been a nightmare. However, the throbbing pain in her head and the bruises marring her face told a different story. She looked around and noticed that it was dark, past midnight, and she was in her bed. Tears began to flow, her usual glass of sorrows spilling through her eyes. *How could this have happened? Why would Dad do that?* She knew the answer.

Love.

What a dangerous thing to feel, she realized.

Why have the townsfolk been so cruel? What had taken over them to go against a good man? I am no good, but him? For the first time, Seraphine yearned for vengeance for her father, for the ones who were trying to be ordinary like her, and for anyone who would have to face a crowd of frozen hearts and black souls, which were overwhelming in Coldhaven.

"You're awake," Aeliana murmured from the corner of the bed, her eyes red from crying.

Seraphine had not even noticed her presence. She couldn't muster a single word, so her sister opened her mouth to speak, no smile or shine in her eyes anymore.

"You passed out, so we moved you here. You were out for a whole day and more." Her gaze was distant, as if she no longer recognized Seraphine or anyone else. Maybe her sister believed that she truly was the cursed creature the townsfolk had accused her of being. *Who can blame her?* Seraphine was not the only one grieving the loss of Leander.

"The city is mourning. Folks have come to apologize," she said with a hollow laugh. "Of course, no apology is enough, no gift sufficient. Nothing will ever be enough."

That's right. Nothing in the realms would make up for taking the life of an innocent soul.

Finding her voice, Seraphine managed to ask, "Where is he?"

Thalassa appeared in the doorway, a picture of despair, tears streaking her face.

"We buried him near the forest border," she said, her voice thick with anger and sorrow—a storm of emotions Seraphine understood all too well.

Pain wracked Seraphine's body with every movement as she started to rise from her bed. Grief weighed heavily on her every breath.

They hadn't waited for her to bury him, but she needed to see his grave, see him. She donned a scarf and some boots. It was almost midnight, and she might freeze to death, but she was determined to make it for him—for her father.

As if Thalassa had read her mind, she whispered, "This is all your fault."

The words struck Seraphine like a physical blow, deepening the chasm of guilt and sorrow that had already swallowed her whole. With heavy steps, she moved toward the door, each movement a painful reminder of the harsh reality that now lay before her. She felt it then, a tingle in her neck.

"Crimson Eyes..." She heard the Grim Wanderer whisper in her ear, his voice ethereal.

Seraphine knew he was close, but she did not look around.

"No."

With that, the tingle on her neck disappeared. Tonight, she didn't need a hero or a friend or ghosts.

Seraphine traversed the city, enveloped in an eerie silence. The streets were somber, reflecting its inhabitants' collective sorrow. With each laborious step, she felt the weight of the world bearing down on her, nearly causing her to faint.

Just breathe. Seraphine needed to find the strength to bottle all her hurt and move, and eventually, she managed to reach the edge of the forest. Unlike the rest of the city, this sacred place was untouched by snow, offering a stark contrast to the cold white blanket that covered everything else. It looked plain, dry.

Dead.

As she approached a particular clearing, she recognized the freshly turned dark earth. She knew, without a doubt, who that grave belonged to.

If Seraphine could describe pain, she could picture this moment here, a dry and cold piercing feeling full of solitude and desperation.

Drawing closer, Seraphine collapsed to the ground beside it, her hand instinctively touching the cool soil. "I am sorry, I am so sorry," she whispered as tears fell. "You were the one meant to outlive the shadows, not me. You nurtured me with love, and now, in your absence, the world feels unbearably empty. You deserved more, Dad. You deserved the ever after filled with joy—the kind you used to weave into my bedtime stories. In my heart, you remain undiminished, perpetually my hero, my guiding star." Her voice broke as sobs wracked her body, her tears mingling with the earth.

As she lay there, crying and cursing—the townsfolk, life itself, Brannon, Nemera, all of them—she spoke with a desperate clarity, talking to the only Ancient left. "In this vast silence, I turn to you alone, Aurum, solemn guardian of the Underworld. Hear my plea amidst the shadows: cherish his gentle soul in your eternal embrace. Please, let him find tranquility beneath your solemn watch..." Her pleas dissolved into more tears.

Then, she recited a quick verse just for Leander, her own mourning words.

"My hero, the steadfast star that pierced the darkest skies.
I will miss you endlessly,
And I will forever chase your shadow,
Yearning just to be near you once more.
To feel your warmth,
To cherish your spirit,
You are the spring amid the winter,
The sun that banishes the night,
The goodness that triumphs over malice.
May your soul be gently shepherded homeward."

The shadows around her began to flicker and stir, as if responding to the depth of her grief. Out of the gloom, ethereal figures emerged, flitting about with a spectral grace. She had seen the small, colorful dots before.

They were sprites and wisps, creatures of goodwill from both the Otherworld and Underworld, gathering in a solemn vigil around Leander's grave. She attributed that vision to her state since they had never appeared in the human realm before.

Perhaps these magical beings were now openly paying their respects. Their soft, mournful weeping for the daughter of a man they respected added a layer of grace to the somber scene. Seraphine could barely watch them. They seemed to be dancing, singing, and mourning, like calling home, calling Leander home. Before collapsing, she swore she had seen snowflakes the color of diamonds falling under her and heard the sound of fluttering wings sing a soothing lullaby.

Please visit me in my dreams. I will be waiting… always waiting for you.

Grim Wanderer

The Grim Wanderer watched as a throng of small creatures gathered around Seraphine and Leander's grave. They were singing songs and paying their respects with quiet prayers, safeguarding Leander's cherished soul. The Grim Wanderer had not summoned these magical beings. They had come of their own accord.

Then, he opened his hand, and snowflakes began to fall over them, the most brilliant snowflakes he had ever conjured—like diamonds sparkling in the dim light.

This moment belonged entirely to Seraphine and her father. He knew she wanted to be alone, but he could not help but watch her. Then, he also wanted to ask Leander for his forgiveness. For what had happened.

For what is to come.

However, something caught the Grim Wanderer's attention and froze him on the spot. Just as the crimson-eyed girl collapsed onto the ground, as if by magic, flowers began to bloom all over Leander's grave—roses of every imaginable color.

Little fireflies joined into this defiant splash of life against the comber snowscape, their lights flickering softly in the dusk.

The Grim Wanderer heard the distant toll of the clock marking two days, but he paid it no mind. Delving into his pocket, he drew forth a pristine white leaf. With a breath as tender as a whisper, he released it to the wind. Before their eyes, it metamorphosed into a cascade of blue and white butterflies. Their wings, iridescent and ethereal, danced in the air, weaving through the night around the grieving girl and above Leander's resting place.

This could never make up for what he had caused, but he hoped that somewhere in the middle of the sadness, his soul could return to where it belonged. At least, that was what they believed in the Otherworld.

Chapter 12

The Hopeful Wolf

After decades of waiting, I finally saw him—a butterfly effortlessly floating toward me. His return breathed new life into my existence, even here in the depths of the Underworld. Tears, bright as diamonds, fell as butterflies of love fluttered around us, celebrating the reunion of our souls after so long apart.

Retrieved from Illyra Everdawn's journal.

The snowflakes no longer cried.

They become diamonds falling from the sky, lighting the cold night.

In the hidden deep of the woods, a soul found its way home.

CHAPTER 13

THE CRIMSON FOX & THE HUNGRY WOLF

Time halts, and with it, the crimson fox ceases to be reborn,
While the hungry wolf savors the feast of cursed souls forlorn.
As snow turns to roses in a macabre dance, the two become one,
A nightmare for the fearful, for dreamers, a muse.

Retrieved from *Prophecies from The Otherworld: The Curse of the Ruling Primal Sith Line* by Dr. Raggart, Ch. 26, p. 260.

One Day Before the Incident
Seraphine Ashcroft

Seraphine woke up in a bed of flowers. *Roses?* She looked around and found herself in a bed of the most beautiful colors she had ever seen. Something tugged at her heart. Perhaps the Grim Wanderer had come by. While she thought that act was meaningful, she also knew it was dangerous. She realized what a horrible thing it was for her to care, to dream, to have high hopes. The girl just needed to stay away from everyone to avoid this from happening again.

Weak and tired, Seraphine kissed the ground one last time before she stood and walked back home. She felt less pain in her limbs, and her clothes seemed dry. For the first time, she saw the sun not as a reminder of warmth but pain.

People eyed the girl as she passed, but this time, she paid them no mind. Whispers around her became melodies of nothing and void.

At the cottage, she moved around the empty house, touching every little mark that Leander had left—the paintings, the memories. She tried to smile at some of her father's little creations while trying to decorate their home, but it felt wrong, as if an invisible rope was tugging down her lips. Then, Thalassa appeared, almost like a ghost.

Seraphine just looked at her. Thalassa moved and sat near the dinner space, grazing her fingers across the wood, as if she could somehow feel Leander there. "Evren Wraithwood has decided not to cancel the ball. He wants us to go as he wishes to pay respects to your father," she said, her voice laden with hurt. "At least there is that. Now that he—" Her voice shuddered, and Thalassa closed her eyes. "I wish nothing more than for you to stay away from that place. People will go there to pray and commemorate your father's death."

How can Thalassa go to such a place? "Are you telling me you are going to a ball with the people that beat my father, your husband, to death just because Evren Wraithwood, who never paid mind to us, says so?"

"It was an accident, Seraphine, and they are still investigating who started the riot."

"It was not—" she started, anger replacing the hurt.

Thalassa stood up from the chair, her eyes crimson from crying. Her usual pretty face seemed older, wasted, as if the source of her light and elegance had vanished alongside Leander. "It should have been you," she whispered, moving toward Seraphine.

"I know."

"I want you as far away from the ball, Seraphine. You, you..." she stuttered. "Your father took pity on you, but this stops now. You have until the ball, and as soon as we are back with my daughter, I want you gone from this place. I don't care if you end up lost in the forest or even go mad—just be gone." At that, she moved out of her sight.

For the first time, she and Thalassa agreed. Still, Seraphine had nowhere to go. *Dorah might give me a home in the Otherworld, but for how long?* Or perhaps she could escape this cursed town and travel across the woods until she found another town.

Maybe she could find a way out and, one day, call for her sister to join her. If she did not hate her just like Thalassa did now. Seraphine shuddered at the thought.

She rushed to her room and began looking for clothes and items for her journey. She would figure out the details later. Now, she just needed to leave this town. Then, she noticed a small box with a letter on her desk, probably overlooked in everything that had happened. Right beside it was the red rose, still untouched, alive.

The red box seemed elegant and polished, something not meant for her. Yet on top, there was a small note in her father's handwriting. Stumbling, the girl opened the letter first.

My dearest Seraphine,
I know it is early and you are angry, but your birthday is two days away. I wanted to make sure you found this little present beforehand. In this box, you'll find a token of my deepest love. It's intended to remind you of the enduring support that surrounds you, even in the most challenging moments. Know that our connection is unbreakable, transcending any distance or silence that may come between us. Hold this gift as close as I hold you in my heart, eagerly awaiting the day we can share our stories and laughter again.
I will see you after the ball. There is so much I need to tell you.
I hope you can forgive me.
With all my love,
Your father

Tears streamed down her face. Her birthday was tomorrow. She was born just a minute after midnight. Seraphine had forgotten about her own day since it felt like a reminder of the beginning of a cursed life, only blessed by light occasionally. However, Leander would never. Guilt deepened the wound in her chest. Her last words to him were a mix of anger and hurt. If she had listened.

If, if, if.

If life were measured by ifs, one could drown just with the sound of it.

She took the box and opened it. Inside was a breathtaking necklace with a small fox pendant, likely made of diamonds. It represented all the things she loved—reminders of what she used to cherish.

A reminder of what I have lost.

Regardless of where she went, her guilt would follow her. Even in the Otherworld, this would haunt her. If she was ice, perhaps moving on could make things easier.

"A frozen heart…" Her eyes widened as she remembered the Grim Wanderer's tale about freezing one's heart. A cowardly move from her side to numb it all, but she was tired of drowning in all the sorrows and hurt. Perhaps starting from scratch by removing those feelings wasn't such a bad alternative.

Coward. Coward. Coward.

Indeed, she was one, but if Seraphine could secure a deal, she wouldn't care about it anymore. A smile pulled at her lips, not because this felt right, but because in the torment of it all, she yearned to breathe and forget—to wander alone, never haunted by fear, shame, or love. It was a punishment, too, for she would forsake her heart. Yet, she was to blame for a good heart being gone, so abandoning hers seemed like a fair trade.

Seraphine retrieved the purple leaf the Grim Wanderer had given her and dropped it into thin air. Taking the fox necklace, she watched as the leaf began to float slowly, waiting for her. So, she followed, knowing it would take her to him.

It led her through the city center, past the clock tower, and into the Weeping Forest. This time, the leaf guided her under some trees to the hidden and mysterious Wailing Forest.

It wasn't quite dark yet, but Seraphine knelt in the snow, her tears falling like diamonds, one after another. Her heart was full of hatred, and she despised that she might not feel hate if she played her cards correctly. The wind seemed to stop, and she could see the trees arching like her all around her.

"I-I wish for my heart to be voided and frozen. I do not want to cry or feel pain. I want to run away. I want to breathe for the first time. Help me. I know you are there, please."

The girl felt a tingle in her neck and looked up to see the Grim Wanderer approaching. He looked regal, still hidden in shadows, and she swore her heart skipped a beat. Out of fear, out of wonder.

The only visible part was his mouth, and she knew he felt for her, that he knew she was coming, not for playful conversation, but out of sheer desperation.

Grim Wanderer

Then, the Grim Wanderer knew he had won. Just as he had planned, the crimson-eyed girl appeared, driven by despair to request the deal he had intended for her.

I have won.

However, the victory was bittersweet, tainted by the palpable sorrow that enveloped her.

It feels wrong.

However, there was no going back now. Seraphine looked like a broken mirror, disoriented, shattered but still sharp, so he pulled his hand out and gave it to her.

She shall have everything, he reminded himself. Still, for now, she had nothing.

Seraphine Ashcroft

Seraphine stood up, marshaling the remnants of her strength, and took the Grim Wanderer's hand. It felt cold, like the touch of winter itself. *Not his usual warmth.*

"I don't care what is required of me, but I need you to grant me the wish you spoke of—the one that will freeze my heart and lessen my pain. I have nothing left—no family, no love, no home. The only thing I can offer is this." She placed her father's gift in the Grim Wanderer's hand. "This is all I have left, my most precious possession."

The Grim Wanderer appeared somber, almost sorrowful. He examined the necklace. "A frozen heart deal requires two things," he explained, holding her hand. "First, something precious that you are willing to sacrifice, and second, a quest that you must complete before midnight. Seraphine Ashcroft, if you accept these terms, and once the quest is completed, your heart will be as ice, frozen like the perpetual winter of this place."

Seraphine trusted his words, even if she felt there was more meaning to them. "I do."

At that moment, the trees around them seemed to moan, and the snow hardened like ice underfoot. The Grim Wanderer closed the distance as his cheek touched hers, and she felt a smile tug at his lips. "Such a pretty thing to say. I would have loved to hear you say that in another circumstance, Crimson Eyes."

Before she could question him any further, he pulled away from her and looked at the sky. "Thanks for the necklace. I will treasure it." He moved again, and this time, he looked mighty, deals and tricks invigorating him like they would any other being from the Otherworld. "Now, to your quest. It is quite easy. Ready to hear my terms, human creature?"

"I am." *Whatever it is, it can't be worse than what I've already been through these past few days.*

"I do like that," he purred, and she felt the caress of his tone on her entire being. "Smitten and unfazed. Can't wait to see more of it."

Licking his lips, the Grim Wanderer asked again, "You know what, Crimson Eyes?"

Seraphine had the urge to close the distance and feel it all from him. However, caring, liking, and loving were enemies in her mind and heart now. "What?"

"For you, I will make it fun. Your quest is to attend a particular ball. There are instructions you must follow. Ensure you adhere to them, but my guess is that you will mostly enjoy the quest." He handed her an invitation.

She recognized it as being the one for Evren Wraithwood's ball.

"Is that my quest?" she asked, a little confused. She expected something more life-threatening, like hunting an unusual creature, perhaps catching a brownie, or cursing a house.

Maybe it's some kind of trick. From Seraphine's experience in the Otherworld, one thing was certain—there was nothing as easy or truly inoffensive when dealing with them. *Ever.*

The Grim Wanderer laughed, wearing a wolfish smile. "You think it is a trick, don't you?"

Then, just as soft as the touch of a leaf, he moved his hand and wiped some of the frozen tears on Seraphine's cheeks. Her breath caught in her throat.

"Well, it is not. But I wouldn't say it is a simple quest, either. The real obstacle here is your lack of social skills and dance practice. Those may come as a barrier."

He was mocking her. "Well, going to the Wraithwoods' household does seem like a painful and miserable quest, now that I think about it. And everyone thinks I am a murderer, so I guess that's going to complicate things," she said, holding the invitation. She was trembling and not exactly from the cold.

The Grim Wanderer moved her hand, the one holding the invitation. Her heart skipped a beat again. *What on Brannon's earth is wrong with me?*

"Save a dance for me, Crimson Eyes." He took the invitation and opened it for her. The words on the invitation shifted and swirled, forming a new message.

Dear Crimson Eyes,
You are invited to a ball of infinite endings and beginnings, a masquerade of monsters and beauties. Please be present and remain until midnight. You shall not consume any food or drink but are required to accept all dances from those who ask.
I await your presence and hope you enjoy your last night.

Before she could question him further, the Grim Wanderer vanished. Calming her heart, Seraphine thought about this. She thought she might regret it, but it seemed like a fair quest.

"No regrets, no feelings," she said to herself.

Enjoy your last night.

Seraphine knew the Grim Wanderer would be at the ball, and for some reason, she wanted to spend some of the final hours tonight talking to him. Maybe she was lonely, but she wanted to feel her heart beating in different rhythms before turning cold as ice. As naive as she was, she thought that perhaps he did too.

Perhaps he felt just like her, lonely.

Feelings. Seraphine was leaving them all behind because she was done with them. Still, there was a feeling she was sad to let go, one that she had enjoyed since meeting him.

Back through the silent streets of Iceveil Square, Seraphine stood some minutes in front of the tailor shop. The town was shrouded in a somber atmosphere. *Everyone is at the ball already*, she guessed—a ball to mourn her father, a ball that hosted the same people who killed him, who had wanted to kill her before.

Driven by a strange compulsion, raw anger, or pure desperation, she threw a rock through the familiar shop window and entered. She wandered around the small shop she had worked at for years, watching ladies come and go with stunning fabrics and dresses. She had been a fly on the wall, always watching but never the one in those dresses, never the one people would pay attention to.

As she moved past some dresses, she noticed an oddly-looking figure in the middle of the shop. As she neared it, she noticed it was a dress—a stunning crimson gown adorned with scarlet diamonds that glittered across the bodice, its skirts flowing like something from a fairy tale.

It must be a new collection. Those fabrics and colors were unusual, as though they were made of petals and diamonds and tears. "Beautiful."

"It is just as beautiful as the one this was designed for." The Grim Wanderer's ethereal voice once again intruded on her thoughts. Instead of feeling like she was losing her mind, this time, it felt like a comforting melody.

"I see, must be a beauty beyond comparison," she replied to the emptiness of the place, a little jealous of whoever that dress was made for. It was surely a masterpiece.

The shop stirred, and white and gray smoke started to appear. Seraphine heard the Grim Wanderer laugh in her ear, closer, as if he was standing there. Perhaps he was, camouflaged in shadows and smoke.

"Go and check it yourself, Crimson Eyes." Then, the smoke vanished just as his voice did in her head.

Alone in the shop again, Seraphine noticed a new addition on top of the dress. "Silly," she muttered while picking up the yellow leaf. She wondered if the colors had some meaning. Dorah used leaves, but only dark green ones. He seemed to have a whole forest in his pocket.

There was a message on the leaf. "Made of starlight and roses, for a crimson-eyed beauty to behold." Then, the leaf vanished too.

It's for me. The Grim Wanderer knew she would come here and placed the dress for her. He told her to enjoy her last night, and he was making sure it would happen. Seraphine couldn't help but wonder how much she would miss the feeling of being marveled by him after the deal was completed.

"Better get to it then." Sighing, she donned the dress. The fabric was softer and lighter than she would have guessed. Perhaps it was indeed made of petals and starlight. With him, one could never know. She moved across the shop and gently picked up some accessories, things she never thought she would dare to use—bracelets and earrings. There were some trinkets she guessed were for the hair, but they kept falling from her hair.

"Need a hand?"

The girl spun back and found Mr. Eliah at the door of his shop.

Guilt rose to her cheeks and throat. "Mr. Eliah, I can explain—" Seraphine could not.

However, to her surprise, he just smiled, paying no attention to the broken glass. "Just Eliah. I am not nearly in my thirties. Sit here?" He motioned her to a soft couch in front of a vanity mirror.

She could not hide her shock as she sat and looked at herself. Her face showed no signs of the ordeal—no bruises, scars, or wounds. *Impossible.*

"I thought you would be at the ball already," Seraphine said, breaking the silence.

"I have no interest in attending this one. But I'm glad to see *you* are going. Never understood why you were not invited to any before. Twisted that it was at this particular time," Eliah said while brushing her hair, adding curls and weaving in silver metallic flowers and pearls.

"Guess I do not match with the classy and socialite of Coldhaven."

Eliah choked on a laugh. "I would dare to say the opposite, Seraphine." He brushed some color on her eyelids and added tint to her lips.

He finished up her cheeks, his eyes sad in the mirror.

"I heard what happened. There are no words that could make up for the tragedy you oversaw. You did not deserve that kind of heartbreak."

Seraphine wanted to thank him, but her words got stuck in her throat. She tried not to cry and ruin all the effort he had made on her face.

"And… I saw you," he finally said.

"What do you mean?"

He offered his hand to her and pulled her up. "I saw you leaving to the forest without your cloak. You left it behind. I knew it was not you, but—" But Eliah couldn't do anything for her. She knew that.

Seraphine turned and hugged him. *Maybe there still are good people in this cursed town.* Not that it would matter tomorrow. "I know, and thank you for the makeover." *And for believing her and being nice*, she thought but did not say aloud.

A blush crept to his cheeks. "Not at all. You barely need it." Eliah moved away from her. "I will go now, and no worries about the… glass. I was planning on re-decorating the place."

Relief filled her lungs, and she almost laughed.

"Seraphine?" he said from the door.

"Yes?"

He smiled widely. "You'll show them all," he said, moving out and leaving her alone once again.

As the clock neared the beginning of the dark evening, she looked at herself in the mirror one last time. Seraphine scanned her face and dress. Her eyes were the stars of the show, surrounded by blackness. The dress matched her eye color and skin.

What will the Grim Wanderer think when he'll see me? What will the townsfolk say? Evren?

Perhaps they wouldn't even notice her. The dress was a good disguise. Plus, she could play this safe. Seraphine just needed to find a corner at the ball and hide.

Like a ghost.

Carefully exiting the shop, she moved through the streets of Coldhaven. She would not miss this place, but she feared her sister, those who were good, the old clock would also vanish with her emotions. *Without feelings, what is left?*

As soon as this deal was fulfilled, Seraphine would return to the Otherworld and figure her fresh start out. *There is always a new tomorrow.* At that, she looked up at the sky and marveled once more at how pleasant the darkness could be, a deep red hue tinting it that time rather than the usual blue.

Perhaps a coincidence.

"It rare is," the ethereal voice said in her ears.

She rolled her eyes.

Chapter 14

The Dancing Fox

Gold starlight wove through her hair,
Her eyes a blend of roses and rubies,
Her dress flowed like a dream,
One I could neither grasp nor claim.

Retrieved from Leander Ashcroft's journal.

Seraphine Ashcroft

The imposing Wraithwood household was large and opulent, its halls a labyrinth of gold and mirrors that multiplied the glittering lights and the laughter echoing through the grand spaces.

"This better be over soon," Seraphine muttered, lowering her head and moving between the townsfolk.

As she stepped farther into the castle, the atmosphere was lively, perhaps overly so, with guests indulging in the abundant feast before them. Tables overflowed with dishes of every kind, and beverages of all hues sparkled in crystal glassware.

Seraphine remembered her instructions. *No food, no drinks, and accept every dance invitation.* It seemed unlikely that anyone would notice her hidden in the corner, let alone ask her to dance, especially since many guests appeared inebriated.

What a relief. Seraphine was saving a dance for one in particular and had no interest in being touched by anyone else. Nor have a conversation. Knowing her circumstances, she might end up kicking or punching some of the folk.

"Do not think about it," she said, shutting her thoughts.

She wandered through the crowd and spotted Thalassa from afar. Seraphine quickly ducked under a table laden with food to avoid being seen. She then caught sight of her sister conversing somberly with some townsfolk. They seemed apologetic. Both Thalassa and Aeliana were wearing black dresses.

At least there was a reminder here that this ball was nothing more than a masquerade for murderers and hypocrites.

She wanted to talk with her sister, but it would be pointless. Seraphine knew that after tonight, she would not hold any tender feelings toward her. *That's for the best.* Seraphine needed to disappear so Aeliana and even Thalassa could move on and live in peace.

Yet, Seraphine was mesmerized. The place buzzed with activity. Servers darted about, offering sweet wine and exquisite delicacies. The music filling the air was enchanting, igniting Seraphine's desire to dance and lose herself in the rhythm as if it were her last chance to experience such passion and joy.

Maybe something here was indeed enchanted. *What a shame it has to be in this household.* The association with Evren Wraithwood did not help the cause. She bet her sister would have loved to dance with him.

Most of the ladies here, actually.

Thalassa and Aeliana moved to the other corner with other people. Seraphine took that as her cue to step away from the shelter.

Someone started to play the violin. The girl tried to find the source, but somehow, she couldn't see anything beyond drunk and way too giddy town folk. The songs played previously carried a tone of mischief and festive vibes, but this one reached her soul.

I've heard that song before.

Seraphine could not remember where exactly.

Closing her eyes, she envisioned her Weeping Forest, reliving moments of joy and freedom when she ran across the snow and trees—from conversations veiled in mystery with Max and childhood games of hide and seek with Leander and her sister, and jests thrown at the sentinel tree.

"May I have this dance?" a deep, familiar voice asked, interrupting her reverie. Seraphine opened her eyes to see Evren Wraithwood standing before her.

This was why the Grim Wanderer said it was not a simple task. *Then again, where is he? Didn't he promise me a dance?*

Evren stood there waiting for her to take his hand. The last she remembered of him was the look of horror as he realized the tragedy that had unfolded with her father. It did seem honest, but she could not help but dislike him. He was the image of what human cruelty was—power, arrogance, and yet he was absolutely beautiful. Mysterious, like winter itself.

Despite her deep-seated contempt for him, she had vowed to accept any dance, so she regally placed her hand in his and allowed him to lead her to the main dance hall. There, it was just the two of them. She heard people whispering and gasping. Still, she paid them no mind. Tonight was all about her, and if this was her quest, so be it.

With that in mind, Seraphine pretended she was just in her forest, running toward the veil, jumping and moving like a snowflake from the cold and wintery sky, each step moving delicately with the violin strings.

To her surprise, Evren, who was silent, seemed to anticipate her every move, mirroring her steps as if they were both dancing through a snow-covered landscape. Maybe she was not a bad dancer after all.

Or he was *very* skilled.

Or we are both really *bad.*

The music was slowing, the melody still beautiful but somehow mournful. Seraphine moved her head up, daring to gaze into Evren's eyes—gray and blue with specks of white, hauntingly beautiful like a snowstorm. Yet, she couldn't deny something was tugging at her heart. There was a certain familiarity in Evren and the way they were dancing.

Maybe in another life, they could have been friends.

What a silly thought, she thought.

Then, he lightly pulled her closer, tugging her by the waist. His touch was warm, almost too warm, and she felt a strange heat spreading through her again, making her pulse quicken. The realization that comfort could be found in his embrace confused her. The few encounters with him had led to disaster, but her body was responding to his nearness in ways she couldn't control.

"Why dance with me?" Curiosity filled her voice.

He arched a very well-defined dark brow at her. "Is there a reason why I should not dance with a beautiful lady?" he countered, seriousness in his voice.

Feeling quite daring today, Seraphine rested her hand on his chest and embraced the conversation. "Well, based on the fact that you completely avoided inviting my family to your balls till this day, I guess an undistinguished lady like me could question your sudden interest."

To her surprise, his lips twitched, hiding a smile. "You are very mouthy, aren't you, Seraphine Ashcroft?" he said while looking her in the eyes, confirming that he had known who he was dancing with from the start.

Evren stared at her as though she were a riddle to be solved. "And I shall apologize about all that and more. I wanted to."

She had seen liars and tricksters, and it was easy for her to tell if one was being honest. He was.

What a contradiction of a man—apologetic but egocentric, handsome but somehow wicked, serious and quite daring.

Seraphine had to admit she kind of liked that, and she hated herself for it.

"About what? For making me look like the joke of the town with Max, or when you ignited that tale about me being a killer, which—" She could not finish the phrase. Remembering her father would bring tears, and she needed to be a veil herself tonight.

"For everything." Evren looked at her, and while it seemed impossible, she believed him. There was just something about his eyes and voice that seemed real. "It is no excuse, but I wish things were different."

"How come?"

He pulled her closer, slowly using one hand and grabbing hers, lifting it and spinning her around in a way one would feel like a princess. His eyes never left hers.

"If I tell you, you may lose interest in knowing what could have been." His breath mingled with hers just as his eyes dropped lower. "And what will be."

"What... will be?" There was no future here, but something about the conversation sparked her interest.

"I won't spoil that either, Seraphine. The future is unpredictable. And you know what the present is?" His voice turned darker. A chill went through her as she marveled at his eloquence, his voice caressing her ears like dark, enchanted melodies.

She thought about not responding, but she fell into the trap of his eyes and raven hair. *Damn it.* "What is?"

Evren moved her head so it rested on his shoulder, and she sensed a brief smile from him. "A dance."

As if in a trance, they kept dancing. It was comforting and felt natural, and for a moment, Seraphine lost herself in the rhythm, in the warmth of Evren's arms, in the music, in the splendid castle.

Closing her eyes, she imagined a normal life full of dances and friends. *An ordinary life.*

She hadn't drunk anything, but she felt dizzy, as if her feet were in the clouds and her mind shattered into stars. Evren was poisonous like dark wine—just a dance, and she barely could keep it together. The feeling of his hand resting on her waist, the warmth of his palm seeping through the fabric of her dress, his cheek on hers, she wished to pull away, but she kept leaning closer and closer, like a moth to a flame.

Although absorbed in this thought, Seraphine opened her eyes and noticed her sister beside a peculiar figure.

Shocked, she closed and opened her eyes again.

Impossible.

Aeliana was accepting an odd drink from a boggart, which seemed familiar.

What is happening?

Seraphine stopped dancing.

She could feel Evren looking at her and still holding her, but this time, she pushed that aside. For the first time, she really looked at the hall.

The beautiful ball was melting into something akin to terror in front of her eyes.

Seraphine looked at the mirrors that lined the hall. The reflections did not just show inebriated guests but creatures among them, sinister beings mingling undetected. Townsfolk were too drunk to notice them. There were many Otherworld creatures, many unknown to her. *Perhaps they are trapped in the human realm like the Grim Wanderer.*

"You surprised me," Evren said, pulling her out of her thoughts and the cruel realization that this ball was nothing like it seemed.

Whatever Evren was saying made no sense. He was probably enchanted too. *Was this his plan?* Seraphine should have known better than to think there was no twist.

Seraphine focused on the mirrors showing the horrendous creatures seemingly having fun, luring over drunk people and whispering things to ladies whose eyes started to look vacant.

Is my sister aware of what is around her? She tried to find Aeliana again. Quest or not, she would not leave her sister in the monsters' grasp.

"I see you are very observant. But nothing to worry your pretty head about. They cannot see them. The creatures here have been glamoured to look human, and most humans cannot see them regardless," the owner of the hand on her waist said, whispering in a way that seemed like he was enjoying himself.

Seraphine looked at Evren, alarms ringing in her head, needles of fear crawling along her spine. "How do you know that?"

Evren smiled, and then the mirrors around the hall cracked. The gold that painted the walls began to darken with deep scarlet hues. Seraphine could see the creatures in the cracked mirrors smiling at her.

The violin stopped, and Evren's laughter rang out, unsettlingly wild. She tried to pull away from his embrace, but he was strong.

She was trapped.

As Seraphine turned her head to look at Evren, in his mirth, she saw it clearly—dimples.

Not any dimples, but ones she had come to dread, to anticipate, to want and run forward to embrace.

It made sense now, the familiarity, why the Grim Wanderer was hooded and seemed to know her, why he veiled his voice. Why Evren barely smiled when he saw her, the worry in Evren's eyes, and true concern for her when her father died.

It had all been a lie.

Evren Wraithwood is the Grim Wanderer.

Evren Wraithwood was indeed a trickster, and now he was laughing, gripping her hand tightly. Fear and betrayal drowned Seraphine's heart. "Well, Seraphine, my crimson-eyed creature. You've fulfilled most parts of the deal—you danced, you avoided the devilish food, and it's almost midnight. There's just one thing left."

"How is this possible?" she asked, trying to puzzle everything out.

He ignored her. Just like before, he raised his hand, and the world froze for a moment, static in time. People lay drunk on the floor, a cup of wine spilled with its drops suspended in the air like pendants. "And you saved a dance for me. What an honor! Ah, wasn't this such a pleasant dance? Did you enjoy dancing with me? The real me? Or were you expecting a hooded coward?" The white-furred cloak appeared, enveloping him again. This time, Evren did not use the hood to cover his face. There was no reason to hide his identity.

If Evren is the Grim Wanderer, how long has he been playing with me? What's the purpose of it?

She felt the air coming short, barely filling her lungs.

Seraphine knew that this deal would be the end of her. *Why plot so much to give me what I wanted?* No, the girl knew she had sealed her fate in the grasp of something worse than a hunter. *Than a wolf.*

"You are a deceiver," she sneered, her voice trembling with disbelief. "You were there all along—with Mr. Vale, with Max. You were at my father's..."

That seemed to trigger something in Evren. His eyes turned black, the sparkle dimming. "Yes, I was," he said. "But you should know something, Crimson Eyes. This, all this, is part of something bigger. It needed to be done."

How am I supposed to merge these two? It seemed like this was his real personality, not Evren nor the Grim Wanderer. Something else. Lost.

No, fake. What Seraphine was seeing here was the truth. Whatever she felt for her friend and for Evren, whatever she thought they were, it was all a ruse.

Evren took her face in his grasp and looked her in the eyes. She trembled with fear and sadness. Yet, she could not look away. "Yes," he hissed, his eyes clearing. A trail down her cheek marked where a tear had unexpectedly descended.

"I intentionally planned some things, little steps that I knew you would take. All so you could reach this breaking point. But what we discussed and shared? What I said... It is real. All of it, Crimson Eyes. Nothing can change that."

At that, Seraphine pulled away from him, not wanting to see his eyes or yearn for his embrace or comfort. She was not weak, not naive enough to fall for this again.

Not now.

Not ever.

She lifted her gaze, and this time, there was no doubt in her voice, in her heart soon to be gone, in her mind soon to be voided. "This changes everything. The past is written on stone, and the future is volatile, but just like the moon, I know it will be there tomorrow. Just like my words. Today, tomorrow, and the day afterward, I will never forgive you."

"That is acceptable. I expect nothing less than that."

"I am not finished," she snapped at him, growling even. "I will never forgive you, and I promise to haunt you and destroy you. That, I can assure you. And that seems like a fair future for both of us."

Evren tried to move closer, the mirrors showing a reflection of him, and her eyes hurt because she couldn't bear more tears or look at him. It was a reminder of how foolish hope could be. "I guess it is a deal then. Until my undoing breaks us apart, it seems," he joked, but it felt empty.

Then, closing the distance, unafraid, she held his broad arms in her grasp, her nails digging into his skin. "Tell me, was it all necessary? Killing my father was part of this all? Because if I am connecting the dots, then you are the one who orchestrated his death," she hissed, his white fur no longer white but stained with the blood from her strong grip and sharp nails.

There was no pain, nothing in his eyes. "No, that was something I did not plan, but I still triggered it, so I won't lie to you and tell you that it wasn't partially because of me. I will, and I mean this. I will regret that for the rest of my life. But that was not supposed to happen," he confessed, his voice carrying a weight that seemed almost genuine. "But listen carefully, or you may end up with even more regrets." His voice was commanding this time.

How have I not recognized that distinctive tone, that presence before?

"See your sister over there? She was given a special beverage from the Shadowmarket," he revealed in her ear.

Shivers traversed her body.

"What have you done?" Her eyes rushed and found Aeliana, little drops of sparkling substance on her lips.

"She will die in about... twenty minutes. Part of the deal was to give me something of value," he declared coldly.

Seraphine crumbled to the floor, her crimson dress shining, her eyes similar to the golden and dripping walls of crimson. She looked like one of the paintings in her magic library.

"I gave you the necklace! That was possession enough! This isn't fair, you liar!" she screamed and lunged at his legs, trying to drag him down with her, but he was stronger, his eyes darkening again.

"I would advise against such actions, Crimson Eyes. I do love that violent nature of yours, but the clock is ticking, and I do not want to play this game any longer."

What is that supposed to mean?

Moving to the wall, Evren saw the broken mirrors showcasing every perfect angle of his face. A smile appeared, as sweet as rotten apples or raw fish. "I said I needed something of value, but I never agreed to accept the necklace as part of the deal. But, I will cherish it forever."

"You son of a—"

"No, no, let me finish!" He moved his other hand, and Seraphine's mouth closed.

"I chose something else for you! I am always that thoughtful! A life for a frozen heart seems fair," he stated with chilling calm.

The apologetic Evren was gone, and the friend she met in the forest had vanished too. With a quick movement of his hand, everything and everyone started to move again. Most humans were drunk, and all creatures were looking at them. Waiting for him.

Seraphine stumbled back. *Who is this creature to hold such power?* Her mind reeled from the horrifying prospect of losing not just her father but now her sister as well, and she was terrified of who she had in front of her. She tried to speak, but he was holding her mouth shut.

Evren noticed her trying to signal her sister, tears streaming down her face. "My apologies, you can talk now, but fast. There is barely time for you both."

One day, there will be no time for you. That, I am sure.

"Please, don't hurt her. I'll do anything. You can break the deal! I will do as you please without it," she pleaded desperately. She should have known better. Dorah had told her never to trust a soul from the Otherworld. *How fragile I am.* The first sign of affection from someone was enough to deceive her.

He quipped, looking around and pretending he cared. "I cannot undo it. You completed the quest, and you know the rules." Evren crouched and looked eye to eye with her. "But I can offer a new deal that will spare your sister. I can give her the antidote, and you will retain your frozen heart deal."

"What's the catch?" she snarled. There was no escape. Everything happened because she was too scared to feel. Now, everyone else would pay for the consequences of her immaturity.

"I'll administer the antidote, and she will live. But you..." Evren curled his lips into a sinister smile. "You, my dear crimson-eyed creature, must make a blood oath to me."

Seraphine could barely hold it together. She would accept anything at this point.

He continued. "You will agree to accompany me on a quest, and during this time, you must not attempt to harm me in any deadly possible way. Your life will be linked to mine for the duration of the quest."

"And after that?" Venom came from her words. Her eyes were bright and deadly.

"If we both survive, you'll have your freedom and can do as you please. I will grant you any wish, asking nothing in return, even if your wish is for my demise," Evren promised. "No loops, no tricks. A fair deal. You get your frozen heart, your sister's safety, and, in the future, freedom. Isn't that what you always wanted?"

Exhausted and cornered, Seraphine pondered if the mystical roses and creatures she'd encountered had been warnings about him all along. The wolf, the one covered in winter and snowflakes on his eyes. Evren knew he had her.

She would not lose Aeliana, even if this meant losing herself. "Deal."

Evren's laughter filled the air once more. "Ah, I do love a good deal, especially when it favors me." Then, he winked at her and pulled her up.

He led her toward Aeliana, who was both laughing and crying, her eyes nearly black from the poison. The dance had been probably a distraction. Aeliana seemed to be in a daze. Whatever they had given her, it was drowning her from the inside out, drops of black blood running from her ears and mouth. *Please, just save her. Please, Brannon. Nemera, help me.*

Unexpectedly, the creatures, small fairies and horrible terrors and nightmares from the Otherworld moved away while Evren took a glass with a clear, almost like water substance and held it to her sister's lips. Seraphine wanted to push him away from her, but for some reason, she felt weak and out of her body.

For a moment, she thought he had lied again, but then Aeliana stopped laughing, and her lips started to gain color again. Her sister's eyes slowly shut, but she was breathing. No dark blood coming from any part of her face. Seraphine looked at Evren, questioning if he truly did something to help her sister.

Evren put the glass in her hand. It contained water.

"How?"

Looking at her, mischief gleamed in his eyes. "I gave your sister a bit of beithir venom. Actually, your friend Dorah was kind enough to lend that to me. You were there," he said, looking around and signaling for some small creature to go away. "This venom is deadly, but curiously, just a few drops of water neutralize it! The magic of the Otherworld, the cures are sometimes quite fun, never obvious but always tricky," he revealed mockingly. "And the best part? I did accept your necklace and would have saved your sister anyway. I am not a monster."

No, you are not. You are a breathing nightmare.

Seraphine fell to the floor once more. This time, she moved toward her sister. Her eyes were shut, her hair was all over the place, and a maze of chaos surrounded her.

"You were so easily tricked, Crimson Eyes. Despite your knowledge of the Shadowmarket and the Otherworld, despair blinded you, deceiving you for years," he taunted as the Otherworld creatures around them laughed.

The partygoers continued to spill wine all around, unaware of what was happening. She pondered if there was something in the drink to make them like that too.

"You are what nightmares are made of. There must be a way to break the deal. I won't—" She started to pull herself up, ready to do whatever it took to break their deal. She wasn't a killer, but she still had some time. Perhaps a bargain, offering her soul. Something that could benefit her somehow.

There is always a way. That was what Dorah had told her years ago when she taught her the ways around the Shadowmarket.

As soon as she launched herself toward him, as much as Seraphine longed to strike Evren, he carefully pulled her once again toward his body in a disgusting, sweet embrace.

He laughed softly as his mouth caressed her cheek.

"Time's up."

Then, the clock struck twelve.

Chapter 15

The Masked Wolf

There was a tale of love and death intertwined,
Twisted and sorrowful, unraveling to its bitter end.
But what they missed was the truth beneath the pain—
That though things shatter, they do not truly end.
And so, love became something beyond death,
And death was no longer the final breath.

Retrieved from *Otherworld Tales: A Route to Doom*
by Lyra Sorrowspring, Ch. 3, p. 54.

The Day of the Incident
Seraphine Ashcroft

The world around her seemed to pause, and Seraphine felt her heart slow—each beat a languid thump against her chest, as if her heart was made of metalwork and not veins. A chill crept into her veins, spreading through her bones and leaving a trail of ice in its wake.

Then, her mind halted, frozen in eerie tranquility, peaceful nothingness. Inexplicably, she laughed—a soft, hollow sound that echoed the situation's surrealness.

She felt empty, as if any concern in her mind had blown away just like the spring in Coldhaven, leaving only white, pure cold.

The mess, the spilling wine, the creatures, Evren became a blur. Touching her neck, she sensed a faint cut.

Driven by a ghostly curiosity, she approached the mirror. Moving her head, she saw nothing but a mere human.

Good.

However, just right below her neck, close to her collarbone, Seraphine could see an inked symbol, a fox tattoo etched delicately on her skin. Seraphine recalled it was similar to the one the cat sith bore in the Shadowmarket, the same mysterious emblem she had seen in the ancient paintings at the library.

"At least it looks good," she muttered, gazing at herself. Oddly enough, she felt nothing.

Evren Wraithwood

It worked.

Evren wanted nothing more than to collapse and let his emotions out. Seraphine was still alive and bound to him.

He surveyed his ballroom—a grotesque tableau of guests sprawled on the floor amidst a macabre mix of wine and blood. Yet, after years, decades—he found a loophole for a curse that bound both him and her—he finally saw a glimmer of hope.

Now, blood-bonded with Seraphine, who somehow could jump across realms, he could use her blood to gain entry to the Otherworld. He still needed to test that out, but after that, they could begin their quest to break the curses binding them. There was so much he could explain, but in his mind, there was no need to tell her more. He would rather have her thinking of him as evil incarnate.

Evren preferred her hatred to her remembering their shared past.

Somehow, he marveled at her. Dancing and holding her close was all he needed. As soon as she entered the ball, Seraphine was the one his eyes could see. She was as beautiful as the strange crimson moon. She was his dream, his doom, his prayer, and his hunter all along. *She is everything.*

Turning around, he saw Seraphine laughing, totally distracted from the chaos of the castle. Aeliana watched her from a distance, eyes wide with fear. Evren could have told her that it would wear off, that the numbing feeling was just a side effect. *But what good would that do for her sister or even Seraphine?*

"Didn't I tell you? That you could become the greatest villain the world has ever seen?" he said to her, moving closer. Her striking crimson eyes looked at his through the mirrors on the wall.

Seraphine gave him a sweet, forced smile, as if she were a doll made of nothingness. "Didn't you?" she said plainly.

Then, she turned around, and again, he could have fallen to his knees, but for the sight of her. Emotionless or not, she was alive. "Perhaps I will be. Perhaps not. You know what I do know?"

"Have no idea," he admitted.

Closing the distance, she moved her head so her lips were almost touching his, her eyes a vacant, torn red. He felt every breath, every inch of her body, her hand near his chest. He was a magnet drawn to her, and he wondered if she knew how much power she had over him.

"I know I will kill you. As soon as the quest is over, I will kill you," she whispered each word into his mouth.

"Ah! That is not a surprise, Crimson Eyes! I do know that. I expect nothing less." He moved to her side, eyeing her again in that stunning dress. "But for now... shall we?" Evren extended his arm, which she took, her nails cutting into his arm, painful and strong enough to make him bite his lip. She had a dangerous grasp. As twisted as he was, he liked it.

They walked out of his household. There was nothing of value there for him. All of this had always been about Seraphine. Evren dismissed most creatures and commanded the others to set everything straight. The drinks were tinted with a rare herb. None of them would remember a thing from today.

Silently, they walked toward the forest, Evren ensuring that crimson snowflakes surrounded their path. The white snow was tainted in red—a cruel yet breathtaking spectacle. He had promised to paint the world in crimson just for her.

How better to celebrate a plan concocted for centuries than with snow matching the color of her eyes? Yet, as he stole a swift glance at her, she seemed bored.

When they reached the Weeping Forest and the veil, the sentinel tree made no sound, but Evren swore he saw a tear fall from the wood-crafted face.

Bound by a blood pact, he took Seraphine's hand. "Take me there."

"Where?" she asked, moving her head as if trying to decipher him.

He signaled the arched entrance from the tree. "The Otherworld."

Yawning, she took a step forward. "Are you not forbidden to enter?"

"Yes, I cannot enter, and no creature from my realm can pull me there. But you are human."

"Well, sounds like fun. I hope you end up face-planting in the snow." Emotionless as she sounded, he almost laughed at her words.

As such, Evren held her hand while moving across the arched branches, and just as she wished, he almost face-planted but not on the snow.

In the Otherworld.

Evren thanked Nemera for whatever had been done to make Seraphine able to cross to the Otherworld and hide him under her human essence. When the world turned upside down, and he moved his feet forward, too eager to even look at what used to be his home, he felt everything tremble.

The clocks stopped ticking.

The talking roses and creatures, selkies, kelpies, hags, boggarts—everything went silent, and the night seemed darker, no moon visible.

A welcoming, he thought. Evren was home.

The trees arched, almost screaming—a beautiful, haunting melody to his ears.

Still holding Seraphine, he looked at the sky and smiled, truly, wickedly. He was indeed home and finally had a chance to make it right. Opening his hand, he let some grayish leaves flow into the darkness.

This time, there were no butterflies, no colors or coins. The leaves turned into oily shadows, dark, consuming, veiling him and the whole Shadowmarket.

When the world turned dark, Evren could hear the chaos.

Drip, drip, drip.

Blood ran, and creatures hid.

He was chaos.

This is just the beginning.

At his side, he saw Seraphine, expressionless. She was still becoming used to her heart and their bond, which was more complex than he had ever dared to explain.

However, Evren knew he had made the right choice. One thing was for sure: she would kill him. *Sooner rather than later*, he hoped. In the meantime, there were deeds to be done.

"Can't say I missed this place," he muttered, releasing Shadoweater and Grimnight along the path filled with creatures. Most were hiding and screaming, and some were even praying to Nemera.

As if that will work for them this time.

Crimson Memories

"Who are you?" the five-year-old girl asked. She had been running around the Weeping Forest, playing hide and seek with her father, until she noticed a man sitting near a tree.

"No one. Just… another wanderer," he replied, and she tilted her head.

What is a wanderer?

"Well, you look sad."

"Yeah… Sad is too shallow. I would say grim," the stranger said, but the little girl laughed, not knowing what grim meant either.

To her surprise, the stranger seemed to smile at her. "So, am I funny to you, little creature?"

She nodded. "Yes." Before she could say anything else, a voice called her name.

"Goodbye, Crimson Eyes. It seems like they are looking for you." He waved at her.

"Goodbye…" she started but realized she did not know his name. "Goodbye, Grim Wanderer!"

The man laughed. "Clever. Okay, Grim Wanderer, it is, Crimson Eyes."

PART 2

A Crimson Fox & A Hungry Wolf in the Otherworld

An ancient whisper softly speaks,
Of a being bound to realms three,
An omen of change, a muse for ballads,
A creature so rare, it shatters and forges anew.

Such potent blessing, perilous threat,
To belong to none, yet be of all,
A harbinger of change and fate,
In shadows deep, it heeds the call.

From realms unseen, its echoes rise,
A mystery in a veil of lore,
To dance with stars, to weave the skies,
A myth reborn forevermore.

Retrieved from *Golden Tales from the Otherworld*
by Galen Sorrowspring, Ch. 7, p. 153.

PRELUDE

Evren Wraithwood

500 BGW Years Ago. Before the Great War

Evren was the youngest of the Wraithwood lineage. His lineage was made to rule over the Otherworld creatures, blessed by Nemera herself. "Humans are the least of my concerns," Evren Wraithwood told his friend Theron Galehollow.

Theron smirked as they walked near the Weeping Forest. "You should care, though. Ren, we honor Nemera by keeping balance, tricking or gifting those humans." Theron, part of the Galehollow lineage, oversaw air creatures. Evren admired that Theron could transform into a hawk. It was a better way to traverse the woods rather than as a wolf, which was the form he could take.

"Why are we discussing useless humans anyway?" Evren grimaced. "Lesser creatures can handle that. I actually enjoy seeing them trick those humans. It's delightful to watch them suffer for their selfish wishes and desires." To Evren, most humans sought help from Otherworld creatures for money, fame, or even love. *What a pity it is to be a desperate human.*

"I wouldn't expect you to handle that or anything. I guess, you are lucky," Theron muttered. "I must go. There are a couple of matters I need to attend to. But have fun, Ren. The woods are usually empty of humans, and there's a waterfall a few minutes from here." With that, Theron transformed into a hawk and soared into the sky.

"Lucky," Evren grumbled. Transforming into a wolf, he wandered around the exuberantly green and alive forest, feeling fortunate to be a prince without the burden of ruling.

Leaves flew around him as he moved faster than any creature in the woods.

"Where are you going?" a female voice asked.

Far enough, but with keen hearing, Evren thought this could be the perfect scenario to scare some useless humans. So he approached the voices, remaining in his wolf form.

"Nowhere," a softer voice, tinged with mischief, responded.

Evren recognized that tone well, having used it himself.

"Look, you cannot wander here alone. There are creatures and—"

The girl with the soft voice cut her off. "Yes, very dangerous and scary. I am trembling with fear."

I like this human, Evren thought.

"But—"

"But nothing. Here, take this book back to the library, could you? I will be back in an hour. There are things I must do, so if you would excuse me," the pleasant human said firmly.

Evren heard her moving deeper into the woods.

The human was walking fast, and while Evren's plan was disrupted, he could still follow the girl. *Maybe trick her. That way, I'll have a fun story to tell Theron.*

They both walked—he, hidden in the woods, and she, glimpsed through flashes of her long hazelnut hair and figure.

She moved like she was dancing. *A bad dancer, though.*

A few minutes later, the hazelnut-haired girl reached a waterfall, probably the same one Theron had mentioned. She turned her back to Evren, searching for a dry spot near the crystal waters. Evren was there, camouflaged between the trees. *Maybe I can jump and scare her, summon a creature and trick her into a deal, or ask a selkie to mesmerize her with its beauty.*

The girl turned around, a journal in her hand. She was writing, her face concentrated. Evren could faintly think of one word to describe her. *Beautiful.*

This kind of beauty was found somewhat in creatures from the Otherworld and Underworld. The kind of beauty one would want to capture in a painting forever. The human had the biggest green eyes he had ever seen, and her pale skin was like snow. Her face was a work of art—classy and delicate but with a dazzling fierceness. Her dress was torn, but she smiled. Whatever she was writing must've been delightful. Evren couldn't help but want to see what it was.

For the first time, he wondered if there was more to humans.

Nonsense, he thought. Evren decided it was too troublesome to bother scaring her, so he stayed there, watching the waterfalls until it was late at night. Then, she stood, ready to head home. He went in the same direction until she returned to her rickety town.

Evren told himself it had been a boring day and humans were a nuisance.

He told himself he hadn't been following her. It was a mere coincidence.

He told himself he had been too tired, which was why he stayed with her until she was ready to leave.

He told himself she was plain and not as beautiful as he had thought.

The prince of the Otherworld also knew he was lying.

Chapter 16

The Voided Fox

A frozen heart deal is never what it seems. Certain humans before the Great War and the veil's creation used to accept that in exchange for eternal life. It was one of the biggest blessings, but not all humans could not bear the weight of immortality, which meant forsaking their humanity.

Retrieved from *Golden Tales from the Otherworld* by Galen Sorrowspring, Ch. 30, p. 210.

Seraphine Ashcroft

Seraphine no longer saw colors or the beauty of the foliage in the Otherworld. She just stood there, as frozen as her heart. She watched Evren move across the Shadowmarket, shadows surrounding him, screams echoing, creatures hiding from the darkness that emanated from him. As much as she wanted to delve into what was happening, she could barely speak or move.

It was as if she were caged in her own mind, her body a machine built to move her limbs. An object to be used. A heartless tool. She wanted to feel—fear, hatred, guilt—but the deeper she searched, the more she could find nothing more than void.

Evren held her firmly, his arm on her back as if he knew her body was barely able to act by itself. Seraphine found no meaning or excitement in that anymore.

Her heart barely beat once or twice per hour. She had been counting. Breathing deeply, she decided to play along. Evren held the strings, but he had promised to free her after whatever quest he had in mind. Perhaps she could learn about him. It was a better use of her time than staying silent and letting the void in her heart consume her.

"I guess you delight in scaring poor creatures," she said, slowly scanning the scene. Shops were closing, and beings of all kinds—hags, siths, selkies, merrows—were running away.

"Who are you truly, Evren Wraithwood? Is this part of your plan, that so-called quest? Scare innocent creatures for fun?"

Evren stopped and surveyed her, his face the essence of smugness and smitten affection. He almost looked like royalty. *A prince of nothing.*

"Curious, aren't you?" he smirked, yet she recognized a flicker of concern in Evren's eyes. "There is someone I need to talk to first before we start our quest. Shortly after that conversation, I will share all the details," he promised, as if it would mean something to her—as if it were proof of trust.

"I remember that one there," she said, changing the topic to something more vain and less boring. She was looking at his cat sith.

"Ah yes, Shadoweater was my trading pal since I was prohibited from entering the realm."

Turning her head to the side, she stifled a yawn. "Why were you not allowed here? And why are you allowed now?" Seraphine was far from curious, but she needed to obtain some information from Evren to use to her advantage.

Feelings can be overshadowed by purpose, it seems.

"That, Crimson Eyes—" He tugged her close to his body with the hand he had on her back. The closeness sent warmth through her body, melting a little of the ice in her veins. "I cannot tell you just yet. We barely know each other," he mocked but kept her close, as if he knew she was cold to the bone.

She followed him. Somehow, the route was vaguely familiar. "Who are you searching for?" she inquired, noting there was nothing appealing about the Shadowmarket now.

"A friend of yours. Your beloved Dorah."

"Why her?"

"Why not?" he said.

"That is not an answer. You cannot answer my question with another question." Seraphine found his answer a little frustrating.

"Can't I?" Evren once again answered with a question.

Seraphine closed her eyes, took a breath, and then looked again at the sky. The Otherworld was different, inverted. The stars were closer.

Evren took off his furred cloak and put it on Seraphine. "She used to be an old friend of mine too. Just that."

The cloak was warm enough. Although a gentle and useless gesture, the girl tugged it closer to her body while they walked toward Dorah's shop.

Evren Wraithwood

Evren noticed Seraphine's usually pale and lively skin was dull. Perhaps it was due to the deal or hunger.

If only I were brave enough to be honest.

The truth was that he, born to unfairness and darkness, was afraid of what the truth could do to her. *Would she remember? Would she think of me as a monster?* Evren was a monster, nevertheless. For now, the best thing he could do was to find a way to end the quest and succeed. He could master the role of the villain anew. He could lie again, he could kill one more time, he could drown himself in the darkness once more.

He watched as Seraphine moved slowly beside him. In his white-furred cloak, she looked regal despite her tiredness. Her wavy, long hair and her eyes were the ones that made his breath hitch whenever he gazed upon them. However, once full of stars and light, her eyes were voided. *And it's all my fault.*

Not for long, though.

The Shadowmarket looked as he remembered, full of shops selling the most disgusting items. He had traveled here a few times but was always told to avoid it. This was a place for mercenaries, black magic, and the worst kind of trading. Evren, too, had been tricked here.

Still, now that Dorah knew Seraphine, he hoped he could leverage that to get some information from the hag.

As they walked, he couldn't help but breathe in the air of the Otherworld. When the veil was created, he barely glimpsed how the realm was transformed. Some parts remained the same, like the Shadowmarket, eerie and dark. Other parts stayed in the human world, like his forest. The world was crafted so the human and the Otherworld realms would lay in the same space. Still, Evren could sense something was off—mixed, unbalanced, unnatural.

There was so much he needed to understand about his realm. *How ironic.* If he had been more careful years ago, the veil and the war would have never happened.

"What an unpleasant visit," an ethereal voice said, moving out of the shadows and resting close to a dark old storefront.

"Likewise, Theodorah," Evren said, bowing to the hag.

Seraphine Ashcroft

Seraphine expected to feel something when seeing Dorah, but there was nothing. Still, she tried to soften her eyes a little, faking some politeness for the sake of her old friend.

Dorah approached her, her hair a mess with sharp roses. Still, Seraphine let her take her head in her hands, her nails sharp and long. "Seren, what happened?" she uttered quietly, concern in her old eyes, the flowers in her hair opening and closing.

"Nothing," Seraphine muttered. "Everything is all right, Dorah." She could pretend, even if it hurt to pull her lips in a smile. If Dorah was part of whatever Evren required to complete this quest, she had to ensure that her current state would not interfere with whatever they needed to discuss.

Dorah's eyes seemed to flicker with an emotion Seraphine could not comprehend, her uncanny brows moving down. As she opened her mouth to say something, Evren cut her off.

"Stop fussing over her, Theodorah. At least be kind. It's her birthday," he hissed, his voice deeper and more dangerous. Seraphine had never heard Evren sound like that.

How did he know it was my birthday?

Dorah seemed taken aback. "How?" she asked Evren, her voice small, scared.

Seraphine couldn't understand a single thing about the conversation or its importance. She almost laughed at the stupidity of it.

"That is impossible," Dorah continued. "You know that! What have you done, Evren?"

It seemed that while she was yawning, Seraphine missed something in the conversation.

"I did what you should have done, Theodorah. I fixed what you did," Evren said, his voice sharp like spikes of ice on the trees.

Seraphine eyed Evren, who was standing somehow taller and closer to the hag, like a hunter, a wild animal without control. "Do not come at me so high and mighty with the right to ask questions or doubt my decisions."

Evren moved closer and whispered something in Dorah's sharp ear. Whatever it was made her flinch and nod. This was the first time Seraphine had seen Dorah so subdued.

"Come inside. I guess you need something from me besides this... unexpected news," Dorah said to Evren.

Are they still talking about my birthday? Seraphine was failing in her plan to learn whatever could be useful against Evren. Dorah looked her way, a small smile full of sharp teeth this time.

"Child, I'll grab some new clothes for you. The dress is lovely, but you may need something lighter."

"For free?" Seraphine looked down. No wonder she was cold. Her dress was torn in places.

Dorah puffed at her. "Are you up for a deal?"

Seraphine found the normality of the conversation comforting.

"Always," she said to Dorah, briefly glimpsing at Evren, who seemed lost in his thoughts. Whatever it was caused him to hit his hand on the door's sharp edge.

Entering the shop, she noticed Evren trying to hide his now bloody finger and the straight line on his mouth. That was contrary to her, who pulled off a real smile.

"Ah, I must have been cursed by Nemera or something worse," Dorah sighed, looking at Evren with disdain. Evren smiled—a handsome smile.

He was, indeed, handsome, but who gave him the right to smile?

Seraphine made a mental to erase that smile from his face soon. A pained smile might be better.

Dorah pulled out a piece of paper and started drawing with a pen filled with crimson ink. *Probably blood.* Seraphine rolled her eyes at the dramatics of the Otherworld. She approached them and saw Dorah lining a map.

Despite her lack of taste, Dorah was kind enough to lend her a pair of old-looking pants and a soft shirt. Seraphine still had Evren's cloak.

The thought of getting on Evren's nerves by stealing his cloak tempted her.

"Here. Our realm is misplaced and somehow hidden over the human realm. There are a few places that remained, but—" She cleared her throat. "Since you were gone, King Malvrek took the opportunity to expand our realm."

The infamous Malvrek. Seraphine had read about him.

Malvrek, king of the Otherworld, had been created by Nemera to oversee all matters here. *Not much is mentioned about him besides that his word is power and that one of his three children will inherit his position one day.*

Evren looked lost in thought, tapping the map on the table. It seemed he was fine after hitting his hand. There was no trace of blood anymore. *He heals quickly*, she thought. "If the veil were to fall, these new lands would create a major catastrophic event in the human realm. It would be a collision," he muttered to himself while dragging one finger across the map.

Seraphine could not help but track that finger, up and down, moving from one drawing to another. It was so elegant and polished, different from hers, full of scratches and dirt.

"Why would the king do something like that, knowing it could lead to major destruction in both realms?" He finally stopped, but his brows were furrowed, his eyes darker.

"Because he thinks the veil will remain," Dorah said, giving him a knowing look. "Now, could you please zip that unpleasant mouth of yours and let me finish explaining?"

Evren smiled and covered his mouth with his hand, like a child pretending to sew his lips shut.

Seraphine *almost* laughed at that.

Dorah sighed. "What you are searching for, I do not have knowledge of. But I am sure that regardless, you wish to reach this place, don't you?" She pointed to a high hill at the border of the map.

Evren remained silent, still holding a hand over his mouth.

Moving forward, she stood near them at the table. "Oh, for Nemera's sake, stop playing around and talk," Seraphine hissed at Evren, pinching his arm along the way.

"Ouch!" Evren jumped at that and looked at Seraphine with a smirk. "Such playful grasp. Those might come in handy." He winked at her.

Seraphine rolled her eyes.

What an egocentric, confusing, and smelly wolf he was.

Then, she suddenly felt warmth. Evren, silently as a predator, wrapped an arm around her shoulders and muttered close to the shell of her ear. "Did I ever mention how much I enjoy you bossing me around?"

Perhaps it was the hunger because she could not deal with him anymore. Still, she felt a burning sensation that started in her stomach and traveled throughout her body. "You are a narcissist, a maniac with a self—" Seraphine stopped as her eyes met Evren's, just mere inches apart, and she could see them perfectly, every small detail. His eyes were gray-blue, like ice and full of white drops. This close, she could finally see that those were real snowflakes moving across his iris—dancing just like the ones she used to love in the Weeping Forest.

Seraphine wondered if she could live inside his eyes eternally. *That would be a good place to live, in the snow, in the frozen gaze of my enemy.*

Evren's eyes warmed, more blue than gray in an instant, and then he closed them. *What a shame*, Seraphine thought, since it was the only nice trait about him.

Liar, liar, liar.

"Don't," Evren whispered again, his eyes remaining closed.

She could see Dorah making a face of pure disgust.

"Don't what?" Seraphine said back, unfazed.

"Look at me like that," he muttered, opening one eye, almost timid.

She puffed, surprised. "Look at you, how exactly?"

He smiled then, an open and wide smile, dimples included. "Look who is answering my questions with more questions now."

Perhaps he was relieved that he had not completely broken her. Yet, she found herself raising her voice a little. "Why would I bother to answer your silly, poorly—" Seraphine started, but Evren moved faster than she had anticipated and placed a brief kiss on her cheek, like the touch of a leaf.

She felt hot. It was an unusual sensation for her frozen heart, which was not melting but merging with the warmth. Seraphine did not know what to say or do.

Is the deal wearing off? Perhaps she could ask him.

No.

The less Evren knew, the better.

One nightmare at a time.

Annoyingly boring and comforting, she could still feel the mark of the kiss there, lingering, warm.

"Now that my companion is beyond speechless and ready to not overwhelm us with a diverse number of adjectives toward me," Evren said, clearing his throat to suppress a laugh, "Yes, I need to get there, but there is research we shall do before that. About the lands, the current state of things, and some other relevant matters. There must be something I could use, something that could give me an idea of how I can—" He paused, choosing his words. "Clear up all this mess."

Dorah looked at Seraphine, who was frozen on the spot, and then at Evren. "There is plenty of information stored in the Mystweave Library."

Evren's head moved so quickly that Seraphine thought he might collapse. "Is my library still standing?" He was shocked, his eyes widening and his hand gripping the table strongly.

"What do you mean, your library?" Seraphine turned and faced him again. She had proclaimed that place as hers years ago. She had been the only one going, having never seen any other creature visit it.

"Mystweave Library was built and formally owned by this unpleasant being," Dorah said, pointing her long, sharp nails at Evren. "And yes, Theron hid the place. There are multiple entries, and there is one portal right here in the Shadowmarket. Seren is a frequent visitor."

Evren muttered, "You don't say." He moved, not looking at anything in particular, and took the map from Dorah. "I suppose there are hidden doors that will take me to some areas of the Otherworld from the library. Am I right?"

Dorah nodded.

"Theron made sure you had a way to reach out if you ever came back, which you sadly did," Dorah said.

Seraphine wanted to ask who Theron was, but she bit her tongue. Her head was still spinning around the fact that the muddy wolf beside her was the owner of her favorite place in the world.

Evren nodded. "Then, we shall begin our research," he said to Seraphine, facing her, this time his eyes hooded and looking at his feet. "As soon as we get to Mystweave, I will talk to you and answer the trillion questions that are in your head. But first..."

Evren moved his hand to her neck, closer to the odd ink on her skin, the mark that now bonded them together. Still, she did not want his grasp that close to her pulse, so she took a step back. "What are you doing?"

He sighed. "Calm down, Crimson Eyes. You kind of messed up the cloak's buttons." His hand moved to the top of her cloak, and she, indeed, had misplaced them. Evren unfastened the cloak and buttoned it again.

He proceeded to thank Dorah and moved across the shop. Seraphine followed after him.

"Evren," Dorah shouted just before they exited the shop.

They both looked at her. Dorah seemed to want to say something to Seraphine, but instead, she closed her eyes and said, "I won't forget what you did, Evren. The bad and the good."

What a terrible mistake. Thanking him will just inflate the man's ego… creature, whatever he is.

"Also, you must wander with care and remain hidden, Evren. The political state of the Otherworld has changed, and there is chaos. The balance of power is holding by a thread."

"Why? Is this something to do with the Underworld?"

"The two eldest sons of Malvrek were killed," Dorah clarified.

Evren's eyes grew colder and darker. His posture stiffened.

"I understand. We'll be careful." He used a very well-polished and practiced fake smile. Then, he looked at Seraphine and motioned for her to lead the way to her precious library.

Chapter 17

The Shattered Wolf

I found a way to dispel the curse placed upon Evren Wraithwood. After years of research, I finally found it. But all my intents to deliver that to him have failed. I just hope he can return home someday. And when he does, that it's not too late.

Retrieved from Theron Galehollow's journal.

Evren Wraithwood

Evren followed Seraphine through the alleys toward the Mystweave Library, his head clouded. *Thorne and Kaelan are dead.* His dearest confidants were dead—the only ones who had ever cared for him, the rightful rulers of this messed-up realm. *Who could have done such a thing?* The king was vile enough, but he doubted he had any interest in killing his own blood.

They must now be eyeing the remaining son and the king. Evren's presence in the Otherworld at this time might prove dangerous.

"Here," Seraphine said, her tone plain, pulling him out of his thoughts. Still, there she was, stunning even in worn-out pants. He closed the distance and stood in front of a broken mirror ensnared by black roses.

Evren rolled his eyes and nearly laughed. *Theron, such dramatics.*

He was about to ask her how long she had known about this place, but his words got caught in his throat when he noticed her looking at him.

He had long admitted that her eyes were his undoing. They seemed a little shinier, no longer fully empty. Seraphine was probably still feeling cold and unsteady, but she had been more chatty. More alive. That could only mean one thing, but he had no time to dwell on that.

She is a dangerous distraction.

"If you keep looking at me, I may have to kiss your other cheek," he drawled slowly, moving his gaze to her lips, knowing it would fluster her. Ignite something there.

She shot him a weary look and moved to his side to avoid eye contact. *Cute.*

"There is something very wrong with you," she spoke under her breath.

Moving deliberately, he positioned himself in front of her. Gently, he lifted her chin, his fingers lingering against her skin, guiding her gaze to meet his once more. "Shall I discover a more delightful place to kiss you, then?" he murmured, a roguish grin tugging at his mouth.

A spark of warmth appeared in her eyes. Seraphine pinched his side as before, and he released her chin slowly, the memory of her skin against his fingertips tender.

"All right, no kissing, then. I have absolutely no interest in that whatsoever. After all, you're definitely not my type... not even close."

She totally was.

Evren couldn't deny the thrill that surged through him every time he teased her. Her reactions were always priceless—those sharp retorts, the subtle flush of her cheeks, a hint of color coming alive on her again. He savored each moment, finding it hard to keep it together.

"Good," she snapped, her voice firm. "Because you are definitely not my type either."

He raised an eyebrow, a smirk playing on his lips. "Is that so?"

"Absolutely," she said confidently, though the heat rising to her cheeks and eyes betrayed her.

Evren leaned in closer, his breath warm against her ear. "Then, why do I catch you staring at me so often, Crimson Eyes?" he teased, his voice devilish.

She turned her head sharply, their faces inches apart. The tension between them was palpable, a magnetic pull that neither could deny. He could see the defiance in her eyes, the challenge, but something else was there too.

"Don't flatter yourself," she breathed, her gaze darting upward in exasperation as she moved around him, facing the mirror. "I found this place a while ago. It took me months to discover a way in, and—"

"You just have to let them bite you," Evren interrupted.

He knew the trick. It was an old way to keep things hidden. Still, there was something about it that he could not fully puzzle out.

"These roses are called nightsiths. They are mostly found around the north, at the edge of the Galehollow region, which is extremely dangerous since it is closer to the now closed entrance of the Underworld." He pushed his fingers toward one of the roses.

They opened their sharp teeth. Then, they started with the usual riddles. Evren pulled his hand back, teasing them.

"That is very insightful and useless information, thank you," Seraphine muttered, her expression stony.

He couldn't help but laugh.

So very hard to impress.

"But, did you, Seraphine Ashcroft, know that nightsiths only allow certain individuals when placed as a protection spell?" Evren's voice was a velvety whisper as he took her hand, his touch lingering and warm. He held it close to the roses, savoring the softness of her skin against his fingers. "Did you know that not everyone's blood is accepted?" he murmured, his eyes locked onto hers, a smoldering intensity in his gaze. As he moved her hand closer, the roses began to stir, eagerly responding to her presence, as if they were crying out for her.

"Why would they accept mine then?" Her tone was devoid of curiosity.

Evren knew it would take time for her to get used to the effects of a frozen heart. Yet, he missed the little reactions she used to have—her curiosity over everything in the world, the spark in her eyes whenever she walked from the Otherworld, the mischief in her lips when she was about to do something maddeningly fun.

All gone because of me.

He moved her hand, and a rose bit her deeply. She made no sound. Seraphine hadn't even blinked. "Exactly. Why would they?" He wanted to tell her that he had built the whole library centuries ago for her—for who she used to be.

However, he hadn't placed the nightsiths, and Theron didn't know about Seraphine. Even if Theron knew, he would have chosen a different type of protection, not nightsiths. These roses hated humans. In fact, a bite from one was deadly poisonous for humans. Yet, the roses seemed more eager for Seraphine's blood than his own. They were aching for her. *Strange.*

As the roses unfurled from the shattered mirror and it began to piece itself together, Evren felt a pang of confusion and curiosity. He watched Seraphine move through the mirror toward the library and wondered if Seraphine was not a mere human after all. If maybe all those rumors, which he had started, were tinted with some truth.

But if she is not human, what exactly is she?

Seraphine Ashcroft

It was just as Seraphine remembered, though it felt like a lifetime since she had last been here. She sensed Evren moving behind her, his presence as massive as a majestic wolf—and just as overbearing.

"Ah, I see someone kept adding more floors to this," he said, sounding pleased.

Seraphine watched as he wandered around the crystal library. It was still dark, and she considered mentioning the usual offering to the librarian but held back. Evren seemed lost in his own world, perhaps reminiscing. She wondered what kind of being he had been to create something so magnificent and what events had turned him into the creature he was today.

Evren finally approached the table. Instead of placing something of value, he laughed, holding a note with the usual warning she always saw.

"I can't believe you trick people with this type of nonsense," he said to the air, still laughing.

"Who are you talking to?" Seraphine asked, beginning to think Evren was losing his mind.

Out of the blue, the candles lit up, and the library shimmered with crystal colors. He hadn't even given an offering. *Perhaps his laugh had been the gift?*

Evren finally looked at her again, and she could swear there was something akin to nostalgia in his eyes. "Do not tell me you were tricked into giving food and other stuff to the library keeper?" he said, holding the paper in his hand. Moments later, the paper disintegrated.

Seraphine shifted awkwardly. "Yes, the Otherworld is based on exchange and—"

"What on Nemera's wings makes you believe that?" Evren asked, stepping closer to her.

"Dorah taught me that in the Shadowmarket, you must—"

He cut her off with more laughter. After composing himself, Evren looked at her, his eyes sparkling with amusement. "Crimson Eyes, those are the rules of the Shadowmarket. My library is not part of the Shadowmarket. It is not a place to trade. This is an extension of me, a part of what my home used to be. There is no business or deal-making here."

"That's nonsense. I tried to take a book once, and the librarian, or whatever keeper here, threw a book at my head," Seraphine muttered. *How much cheese and precious objects have I wasted on this place?*

"Did he?" Evren looked around as if searching for someone. His eyes darkened, and when he opened his hand, a red leaf appeared, floating around the library. He followed the leaf.

Seraphine wasn't sure if she was supposed to follow, but she did. The leaf flew across the first floor to a bookshelf. Evren crouched and removed the books from the first self.

"Where are you, Raggart?" he whispered, his voice rough.

As he cleared most of the shelf, Seraphine saw a creature hiding, clutching the last book.

This was the first time she saw the librarian this close. The creature had two long, pointed ears and a trunk-like nose. It was golden and not very friendly-looking. She had thought he was a regular brownie, but there was more to this one.

The creature looked at Evren and hugged the book tighter.

Evren smiled widely. "Found you."

Chapter 18

The Clever Fox

Once upon the snow,
A prince from another world fell in love.
Instead of roses and jewels of all types and forms,
He gifted her a house made of words and tales to behold.

Retrieved from *Old Tales & Stories*
by Luke Hollowspring, Ch. 1, p. 3.

Evren Wraithwood

He was going to throttle the little kilmoulis. *What in Nemera's name had Raggart been thinking, hitting Seraphine on the head?*

"Mr. Wraithwood," Raggart finally said, still holding the book like a shield. "It's been centuries. It's such a pleasure to have you again."

Evren smirked and signaled behind him where Seraphine stood.

"Who on this realm told you you could use my library for grocery trading?" Evren asked. Before Raggart could speak, he continued, "And why were you hitting my lady with a book?"

"I am not your—" Seraphine started, but he hushed her.

"I am trying hard to make a point here, Crimson Eyes," Evren said. To his surprise, she remained silent, though he could almost hear her eyes rolling. "Is there anything I should know to make sense of all this nonsense?"

The kilmoulis dropped the book and stepped out from behind the bookshelf. He was quite small but very clever. "Mr. Wraithwood, Mr. Galehollow came a few years after..." Evren narrowed his eyes at Raggart. "After the incident."

Raggart cleared his throat and continued more eloquently, "He protected the library and asked me to keep it safe from any intruder. He also told me to have that note ready for your return. Mr. Galehollow thought it would be a very fun and delightful welcoming joke..." Raggart trailed off when he noticed that Evren found the situation far from funny.

Evren patted Raggart on the head. "Isn't Mr. Galehollow a trickster?"

I am so going to pluck your eyes out, Theron. Just you wait.

He sighed. "Well then, I guess you took his word and ended up hurting her in the process under the guise of 'protecting the library.'" Evren stood up, and Raggart moved in front of Seraphine, a certain sparkle in her eyes. Evren realized that Seraphine had probably never seen a kilmoulis before.

"Seraphine, this is Raggart, the library keeper," Evren said, pushing Raggart slightly with his foot. "He shall apologize for the stolen food and the bump on your beautiful head."

Raggart finally looked at Seraphine, his small eyes widening in recognition. If Raggart had seen her properly before, he would have never dared to touch her.

Evren kicked him a bit harder this time, and Raggart composed himself. "I shall apologize for the stolen food and the bump on your beautiful head, Lady Wraithwood."

Evren stifled a laugh as Seraphine's eyes widened slightly. "I am not Lady Wraithwood!"

He put an arm over Seraphine and hushed her again. "Yes, I know. Could you please accept Raggart's offer of peace so we can move on with our lives?"

He saw Seraphine narrowing her gaze. "Of course, I do not blame you at all, Raggart," she said, her tone forced but at least polite.

Raggart smiled, revealing a set of tiny, razor-sharp teeth. "Your benevolence, Lady Wraithwood, knows no bounds. I shall be forever grateful—" Before Raggart could continue his fawning speech, Evren kicked him out of the way.

"Glorious. Now, let's begin our research." Evren looked at Raggart, who had been pushed a few feet away. "Could you handle a proper supper? This may take some time, and we've barely eaten since we left the human realm. Actually, Lady Wraithwood—" Evren felt Seraphine pinching his side again, hiding his smile. "Has been starving for longer than that. Could you arrange something?"

The little creature nodded eagerly. "It would be a delight for me to arrange supper preparations."

Evren smiled in gratitude.

"Mr. Wraithwood," Raggart called once again.

Evren sighed. Time was of the essence, and Raggart was proving to be a hindrance. "Yes, Raggart?"

Raggart hesitated for a moment before nervously saying, "I wonder if you heard about Thorne and Kaelan." He glanced at Seraphine.

Evren felt a sharp pain in his head and chest. "Yes, we'll discuss it in private later, Raggart."

Raggart nodded and disappeared, leaving them alone.

Seraphine Ashcroft

"What was that?" Seraphine asked.

Evren traced her with his eyes, somehow confused. "You must be starving," he said, as if it were the most obvious thing.

"Yes, but what was that creature?" she said, pointing to the path the library keeper had followed. "I have been here for years, and I've researched all types of Otherworld creatures, but I have never seen something like it."

"That is a kilmoulis," he said bluntly.

Seraphine narrowed her gaze at him.

"Could you stop the pettiness for once and explain at least that to me? Since you are still so tight-lipped about this quest."

He laughed and moved toward the second floor of the library. "Ah, you have been in my library and never looked into the main encyclopedias. What a shame, Crimson Eyes." He was clearly trying to annoy her.

"Let me remind you that I don't have a millennium of years to live and see," Seraphine continued, walking in front of Evren and looking him in the eyes. "My time is limited in this world. If it were up to me, I would spend it all here, reading. But I have matters to attend to. My life is a ticking clock."

He glanced at her and continued walking. "Was."

"Was what?" Seraphine was overly exasperated with the vagueness of his explanations.

"A ticking clock."

"And that's supposed to mean something?" she said, following him across the second floor. He seemed to be looking for something in particular.

Evren paused and smiled. "It will."

She caught the back of his tunic. "Evren," she said, realizing it was the first time she had called him by his name. He realized it, too, as his eyes widened in surprise. Seraphine cleared her throat. "You doomed me in ways that a human shall never forgive. Yet, I am bound here to you. The least you can do is to give me proper answers."

"I will explain everything to you, Crimson Eyes. I promise," he muttered, sincerity in his voice. "In exchange for something."

I will kill him.

"As if I would agree to more deals with you! Aren't we working together, Evren? Basic etiquette would be to share all the information you have with me."

"Give you all so you can use it and kill me after the quest?" he replied, somehow amused.

She remained silent.

"Well then, want to play?" he said once again.

Maybe it was her voided and frozen heart, but she felt confident enough to say the most terrible thing to an entity that had only brought her misfortune. "Let's play then. What's the deal?" she said, closing the space between her and Evren. "What is it that you want so I can get all of you?"

Evren's eyes sparkled—not mischief but something else entirely. "I want many things, Seraphine Ashcroft." He moved a step closer to her, and she could feel his breath on her lips, like the caress of a petal. "But if you want all of me, the right thing is to have all of you too."

Seraphine's heart sped up a beat. This time, she wondered if he had truly tricked her, and her wish was wearing off. Yet, she was so focused on him and his closeness and familiarity that she couldn't speak that thought aloud. She fought to keep her expression neutral, not to betray the effect Evren had on her.

Evren continued, "But I am smart enough to know that you would never agree to that." She would have if he were the Grim Wanderer—if he had not deceived her. "So, in exchange, I want you to find something for me in the library."

That sounds easy.

"It's a deal. I will find whatever you want, as long as it does not attempt to harm or is something that I would not be able to reach due to my human nature," she said decisively. The more detailed, the fewer chances of her getting tricked into something she couldn't accomplish.

"Ah, someone knows the rules," Evren said, moving his hand and caressing her ear. Seraphine was unmoving, feeling the warmth pouring from Evren's touch. She made sure to remain unfazed.

He smiled at her. "Fair enough. I'll make it easy for you, Crimson Eyes," he said, finally moving away.

Great. Room to breathe. Having Evren too close to her was unnecessary and unwanted.

Liar. Liar. Liar.

"There is a box hidden in the tales section. Find the box and wear whatever is inside. It shall not harm you, that I can assure you, but you must find it and use it all the time. With that, I will commit to telling nothing but the truth I can afford whenever you ask."

Seraphine knew that he would be compelled to tell her the truth if the deal was completed, yet all creatures here were masters of deception and half-truths. Still, this was worth the risk, so she lifted her chin and looked into Evren's eerie gray-blue eyes, snowflakes falling.

She said with a smile, "Game on."

Shortly after that, Evren told her to meet up in two hours on the first floor of the library. It seemed like he wanted to talk with the library keeper and arrange some tables so they could both get comfortable with the upcoming research they needed to do.

Not that Seraphine knew about that.

This time, she let herself marvel at the beauty of the place, the books lining up, the crystals all around. Seraphine had to admit that Evren had quite the taste.

She moved and passed the hall with the eerie paintings, and shortly, she was in the tales section.

What in Brannon's name?

Seraphine thought she would have to check every bookshelf and maybe do some digging. What she did not expect was to see a little white box lying in the center of the section. It was the only item besides the books. *Is this some kind of trick?*

She sauntered toward the box on the floor, just in case it was a trap. Once she reached it, she hovered over the little white box. *Small and quite pretty.* Still, it was bland-looking but quite familiar.

She bent down and stared at it, waiting for something to happen. A monster to appear. Maybe books would fall on her head again. She laughed at that a bit. *Poor Raggart.*

Nothing happened. Seraphine eyed the box for minutes. *Whatever.* She muttered a curse and picked up the little box, closing her eyes.

She was frozen on the spot, waiting for something to come for her, but the only thing she noticed was the smell of food. Her stomach screamed at her. Now that hunger dominated her mind, she opened the little box. According to Evren, the deal was to find it and use whatever was inside. Hopefully, it is not something indecent. *With him, one could only imagine.*

Slowly pushing the lid open, Seraphine looked inside the box, and her hands started to tremble. Sweat dotted her forehead, and once again, her heart seemed to beat a little faster. As cold as she felt, there was cracking fire moving inside her, so annoying and burning she wanted to tear her hair and clothes apart. She wanted to scream, to break something, to cry.

Below all that, she felt it. Emotions started to rise from the bottom of her voided darkness. A small one was the first to surface.

Sadness.

It was brief, and it disappeared right away. Somehow, Seraphine wished she could have wrapped that feeling instead of returning to nothingness.

Of course, the task would not be easy. It was a painful reminder, something she would gladly wear. She felt a liquid fall on her cheek. She touched the red liquid.

No, it's not blood.

Whatever she had felt for a few seconds was strong enough to make her shed crimson tears. Using her hand to clean her cheek, she saw nothing interesting in them. They looked plain now, just a brief reminder of an emotion that she once didn't want.

Still, she needed answers, so she grabbed the fox necklace in the box. It was the same necklace she had given Evren as part of the deal for her heart—the necklace her father had bought for her birthday, the necklace Leander should have delivered himself.

"Lady Wraithwood?" Raggart said.

Although startled, Seraphine steeled herself. "Yes?" She did not correct him on the title he used and turned around, faking a polite smile.

"Would you…" He stuttered and moved his little feet nervously. Raggart was a bizarre creature, but Seraphine sensed he was somehow more akin to kindness than any other. "Could I help you with the necklace?"

Seraphine nodded, thinking perhaps she could win Raggart over, seeing as he was close with Evren.

With that, Raggart, small as he was, took the necklace, and Seraphine bent down enough so he could put it on her. She heard a soft clack and then felt some light pressure on her neck. Before she could thank Raggart, he was gone.

Seraphine stood there on the floor for some more minutes. Then, just like she was about to touch a sharp or dangerous item, she moved her hand across the necklace and closed her eyes.

She realized that while her feelings seemed to be in a frozen, odd state, her memories were still intact. So, she held the small little fox pendant and let herself, for a minute, think about her father. Somehow, the memories of him were clear, like a vision. He was smiling in one. In the next, he was holding a younger Seraphine. Then, an unusual memory followed. Leander was smiling at a young lady. He seemed younger, and Seraphine could not place where this memory was coming from.

Seraphine kept her eyes closed, trying to hold onto the odd image. The woman was stunningly beautiful, her hair a mix of crimson and white. Still, what took Seraphine's breath away was how genuine her smile was, and Leander had never seemed so happy, so free.

The woman and her father were chasing each other in a place far from the wintery forest. She guessed that was how spring must look like, but she didn't understand how it was possible. Then, purple butterflies surrounded them.

Finally, as the image in her head blurred, Leander caught the woman in his arms, hugging her.

The woman turned around, and Seraphine saw her eyes were crimson.

Before any conclusions could be drawn, the image vanished. Seraphine felt close to fainting from the lack of food and exhaustion.

If that was really my mother, where was she? Does she know about all of this? If so, why has she left?

Seraphine thought it was better to abandon the thought rather than consider another cruel twist to the reality of being unwanted. It did not hurt her anymore, but she could not keep tabs on how many of those twisted fate scenarios she could endure before she broke.

Chapter 19

The Twisted Wolf

One being from the Otherworld shan't hold dear another from the human and even less so the Underworld. If that were to happen, the punishment would be absolute death.

Retrieved from *The King of The Otherworld*
by Kamera Willowpeaks, Ch. 10, p. 130.

Evren Wraithwood

He sensed Seraphine before she appeared in the main hall on the first floor of the library, still wearing his cloak.

It has always looked better on her.

"Did you complete your little task?" Evren asked while his stomach rumbled, craving real food from the Otherworld. Still, he was excited to see Seraphine move her hair, her eyes eerie and careful. As if she should somehow keep her distance from him. As if he would hurt her.

He felt shame fill his veins. His guilt was heavier than blood.

From under the cloak and clothes, Seraphine took out the fox necklace. It was no quest or deal. He owed her that, a reminder of what she was. Evren had taken everything from her. Still, Evren couldn't hold back his reaction, a sense of peace. Leander procured that for her. Leander had all the right to hate him, but again, this was not about him.

Examining the necklace, Evren noticed Leander had been aware of certain things from the Otherworld. He pondered if perhaps he knew he was destined for that. If so, Evren could not change destiny, but he would keep his name alive.

Seraphine cleared her throat, bringing him again to a reality where she was her enemy, something he found quite hard to resist. A reality where the face of dreams and eyes of starlights were masked in a mastered impassive expression once again. "I fulfilled the deal, so you better do your part, Evren."

Ah, even if she sounds annoyed, the way she says my name is beyond delightful. Evren was in no position to bargain.

"I made a deal, and I am caged. I am yours—my truths and my thoughts. And my soul. You just have to ask," he said, shrugging.

Seraphine moved closer to him, and her essence enveloped him. She seemed ready to say something, but Evren cut her off.

"There is a lot to talk about, but Raggart put in a lot of effort, so shall we converse with food and wine?"

Seraphine's stomach growled.

He took that as a yes.

Evren led Seraphine to a hidden room in the library.

"Rooms?" Surprised, she turned and looked at Evren, waiting for an explanation.

"You know, those square things where you sleep or store things? Those are very common in the human realm."

Her eyes darkened, and Evren was sure she was about to hit him, but she held herself in a perfect picture of nothingness. "You have been sneaking into my bedroom for how long? You know what? Doesn't matter. I just did not know these rooms existed. I feel like I missed the whole mystery part of the library and just did the boring thing by reading books."

He laughed at her surprise. The library had many tricks and doors, and for some reason, he was eager to show them to her. It felt like a second chance. "Books are the fun part."

The doors were pretty secluded. Even Evren was having difficulty finding most of them now. The place was massive and full of secrets.

And bittersweet memories.

A long time ago, he built the library as a gift. He also wanted it to be a safe place, so he ensured it was packed with enough rooms and spaces besides the most important items—books.

Evren made a mental note to organize library expeditions. Hopefully, Seraphine could enjoy those since it seemed like they would be staying there for quite some time.

As they moved across the space, he recognized an ancient and dusty reading room equipped with a long table covered in dishes of all kinds—meat and color-changing fruit from talking trees, plus Evren's favorite beverage.

"This looks… like a banquet instead of a regular supper," Seraphine muttered, her head angled curiously. She moved across the room and took a seat, her crimson eyes scanning every detail about the room and the food. She took a glass of the dark blue liquid. "Is this wine?" she asked while smelling the content briefly.

"It is. Dark blue wine, popularly known as starlight wine," Evren said, moving behind her and taking the cloak from her. It was warm enough in the room with the fireplace.

She stilled for a moment and then let him take the cloak away. Moving to another seat, he took a glass of dark blue wine and swirled its contents. As soon as the wine moved, a couple of colored dots and sparkling dust started to appear in the wine, making it look like a dark sky full of stars.

Seraphine imitated Evren, and, to his surprise, she smiled. "It is so pretty that I do not wish to drink it." Her eyes seemed to follow the trail of starlight moving inside the wine, as if she was chasing the little dots.

Raggart jumped onto another seat, his face barely reaching the table. "We have plenty of it stored. It would be a shame if you bothered with the prettiness of it instead of experiencing it." He pointed to the other dishes. "There is also plenty of food you would probably enjoy. I especially recommend the berry roses over there. They are a delight," Raggart said, almost drooling.

"Make sure to eat just enough of them," Evren said, cutting Raggart's explanation off, all too familiar with his ramblings.

Her hand stopped as she was just about to take one of the berry roses. "Why?"

"Because while the wine here is considered like water, berry roses tend to have a… numbing effect."

"So you can get wasted?" she said.

He bit back a smile.

"Yes, something like that," Evren said, faking a cough to stop his imagination from running too wild.

Clearing her throat, she sent him a challenging look and took a bite of the berry rose, her eyes closing slightly. Evren felt a tug in his heart. *How is it possible for me to get so overworked by the simple act of eating?* He was such a pitiful creature.

"Well, those are delicious. I better be careful then." Then, she took another one.

I am done for.

As such, they dug into the food. Evren noticed that Seraphine had picked another of the berry roses. He also noticed Raggart trying to grab one, and Evren kicked him from below the table, which ended up with Raggart flying across the room. This rewarded him with another quick smile from Seraphine.

Cautious, Evren decided to have some meat instead, purple pineapples, which were spicy but forever his favorites, and golden strawberries covered in silver chocolate. His longing for food was equal to his longing for her, which felt overwhelming.

"I am ready for some answers," Seraphine finally said from her seat, her voice a tone higher and her cheeks full of color.

They were both facing each other at the table, close enough for him to touch her legs and never close enough to reach her. Evren cleared his throat and signaled Raggart to leave the room. The kilmoulis was more than happy to do so since he sneaked some berry roses under his small arm.

"Before you question me, I would like to explain some details about the quest and my plan. Hopefully, that will answer a couple of things, and I can save some of the precious words that come from those stunning lips of yours," Evren purred, putting his head in between his hands.

To his surprise, she just nodded. He took her silence as his cue to begin.

"I was cast out from the Otherworld years ago. While I found a loophole through you, I am not fully in my power, and power is all here in the Otherworld. Without it, we are…"

She sighed and bit some sparkling strawberries. "Yeah, yeah, I know that part. Go on."

"I need to find something that can break whatever seal they put on my power, my essence." It was more than his power. They had taken part of him—of her. "That is why we are here. There must be something that can help us. Maybe a book, anything at all. Then, I shall be able to amend a couple of things I messed up years ago." Evren chose his words carefully. While he promised her the truth, there were some things he could not reveal.

Seraphine took another berry rose and ate it fully. Her eyes were a little blurry and unfocused, and Evren knew she had eaten too many of those berry roses. "What exactly are you?" she said, a little tongue-tied already.

That was a tough question, especially because she had said "what" and not "who." "I—"

She interrupted him by standing up. Seraphine took a final berry rose and gulped her glass of wine. Glitter spluttered around the corner of her mouth. Suddenly, she moved to the other side of the table and sat in the seat right next to Evren. She licked her lips but failed to remove the little drops of starlight from the corner of her mouth.

Evren gulped nervously and decided to take a sip of his wine and not look at her. She was too close now.

And probably a little drunk.

Yet, Evren couldn't help but notice how the soft light danced on her skin, the way her eyes sparkled with a mix of mischief and something deeper, a look he had missed. Her nearness was intoxicating to the point that he could drown in her view rather than berry roses, and he fought the urge to reach out and touch her, to feel her warmth against him.

Get a hold of yourself.

"Were you saying? I just want to make sure I hear every detail," she said, placing her elbows on the table and putting her head in her hand just like he had done a couple of minutes ago and looking expectantly at Evren. He thought he was safer in Aurum's grasp than under the eyes of the crimson-eyed girl.

"I am a primal sith." He looked at her.

Seraphine froze on the spot, her eyes sparkling again. Evren could see little stars moving inside of them. He composed himself and continued, "My family lineage is distantly related to some of the high and noble arcane courts that rule the Otherworld." His family lineage was well known but far from being a court. Still, he was not close with other lesser courts and lineages. "As you probably know, the closer to royalty, the more human-like. No curious features or things like that as other lesser creatures. Yet, there is a part of me missing, which I hope to get back when I find a cure or a way to fully release my power."

To his surprise, she giggled, the sound new to his ears. "You don't look human at all," she said, taking the glass of wine Evren had and moving her fingers across the edge of the glass.

"Of course I do. I do not have any horns or canines!" He opened his mouth and faked an indignant voice.

They were facing each other, a few inches apart. It was a stupid move since the closer Evren was to her, the emptier his head became.

Seraphine lifted a delicate finger, stumbling a little. "No, you are too handsome for a human."

Evren could not help but laugh at the cuteness of her stumbling. Her laugh, her playful tone—it was all driving him mad. He wanted to pull her closer, to feel her lips, explore every inch of her.

Is she aware that her emotions are showing more and more? "Crimson Eyes, there is one—" Before he could finish, Seraphine's eyes opened, and she put both of her hands on Evren's mouth, silencing him.

Too close, this is too close.

She hushed him and then began again. "Wolf." Evren stiffened at that. "The first time I saw you, I thought you were like a wolf." He eased up a little. "A muddy, smelly wolf," she said and giggled again.

Evren pretended to be annoyed at her. Still, she had told him this before when he was under the guise of the Grim Wanderer. "I am not smelly," he said, muffled by her hands, and rolled his eyes.

Seraphine giggled.

No, that was not just a giggle. *That is a whole crumbling event.* Evren wondered if there was a way to encapsulate her laugh in a bottle so that whenever he needed a reason to smile, he would hear her giggles and voice. He thought he missed the dark blue wine, but he realized he missed this more. The sound of her. The feel of her so close, even if it was torture.

Sweet torture, they call it.

Her touch was light, her hands soft against his mouth. He imagined what it would be like to have those hands roam freely over his body, to taste the sweetness of her skin, to drown in her presence. He might not get drunk with berry roses, but he was drunk on her laugh and eyes already.

However, it was getting late, and she was already too dizzy. *Better to take her to her chamber.* Seraphine might pinch him tomorrow if he let her continue with this gibberish any longer.

She might pinch him anyway, but still, it was the right thing to do.

Reluctantly, Evren removed her hands from his mouth, lingering for just a moment longer than necessary, savoring the contact. "All right, Crimson Eyes. It's time to get you to bed," he said softly, his voice betraying the desire he tried to keep hidden.

He held her hands in his and stood up, pulling her up with him. Seraphine stumbled a little. "It is time to rest. You can continue with the failed interrogation tomorrow," Evren said, and Seraphine nodded.

She took a step forward. As soon as she did, she almost fell, but he pulled her close to his body. There was no space between them, not a single barrier, just the slow movement of her chest against him. "Just kill me now, Aurum," Evren muttered, taking Seraphine by the waist and slowly sliding his other hand down her leg.

"W-what are you doing?" she whispered, her eyes wide again.

He picked her up and gathered her in his arms. Her head rested on his shoulder, and her legs flowed in the air. It was the image of a damsel never in distress held by the farthest thing from a hero. *What a fairytale,* he thought. "I am making sure you don't kill yourself on the way to your resting chamber, and I am avoiding a possible murder attempt from you in the morning," he said, stroking her hair a little, moving some strands off her face while exiting the room.

He carried her up the staircase. The windows and glass panes reflected the moonlight. It was late, and Evren could only guess how many days had passed since the incident in the human realm. *Two, probably three.*

"Warm," Seraphine muttered as he moved from the fourth to the library's fifth floor.

Evren looked at her. Her eyelids were closed. "What is it?" he asked, not expecting an answer. She was probably fast asleep.

In those moments, he hoped she was dreaming. Her life seemed more akin to a nightmare, so he prayed to the Ancients that she could have freedom in her dreams.

"I am always cold," she continued, almost whispering. "My heart, my head, and my body. It feels... like ice. Like my veins are..." She sighed. "Alive but feeding me with frost."

Evren recognized the feeling. However, he also knew that her body was still adjusting.

She moved her arms and shifted closer to him, her head now resting in the crook of his neck. Her breath caressed his skin, and he stopped on the fifth floor. Not because this was his destination, but because he dreaded to separate from her.

It was a selfish movement, but he just wanted a moment. *One is enough.* Still, he wished to hold her forever.

"You are warm," she spoke softly, and he moved slightly so he could look at her, her eyelashes down and her cheeks turning crimson. "I… I like to touch you because you—" She yawned. "You fill my veins with warmth. With you, there is no frost. You are the snowflakes and the soft snow spots on the trees that lighten my lonely days."

Evren could not muster a single word. His heart was beating like it caged a thousand butterflies, trying to make a hole in his chest so they could fly. He wanted to kiss her, to tell her how much he wanted to be that warmth for her forever, but he held back. She was vulnerable now, and he didn't want to take advantage of that. Plus, he did not deserve it.

"I know," Seraphine finally said, her head falling, a cascade of hazelnut hair glowing in the moonlight. Somehow, she sounded more energetic than before.

"What is it that you know?" he whispered while caressing her cheek.

Her skin was soft under his touch, and Evren marveled at the contrast between her usual cold words and the warmth she craved. She fell asleep after that, her chest rising and falling slowly as he continued carrying her.

Chapter 20

The Sneaky Fox

Sneaky little thing, come out and play,
Wouldn't you like to be painted in red today?

Retrieved from Evren Wraithwood's journal.

Seraphine Ashcroft

Seraphine was running again. She was overwhelmed by the feeling of being chased, like so many times before. Still, the forest seemed familiar now, so she turned to the left and ran toward a path. She knew it would lead her to some waterfalls.

Her waterfalls.

Their waterfalls.

She ran and peered behind her, searching for the predator she had faced in previous nightmares she could now recall. She saw no one, so she took a breath and looked at the beautiful waterfall, blue as the sky itself. She neared the edge to look at herself in the water.

Maybe this was a dream.

Perhaps I've been killed, and this is the afterlife?

She almost laughed at that.

The reflection that greeted Seraphine had the same crimson eyes as her. Still, the woman staring back at her was someone else. She had seen her before somewhere.

Then, the sky turned dark and red, and the waterfalls blackened.

When Seraphine looked at the reflection again, the woman mouthed two words. Suddenly, the world became black, and screams filled the air.

Her screams.

Seraphine opened her eyes. She breathed rapidly, disoriented and confused. *A nightmare.*

She moved to stand up, but a sharp pain throbbed in her head. *Curse you, berry roses.*

She was supposed to get answers from Evren but somehow ended up indulging in those delicious fruit. She took her pillow to her face and screamed into it. "This is not going as I expected."

Wait a second.

She focused on the pillow. Then, Seraphine realized she had no idea where she was and why she had her own pillow. In fact, her own bed.

Where in the world am I?

She stood up from the bed, which was massive and cream-colored, and glanced around. The bedroom was all cream and black, with crystals all around and walls covered in books. She noticed a desk and a wardrobe. The room seemed bigger than her cottage in the human world.

At that, she stopped and wondered about Aeliana. *Is she well?* Seraphine wondered if her sister missed her or hated her. She shook her head and decided to push those thoughts to the back of her mind. She was emotionally unattached and planned to keep it that way.

Wandering around, she found that the wardrobe was full of elegant dresses. *Did this room belong to one of Evren's lovers?* Not that she cared.

Liar, liar, liar.

Then, she scanned the books on the walls. *Mostly fairy tales.* She smiled. There were some interesting ones she might love to read. Maybe she could borrow one or two.

"I must be in the library," she said to herself. The decor and style matched the library.

Then, Seraphine felt the need to see Evren. She barely remembered anything from last night, and she had many questions. Not to mention, she felt better. There was ice in her veins, but it was manageable. She would never say it aloud, but Evren did well in making sure she ate something. Hunger was no longer ruling her.

With that, she put her hair up a little and took one soft black dress from the wardrobe. *What could this be made of?* It fit perfectly, and she turned to the door but stopped once something caught her eye.

She moved back and looked at the frame of her bed. Something akin to shock was bubbling in her throat.

Softly, she ran her fingers along the frame, detailing the crafted foxes. They were just like the ones she had in the cottage. No, exactly like the ones Leander had painted in her room.

Impossible.

Coincidences were common, but Seraphine was starting to sense that whatever happened to her was far from accidental. She took a step back. *Why would there be a room with the same drawings as in her cottage?*

Then, the two words from her dream returned to Seraphine, and she wondered if they were connected.

"Lady Wraithwood?" Raggart said from the door to her room.

Seraphine hadn't heard him enter. She stole a look at him, arching a delicate brow. "What are you doing here?"

Small as he was, he still appeared like a nightmarish thing. "I heard screams, so I came to check if my lady was in trouble." He moved nervously. "I did knock a few seconds ago, but there was no answer. I decided to enter. Still, I do apologize for intruding."

Seraphine sighed and decided not to correct Raggart again about the title he had been using for her. "It is fine, Raggart. I appreciate your concern. I might still be a little sleepy. Hope I did not trouble your rest, Raggart," she said sincerely.

He smiled, and his sharp teeth shone a little. "Not in the least. And if I may say, you look regal in that black dress."

"Thank you. I hope the owner won't mind."

Raggart glanced at the floor and cleared his throat. "I can assure you she won't mind at all."

That piqued Seraphine's attention. "Ah, so they do have an owner."

"That is not—" The little creature cut himself off. "I mean they do, but it is not—"

"I could not care less about it," she interrupted him. "Now that I have you here, I need to find 'Mr. Wraithwood.' Can you lead me to him?"

The creature seemed happy not to have to explain anything else. Raggart motioned for her to follow him.

As soon as she exited the room, Seraphine confirmed she was still in the Mystweave Library. The room was in a hidden hallway on the fifth floor in a labyrinth of shelves and books. They moved to another oddly-looking hallway that she had never seen before. She could see minor rays of light coming from the windows.

Raggart stopped in front of a bookshelf. "Here. It is still early, so I assume—" Raggart started, but Seraphine cut him off again.

"Is he... inside a book? Or am I going mad because I cannot see anything but a pile of books here?"

The little thing laughed. "It is a hidden door. The bookshelf here. When you are ready, just remove the book that has the symbol of a key." With that, Raggart ran like this was the last place he wanted to be, leaving her alone.

"Well, that was helpful," she muttered to herself and spotted a book that had a small key painted on it.

She removed the book from there as Raggart had instructed, and the bookshelf moved to the left, revealing a regular door. She sighed. *So theatrical.*

Then, she pushed the door open, ready to get some answers.

Still, Seraphine was not expecting the room to be this massive and comfortable. She was not expecting to see Evren, shirtless, lying on his massive bed. Asleep.

This could be my best opportunity. Maybe she could use a heavy book and casually drop it—slap it—on his face. No one would know.

It will be totally worth it.

Yet, she decided to look around to see if she could find something of value. There were books just like in her room, but his desk was bigger, with a bunch of papers scattered everywhere—maps, drawings, scribbles of some kind. *Someone needs to ask Raggart to tidy up this place.* She glanced at the drawings and maps, stopping on a paper containing a list.

Various names, perhaps 80 or so, were scratched out. There were notes beside each name.

"Died in her sleep."

"Killed by her friend."

"Jumped off a cliff."

Still, one name at the top was not scratched out. There was no cause of death, but the letters were hard to read, like someone had poured liquid over them many times and rewritten the name. It was hard to read, but she could make out the name Seiren Wraithwood Elaris.

Was she the owner of this dress? Somehow, she felt as if her heart was one degree colder. Shocked, she took a step back.

Unknowingly, she hit Evren's bed. She turned around and stared at him, still fully asleep.

Seraphine could never deny that Evren was absolutely beautiful in an eerie and mysterious way. Still, he seemed so peaceful sleeping that she wondered if he truly was Evren, no concern on his face or that stern and stubborn bow on his lips.

Dreamy.

That one degree in minus warmed.

Seraphine did not miss his well-toned and lean body, and the scars on his chest were oddly appealing. She wondered what had happened. Now that she thought about it, he did not seem much of a fighter—a warrior, yes, but not in the sense that most would think. Evren was a mastermind, the whisper that triggered the gun and the blade to draw blood.

Again, not that she cared.

Then, her eyes stopped on two tattoos on his arm—moving, alive, like smoke on his skin. She could not detail them, as if they were hiding from her. She moved closer, trying to catch them, but stopped, her eyes focusing on a small, mostly hidden tattoo. This one seemed different, alive too but somehow unafraid to be seen, static. *What is it?*

A feeling of déjà vu overtook her, as if she had seen it or perhaps been in this position before, and she did the most obvious thing. Seraphine neared him. Putting her hands on his bed, she sat down softly, trying not to wake him, but she could already feel the warmth coming from his skin. Arching down her head a little, she could see more of the tattoo. It was large and red. There were some symbols she could not make sense of, but there was a tail connecting to something on his neck. *If I could see his neck a little bit closer...*

Her hand moved as if enchanted toward the tattoo, and her pulse quickened. She imagined tracing that tattoo with her fingers, an unfamiliar heat pooling in her core. *What is wrong with me?*

Before Seraphine could even dwell on that, someone pulled her by the waist and pushed her right on top of Evren's body. She was ready to scream and fight her way out of the nice and warm body below her, but before she could even move a finger, Evren laughed.

Oh, Ancients, help me now.

Drowsy, he said, "Well, I don't mind this method of yours for waking up people." She looked at him and slapped herself internally for getting caught. *I won't see the end of this.* His eyes were a little hooded but open, stormy but extremely beautiful. She could accept that—not to him, but as a sad reality and undeserving for him.

Yawning like a cat, one hand fell close to her thigh, and the other one was slowly moving up her waist, leaving small trails of fiery kisses. "Unless you use this with other people. In that case, I would mind and probably curse them all." He smiled fully, showing his dimples, and her heart sped a beat once more.

What a misery to be so enchantingly repulsive in the best way possible.

Evren's dimples deepened, and his eyes softened on her.

Take my soul, Aurum.

Chapter 21

The Tempted Fox

Blood is a funny thing when coming from another being.
It can mend, it can cure, and somehow heal the sore
But cannot be trusted or deceived.
That is why in the Otherworld water is thicker.

Retrieved from *Ancients and Primals*
by Elowent Sorrowspring, Ch. 2, p. 10.

Evren Wraithwood

Evren couldn't hide his smile even if he tried to. *Oh, how much I will enjoy this moment.* He had sensed Seraphine and pretended he was asleep, and it was entertaining to see her all over him, even if she was trying to check his room for something she could use against him. Daring enough, she approached him to peek at his tattoos, which was torture enough. *It was so hard to keep my facade of the sleeping beauty incarnate.*

Evren could not resist the idea of pulling her close to him. It was early, and he had never been a fan of mornings, and he undoubtedly found her so deliciously perfect against his body that he could not help but snuggle her closer.

However, things worsened when he finally fully opened his eyes to see a shocked Seraphine, stunning against the sweet light. The worst of all, she was wearing a black silk dress—a very tight and soft black dress made of linen tree. It was a treasure, and his heart, or whatever was left of it, became stuck in his throat as a memory returned to him.

"*I made this especially for you,*" he had said centuries ago, yet she never used it.

For once, I shall thank you, Nemera, he thought. This view—he could get used to it. The dress, her hair slightly pulled up, her eyes.

Her.

However, for that, Seraphine needed to like him. While they had become closer in the past few days, closer as he forced her into a blood pact, he knew she still hated him.

And with reason.

Evren knew he should pull away, but he was selfish and wanted her closer, at least for a few more seconds. *Is it because of what she said when she got drunk on those berry roses?* No, but he could use that as an excuse for himself.

"Were you spying on me, Crimson Eyes? Drooling over my handsomeness while I was asleep?" he said, pulling himself and her up so he now rested on the frame of his bed, and Seraphine was straddling him. Something else replaced the shock on her face.

She huffed and put on the impassive expression he knew so well. Luckily, he knew the game well too. "I was not." However, she made no movement to get away from him. If anything, he felt Seraphine arching slightly closer to him.

"Hmm," Evren purred at her. "Did not seem like you were not, Crimson Eyes." He moved his hand and motioned to her hair. "You look beautiful this morning. Tell me..." He moved his head closer to her until there was not a single inch of space between their bodies, and he could see Seraphine's lips parting. *Oh, she may hate me, but I know she wants me.* There was a primal necessity that could not be erased and had nothing to do with feelings.

"Tell you what?" Her eyes were a little hooded, her lashes lowering, and Evren could see her chest rising and falling more rapidly. That dress was the greatest investment he had made, tight in all the right places.

"How is your headache?" he muttered. While he intended to mock her, he was truly concerned about her well-being.

She moved nervously, and Evren had to shut his eyes for a moment to suppress the feeling of her. Somehow, she was unaware of the effect of her moving on his lap. "It still hurts. I feel like my head is cracking and slowly killing me, and I do not remember a thing."

"I told you to not—" he started, but the look on her face was enough to shut him off. Evren was smart enough to know what battles he could win. With her looking at him that way, he had already lost.

Instead, he went to a safer approach. "I can help you with the headache. And after that, we can get something to eat... and start the research for the quest," Evren muttered, way too focused on Seraphine's neck, where the bonding-inked tattoo mingled with some beauty marks.

How many does she have? Do they make a constellation?

Seraphine bit her lip a little and said, "I do recall that part. You mentioned that we need to look into something that could lift whatever curse was placed on you, but I still have a lot of questions."

"Of course you do. I expect no less."

"So, you will help me with my headache?"

"Yes, my blood does have healing properties. You can just take one drop, and you will feel better." Evren's lineage blood was highly desired due to its healing properties. People would trade blood from lesser-related people linked to his heritage all the time.

"Right. Of course. You are so wholesome and holy that your blood is the key to the health issues in the realms."

He laughed slowly. "You said it, not me. And it is the truth. Now, you can also deal with that headache. Berry roses are as deadly as they are holy."

Seraphine scrunched her face, and Evren laughed again, louder. "It is just a drop, Crimson Eyes. And it's not like it's normal blood. Besides, you will feel like new. And we need to move with this, Seraphine. While I do enjoy having you here, I do wish to complete this quest and, for better or worse, free you."

That seemed to trigger something because her eyes were now stormy, Seraphine experiencing too many thoughts in a second. "That is really what you want? To free me?" she asked, doubtful.

However, Evren was being honest. "Yes. While my ways were not exactly beneficial to you, which I will regret for the rest of my life, I do wish you to have your freedom. That, I can swear."

After a moment of silence, Evren saw how she took a deep breath and looked at him again.

"Well then, how do I take your blood? Should I bite you? Are you a vampire of any kind?"

Her mind is perfection. "I am not a vampire. I do not think they exist here in the Otherworld," he said, more amused than anything.

"Then how?" she asked, genuinely curious. "Should I cut your whole finger and be done with it?" The shine in her eyes appeared. Evren loved her cunning nature, and each day, he knew he would see more of her come alive.

Evren proceeded to bite his lip, strong enough to cause an open and small cut. "There, just take a drop and drink it. It is tasteless, but you shall feel good immediately." He was teasing her, but he had no control. The closeness of her was driving him to the edge.

Seraphine furrowed her brows. He then moved his finger and touched his lip, slowly smearing the drop of blood provocatively. "Like this. Just take some—"

He never finished the phrase.

Seraphine moved and put her lips on his.

Seraphine Ashcroft

Seraphine told herself she should have asked for an alternative. However, being close to Evren made her feel an intoxicating warmth. Despite him being the mastermind behind all her suffering, his nearness clouded Seraphine's mind.

The closer I am to him, the fewer shards of ice I feel. When Seraphine felt him beneath her, and he bit his lip, something primal ignited within her.

My reasoning is gone.

There was just necessity, like the need to breathe and eat. Even was that—a need and want she couldn't understand but felt deeply natural.

Seraphine bent a little, her initial intention to draw a drop of his blood. Her head pounded, feeling as if rocks were being thrown at her. However, as soon as her lips touched his, everything changed.

Perhaps it was the lack of warmth, the years spent in shadows, or the events that had transpired, but she felt a deep hunger—a need for more. It was the same need that emanated from Evren when he had pulled her closer and opened his mouth to hers.

Seraphine had read enough books to know the basics of a kiss and had kissed Maxwell once. Still, this was different. For once, she let herself go, losing herself in the softness of his lips and his sweet, calming warmth.

Evren's hand moved in slow, tantalizing motions up and down her waist, and she moved her hand to his chest, surprising herself by pulling him closer. The kiss was everything a tale should be: sweet and caring, yet devouring and igniting.

She had never felt anything like this before. When Evren broke the kiss, she wanted to protest, but he had other ideas. He trailed a path of kisses down her neck, and she swore there was no better feeling than that. She could survive on those.

Somewhere between the kisses, Seraphine sighed in bliss. She knew she would scream into her pillow about this later.

One nightmare at a time.

However, this didn't feel like a nightmare at all, and that was very troublesome.

"You are the most exquisite being I have ever seen," he murmured, kissing her neck and lower, caressing her cleavage. "And I love these little spots, like constellations."

What is he talking about?

She needed to remind herself that she had marked him as her enemy and promised to destroy him, even as he gave special attention to the corner of her ear.

Still, Seraphine couldn't understand why she wanted this so much, why she needed it. She decided she wouldn't care. *Trouble is overrated today.* She moved her hand, unlocking the pin of her hair, letting it fall around her shoulders. Using her other hand, she guided Evren's mouth back to hers.

This time, they kissed like they had been waiting centuries for this moment. Perhaps they had. Yet, she noticed how Evren remained controlled, caressing her but also keeping his hand from moving too far. That warmed her veins.

Yet, she wanted more.

Seraphine broke the kiss, making Evren sigh, and then she closed the distance, trailing kisses from his cheek to his ear.

I may regret this someday, but that's something for later.

She whispered, "Morc."

Just like that, Evren was no longer still. He moved, lifting her for a moment, and then, he had her on her back, kissing her softly, biting her, drowning her in warmth and light.

She let her hand roam freely over Evren's chest, marveling at him and the sensation of it all.

"Seren..." Evren said between kisses as she drew him down on her. He slowly drifted, his mouth never leaving her skin, his hand slowly moving the hem of her dress, drawing small circles on her thighs until she opened up for him, waiting for more. She wasn't sure exactly what, but it felt right.

Evren followed her lead, once again covering her mouth with his, letting his hand roam freely to a spot below her navel, lower and lower, until her breath quickened, and he moaned against her lips at the feel of her.

"Evren," she gasped his name as his talented hand continued to caress her most sensitive spot. "Please," she sighed, her voice barely audible.

He smiled, a predatory grin, watching her squirm and arch as she continuously asked for something she couldn't name. Then, he lowered his head again, biting her lower lip as he pushed harder into her sensitive spot, and she cried out, her hips lifting to meet him. She was on fire, every nerve ending alight with sensation. She writhed beneath him, lost in a sea of pleasure.

Then, just when she thought she could take no more, he brought her to the brink and pushed her over. She shattered, her body convulsing in waves of ecstasy. And somehow, she wanted more, as if whatever she had lacked had been transformed into an insatiable hunger for this. For him. For whatever could make her feel alive.

"There is time, Crimson Eyes," he said under his breath against her mouth, as if he had read her thoughts, his hand caressing her waist and hair, kissing her one last time before he pulled her up to his chest and held her.

It felt like the most natural thing in the world.

For a moment, she lay there, hearing Evren's heartbeat and wondering if all of this was a terrible reaction to everything she had gone through.

Seraphine had never experienced anything like that before. While part of her thought she was mad to let Evren go that far, another part of her wanted him. Badly.

I am still going to be his doom. Without a shadow of a doubt. However, somehow, she did not regret what had happened. Maybe this could be a distraction. A way to own him.

It wasn't that good anyway.

Liar, liar, liar.

"Seren, I—" Evren said a few minutes later, both in his bed, his voice unsure. "I swear my intention was not…"

Seraphine studied him, her face still flushed. "Mine neither," she said shyly, though she knew she was lying to herself.

He cleared his throat, avoiding her gaze. "I-I just…"

She laughed, a bright sound that broke the tension. Clearly, he was more shocked than she was about what had just happened. "I liked it. I still despise you. But maybe we both needed that? I know I did… I've never… you know."

Evren's eyes softened, and she could see snowflakes in his gaze. She found that trail very calming to her heart. "Good. I deserve nothing but your hatred. But—" He moved and kissed her nose quickly. "If you want to use me in any way… this way, fantastic. You are… better than berry roses. But if you want to one day yell at me, tear me to pieces, do it. It is only fair."

Seraphine nodded, feeling somehow relaxed and warm. There was a thrilling comfort in his words, as twisted as that was.

"But," he said finally, a mischievous glint in his eyes. "I would prefer you to use me more frequently this way." He winked at her, and she pinched his side in response.

"Ouch," he said, smiling. "Such devastating fingers, Crimson Eyes. Now, let's have something to eat and get to work, shall we?"

As he dressed, Seraphine couldn't help but steal glances at him. His well-built body, the scars that told stories she wanted to uncover, the way his muscles moved—it all made her pulse quicken. She found herself imagining what it would be like to touch him again, to explore every inch of him.

Evren caught her staring and smirked. "Enjoying the view?"

She rolled her eyes. "You wish."

His eyes darkened with desire. "I do."

The way he looked at her, like he wanted to devour her, sent a shiver down her spine. Seraphine bit her lip, the memory of his touch still fresh on her skin. She could still feel the way his hands had roamed her body, the way his lips had teased her, driving her to the edge.

However, she wouldn't give him the satisfaction of knowing just how much she wanted him.

They headed to the same room where they had enjoyed supper yesterday, a spread of food awaiting them. Seraphine's stomach growled.

Evren pulled out a chair for her. She sat down, trying to maintain her composure, but the heat between them was palpable.

As they ate, their hands would occasionally brush, sending jolts of electricity through her. He would smile at her, a knowing look in his eyes, and she would have to remind herself to breathe.

"So," she said, trying to change the subject. "What's our next move?"

Evren leaned back in his chair, looking every bit the confident, infuriating man she had come to know. "We need to find information, perhaps a book that will guide us on how to lift any type of curse."

She nodded, trying to focus on his words and not the way his lips moved when he talked. "Right. A book. Do you have any idea where it might be, one that mentions that?"

He shrugged. "Somewhere in this library. It's a massive place, but we'll find it. There are some sections we can start with, and Raggart can always guide us."

As if it would be easy to explore a castle made of books.

She inhaled deeply. *Perhaps I can distract myself with books rather than him.*

"I have a question," Seraphine said.

"Of course you do," he muttered, not lifting his eyes from his plate.

"Can a hag or maybe another being lift whatever curse was placed on you?" she wondered. She knew that there were some creatures powerful enough to remove curses.

"No, this type of curse can only be lifted by the one who placed it, and trust me," he said, lifting his head and looking at her directly in the eyes. "He has no interest in doing it. Ever."

"Why not? It's been... decades? What if you ask him—"

Evren moved his plate, cutting off her reply, and moved to the side of the table, leaning down so they were both at eye level.

"Mmm, you are so very curious about it, aren't you?" he said, his eyes warm enough to melt her resolve. She tried hard to push away the memory of his closeness.

Seraphine cleared her throat. "I just wish to understand more. That way, I know what I should be searching for," she said, smiling politely and ironically.

His eyes moved down to her lips, and he purred, "That you do." Then, he broke whatever was happening there and stood up, offering his hand to her.

She looked at his hand as if it were a trap.

An alluring trap.

Put it together, Seraphine.

Evren laughed. "I want to show you something, please."

She grabbed his hand and let him pull her up from her seat. Then, he motioned her toward the second floor through a hallway she knew very well.

Evren Wraithwood

They moved across the second floor and reached a particular hallway where certain old paintings were hanging on the wall.

They used to be different. The paintings showcased what was once a beautiful story, and Evren had cherished them. Then, when everything had gone down centuries ago, the paintings twisted and changed. Instead of showing a love story, they displayed the tale of his own downfall. At that time, Evren had been so angry that he ripped them apart. Still, there were some pieces nobody could capture in the paintings.

Pieces of him.

Pieces that he hoped could help the crimson-eyed girl understand that he was not the greatest evil.

He wanted her to understand him, not to hate him as much as he hated himself.

Such human desires, he thought.

He looked at Seraphine, who was gazing at him expectantly. Her crimson eyes shone with curiosity.

And want.

Evren needed to remind himself that whatever desire he had should be shadowed by the objective of it all. *Her.* He sucked in a breath and focused on the painting once more.

"Did you have a chance to look at this stunning work of art?" he mocked, knowing full well this was by far not a work of art. The canvas was dirty and old.

Chaotic and torn, just like him.

Seraphine took a step forward, touching the canvas. "I have," she said, moving her head as if thinking of her next words. "I have tried to piece this together. Searched for books that could give me some idea of what this story was about." She lifted her eyes to him. "I asked Dorah, but it was like there was no record of it. I even tried to illustrate the paintings on paper, but as soon as I left the library, everything I drew was erased."

"Those are enchanted paintings."

"You don't say," she said in jest.

Ah, I could drown in her irony.

Sighing, Evren moved. "I placed these when I built this place. The paintings, the content at least, were linked to my memories. They are rotten and dark now, but they used to be bright. The images used to be something I once loved, the remains of what could have been but never was."

Seraphine moved across the paintings and reached the last one. A visible neck, his neck, was the only thing left intact. That one he had ripped apart, leaving behind a glimpse of him on the painting. He could recall that day, centuries ago, how much he hated him, hated the library, his memories, and he wanted to tear it all down. *How incredibly hypocritical of me to lead Seraphine to the same fate.*

"This is you, isn't it?" she said, looking at the painting, focusing on the visible neck. It was a fox, a replica of the one she also had on herself, just slightly larger.

It wasn't a tattoo but something Evren had done by cutting himself for years and years until his skin couldn't grow or heal. Looking back at her, Evren noticed she didn't seem to be waiting for him to confirm her words. Her eyes were trying to piece the story together.

"Why did the content of the paintings change?" Seraphine finally asked, and for a moment, he wondered if it was better to let this go.

Still, he needed to remind her that he was no good. That while he was a victim too, he should keep his word and focus on the matter at hand and not the impossibility of it.

"Because the one I loved died, and the memories of her too. What replaced them was a moment of darkness that took over me completely. A moment I wish I could erase, but ironically, it is placed in the canvases." Evren closed his eyes, remembering very well what lay on the paintings before and what was now.

The story of how I killed the one I loved the most.

"I am sorry," she whispered, and he looked at her with surprise. *Always kind, even to me, the person she should hate.* "After my father passed…

I realized heartache and losing the one you love can trigger darkness within you. Wasn't that the reason I reached out to you and let myself into this mess?"

"Seraphine, I am—"

She cut him off. "I know," she said, looking at her feet. "It was my choice. I could have run away or done other things, but it was my choice. Whether you interfered or not, it was meant to be that way. So I get it, the need to numb it all, run away from the overwhelming pain. Now, was your... I mean..." Seraphine once again turned to him and focused on the paintings. "Was the one you loved why you built this whole place?"

"Yes." *It was an engagement present.* "And I still love her."

"That must be nice. To be cherished like that still after death."

When Evren looked at her again, she darted her eyes. Seraphine examined her black dress, a look in her eyes he could not decipher, but then she gazed at him again, her expression impassive.

"Does this have anything to do with your curse?"

It has everything to do with it.

"Before she died, my... father did not approve of our union. He is a very well-connected being here, and he decided to rip most of my essence. At that time, the veil was created, and he also left me in the human realm and forbade my return." His voice shook a little. "Then, he orchestrated the assassination of my fiancée."

"He killed her just because he did not approve?"

It's more complicated than that.

"Well, he might do something worse if he finds me, and he will find me. I just need to be whole and have my power back before that happens." *Otherwise, my father will kill me and eventually you.*

"What if there is no way to break your curse?" Seraphine muttered slowly, her back stiff.

If there is no way... No, there has to be. Evren turned her life upside down just for this. He would find a way. "Then, you'll need to kill me. I'll be freed of my pain, and you'll all be free of me."

Chapter 22

The Jealous Fox

And there, upon the dirt and below the crimson sky,
The Ancient one of the Underworld did rise.
When he opened his eyes, the world was drenched in crimson black,
But when he opened his hands, the souls ignited, burning alive.

Retrieved from *The Garden Poems: Madness & Rosses*
by Lyra Sorrowspring, Ch. 5, p. 78.

Seraphine Ashcroft

After that conversation, Seraphine felt a twang of something she could only describe as discomfort. She was wearing a mysterious woman's dresses, probably sleeping in *her* room. Staying in *her* library.

Evren had indeed used Seraphine to get back to the Otherworld, but he had no idea why she was allowed, which she planned to figure out. However, due to the blood pact, she served as a conduit for him to loophole himself back into the realm. She felt used. He could have just told her he needed her for that. *There was no need to create this mess.*

She also did not know what he planned to do after he lifted whatever curse had been placed on him. Evren had told her that she didn't need to know since, at that point, she would be fully free of him. She did not push it.

However, she felt there was more to this. Then again, this was not a matter of her concern. There were more pressing things, such as the fact that she had started to feel certain emotions again.

Brief but constantly increasing—grief, sadness, guilt. They would come in waves and then disappear. Yet Seraphine would not trust Evren with this.

Days passed, and they both kept reading and looking into books of all kinds. The reminders of their connection seemed to have dissolved after their conversation in the hallway.

Evren also seemed colder. They would meet for supper and snacks, but he tried to be as far from her as possible, barely talking. Not even an ounce of mockery. As if there was no use for her anymore besides as a tool to an end.

While Seraphine told herself it was for the best that they both realized whatever happened was just a simple act of desperation, she also felt a twinge of loneliness. While he was morally incorrect, she understood that Otherworld nature was prone to that. Yes, he had caused major pain in her life, but she had also made her own choices.

Plus, she missed the playfulness, even if it was a distraction. She realized she missed her Grim Wanderer, Evren.

Seraphine would probably never forgive him entirely, but they could rely on each other to achieve their objectives. They both wanted the same thing.

Freedom, in its own twisted way.

The more she thought about Evren's story, the more she was reminded of the one he loved, the one who still owned his heart. Frustration would gather in her, so she would go to Dorah's and help her, and there, they would play shadow chess. In her loneliness, Seraphine would also indulge in little conversations with Raggart. However, it was not the same. The sense of boredom that had seemed to ease a few days before was now overwhelming in a way that angered her.

Evren would never accompany her to the Shadowmarket, preferring to remain in his room, reading books. Yes, he was ever the gentleman, but the distance irked Seraphine to no end.

She sighed, took the next book, and decided to continue the search.

Then, Evren appeared, standing so close she could feel the heat radiating from his body. His eyes were dark with desire, the snowflakes falling inside his eyes. He reached out, cupping her face with a teasing smile.

"Lost in the library again, Crimson Eyes?" he whispered, his voice dripping with irony.

Before she could respond and fight about the sudden change in his behavior, his lips were on hers, kissing her deeply, passionately. She melted into him, her body reacting instinctively to his touch. His hand roamed over her, tracing the curves of her body, slipping under her dress.

She gasped as his fingers brushed over her, teasing and caressing until she was breathless with need.

"You like this, don't you?" he murmured against her skin, his breath hot and tantalizing. "Admit it, Seraphine. Say you want me."

"Evren," she moaned, her voice a desperate plea.

He continued to tease her, his mouth trailing kisses down her neck, his breath scorching her skin.

His voice was a dark whisper in her ear, "You're mine, Seraphine. Say it."

"I-I—"

Suddenly, the world shattered.

Seraphine jolted awake, her body still tingling, her heart racing with unfulfilled desire. She felt a flush of heat and red anger rising within her.

"I hate this," she muttered, slamming the book shut. She must have fallen asleep while reading. She stood abruptly, noticing Evren frozen on the side of the desk, watching her with a mix of concern and longing.

When did he get here?

As she stormed past him, not sparing him a glance, Evren's eyes followed her for a moment before he looked elsewhere, refusing to meet her gaze. He stood there, blank and silent, as she made her way to her room, each step fueled by frustration. The dream had left her shaken, her emotions a tangled mess, and all she wanted was to escape the turmoil inside her.

"No," Seraphine said firmly as she put on a black-furred cloak she had borrowed from Dorah. She didn't dare use the white-furred hood Evren had lent her. She wasn't returning it either.

"No?" Evren said, dumbfounded, as if he had never heard that particular word.

Muddy and self-centered wolf.

"Would you like me to spell it? It's pretty simple, but I guess you missed the basics. It's—" she started.

"I know how to spell words!" he said a little louder. Today, he seemed irritated. This morning at breakfast, he had barely talked to Raggart, and he seemed like he hadn't slept well.

Today, Seraphine decided to visit the Shadowmarket. She was tired of wearing Evren's deceased fiancée's dresses and needed to feel like herself. *No more borrowed items.*

She was about to leave the library when Evren appeared, blocking her way out.

"Do you mind?" Seraphine retorted, trying to move past him.

He closed his eyes as if trying to suppress whatever was on his mind. "Is it too much to ask you to pick up something from one of the Shadowmarket vendors? The owner, a Leprechaun, is very nice! It's not like it would be a burden since you're heading there anyway. It's just a small—"

"You can go yourself!" Seraphine was on the edge of screaming. After ignoring and avoiding her, fetching items was the last thing she wanted to do for him.

Evren furrowed his brow. "It is better for me to be hidden. It might be risky for all of you, including you and—"

"I do not care!" she snapped. "You barely talk to me. You treat me like I am nothing but a ghost! Do you know how lonely this all feels for me, Evren? For Brannon's sake, I know I am not your fiancée, but at least you could make an effort to make this situation we are in more bearable!"

Seraphine knew she had said too much. She looked away.

He looked surprised, taken aback. "What does that have to do with anything? I thought you wanted me to keep my distance and—"

"I am tired, Evren! I might be an emotionless shade, but that does not mean I can handle using *her* clothes, *her* room! I am my own person! I am not asking you to want me. I just want to feel like *me*!"

"Seraphine, wait a minute—"

"No." Seraphine closed the distance and sneered at him. "Did you kiss me because you were bored? Were you looking for a replacement and realized I was not worth it enough? What happened to the one who was my friend, the one who appeared hidden in shadows and made me feel seen?" Her voice broke because she sensed and felt too much. Her heart wasn't numbing her feelings at all. It all came rushing to her. She could not hide from them anymore. *Especially not after* that *dream.*

"My exclusive use now is to help you get rid of this curse? You are no better than any human. You are a deceiver. From now on, I want to get a new room—for me. And I no longer want to spend time with you, so make yourself scarce. And, no, I won't pick up anything for you." With that, she pushed him and moved across the mirror toward the alleys and the Shadowmarket.

"I am sorry."

She heard him whisper in her head, soft and similar to the times he had done it in the human realm. However, if apologies were coins, she would be rich and living in a castle of spring.

However, what mattered the most was that he did not follow her.

Still, she wanted him to. She was unsure why.

While she expected to feel relief after what she had said, the only feeling she found inside her not-so-cold heart was disappointment and, at the bottom of it all, guilt.

I hate him.

Seraphine found a way to obtain some goods from Dorah and trade them in various places for new clothes. They were nowhere near as elegant as the dresses she had been wearing. The abhartach—a pale, bony figure with rusted, kind eyes—had given those to her. Old as time and known for his thirst for blood, she often wondered if he belonged to the Otherworld or the Underworld.

Still, at least those were her dresses.

In her mind, she replayed that stupid dream. "You are mine, Seraphine," he had said there. *Of course, it was a dream.* Not that she wanted to be his, but it was enough to see him every day. Seeing him in every nightmare changed things.

I hate this.

Seraphine wandered across the Shadowmarket, trying to focus on what she could do to fix this mess inside her not-so-frozen heart. The Shadowmarket was like a second home, and she wanted to be away from Evren longer. She had been harsh, and it was not fair. While she hated to admit it, she might have been a little jealous. Maybe because she realized that all the things she loved, her library, her books, belonged to another.

And who was she anyway?

She was angry because she felt used. In truth, it seemed like she was just another book for him to read and discard.

Not someone to truly cherish.

Seraphine was all alone in this massive world full of realms. Her heartbeat might still be slower than usual, but her feelings had started to resurface with a lot of power. She was trying not to drown in her emotions.

In the memories.

In thoughts of his father.

In the fear for her sister, who had almost died from being poisoned.

In the odd feelings she had for Evren.

Air. Seraphine needed air and space, so she took a detour and wandered until it was beyond midnight. She knew she should return by now, as Dorah had said things were lurking there at dawn. Plus, she was still human. Yet, she just couldn't go back. She needed to bottle up whatever was inside her before facing Evren.

Seraphine stopped near some whispering trees and decided to lie down there a bit. *Better to hear their nonsense than to hear whatever is in my head.* She closed her eyes and let the breeze of the Otherworld caress her face.

"I am so tired," she whispered to no one.

Other questions surfaced in her mind. The crimson-eyed girl with Leander, the feeling that something was missing, the carved foxes, the list of names in Evren's room.

Her.

She was an enigma on her own.

She just wanted a place to be quiet.

To be herself.

Seraphine did not know how long she lay there, but when she opened her eyes, it was dawn.

Oh no.

She pulled herself up and decided that it was time to go home.

Home.

She shook her head. That was not her home. *I don't have a home anymore.*

Suddenly, something hit her from behind, strong enough that she fell to the ground, full of colorful leaves and cloudy grass.

"What in Brannon's..." Seraphine looked behind her, and her eyes widened.

A soul eater.

Chapter 23

The Wanting Wolf

The poor, sad wolf lay on the floor,
Waiting for her return.
And when she did,
She was the same as before,
And the wolf basked in a world of happiness and longing.

But when she left, the world cracked,
And the poor wolf wondered,
If it was better for her to be gone than to stay by his side.

Retrieved from *The Great Love Story of The White Fox*
by Illyra Everdawn, Ch. 17, p. 105.

Evren Wraithwood

Evren couldn't believe it.

"What do you mean you lost sight of her? It's dawn, and the Shadowmarket is not a place to be wandering around during dawn, Raggart!" He had sent Raggart after Seraphine every single time to ensure her safety. After what Seraphine had said to him before leaving, Raggart losing her, and his increasing lack of sleep due to keeping his distance from her, he thought he might be the most misfortunate being in the whole realm.

"I-I— She was there, and then she was not," Raggart stammered.

Evren fought the urge to kick him. *What kind of excuse was that?*

Evren had decided to keep his distance for her well-being. He thought it was the right choice. Still, it was hard, and he couldn't stop thinking about her. Her voice, the way she felt whenever she was close to him, her lips. How beautiful and dazzling she looked when she focused on the books. The way she delighted in food.

Evren would wake up in the middle of the night, thinking about her crimson eyes and how much he would delight in painting the whole library with that color so he would be reminded of her forever. He would stay up, restraining the need to go to her and see her.

Evren wanted so much more than just seeing her or talking to her. He couldn't deny the deep longing that stirred every time he thought of her. He wanted to hold Seraphine, kiss her again, lose himself in her warmth, and hear her whisper his name for an eternity. He wished to take her everywhere, possess her, and let himself be possessed by her—in his bed, in the library, in the woods, everywhere.

Ah, the restraint he had to maintain whenever he saw her leaning to pick some new books, imagining how her body would feel pressed against his, her breath hot on his skin. *And when she had moaned my name when she fell asleep in the library… Was she thinking of me?* He almost broke there.

After what she had said at the doorway to the library about him deceiving her and implying he had used her and then thrown her away, he wanted to wrap her in his arms and explain everything to her. However, he knew that was not a good idea, not when she was in that state. Still, he decided that while he might withhold some information from her, he could start over and be there for her. He would find a way where both could still have a happy ending.

He almost laughed at that. *A being of the Otherworld believing in happy endings.*

Evren should have talked to her before distancing himself and hurting her, but first, he needed to make some arrangements. So, he made sure Raggart followed her while changing the Mystweave Library to show her that he had been wrong and wanted to be her friend. *Maybe more, if she allows it.* Most importantly, he wanted to see her.

Seraphine was always haunting him, but she was far from a ghost. She was the reason he did not end up wandering alone and why he still pushed himself to do what was needed. She was the reason for everything, the sole thing that kept him from falling into chaos. Seraphine was his hope.

"I will look for her," Evren finally said, putting on a dark cloak that would hide his face.

Raggart looked at him. "Mr. Wraithwood, it is dangerous for you! Someone might spot you and—"

"I don't care. I have to bring her back. Plus, I doubt someone from my father's army is looking for me, especially at dawn and in this place. I can handle myself," he said, adjusting his boots and taking a red leaf, a tracking type of leaf that would lead him to her. Next time, he would give Raggart a couple of those so he wouldn't lose her like she was some kind of stray cat.

"But, sir, I know she is—"

"If you value your life, Raggart, I suggest you don't finish that sentence," Evren said, rubbing one of his tattoos. At that, the ink disappeared, and Shadoweater appeared.

With a sigh, he let the red leaf move across the mirror, and both he and Shadoweater followed it into the Shadowmarket.

I won't ever let you out of my sight, he promised, his heart pounding with anticipation.

Shadoweater moved across the empty streets and alleys of the Shadowmarket. While Evren lacked his full essence and power, he was still more dangerous than any nightmarish creatures that lurked in the area.

They crossed the main center of the Shadowmarket until the leaf floated near some enchanting trees.

Where are you hiding, sweet and cunning fox?

Evren moved through the foliage, but Shadoweater's hiss froze him in place. *A warning.* He took a silver leaf from his pocket and turned it into a sharp dagger. He was well-trained, but he was not very fond of using weapons. He had always preferred fangs and claws, but since he could no longer turn into a wolf, a dagger would do the trick.

Another scream came from afar. Something twisted in Evren's heart, and his head clouded with memories. *How many times have I witnessed her death?*

No, he would not entertain that thought.

Dagger in hand, Evren moved faster than he thought possible.

Please be safe. Nemera, Brannon, Aurum, just let her be safe.

The red tracking leaf fell to the floor, a soul eater in front of him. The creature from the Underworld was holding Seraphine against a tree, strangling her. Blood trickled down her head to her face, matching her crimson eyes.

There were three of them. They were fast and skeletal but deadly, and their only purpose was to devour and feed on souls. A human soul was the most desirable for them since the Underworld had been lacking them for decades.

Evren dashed toward them. Shadoweater caught one of the soul eaters by the throat and sliced its neck open, purple blood splattering on the leafy ground. The trees screamed as Evren moved to the one holding Seraphine, throwing his dagger at its head and knocking the monster off balance.

He caught Seraphine before she could fall. She was breathing, but there were marks on her neck, and she might need stitches on the back of her head.

"Hey, Crimson Eyes. Can you hear me?" he said, holding her closer while the cat sith moved to the second soul eater.

She blinked at him, like she was in a daze. "I... I fell asleep and then tried to go back, and one of them punched me. I..." She was trembling, and before he could stand up, laughter came from behind them.

"What a ravishing hunt! What is a soul in comparison to the most wanted being in the entire Otherworld?" the soul eater Evren had hit said. The monster was smiling, sharp canines showing, and its shadowy skeleton body seemed to be recovering.

Evren put Seraphine behind him, covering her. "I can assure you they won't give you a penny for me."

"Is that so?" The soul eater approached them, and Evren was ready to tear him to pieces. *If I could only use more of my power.* The monster continued, "I am sure Malvrek would be pleased to have the one who killed his two elder sons."

Evren stiffened. *Kill my own brothers?*

Seraphine moved from behind him, cutting his thoughts short. She snapped at the soul eater, "He is not the killer, you disgusting thing."

Evren's heart skipped a beat. Despite everything, Seraphine believed in his innocence. Still, the thought was maddening, the accusation shaking him to his core. His father had always been ruthless, but to paint him as the murderer of his kin was a lie so twisted it almost felt real.

The soul eater looked at her, something flickering in its eyes, and it laughed. Shadoweater was still focused on devouring the other two fiends. "Let me correct myself. I just found the most wanted being in the Otherworld and a rare oddity worth a mile of souls."

Evren launched himself at the monster, producing a couple of other daggers from some silver leaves. He moved fast and pushed the soul eater to the ground.

The Soul Eater scratched Evren with its dark, sharp nails. The monster was fast, and Evren hadn't fought in a while.

Evren dug one of the daggers close to its heart, but the thing just laughed. Quicker than he had anticipated, the soul eater dipped a sharp nail inside Evren's side and bit his shoulder so fiercely that Evren froze. Then, he felt it—the soul eater was feeding. His strength and mind were slipping away, and he slowly lost grip on his dagger and himself.

Evren gazed softly at Seraphine, who was barely standing. *If I am to die getting lost in this universe of crimson, it would be worth it.* Shadoweater had long been instructed to protect her no matter what.

However, Seraphine moved toward them.

No, no.

He tried to shout, but no words came out.

She stumbled a little, and Evrens eyelids grew heavier. Then, like a shooting star, Seraphine jumped over them, pushing the soul eater off Evren. He tried to regain his strength, call for his cat sith, or maybe call for his other familiar, but he couldn't move. He had been out of this realm for too long and was too weak. Seraphine pushed the soul eater, and the monster swiped her side, his claws ripping flesh and breaking a bone. She bellowed, a raw scream full of frustration and hurt.

Evren started to move, but the soul eater froze. Seraphine used that moment to grab the monster's head. She pulled the thing closer, as if trying to break it, but it was no use, and fear overcame her when the soul eater laughed again. "Do you still know who he is?"

"Should I care?" she mumbled, holding the head of the soul eater firmly, continually pressing.

The soul eater grimaced, its voice slowing, as if he was also tired and drained. Suddenly, purple blood came from its mouth and eyes. "You should. He is a murderer—"

"He is not," she said so confidently that Evren almost believed her.

"Ask his beloved father," the soul eater coughed, purple blood splattering around them.

Perhaps Evren had hit the thing harder than he thought because it was not hurting Seraphine. It almost seemed as if it was slowly dying.

The soul eater looked at Evren, a smile forming. "Tell her, 'prince.' Tell her that Malvrek, your father, is looking for his remaining son. Tell her how you killed your other—"

Seraphine pushed her hand deeper into the soul eater's head, and before it could react, the monster fell to the ground, limp. It was paler, its eyes black and vacant.

What in Nemera's name happened?

Seconds passed, and Seraphine remained on her knees, unmoving. Evren somehow regained his strength, and with Shadoweater's help, he pushed himself toward Seraphine and the soul eater's body.

Is she hurt? As soon as he approached them, he realized that the soul eater was indeed dead, but more than that, the monster had been fully drained. Its magic, its essence, it was gone. If it had a soul, that was drained too.

Before Evren could ask what had happened, he saw her.

The hand with which Seraphine had grabbed the soul eater's face had black veins spreading upward. Her eyes were vacant too, the crimson in them dense, as if they were pools of dark blood. Around her eyes were spiderwebs of black ink coming from the corners, as if feeding her. Or poisoning her.

"Seren?" Evren asked softly. To his surprise, she turned her head and looked at him. She tilted her head to the side, like a predator evaluating its prey. The person standing there was not Seraphine.

It looked at him as if he was next. Evren steeled himself, aware he would never hurt her. Suddenly, Seraphine fell on top of the soul eater, and Evren quickly jumped to her. He breathed a sigh of relief.

She is breathing.

He sensed Shadoweater behind him and motioned him to leave, turning back into a tattoo on his upper arm. Evren, still hurting and weak, held her up and carried her limp body.

Her hand was still dark with protruding veins. Evren tried to rush, the mirror portal not far from his location.

She is well. You will figure it out.

He allowed himself to consider what Seraphine's action truly meant. She had just drained a soul eater's soul, something that no creature from the Otherworld could do.

He was unsure of what this made her, but she wasn't a mere human, and she wasn't a soul eater either.

Which means that she is probably something far worse. Far more dangerous.

Evren finally understood why she was allowed to move across realms. If what he was thinking was correct, then it all made sense. Few creatures were allowed to wander across realms, and perhaps someone in her family tree had been part of them. Still, he was unsure how she had been born in the human realm. Mixed races between realms were forbidden and usually executed, but like soul eaters, the only ones who could feed on a soul like she had done was their ruler: Aurum, the Ancient of the Underworld.

Chapter 24

The Soulless Fox

There was a song I once loved,
A haunting melody of two beings from different worlds.
I thought it was sad and twisted,
But something was missing, a piece left untold.

The story wasn't complete,
For she had indeed become part of a tale,
A tale she never intended to be written into,
A destiny she never sought to claim as her own.

Retrieved from *The Mad Love Story of The Haunted*
by Illyra Everdawn, Ch. 1, p. 5.

Seraphine Ashcroft

She is burning," a familiar voice said, and then she felt something wet and cold against her neck and head.

Where am I? All she could see was blackness around her. She felt a brief touch on her cheek.

"What happened? You can barely stand on your own," another voice said, ethereal and female, familiar but not as pleasing as the first one.

There was silence until the male voice spoke again. "She took its soul."

More silence.

"No, that is not accurate. She fed on its soul," the male voice corrected.

Seraphine felt off. Her memories were a haze of gray eyes and sharp teeth.

"That is not possible. She is not a soul eater. Don't you have eyes to recognize the difference between a human and a soul eater?" the ethereal voice replied ironically and almost angrily.

The male sighed. "Of course, she is not a soul eater, Theodorah. I suggest you refrain from such offensive remarks. Now, I wish I had no eyes so I could avoid seeing *you*," the pleasant voice remarked while the other laughed.

"I would gladly take those off your face if you so desire to avoid my presence." There was a brief pause, and Seraphine could swear that whoever was talking was smiling now. "Prince."

Her head hurt, and a voice echoed in her mind.

"Tell her, 'prince.' Tell her that Malvrek, your father, is looking for his remaining son."

She had heard that before but could not place where or when. She could barely remember her name.

There were whispers, but she could not make out whatever the voices were saying.

"I'll send him a letter," the male voice said again. "Maybe he knows something."

"Ah, the smart one," the ethereal voice said again, and she felt something cold on her head once more. Seraphine sighed in relief.

"For Nemera's sake, Theodorah! Can you just stop? You are partially the reason why we are in this mess," the male voice said, a little frustrated.

The ethereal voice laughed, sharpness and pure hatred emanating from her. "I did what I could. I kept her alive."

"Barely."

"You are one to talk," she countered, and Seraphine felt something sharp piercing her skin. She felt dizzy, and her mind began to shut down, slowly drifting from the conversation. "Weren't you the one who killed her in the first place?"

Seraphine felt something soft against her skin, like the gentle caress of feathers. Warmth surrounded her, seeping into her bones.

Slowly, she opened her eyes and stretched languidly, much like a cat awakening from a nap. Then, she suddenly remembered Scarlet. Seraphine closed her eyes, berating herself internally for forgetting her poor little companion.

She cast a look around and realized this wasn't her room. Sitting up slightly, she noticed she was alone, not in her familiar quarters at the Mystweave Library, but in Evren's room.

What is happening?

Then, it all came rushing back—fleeing from the library, falling asleep under a tree, the soul eaters that had tried to kill her, and Evren becoming badly wounded. Without any rational thought, she had jumped to help him.

A shiver ran down her spine as she remembered what had happened afterward. Or what she thought had occurred. Maybe she was delirious, her memories fractured and incomplete. However, something told her that wasn't the case.

She couldn't quite describe the feeling, but it had been some kind of unknown hunger, a primal need to touch the soul eater. After she did, she felt warm and lost, like she could reach out to the night sky and touch a star.

Then, everything blackened.

Seraphine looked at her hands, looking for scratches, but they were clean. She touched her neck and head. No pain. She seemed completely unharmed, which was impossible. She vividly remembered one of the soul eaters pushing her head down, the sight of her own blood everywhere.

And Evren... How could he have survived his terrible injuries? He could heal easily, but he had lost too much blood. The thought sent a jolt of pain through her body. She should never have said those things to him, and seeing that she was all alone, she felt the worst had happened. *How did I end up here?* She was unsure, but her heart ached.

"I am so sorry," she muttered to no one, burying her head in her hands.

"You should be."

Startled, she raised her head and saw Evren in the corner of the room. His hair was a disheveled mess, and bandages were wrapped around his waist. Yet, he was striking regal, the very embodiment of power.

Thank the Ancients.

"You're alive," she said slowly, carefully controlling her expression. She must remain calm. Right now, she was prey under the watchful eyes of a skilled hunter, a dangerous being. However, she had been too blind to piece things together, to ask the right questions.

Evren huffed and rose from the chair, moving toward her with the slow, deliberate grace of a wolf stalking its prey. He sat at the corner of the bed, still keeping some distance between them. "You sound disappointed, Crimson Eyes. Would you prefer it if I were dead?" he asked, his unearthly eyes—gray with cascades of snow—piercing into hers.

His death would have meant her freedom, but she still felt a strange sense of relief knowing he was alive. "No, I wouldn't. But I guess your father doesn't share my beliefs, isn't that right, prince?" she said, and he flinched. She pressed on, anger flashing in her eyes, "How long were you planning to hide the fact that you are possibly the only living heir of the Otherworld?"

"Seraphine..."

"I want to rest," she said, though rest was the last thing on her mind.

Evren had promised her the truth, and this seemed like something she deserved to know. Their quest to break the curse had been doomed from the start, and he let her believe there was a way out. A hope for freedom. She had been so naive.

He moved closer but paused, noticing how she seemed on the verge of fleeing. "Look..." He closed his eyes briefly, collecting himself. "There is a reason why I—"

"I don't want to hear it."

"Fine, but there is something we need to discuss," he said, his snowy eyes locking onto her bloody ones.

"I don't—"

Evren cut her off. "How in the realms were you able to kill a soul eater by feeding on its soul, Seraphine?"

Memories of her draining the soul eater flooded back. The warmth she sensed had come from a soul. That was why she now felt so filled. She had devoured the soul of a creature meant to take souls. *And I enjoyed it.* She had wanted it.

Minutes passed, and Seraphine still couldn't breathe—couldn't think. Evren had been talking, trying to calm her, but her mind was in other realms.

I have killed.

The soul eater would've probably killed her, but she had enjoyed it.

If that were to happen again, would I kill someone else and drain their soul without noticing?

She was getting sick. This was a nightmare.

I am worse than a monster.

"Crimson Eyes, please just breathe," Evren said, but she couldn't focus. Everything was a blur, and there was no escape. She felt him pulling her toward him, and she pushed him away.

"No, do not get close to me! Ever!" Seraphine screamed. She had always been proud of not being a killer, never the monster they pictured in the human world, but now she could hurt him or anyone else who got close to her.

Still, she could never do that to him. She cared too much. Seraphine flinched at that. *Despite everything that happened, I…*

"Fine! I won't, but I do need you to take a big gulp of air. Otherwise, you might pass out, and I cannot afford that. No one is going to touch you. We will figure this out, and yes, there are plenty of things wrong with us and this situation, but just breathe," he said, concerned, his eyes stormy.

Probably a facade.

Still, she closed her eyes and started to breathe slowly. This was not the time to lose control.

"That is good," Evren said, helping by counting and breathing alongside her.

When she felt like herself, she muttered, "Something is wrong with me. My heart feels cold, but it is beating faster than usual. I am feeling, Evren. Emotions that I should not be. I actually think I am feeling even more than I used to. Shouldn't I be voided and cold? Perhaps the deal went wrong and turned me into this? I am afraid." There, she said it, what had been bubbling for days, the source of her anger. *Fear.* "And that thing I did…" She couldn't finish the thought.

Evren moved away from her, and her heart cracked.

"Seraphine, there is something I did not mention to you, and I think that might explain why you are feeling after our deal," he said carefully, and that just increased her fear. "But the other part? That is something I have no answer for, but we shall find them together. The worst thing that could happen is that you end up having some…" He looked aside. "Type of far relative that possessed that kind of trait."

She huffed at him. "I am not even surprised about you holding back information again." However, she was also curious. "What kind of creature was in possession of that terrible trait?"

"Well… A soul eater is similar—"

"I'm not a soul eater, Evren."

"What I was trying to say here is that soul eaters were created by creatures that possessed that trait long ago, so maybe it's a distant relative of those." Evren was pacing around his room, looking at the books and somehow trying to piece everything together.

"And those relatives are…" Seraphine pushed because she felt like Evren was omitting information.

Like he always does.

"I do not know the name of those, Seraphine," he said, still avoiding looking at her.

"But you know something," she said, standing up and crossing the room. She moved in front of him, far enough to ensure he wouldn't be harmed by her but close enough so Evren would not be able to avoid her gaze. "Tell me."

He looked troubled, as if whatever he was thinking was pure chaos, and his eyes—those snowflakes of his—were swirling in a frenzy. "The only creatures that possessed something like that, that ability, are from the Underworld."

Chapter 25

The Killing Fox

A human was granted eternal life,
But as the years passed, he grew cold, unmoving,
A shadow of the man he once was,
A danger to himself and all who crossed his path.
And so, the wish, or perhaps the deal,
Took on a life of its own,
A curse disguised as an immortal gift.

Retrieved from *Ancient History of The Realms*
by Malvrek W., Ch. 110, p. 2334.

Seraphine Ashcroft

Seraphine almost laughed at the thought of the Underworld. It seemed the rumors were true—she was an omen of death. She had asked Evren to leave her alone for a moment after that, needing time to process everything. Evren agreed that the other part regarding the deal could wait until she felt up to it.

Such a liar.

She sat on the bed and thought about the dream of the crimson-eyed woman. There was something about that dream and her. What she had said to her ears had seemed like a mere dream, but now, she needed to know for sure.

Maybe by touching the fox pendant again, I can bring back some memories.

She moved her hand and touched the necklace. Nothing.

Seraphine sighed, acknowledging that she needed to do some research, not just for Evren but for herself. She knew there were certain forbidden books about the Underworld. Maybe they could find something there.

Later that day, she asked Raggart for clothes and a pair of gloves. She wasn't sure how to trigger that awful ability again, but she hoped covering her hands might prevent her from hurting others.

As she moved to the library, she spotted Evren. He was looking at a book, a mug in his hand. "You look great, Crimson Eyes," he said, glancing from the pages to her with something akin to wistfulness.

She rolled her eyes and moved to the other side of the desk.

"Ah, what an interesting choice of accessories." He motioned to the gloves.

"Better to keep my hands covered until we know for sure."

"Whatever you say."

"Do not mock me, Evren. I am here because there is a lot to talk about. I want to hear it all, prince. I want to know why I have been feeling like something wasn't done properly with the deal. I asked for my heart to be frozen so I could stop feeling everything, but somehow, I am here feeling even more. And I want to know why they are looking for you. Certainly, you did not kill your brothers," she snarled.

"So you have been feeling more? Are you suggesting that you actually like me and—"

"Never in this lifetime!" she seethed at him.

His mouth twisted as if he were tasting something bittersweet. "I see," he whispered, then closed the book in his hand and inhaled sharply. "I lied about the frozen heart deal."

"That is such a surprise, you lying about something." She moved her hand, pointing at him. "Did you still fulfill the deal? Was this some trick you used to have me bonded to you so you could come here? Because if that is the case, you could have saved a lot of time and just asked me, you stupid jerk."

"I told you that I would fulfill the deal, and I did. It was a pact, and you know that a deal spoken is a deal that cannot be broken. Otherwise, you wouldn't be here under a blood pact with me," he said awkwardly, looking away.

Muddy, lying, deceiving wolf!

"Then?" Seraphine spoke a little louder, slamming the desk with enough force that her fingers hurt.

Evren finally looked at her again, resignation in his eyes. "I lied about what a frozen heart deal is about. It is not to numb emotions, Crimson Eyes. It does numb due to the nature of the deal and for your body to adjust, but that is a secondary effect."

"Then what is it?" *If he turned me into a creature, I will remove my gloves and—*

"A frozen heart is a forbidden way to grant eternal life."

Evren Wraithwood

"Are you telling me that I am now… immortal? Are you out of your mind? What benefit is that to you?" Seraphine's eyes widened.

Evren wanted to move closer to her, but he knew she was still uncomfortable. Yet, he couldn't help but notice how dazzling she looked in those beautiful black gloves, like an elegant aristocrat. Plus, those crimson eyes ate at his soul with every single glance.

"Yes, remember the story I told you?" he asked, hoping to pacify her.

She nodded and then narrowed her eyes at him. "That sweet tale about the hunter killing his beloved, prince?" she said, and he couldn't miss the little intonation whenever she used the word "prince." "I might use it as a reference for our twisted tale here, but this time, I may get to be the hunter and just purposely kill you."

If Evren had been fascinated with her before, this enslaved him for life. Yet, little did she know she was already the hunter in this messed-up tale.

"Ah, I didn't know you considered me your lover, Crimson Eyes," he mocked, and she shut her mouth, which only enticed him. "If I knew before, I'd definitely act kinder."

Her eyes looked like fire, like crimson sparks ready to explode.

He laughed. "Easy there, Crimson Eyes." He stood up and looked around the bookshelves, taking a particular book.

"The tale has multiple twists and versions," Evren began, opening the book before her. "Maybe he did ask for a frozen heart, but there are two types of deals." He pointed to a quick note in the book. "One can ask for a frozen heart poison, which will freeze your heart and bones until death." Seraphine gasped. "Or, you can ask for a frozen heart deal, which can only be granted by one of the main arcane courts or—" He winked at her, and she rolled her eyes. "Someone greater like me."

"It took most of whatever power I had left to grant this, Seraphine, since it's forbidden. Centuries ago, it was something that would be granted to certain beings or humans as a reward. Eternal life."

Centuries ago, some humans yearned to be more than humans—endless lifespans, countless opportunities to rebuild themselves, which turned out wrongly. "For better or worse, it does truly freeze your heart, which is why you felt so detached from them at first. But that effect disappears over time—it mostly stops your life clock."

"Why? You could have offered another deal. Why go that far into making me..." She didn't finish the sentence, sounding curious, as if trying to decipher if this was something she could use to her advantage.

Evren felt terrible. He had pushed her to her limits, and the most terrifying untold truth of it all was she wasn't fully human. He was unsure how the deal would evolve in time with this new information. "Because I was certain you'd accept it, knowing that it would offer some numbness. And it did numb you for a while, but that wears off."

He knew he sounded like a deceiver, an untrustworthy wolf, but he couldn't reveal the real reason. She had so much on her mind, and he wouldn't add another burden.

Seraphine touched the book's pages where the notes about the frozen heart deal were. Closing the book, she started tracing the different symbols carved on the cover.

You made those a long time ago.

Evren felt a pang in his chest. There was much of her here, but so much was still missing. A lot of her was new to him, and he couldn't help but love all the versions of her.

"Captivating. Can I keep it?" she muttered.

"The book's enchanted. The only visible page is the one I showed you."

"Just answer the question. Can I at least keep something?" she said, her eyes sparkling, almost hypnotizing him.

He nodded, moving his gaze to another part of the library.

"You can keep it."

You can keep everything.

Crimson Memories

"If you could wish for anything in this world, what would it be?" the little girl with odd eyes asked the sentinel tree.

"I am a tree. It's not like I can wish for more. Aren't you late? What is this nonsense?"

"Not that late…" she said, stretching and hugging her fox toy made of tree roots. She could barely climb a tree and thought the sentinel was very muddy, but she liked the idea of pushing its limits. "But yeah, Dorah is waiting for me." She started moving toward the entrance.

"Well, what would you wish for then?" the grumpy and angry sentinel tree asked.

The little girl smiled at him. "I wish… I could be a snowflake."

"Just that? You wish to be a simple thing meant to be forgotten?" The sentinel tree seemed almost surprised.

She giggled. "Yes, I wish to be free as a snowflake, dancing and flying, free to roam between trees."

PART 3

The Tale of the Fox That Tricks the Old Wolf

At the edge of the realm, they sang
For a fox that had blood on its hand.
Smiling, the fox danced and drank
While the wolf looked from a cage afar.

Times will fly, and the song will last
About the smart fox that beat the wolf in a fight,
About a twisted fate distorted by the fox,
Who betrayed the wolf when it needed it the most.

How bizarre it was,
To see a fox dance and laugh.
And when the time was right, it held its clock in its hand
And turned the time backward one more time.

Retrieved from *Golden Tales from the Otherworld*
by Galen Sorrowspring, Ch. 7, p. 153.

PRELUDE

Seiren W. Elaris
500 BGW Years Ago. Before The Great War

Evren was waiting for her outside the bazaar. “Would you please pick one?” he said from afar, looking annoyingly cute.

Seiren smiled sweetly at him.

“Why the rush? Weren’t you the one who offered to come with me? You can go,” she said, knowing too well that he would stay. He always had. He always would.

She took the material in her hand. It was pretty and soft enough to make herself a nice dress.

Evren sighed, his eyes having a life of their own, a beautiful winter storm in them. “You know, I can always have a kelpie give me some of its hair. It is said that hags create the most stunning dresses out of it.”

Seiren puffed. “Right, as if you were friendly enough to get a kelpie into that plan of yours.”

She felt two arms pulling her closer to a strong chest and then a soft caress of his lips on the shell of her ear. “Should I remind you that I don’t need to be friendly? I just need to ask.”

Seiren couldn’t help but sigh before relaxing in his embrace.

“That is not very princely of you.”

He laughed, pulling her closer, and she adored these moments with him—how normal it was to have a life together. She looked at her hand again, a beautiful ring shining on her finger.

Evren had built a place for them full of books and love, and while they had their haven, she knew there were things to be discussed, like how his family would react when they found out they were getting married or the fact that she would age and die while he wouldn’t.

Sad as it was, Seiren could only hope to spend a small infinity of time with him, even if that was just a couple of years. “I am not that kind of prince. You pretty much thought I was some kind of monster.”

She laughed at that, her green eyes sparkling with amusement because she never imagined he would be this handsome and sweet person when they first met. “You were a wolf when I met you, and you still are, but you are also a prince.”

“Not for long,” Evren said, turning her in his arms, and she rested her head on his chest, breathing him in.

“Not for long,” Seiren repeated.

Softly, he put his fingers on her chin and lifted it so they were looking at each other once more, and Seiren knew that she had fallen in love again with him. This was the third time that day—over and over again, as in an endless loop.

“Have I ever told you that you have the most beautiful eyes I have ever seen?”

Evren had, countless times, and she still could not figure out how someone like him could find beauty in her ordinary self and plain green eyes. Yet, here they were.

My happily ever after.

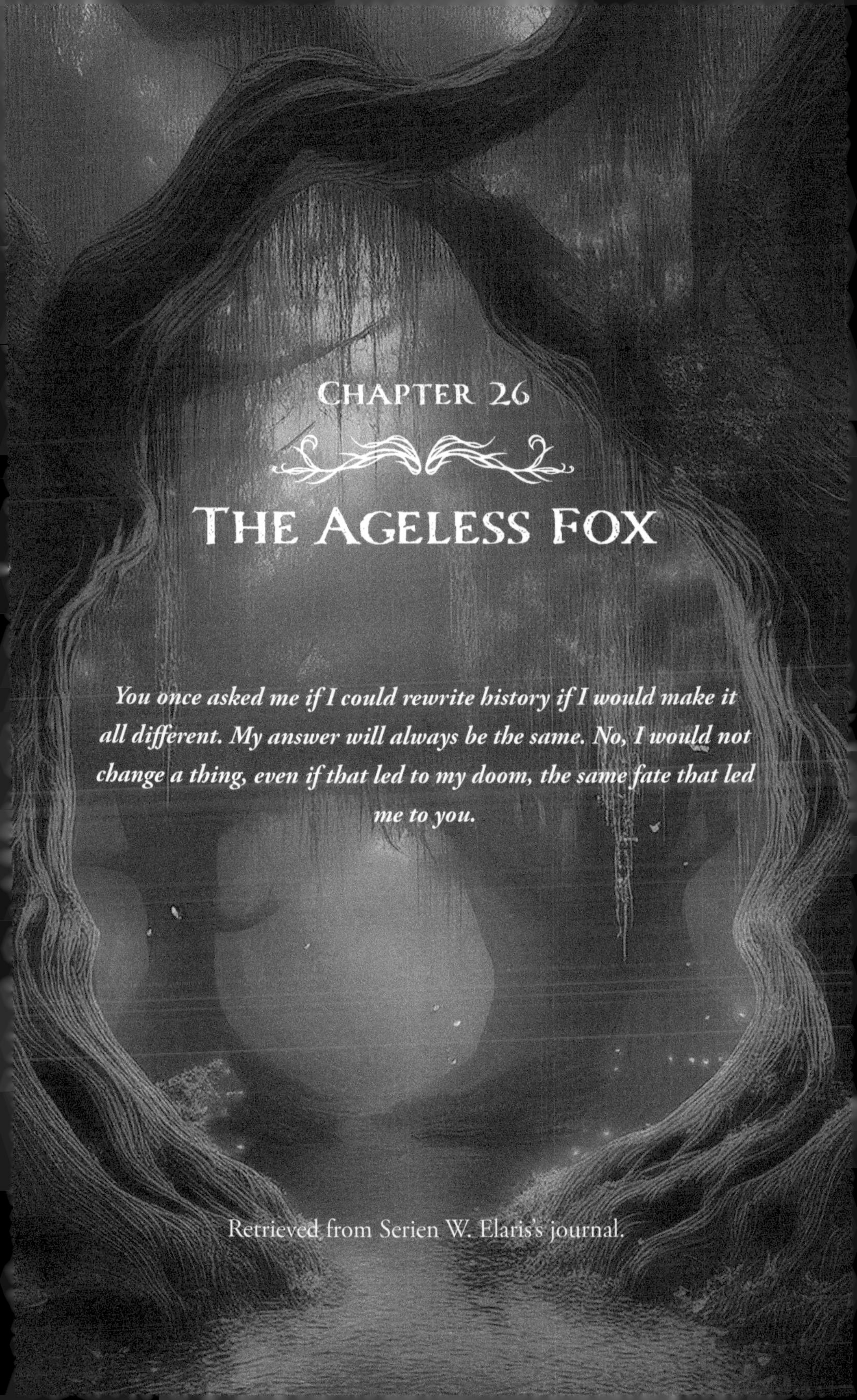

Chapter 26

The Ageless Fox

You once asked me if I could rewrite history if I would make it all different. My answer will always be the same. No, I would not change a thing, even if that led to my doom, the same fate that led me to you.

Retrieved from Serien W. Elaris's journal.

Seraphine Ashcroft

One nightmare at a time.

After talking with Evren a few days ago, everything had fallen into a comfortable routine again. The only difference was that this time, Evren didn't seem distant. Instead, he seemed eager to talk to her. He was his usual trickster and a flirt, and Seraphine had to admit she enjoyed their little chats. It felt as if she had found a safe place inside the eyes of her former enemy.

Seraphine also noticed how warm his eyes turned when he looked at her these days, a storm of soft and sweet snowflakes. The worst of all, his small gestures made her heart flutter—little touches and careful details, the sweetness in his tone and the caring in his voice. Seraphine knew everything in her world seemed like a twisted lie, but she was learning to love those lies. *Or maybe the mouth from which they came.*

She sighed, moving along the high walls full of books and loving their smell. The girl was also loving how much she had been feeling. There was something about losing her heart that made her realize how much she had missed it—the good, the bad, her humanity. Now, some things hadn't changed. Seraphine was still sleeping in the same room as before their incident. Evren had mentioned he was rearranging a new resting place for her. She just needed to wait a little, according to him.

Halting, Seraphine laughed at that. Seemingly, she had all the time in the world now. The girl couldn't help but wonder what she could do after this quest. *Maybe I'll travel around the realms and marvel at wonderful places, unknown seasons, and faces.* She might see every corner of the world with all the time at the tips of her fingers.

Sometimes, that thought excited her, but then she would have to see her sister eventually pass away. She wondered if the reason behind the frozen heart deal name was because, in time, one might wear off humanity—if a timeless body would lead to an immutable heart, stoned and stored by time. Evren seemed fine enough. However, he wasn't born human.

Wasn't being an unfeeling creature, wandering alone in solitude, something I wanted when I asked for this?

Here she was, with enough time to live, but the longer she lived, the more she would miss her father and sister. Seraphine hoped the memories of her loved ones would remain in her so she wouldn't become just a void vessel.

"One nightmare at a time," she muttered to herself, heading to the library.

Today, they were going to the forbidden section, and she was a little too eager. It seemed like she was attracted to everything that was forbidden these days. Evren thought it would be a good idea. Maybe there was something useful about lifting a curse or about her inner curse.

She had started to think of her condition as a curse after a few days, especially since using gloves on her hands was something she did daily.

Seraphine gazed up and welcomed the feeling of being marveled by the library's crystals and colors. It was noon, and the sun was rising high, reflecting shadows and figures in kaleidoscope colors. She had never seen the library bathed in daylight, and while the moonlight cast quite a stunning glow in this place, the sun was warmer. For a moment, she closed her eyes and let her mind rest for a minute.

"There." Evren's voice was loud.

She stayed still, not daring to open her eyes. *Just a few seconds more.* She just wanted to feel the warmth of not thinking at all. However, those around her had other plans.

Unmoving, she said, "Can't I even have a moment for myself?"

Evren laughed, and she knew his dimples had appeared. She couldn't help but smile a bit too.

"Ah, a brief glimpse of a smile!" he exclaimed.

Seraphine opened her eyes to roll them at him, but she didn't find the chance to. He was right in front of her, robbing her air, her privacy, her mind. He was always way too close. Yet, she started to pull away, afraid of hurting him.

"No," he said, touching her cheeks.

Whatever Seraphine wanted to say was lost. Evren looked at her in a way that could be described as watching a rose grow in the winter, like a drop of rain falling in a desert.

"Two things."

"Two things," she uttered slowly, not knowing what else to say.

"I know you are scared of… whatever happened there, but we are under a blood pact. Even if you find yourself in a position where you try to harm me, you wouldn't be able to."

Evren had said that before. She had figured that much after a few conversations with him, but she still wasn't sure how much that blood pact could protect him.

"And second, and most importantly, I need you to do the same thing you were doing before I interrupted you."

"What? I was just standing still and—"

"Exactly. Just close your eyes and stay there. I'll be back in a minute, but… stay there." With that, he moved his fingers, fluttering like butterfly wings against her eyes, and she closed them for him.

Well then.

Seraphine heard him leave, and while she should have moved and done exactly the opposite of what he had said, she did not. She closed her eyes and moved her head up, letting her mind wander to white snow and snowflakes instead.

Minutes passed, and she heard a click. Seraphine opened her eyes and saw Evren carrying a strange-looking box with a rounded crystal in the center.

"What is that?" Curiosity filled her.

Evren gave her the box. It was old and heavy and looked like an oddly-shaped telescope.

"Not sure what this is called, but a hag created it for my father a long time ago. It captures moments on canvases," he said, moving toward the staircase.

"Can I keep it?" She had been asking him that a lot lately and could not help herself.

Running to walk side by side with him, they moved toward the second floor and around some old and dusty parts of the library. At the end, she could see an intriguing door and a bored Raggart waiting for them.

"You did not answer my question," she pushed again, moving in front of Evren.

He laughed softly, almost as if he found the answer to the question too obvious. "You can keep everything."

Seraphine smiled and held the little box in her hands. He started to move but then turned around, blocking the view of Raggart and the door. "Could you go to the tales section and bring one of those stories you like so much? We might stay a while in the forbidden section, so it's better to have something nice to read whenever we need a break."

Seraphine nodded, and as she made her way to the second floor, she passed by the infamous hallway with the peculiar paintings of Evren's memories.

Clack!

The strange artifact Evren had given her fell to the floor, and Seraphine's eyes felt heavier and lighter at the same time, a tear falling down her cheek. The hall of paintings was as damaged and torn as ever, except for a newly added painting in the center, bringing some new life to the area.

She could see the library in the canvas, full of books and starlight mirrors, and in the center of it, there was a long-haired girl, smiling, looking up with her eyes closed, peaceful, melodic.

Seraphine's heart and eyes fluttered with countless snowflakes and butterflies.

That's me.

Evren had used the artifact to save the memory of her on a canvas. Then, she felt a whisper from afar inside her mind, just as he used to do when he was the Grim Wanderer.

"Thought you may like my new favorite painting."

Seraphine smiled, her heart full.

Evren Wraithwood

Seraphine returned with her hands full of books, the memory-taker artifact dangling precariously on top. The sight brought a smile to Evren's face. He moved closer and took a couple of books from her, his fingers briefly grazing her gloved ones.

He could feel the energy bouncing between them and marveled at that. Since the first day he met her, it had always been like this. What was even more entrancing was she looked at him in a way he hadn't seen in decades, the same way she had when she had waited for him at the waterfalls all those years ago. Her eyes were full of yearning. While Evren couldn't fathom how she could barely gaze at him, he also understood that they were fated. In a twisted, peculiar way, they always found a way back to each other. However, this time, it felt like the final one.

One final chance.

Yet, a certain fear clung to him like a persistent shadow, reminding him to be careful. If his father found out about her or what they had done centuries ago, he would use that against him. Killing her would be an act of mercy in his father's eyes.

Evren cleared his throat. "Raggart, grant us access to the forbidden section."

Raggart moved between Evren and Seraphine, holding a large golden key shaped like a leaf with a crimson crystal in the center. "I must apologize in advance, Mr. and Lady Wraithwood," Raggart said as Seraphine rolled her eyes. "We have not entered this place in centuries, so there is probably a lot of dust. I will make sure to have some—"

"There is no need, Raggart. We want to keep this place forbidden," Evren said as Raggart placed the key in the oddly-shaped hole in the small door.

The door was tiny. They might need to crouch to enter. Evren created it when he stole his father's tomes about the Underworld just to irritate him. However, he had barely entered once.

There was a click, and Raggart pulled the door open. Dots of golden dust filled the air.

"Golden dust?" Seraphine muttered, almost ironically. "Nemera must have had very rich tastes to have dust that looks like gold sparkles."

Raggart moved aside from the door. "As soon as you cross the threshold, you'll go through a very narrow tunnel for a couple of meters. Here, be careful with your heads."

Seraphine angled her head to the side, and Evren found it was one of her quirky habits, making every movement a delightful view. "You aren't coming?"

"No, someone must keep an eye on the library, and I am waiting for some important correspondence from a… friend," Raggart said, his ears twitching slightly, implying that it was indeed the truth.

Then, Raggart moved from the door and dusted off the gold particles from his skin. "After the tunnel, there are a couple of pools created when the realms cracked. Just find the one that is crystal clear. Should be at the very end, and…" Raggart gazed at Evren.

"And then I'll lead the way," Evren said confidently.

Seraphine Ashcroft

Evren quickly crouched down and entered the tunnel, crawling mostly on his knees while still holding most of the books Seraphine had borrowed. Perhaps she shouldn't have borrowed so many, as those books were as thick as a sentinel tree. Seraphine followed him, and while she was only carrying the little box, she found it challenging. The tunnel was narrow and pitch black, and she could barely see the back of Evren's neck.

"Why is there a tunnel? This feels more like we're sneaking in rather than just checking a library section," she posed, her knees hurting.

He looked back at her, his eyes light blue and gray, almost iridescent in contrast with the tunnel's darkness. "I wanted to make it difficult to reach, which I deeply regret now."

Seraphine was about to ask why, but she saved her breath. At this point, she felt the air was becoming thicker and denser, as if they were no longer in the library. *Nothing in this realm is obvious or as it's supposed to be, especially with Evren.*

Her eyes sparkled as she noticed a blue light coming from the end of the tunnel. "Almost there, Crimson Eyes."

Moving a few meters more, they reached what should be the edge of the tunnel, and Evren stood up first, offering her his hand. Seraphine hesitated but decided to trust that her gloves would be enough of a barrier to prevent her from hurting Evren. Even with the gloves, she could feel a brief electric push and warmth coming from his hand, feeding her, filling her. Slowly pulling her up, he managed to handle the books with the other hand.

As they both stood up, her eyes widened in pure wonder.

Right in the library, far from the tunnel, lay something akin to a cave. It was full of strangely shaped leaves, unique flowers, and ponds of different colors. Seraphine could stay days here and never count all of them. Water filtered out the walls.

Then, she realized this appeared like the remnants of a waterfall—broken or misplaced in time but still beautiful.

"When I built this place, I thought it would be fun to have a distraction—a setup that would make no one consider this was hiding the most forbidden and wanted books in the entire realm," Evren said.

Seraphine's gaze moved all around, mesmerized by everything she saw. She wondered if she could get permission to dip into one of those ponds one day. It was a place out of a fairytale—it was a hidden spring haven, a glamour that served to protect something outstandingly powerful: knowledge.

"It is a very beautiful facade. It looks like… waterfalls. We had some, but those are frozen and…"

Evren moved his free hand and removed a small strand of her hair from her face, his knuckles grazing her delicately. "It used to be a waterfall before the veil's creation. Instead of ponds, there was a gigantic crystalline waterfall that extended higher than the library and… It was a very magical place, " Evren said quietly, a tone of sadness in his voice. "Now, let's find that crystal pond."

Seraphine followed him, unable to resist touching some of the flowers. They moved past various ponds—some green, others dark blue, and even a rosy one. Near the edge of the cave was a crystal pond. The waters seemed to bubble and sparkle. To Seraphine, it was like watching stars swimming freely in the delicate waters.

Nothing is impossible in the Otherworld. Sometimes, she forgot about that, and her human feelings would still hinder such beautiful impossibilities.

Would touching the pond feel the same as touching the sky? Seraphine could not stop the thought. There was something indeed magical about this place.

She looked around and exhaled. "Now what? Do we get into the waters and pray for the books to appear?" she joked, the words feeling unfamiliar on her tongue.

Joking again felt strange and wrong—and right. When Evren was around, the line between those seemed to disappear.

However, her amusement faltered as Evren stared intensely at her.

"What?" she asked nervously, unsure what to expect.

"Nothing, just that seeing you smile felt like…" His lashes now hid his eyes as if he feared meeting hers.

Curiosity filled her. "Like what? If you don't like it, then I will do it more frequently. Anything that displeases you will surely make me happy."

At that, Evren moved his gaze slowly from the ground to her face, feeling his eyes touch every single part, and a shiver went through her. The books in his grasp disappeared in the air as he moved slowly, circling her just like the predator he was. However, Seraphine was not afraid—not of him.

The only thing she feared was her mind whenever he was around.

Stopping behind her, Evren moved his hand around her waist. His mouth brushed against her ear. "You put me in such a tough position, Crimson Eyes. The issue here is that I like those lips of yours too much. But let's pretend I don't so you can continue smiling at me to disgust me while I secretly enjoy it."

Air flew away from her lungs, and her veins filled with warmth and heat as strong as ice itself. Seraphine let her head drop, and from behind her, Evren moved his hand up until he was slowly caressing her upper stomach.

"Now, let's get this out of here," he said.

For a moment, her mind went wild about what he was referring to. Then, he took the artifact, the mere touch of his hand making it disappear.

He sighed, and she felt his chest expand. With a tone of mischief, he murmured, "And please, do not kill me after this, Crimson Eyes."

Before Seraphine could process the meaning behind his words, he pushed her into the pond.

CHAPTER 27

THE BREATHLESS FOX

Kelpies, merrows, creatures born from the drops of water by Nemera, belong to the oceans. They do not need to breathe, as water itself is their source of life. Other creatures can also breathe underwater, but water is dangerous, tricky, and dense with forbidden desires. Yet, once in a while, it is a place full of wishes and sparkling hope. Beware of the siths that dwell below, but perhaps be even more cautious of the waters you're in.

Retrieved from *Encyclopedia of Wonders and Chaos* Volume II
by Lysara Sorrowspring, Ch. 12, p. 67.

Seraphine Ashcroft

I *will kill him.*

Seraphine hit the water and opened her eyes, unable to help but marvel at the view. As she lay under the water, the crystalline drops reminded her of her beloved snowflakes. Bubbles floated around, dancing and shimmering like silver drops of starlight moving on their own. The water around her sparkled with an ethereal glow, as if stars had descended into the pond. Then, she heard another splashing sound, and Evren was beside her.

She narrowed her eyes at him with a promise for vengeance as she rose to the surface, but he faintly gave her a half-smile and tugged her below the waters again, fear clutching to her.

Underwater, Evren's raven hair was dotted in starlight and flowing as if it were made of water itself, and his eyes could be compared with the crystal water. Then, she realized that the pond was a replica of his eyes.

However, when Evren opened his mouth, still underwater and holding her close, he spoke, "Sorry for that."

Though the water muffled his voice, it sounded clear. She looked shocked while still trying to hold onto the little precious air in her body.

"Ah!" he said, smiling widely and moving closer, his hand touching her neck softly, the sensation as intense as ever. "Just open your mouth, Crimson Eyes."

He must be trying to kill me, she thought. As she started to pull away from his grasp, trying to push herself to the surface, he stopped her, wrapping his arms around her waist, locking her in place. Caged.

The air seemed to be leaving faster as her heart quickened. *I'm drowning.*

Concern marked her eyes, and she started to get dizzy and disoriented. "Just open your mouth, Crimson Eyes. You'll see that you can easily speak," he urged her, his brows furrowed but still holding her in place. Not letting her go.

As if I'll believe that. Seraphine had been holding onto the feeling of drowning all her life but did not expect to die from it.

She struggled hard to swim up, trying to escape his grip, but Evren's hold was like iron. However, she slowly felt herself drifting away, her movements slower.

"For Nemera's sake, Seraphine." Evren took her face in his hands. Her eyes were drifting closed, but she could see a quick smirk on his lips. "Just to be clear, don't kill me for trying to help you not kill yourself. Again."

Before Seraphine could make sense of his words, he pulled her head closer to his and dipped his head, his lips touching hers. It felt as soft as a feather initially, and then it intensified as he kissed her deeply.

For a moment, Seraphine forgot about killing him or drowning. Her heart sped up, almost about to burst out of her chest, and the only thought in her mind was Evren kissing her. *Death by a kiss?* Losing control of her mind and body, she moved closer. Kissing him was like breathing fresh air and being bitten by poisonous black roses. It was a blessing and a curse. It was life and death.

The water around them seemed to hum with energy, the bubbles reflecting the light in a symphony of colors. Seraphine could feel the warmth of his lips through the cool water, the pressure of his body anchoring her in this surreal underwater world.

Steadily, she gave into the hunger of her soul, gripped his raven flow hair, and kissed him back with all she had. If this was her last breath, she chose to waste it on a kiss.

Clinging to him felt natural, and Evren deepened the kiss, his lips exploring hers ardently. His touch was both tender and possessive, as if he was claiming a part of her he had always known was his. She felt his hand move to cradle her face, his thumb brushing gently against her cheek as his mouth moved over hers, tasting, exploring, devouring.

It felt like her soul was filled with fire and air and, at the same time, devoured by him, as if he were a soul eater himself, sucking her soul and life. Magic, torturous, addictive, and warm were recurrent feelings while they continued kissing as if time had stopped just for them. Seraphine breathed sharply, wanting to hold onto the moment.

I took a breath.

She opened her eyes abruptly and moved away from Evren, just enough for her to touch her breathing chest. She could feel air coming in and out of her mouth. It was dense but still enough for her heart to keep beating, for her to be still alive under the pressure of drowning waters.

That's what he meant when he asked me to open my mouth. Evren had been honest, but perhaps she still had some trust issues when it came to him and a lingering fear concerning everything around her.

Evren smiled at her smugly. His lips were shallow, and she felt a blush creeping onto her face. He had been trying to help her, and she had pretty much gone after him as if he were the last meal she would ever get before her death.

"One day, after this quest is over, I will kill you," Seraphine said, but it didn't sound like a threat at all, her voice sweet and airy in his ears.

"I just saved your life with a kiss." He took a strand of her hair and started to twirl it around his finger. "Just like in a fairytale! A prince saving a damsel in distress with a delightful kiss."

"Delightful? Nightmarish would be a more accurate description."

"Crimson little liar," he mocked, and they faced each other.

She pinched his side, and he laughed, his dimples making an appearance. "Now what?" she whispered, still unable to believe they were breathing underwater.

"Now, we swim until we reach the deepest part of the pond." With that, Evren took her hand and started to dive down, her hair moving in a slow, majestic dance as they moved deeper until the water turned from crystal to blue, blue to gray, and then gray to pitch black.

Evren Wraithwood

They reached the dark pond's bottom. There was barely any light, and looking up, the surface seemed far. Between the creation of the veil and the collapse that happened centuries ago, the water here was different, and breathing wasn't a concern for them.

While he would not say this aloud, Evren had to admit that he wasn't entirely sure Seraphine could breathe underwater. He hadn't tested this before, and he felt slightly guilty over that. Still, if she had failed, he would have taken her to the top. If he knew something about her, it was that Seraphine had the odds in her favor.

Evren couldn't hide the smile on his face. She looked so surprised when he had kissed her, and while the kiss was just to help her breathe, both of them knew better. As far as he remembered, she was all over him too.

He glanced around, still holding her gloved hand. It was pitch dark, with black starlight and dust floating around, different from the starlight above. The only thing visible were her crimson eyes. They were a beautiful, stark contrast in the middle of the darkness, shining brighter than everything else. As much as Evren adored them, he knew there was something more about them. Hopefully, he would find more answers in the forbidden library.

"Well? Is the forbidden section in the black waters? Another magic trick you want to show me?" Seraphine's voice was calm.

He moved his other hand and touched the ground. Just like he remembered, it was soft and dense, but it wasn't exactly what it seemed.

Knowing Seraphine, she would love this, especially what lay beyond that. Evren couldn't wait to see the delight in those extraordinary eyes when she realized where the library had been placed. He hoped it remained the same as he remembered. It had been centuries.

"See here?" Evren guided Seraphine to touch the ground. "What do you feel?"

She used her other hand to pat the ground. "It feels dense. Like a wool blanket."

"Ah, my crimson-eyed creature, dense like a blanket?" Evren said, moving the hand he had wrapped around Seraphine to push through the ground. The dense surface started to give in, like a spider net expanding. "But I must say that your lips are way dense and soft—"

She pinched his hand, and he couldn't help but laugh. Somewhere in the depths of the blackness, he heard her laugh too. Evren wondered if he could capture this moment, capture that sound, those eyes with a kiss.

"Such dangerous fingers you have there," he said. "Now, this dense ground is just a portal. We just need to slowly go through it. It might feel sticky, but it shouldn't last more than a minute. Ready?"

"Ready."

With that, he pulled her down, both of them sinking into the ground. He felt Seraphine tighten her hold on his arm as they swam deeper, not only through the waters but beyond the ground itself.

He felt water brushing his fingers first, and then the dense fog and sticky sensation around his body began to dissolve. He moved his hand to find a rocky corner while he pulled Seraphine through with him. Evren used his strength to pull Seraphine out of the ground, continuing to swim up, not down, this time.

"I get it," Seraphine muttered as they saw the waters beginning to lighten again, indicating they were close to the top. "It's inverted, isn't it?"

He nodded. "Yes, a fun trick, don't you think?"

"Stunning. I'm still in awe of being able to breathe underwater. I used to practice holding my breath," Seraphine said.

That piqued his curiosity. "What do you mean?"

"I-I would hold my breath underwater in my tub. There's no pond to swim in Coldhaven."

Evren stopped just before reaching the top of the pond and the entrance to the forbidden section.

"Why would you do that?" he asked, looking at her.

The water was clear, and her hair danced around her, making her look like a water nymph that enchanted men with their beauty.

She hesitated for a moment. "I wanted to see how long I could hold my breath. After a hard day, I'd close my eyes and empty my mind in the tub, challenging myself to see how much I could bear."

A pang of guilt surfaced again in Evren. While he had planned this masquerade and these games for her, he couldn't deny he had time to find a better way. She felt like she wanted to drown her sorrows, shattered and dragged in ways none should suffer.

Because of me.

Still, she rebuilt herself every time. Evren had seen her do it repeatedly.

He wanted to apologize but instead offered her something better. Moving closer, he grabbed the small fox pendant on her necklace that floated between them.

"I will make sure you never have to feel like you need to get underwater to lighten the burden of others' cruelty bestowed upon your life," he swore, a deal imposed on himself for eternity.

Seraphine's eyes widened. "I don't know what you mean by that," she retorted.

He continued tracing the little pendant."You see, you are here, breathing underwater, with no burning in your lungs. So, whatever you thought you couldn't endure, you are doing it now. And it's not magic. It's always been you." He heard her sigh, and when he looked at her again, Seraphine seemed at ease.

Moving slightly closer to her, he whispered, "For me, you are like a fox—smarter than most beings, cunning, the best type of trickster. Regal and beyond the reach of a mere wolf like me."

She laughed, her eyes softening. "Ah! You're missing something. Beyond the reach of a mere smelly and muddy wolf, the adjectives here are quite important, but again, I know you lack those abilities."

"Mmm, you may be right there, Crimson Eyes." He was unworthy of her on so many levels, yet he dared to wonder if, in a world where impossibility was causality and normality, one could dream.

Surprising him, she took his hand, the one holding the pendant. Instead of removing his hand, she covered it with hers, softly like silk. "Good I'm not a mere fox either, Evren. I'm a twisted crimson fox with a particular taste for twisted wolves." Her voice turned softer and richer, and the way she looked at him made him believe for a moment that perhaps his dream was not an impossibility after all.

"Not a smelly and muddy wolf? Just twisted?" he asked, concerned.

"That—" Seraphine removed her hand and smiled shyly at him. "Has yet to be seen." After centuries and decades of boredom, Evren felt an emotion he hadn't fully been able to recover until now: hope.

Evren took her hand again, this time to pull her out of the waters, trying hard to suppress his smile but failing. "Fair enough, Seraphine Ashcroft." Then, they both swam back to the top until he felt the cold air touch his body once again.

Chapter 28

The Enchanting Wolf

In the grandest state of the Otherworld lies the Wraithwood household,
A manor draped in shadows, brimming with treasures,
Gold, and artifacts, the finest riches in all realms.

Yet, the most fiercely guarded of them all are the books,
Histories hidden and silenced secrets bound in leather and ink.

There is a whispered tale of these tomes being stolen,
But the truth remains a mystery,
Just like the dark, forbidden knowledge within their pages.

Retrieved from *Encyclopedia of Wonders and Chaos* Volume II
by Lysara Sorrowspring, Ch. 16, p. 98.

Seraphine Ashcroft

The first thing Seraphine felt was the cold kissing her cheeks. She looked around and, for a moment, felt like she was in a dream—a winter dream.

The pond, or the library section itself, was enclosed in a sphere. It was cozy, with bookshelves lining the curved walls and inviting sofas and tables near a crackling fireplace. However, what surprised her was the sphere's dome, which had a small opening showing the night sky—a deep blue canvas filled with stars. Through this opening, the most magnificent thing fell slowly into the pond.

One after another, snowflakes landed on her nose, just like they had back in her forest. They were cold, almost real, but she knew it was just magic. The Otherworld was full of magic, but this one tugged at her heart. Her memories.

Seraphine remembered how she loved watching those delicate flakes dance, following them whenever she wanted to feel and wander alone. They also reminded her of her father, bringing a smile to her lips. Leander was akin to that—a beautiful, soft snowflake in the midst of a hard storm. She sometimes thought snowflakes were just butterflies that had shapeshifted to adapt to the cold.

"I knew you would like it," Evren said as he gently pulled her hand, guiding her out of the pond.

Such a caring predator Evren is. "I do. Are they real?"

"Yes, you can also find snow here in the Otherworld near the south. I went there centuries ago and made sure to bring back some enchanted snowflakes. I can't help but love the beauty of those icy drops. One day, perhaps I can take you there. You will surely love it."

Evren moved, standing out of the pond and wrapping his arms around her, pulling her up. They were both soaked and very close, so close she moved away quickly, hiding her eyes, hiding every possible clue of what was on her mind.

She made sure her gloves were in place too. "Let's find some answers." Seraphine started to walk to a bookshelf, trying to steady her heart. She saw Evren from the corner of her eye. If she was honest, Evren looked like a dream, washed in sparkling glitter and water.

There is something so *wrong with me.*

"While I love the enthusiasm, Crimson Eyes, let's grab some dry clothes first. You will probably catch a cold," Evren said, sounding like he was enjoying himself.

"You better have something cozy."

He winked at her and moved to retrieve something from a storage box. In a few seconds, he held a pile of clothes. "This should work. I didn't find any fancy gloves like yours, but here—" He pulled out something from behind.

"Mittens!" Evren sounded as if he had just taken a bunny out of a hat like those traveling magicians in Coldhaven.

Seraphine couldn't hold her laugh. "You seem overly excited about the mittens."

"I see, Crimson Eyes, you're mocking my taste in fashion," Evren said, handing her a pile of clothes and taking another for himself. Without much thought, he began to pull off his shirt and unbutton his oddly-designed breeches right in the middle of the place—in front of her.

For Brannon and Aurum's sakes.

His hair was still damp, drops of water and glitter roaming over his body. As soon as he was shirtless, she noticed the intricate tattoos and scars. Then, he moved his hand slowly, touching the edges of his breeches.

"I appreciate you appreciating the view, but I think I'd like some privacy since I'll be removing everything from my waist down," he said mockingly. Seraphine realized she had been practically drooling over him.

Oh, for the Ancients, get a hold of yourself, Seraphine Ashcroft.

Evren laughed. "Unless you wish to see, in which case I can always—"

"No, thank you. I am not interested in the view at all. I just got lost in my thoughts. I barely saw you," she said, stumbling over her words and feeling the heat rise in her cheeks while turning around.

She heard him moving and then the soft drop of clothes.

"Whatever you say, Crimson Eyes."

Looking around, she realized this place was extraordinarily beautiful. A warm feeling enveloped her at the thought of the treasure trove of knowledge before her.

A raspy, fake cough disrupted her. "Ah, I believe you should change now, Crimson Eyes. You're still damp."

She turned around to find Evren fully clothed, wearing an oversized old shirt and soft black pants. She always marveled at how normal he sometimes looked—a prince in oversized clothing.

Feeling rather daring and wanting to fake courage, she took the clothes and looked at him. "Sure."

Without breaking eye contact, she removed her pale dress, letting it pool at her feet, leaving her in almost nothing but mere pieces of undergarments.

"I should look away." His voice was raspier, just as his eyes darkened, pupils taking all over his wonderful clear blue, gray, and snowy eyes.

Lifting her chin and trying hard not to cover herself, Seraphine let a smirk pull on her lips. "Unlike you, I do not care whether you stare or not." She did care, but she was daring him to shy away. She wanted to show that she had all the control over her emotions. *Over him.*

However, he stood there, matching her challenge. Evren gulped as he watched her, and his eyes narrowed, as though he had too many berry roses or human wine. She continued to move her hands around her until she stripped down completely, cold air touching her skin. Still, this was nothing in comparison with the heat she received from his eyes.

Never breaking eye contact with him, she put on a light camisole and a soft cream dress decorated with fur on the top. Finally, she put on the mittens, which were a bit too big for her and looked at him. "You're looking quite pale. Is something the matter?" Seraphine tried to sound confident, but her voice was faint, betraying her own wish to pretend this wouldn't affect her.

Evren moved closer until they were inches apart, and a few drops of water from his hair fell on her cheeks. "You are an evil, pretty thing." He smirked while lowering his head inches away from her lips.

For a moment, she thought he might kiss her again.

Instead, he moved his head to the side, kissing away the drop of water that had fallen on her cheek, his lips staying there for a few seconds, leaving her a little drunk on his closeness. He pulled away, blue fire in his eyes and a knowing, delicious twist on his lips. "But so am I, Crimson Eyes."

Seraphine sighed in delight while settling on the comfy couch. Evren was beside her, both of them surrounded by a pile of books. "This is interesting."

Seraphine had also found the tales book she had borrowed on a nearby desk. It seemed like Evren could shadow the books directly to this place, but he wasn't strong enough to shadow them both here without going through the pond. Yet, she was secretly grateful. She had enjoyed their time underwater.

"What is it this time?" Evren asked for what felt like the thousandth time. They had spent hours here, and every book or note had been useless.

However, there were some fun facts that Seraphine couldn't help but share. "Here, it says that Aurum once fell in love. Is that even possible? For Ancients to fall in love?"

Evren looked thoughtful. "He probably fell in love with himself. I've heard tales of him being overly narcissistic."

"So you both are no different at all," she joked.

Evren tickled her feet, making her giggle. Somehow, a couple of hours before, her legs had ended up in his lap. It felt comfortable. She stretched out like a cat and yawned for the fifth time in barely an hour.

"Anything else that caught your attention?" he said, drawing small circles on the sole of her foot.

Seraphine read through another note on a page. "This is a strange-looking family tree." She pushed the book toward Evren.

He arched a brow, waiting for her to explain.

Seraphine rolled her eyes and cleared her throat. "No Ancient had a direct lineage. I mean, they created you all from whatever magic source, earth, mud, but it's not like they gave birth."

Evren opened his mouth to say something, but she cut him off with a glare. "But here, there is a line connecting Aurum to a descendant. Not the usual lines that represent the creation of beings. No, this one comes directly from him as if—"

This time, he traced the line that Seraphine had mentioned before. "As if he indeed gave birth to someone and not solely created them from magic." Evren seemed curious. A child from the Ancients was something never heard of before.

"She must be quite something, perhaps even a hidden entity, if this is accurate and my line of thought is in the right place." Seraphine was overly excited. The Otherworld was full of wonders, but uncovering secret information from the Underworld, the realm hidden in shadows that had never been visited, felt revolutionary.

Evren tickled her feet again, and she giggled a little, pushing his hand with her foot. "How do you know it's a 'she'? The tree literally just shows a silhouette," he said funnily, arching one delicate brow and looking at her as if she was even more wonderful than discovering a secret child of an Ancient.

A part of her felt—knew—it was a she. Yet, Seraphine shrugged, and Evren laughed. "A daughter. From one of the Ancients. Well, if that's true, then she must be the second most feared and powerful being in the realms."

Seraphine leaned forward a little and took another book that was piled nearby. Now, this one had a pitch-black cover, and there was a thorn in the center. A spike. It reminded her of the nightsith roses.

Seraphine carefully opened the book, and the pages were empty.

Strange.

"Prince Wraithwood," she called. Seraphine knew he hated that title, but she had been feeling more comfortable, and mocking him was just a delight. He made a face that almost brought a full smile to her lips.

This time, he was the one pinching her little toe. "What is it, Lady Wraithwood?"

She rolled her eyes and moved to try to kick him, but he restrained her legs and laughed fully, the two little dimples appearing on his cheeks. "Do not come at me, Crimson Eyes. You were the one who started with the formalities."

"You are a prince," she said matter-of-factly.

"For Nemera's wing, I am far from that. But anyway, what is it that is filling that head of yours this time?"

She handed Evren the book she held. "Careful, there is some kind of spike on the cover, but it seems enchanted. I cannot read it. Can you see any content on the pages?"

He opened the book and went through the pages. "Those are all blank. I see nothing."

"There must be something in that book."

Evren agreed, but there was no way to know now if it was useful or not, so he decided to return to the main hall of the Mystweave Library and ask Raggart or Dorah about the book. Perhaps there was a way to unlock it.

Evren moved to help Seraphine stand up, and she let him. Then, he picked her up in his arms and carried her all the way back across the forbidden section. She was so tired that she did not even protest. He held her legs and body while moving underwater, her drifting eyes focusing on his eyes and his dazzling hair.

For a moment, Seraphine's mind was quiet, and she found that very calming, familiar even. While she hated to admit it, Evren's hold and nearness were always full of light and warmth. Little by little, she started to piece him together and felt surprised by how much sweet darkness and dangerous warmth he was. Before closing her eyes and drifting to the sweet embrace of her dreams and the smell of Evren, she realized she had been accepting that she liked his company a little too much.

A soft caress touched her ear, and Evren kept repeating her name.

Still in his arms, she opened her eyes slowly, looking at him. "What is it?" Seraphine asked sleepily as they finally reached the main hall of the Mystweave Library. He released her of his embrace, and cold air surrounded her right away.

She tried to move toward her chambers, located on the fifth floor, but Evren stopped her. The sky was beautiful through the great crystal roof—different from the human world, with stars that seemed larger, almost as if they were closer. The moon, ever-changing in this realm, tonight glowed white with golden spots, casting a magical shimmer on the shadows.

Evren took her hand, still covered by the wet and funny mitten from their underwater journey. They needed to figure out a way to keep more clothes on both sides. At this point, they might need to change two or three times a day if they kept visiting the forbidden section.

"I must show you something." Evren pulled her hand and guided her across the halls and paths of the library, past the familiar bookshelves on the fifth floor that concealed the entrance to Evren's room.

Seraphine started to say something, but Evren cut her off with a look. He took the key book, opened the secret door, and led her inside. She hadn't been near his room since the incident. At first glance, the room appeared the same, but the more she looked, the more she realized it had changed.

The room felt bigger, more expansive. Instead of just one bed, there were two. Some shelves had been replaced by wardrobes, sofas, and an extra desk. The chamber was now two times more spacious than her cottage and her own chamber, with plenty of room to move around. She noticed a few new details: new crafts on the walls, which were now crimson-colored and adorned with cream figures.

Still, what surprised her the most was the furry little thing, white as snow with the same crimson eyes as hers, sitting on the bed closest to the window.

"Scarlet!" she exclaimed, rushing over to her beloved pet. The small creature leaped into her arms.

Evren Wraithwood

The past few days, they had fallen into a comfortable routine, and Seraphine seemed more at ease with him. Still, the shadows of the past always had a way to sneak up on them. There was so much at stake, and Evren wondered if all these dreamlike moments with her led them both toward an era of terror.

The best course was to keep her close, so he arranged his room to fit her in. Seraphine might torture him for that, but he had some cards up his sleeve, and Evren knew she would eventually agree. That beloved pet of hers was just the tip of the iceberg, and he was thrilled to show her a couple more things he had done to make sure she felt at home.

Because it is her home.

Evren wanted it to feel like that again.

"While I love having Scarlet here, I need to ask, why in the realms are there two beds? Do not tell me that you expect me to share chambers with you," Seraphine muttered, scrutinizing the room. Despite her words, her eyes were sparkling and darkening into his favorite red shade.

Moving around the room, Evren looked to the floor, again, somehow hesitant. He would never force her, so he walked until he stood between the beds. "I know you wanted your own chambers, but I am unable to create one room out of nothing." He was such a bad liar, and she looked at him knowingly.

"As if…" Seraphine's lips twitched as if she was trying hard not to laugh while she petted Scarlet's long ears.

"Yet, I rearranged this place so we both could fit and…" Evren said, opening a new wardrobe. "I also had Raggart go shopping, which was not a delight for him or me. But here, I wanted you to have new outfits. I even got a nice red cloak, better than the one you used to have. I felt like you might want some reminder of…"

He trailed off as he felt Seraphine moving to his side, still wet from their underwater journey but stunning, drops of shiny water covering her hazel hair. *How can a being hold such power over me without even trying?* The mere act of her breathing was enough to bring him to his knees.

Evren saw her delicate gloved hands touching the fabrics of the different dresses and tailor-made outfits, all of them to her liking, he was sure. He could give himself credit for that. Years chasing her had taught him what little things could make her eyes shine.

"These are lovely. Stunning, I mean, I have never seen dresses like these, all colors…" Then, Seraphine moved to the cloak, the same red as her eyes, made of the finest selkie hair and inked with roses. "The cloak is… I could never afford something like this. Still, I cannot share a room with you. That is not—"

"Ah, but you will when you know what I hid behind the pillow on your bed," he interrupted, knowing her curiosity would be piqued. Her eyes shone, the crimson in them twisting until they looked like rubies.

"What is it?" she asked, moving toward the pillow, but Evren stopped her.

"You must accept to be my roommate first, Crimson Eyes," he said, grabbing her hips and pulling her close enough that there was no space between them. He lowered his head until his lips brushed the shell of her ear. "I promise to behave. Unless…"

"Unless?" she echoed, her voice a breathy whisper.

"Unless you wish me not to," he said, then kissed her ear. He could feel her sigh.

A little out of breath, sleepy, and perhaps slightly enticed just like him, she muttered, "I would not wish that, even if the realms were about to crack again and the life of everyone else depended on it."

Evren chuckled, his breath warm against her ear, and brushed his nose across it, softly tracing its shape before moving lower, caressing her face and cheeks. She made no move to pull away. If anything, she seemed to be melting with him, torturing him with the delight of her essence.

"Is that so? Because I would break the realms and even myself just for you. I would paint the whole world crimson just to see your eyes every second of my life. I would create a new library from scratch if that meant seeing a spark in your smile." He moved so close that their lips were inches apart, a breath away from connecting. "And for you, I would behave and never bother you, though it is my undoing since I yearn for your closeness, your little remarks, and the feather touch of your lashes and lips. If I wasn't clear before, I hope I am now. I want you close, as much as you allow me. Even if it is close to nothing, I will take it all."

Seraphine closed her eyes, her lips parting, anticipation hanging in the air like a taut string.

However, Evren had made a promise. "So what do you say, Crimson Eyes? Would you accept my offer? Do we have a deal?" he asked, pulling back just enough to create space between them for her to decide.

When she opened her eyes, it was his undoing, her smile radiant. "I wish I could capture that speech and bottle it up, prince," she said, moving closer and kissing his cheek briefly.

Evren had to remind himself to keep himself steady. She stayed close to his cheek, and this time, his heart felt like it was about to explode.

"Yes, we have a deal." Her breath mingled with his.

"Well then." Stepping back reluctantly, he gazed at his feet again. If Evren dared to look at her, he might just break his promise to behave. "I hope whatever is under the pillow is to your liking."

Moving aside to give her space, Seraphine still brushed her body against his. It might have been intentional. *That cunning fox.*

"If this ends up being some kind of silly thing, I—" she began, but her voice trailed off.

Evren knew she had found the letter intended for her brought here from the human realm, thanks to his cat sith.

Chapter 29

The Traveling Fox

When the world turned dark and cracked,
The realm of souls was painted in red tears and black roses,
A haunting reminder of what was lost, a trail left to be discovered,
A secret whisper of what they would become,
Clinging to the hope that their one would return
To reclaim the throne and rule over the world once more.

Retrieve from *Poems and Songs from the Underworld*
by Lyra Sorrowspring.

Seraphine Ashcroft

Seraphine looked at the envelope with her name on it. She instantly recognized her sister's handwriting. Evren had been considerate enough to leave the chamber, giving her time alone with the letter.

Her heart wasn't beating fast or fluttering like butterflies. It was softening, like the snowflakes that fell on the snow. Evren had gone through all this trouble to make her feel comfortable. *Having him as a roommate will be chaos.*

Still, she was eager to be wrapped in that chaos and so much more. Things were different now, and perhaps, after the quest, she might want to keep something from Evren.

Maybe I just want to keep him.

She unfolded the paper and read her sister's letter.

Seren,

You wouldn't believe the sight I woke up to this morning. A stranger appeared at the front of our cottage. He seemed nice, but there was something more to him, something I couldn't quite place. It made me wish you were here because you were always a source of comfort.

After the ball, you disappeared, and the rumor started flying. They're saying you're dating Evren Wraithwood. Can you imagine? They even say he proposed to you! At first, I thought it was utter nonsense, considering how much you've

always claimed to hate him. But then that stranger showed up, offering us plenty of money on Evren's behalf, enough to cover our expenses. He mentioned you were with Evren on some kind of trip.

I still don't believe it. I hope you'll tell me it's not true. Regardless, know that I miss you, Seren. I miss you as much as I miss our father. I don't blame you for what happened that day. I would have died for you, just like I know you would have done for us.

Come visit us soon. Write me a letter. Anything.

P.S.: I asked the stranger to take some of your stuff to you. And Scarlet! She misses you terribly.

With love and longing,

Aeliana

"I don't blame you," Seraphine repeated, tears gathering. She laughed the tears away because Aeliana's lightheartedness shone through even in a letter. *Maybe after the quest, I could go back and visit her.* The idea of having a future that involved her sister made Seraphine hopeful again. Still, it was thanks to him, to the one that made her life a miserable but beautiful storm.

But why would Evren make up such a tale about us dating?

They certainly weren't. Seraphine wouldn't even want that.

Liar, liar, liar.

Saving the letter in her new wardrobe, she took out what seemed to be a soft, dark and shiny nightgown. Moving into the bathroom, which was impressively large, with a massive tub and mirrors all around, she changed into the nightgown and brushed her hair.

The day had been filled with too many adventures, and all she wanted was to rest. Tomorrow, they would go to Dorah's to check on the enchanted book. Now that she was embracing her emotions again, she needed to see her friend.

As Seraphine exited the restroom, she found Evren lying on his bed with a book in his hand. When he looked at her, she wished she could break the deal about behaving. However, she held herself steady.

"Black looks good on you." His eyes followed her every step. Seraphine made sure to slow her pace, moving in a way that might have shown too much of her skin as she crawled into her bed. "You are making this a sweet torture for me, Crimson Eyes."

She giggled at that, and Evren moved his hand, snuffing the candles that lit the room. She tried to close her eyes, but knowing that he was just a few meters away was devastating in the best way possible.

The worst part was she needed to sleep.

Seraphine sighed exasperatedly, and she heard Evren whisper almost mockingly. "Sleep issues there?" His voice embraced her in the darkness like sweet poison.

"No." *Yes.*

"Want to hear stories of all the shameful things I did when I was younger? There are some fun ones you'll find delightful," he offered.

While she couldn't see him fully because of the dark, she spotted those snowy blue-gray and impossibly enchanting eyes of his.

"I would like that. Make sure to be detailed on the parts where you made a fool of yourself," Seraphine whispered back.

Evren told her stories about how he tricked humans before the veil was created. He made her laugh, and she wondered if this could be their every day and every night.

Slowly, her eyes fluttered closed while Evren spoke. In the back of her mind, which had been embraced by dreams, she heard him say three words that, instead of scaring her, left her breathless.

Two familiar eyes were looking at her, eyes she knew so well she could draw them from memory. The spring was all around, leaves and flowers bursting with colors. Just like every afternoon, she hid in the secluded waterfalls near her town. There was something so peaceful about this place—maybe the sound of the water or the almost knowing silence that enveloped her.

However, she wasn't alone. Nearby, a wolf lay on the ground. The same one she had spotted weeks ago. It was beautiful, and she wondered if it was just a wolf. She had heard stories of Nemera's creatures—tricksters, evil—but she always thought of them as fascinating.

This wolf seemed to enjoy her company too. It was larger than average, its fur a striking blend of gray and white. She had never seen eyes like that, gray with bluish hues and white dots that seemed to move as if they had a life of their own. The wolf moved closer, and she patted its head and ears, marveling at the feel of its fur.

Seraphine smiled at the wolf, and she swore it smiled back at her. Then, she heard it, clear as the water—the wind calling her. It was a name she didn't recognize but had seen the crimson-eyed woman mouth in another dream.

A dream.

She heard the wind or herself saying, "No," before waking up. "A memory."

"Checkmate," Seraphine said, a triumphant smile on her lips. Dorah's roses, nestled in her hair, seemed to snap back in irritation.

"That was barely a checkmate," Dorah retorted, her tone sharp but playful.

Seraphine had traveled to the Shadowmarket with Raggart to ask Dorah about the mysterious book. She didn't mention anything specific about the book or its forbidden nature. While she trusted Dorah, she didn't want to get her friend in trouble.

Dorah explained that opening a book depended on it, which led Seraphine nowhere since she couldn't take it out of the library. *I could talk with Evren about it.* Hopefully, there was a way. Meanwhile, she decided to enjoy the rest of her morning with Dorah.

They assisted some customers with their bizarre requests. One customer, a sith with piercing green eyes and a sly smile, asked for a poison that could induce nightmares. Another, a selkie with skin still slick from the sea, sought ingredients for a potion to make shadows dance. A banshee, her wailing voice like a distant echo, requested venom potent enough to paralyze a spirit. The atmosphere in the Shadowmarket was always a blend of the mystical and the sinister, and today was no exception.

Later, a little close to noon, they decided to play shadow chess. Seraphine had already won three times.

"You seem content, Seren," Dorah noted, her voice lacking its usual warmth. Seraphine observed Dorah, noticing how her friend's hair had become greasier and her eyes, usually so vibrant, were now dull and shadowed.

Seraphine nodded and took Dorah's hand, feeling how cold they were. "Is there something wrong? You seem… off."

Dorah laughed it off, though her laughter was hollow. "Nonsense, Seraphine. Maybe it's Evren's bugs sticking to you." She waved away Seraphine's concern, but she knew better. Something was amiss with her hag friend.

Picking up the chess selkie figure, she examined it thoughtfully. "I'm glad you're safe, Seren," Dorah said, not looking at her. It seemed someone—probably Raggart—had told her about the incident with the soul eater. Seraphine asked about it, but Dorah, as usual, gave another cryptic comment. "Maybe you need to stop praying to the wrong Ancient."

Dorah had said that before. *Could it be possible that Dorah knows more than she's letting on?*

"I'm all right. I won't die and leave you to your boredom," Seraphine said, standing up and giving Dorah a gentle kiss on the cheek.

Raggart stood up with her, eyeing Dorah oddly. Beside him was Shadoweater. Seraphine had asked Evren for his cat sith's company that morning, explaining her desire to take a detour today. He hadn't been pleased, but he couldn't deny her, knowing Shadoweater would be with her.

With that, Seraphine left the shop and breathed in slowly as she wandered across the Shadowmarket, the sun up but shadowed, no soul eaters since they mostly appeared at dawn.

Today was meaningful, and Seraphine was excited.

"You must come here at midnight," Raggart said as they walked through the bustling market toward the well-known arch tree that would take her to the human world.

Seraphine nodded, pulling on Evren's white cloak. If she was to use the red one he had gifted her, they might recognize her. He had also lent her some leaves and briefly explained how to use them if necessary, which she hoped wouldn't be since she barely remembered the meaning of the colors.

"Shadoweater can morph into a human or something akin to that for some minutes and deliver the letter to your sister without putting you at such risk, Lady Wraithwood," he repeated for the tenth time.

"I know, and yes, I know I won't be able to actually talk to her. But I want to see her. Make sure she is doing all right. And I have Shadoweater here, Raggart. He can eat whoever crosses my path." The cat sith purred and moved around her legs, like a giant, monstrous cat. His kind was one of the few that could move across realms, making him the best companion.

Raggart sighed. "If something were to happen to you—"

"It won't. Send the prince my regards," she interrupted, stepping through the arched tree. Just like that, the world once again turned upside down.

Cold snowflakes touched her cheeks, and she took a moment to feel it all. Seraphine had missed the Weeping Forest. She couldn't say the same for her town or most people.

She looked at the cat sith and decided to use one of Evren's magic leaves. She needed to ask him about those later, curious about where he had procured so many.

Pulling one out of her hidden pocket, she chose a red leaf. That one was a tracking leaf. According to Erven, she needed to think about what she was looking for, and it would lead her to it. So, she thought about Aeliana.

The leaf took flight, and Seraphine and Shadoweater—who would be invisible to most humans—moved through the Weeping Forest, across the snow and past the dead trees. *How many times have I crossed this path, feeling anguish and searching for an escape?*

However, this time, she was experiencing it differently. She was marveling at it. The white snow was no longer needed to wipe away all the bad things.

As they approached the entrance to Coldhaven, Seraphine put on the white hood that would hide her face and checked her gloves.

The leaf moved through Coldhaven. The streets looked just as they had before—old and rotten. The people seemed frigid and cold. She guessed one might change, but cruelty stayed the same. She moved slowly through the crowd, knowing she was well hidden. No one would expect her here. No one would care.

The leaf stopped at the frozen clock tower, stuck in time. Then, just nearby, Seraphine spotted her.

Aeliana was laughing with a young boy. She had cut her hair and seemed a little more mature. Her sister seemed happy, and that was all Seraphine needed to know. Mere days felt like years.

She felt Shadoweater pushing against her legs. "All right, I need to send the letter, make one more visit, and we can take a break, okay?" Seraphine voiced quietly. She took the small envelope in her hand. Evren had enchanted it, just like the leaves, so it would appear in the desired place.

Seraphine touched the mark on the envelope, and as Evren had said, it turned into a creamy leaf. It flew across the street and slipped into Aeliana's green and yellow dress pocket.

That was it. *One thing to do and—*

"Seren?" Aeliana's voice cut through her thoughts. Aeliana had reached into her pocket for something and found the envelope. Seraphine had hoped for Aeliana to find it later. *Damn my luck.*

Her sister seemed to be looking around for signs of her, tears in her eyes. While Seraphine yearned to get closer and hug her, she hid farther behind the clock tower. Aeliana seemed torn, and the boy was holding her, trying to calm her.

At that, Seraphine closed her eyes and slowly drifted from the scene, moving between the small buildings toward her final destination. *I will be back for you someday.*

Evren Wraithwood

"Just let me have one more, Raggart," Evren said, his voice slurred, barely holding himself upright. Seraphine was out in the human realm. He had wanted to tag along, but there was still a lot of research to do.

While he was concerned, he missed her the most. Instead of continuing his search in her absence, he decided to indulge in a plate full of those berry roses Seraphine liked so much.

Raggart moved the plate out of Evren's reach. "Mr. Wraithwood, you can barely stand. I suggest not to—"

Evren grabbed Raggart by the ears and gently lifted him off the table.

"Have you received any letter from Theron?" he asked, biting into another berry and finishing his glass of wine.

"I have not. Maybe he is on his own quest. Sometimes, he can stay up in the air for years," Raggart replied.

Evren could no longer transform, which made him feel half-empty sometimes. Still, he hoped Theron would respond soon. Evren needed him.

Evren sighed, his thoughts drifting to Seraphine.

"She will be back. She also sent you her regards," Raggart said, as if reading Evren's mind.

"Of course she did. And I know, I just..." He reached for another glass of wine.

Raggart climbed up again, perching at the corner of the table. "You need to tell her, Mr. Wraithwood. Sooner or later, she will find out anyway."

However, Evren couldn't. Seraphine seemed so content and full of life these days, and there were too many things happening. Adding that specific burden could ruin everything. "I won't burden her with that."

"You won't. She might surprise you, like she always did, like she always does."

He put his hand in his hands. "She will hate me. She already hates me, but she will hate me more if she finds out that… I—"

Raggart looked at Evren empathetically. "She won't. It was not your fault. And she does not hate you. I might say that is quite the opposite."

Evren laughed bitterly. "Lust is not love, Raggart."

It was my fault, what happened centuries ago. Evren took another berry rose, savoring the bittersweet taste, and let himself drown in the memories of Seraphine while waiting for her return.

Chapter 30

The Betrayed Fox

Are eyes just a window to the soul?
Perhaps they are more—a portal to another world,
A glimpse into what lies hidden beneath the surface,
A path leading to a treasure waiting to be uncovered.

Retrieved from Evren Wraithwood's journal.

Seraphine Ashcroft

Seraphine muttered to her father. "Outlandish, don't you think?" The ground was full of flowers and grass, covering what remained of him. In the everlasting snow and cold, the world seemingly offered him a little piece of spring.

The girl smiled briefly and sat with him, Shadoweater cuddling by her side. "Are you happy somewhere in the middle of all these realms? Or perhaps you aren't even in any of the realms." She lay down and cuddled closer to the grass and flowers. "Yes, that sounds more like you. You are probably flying all around like a shooting star, unreachable and impossible to ignore."

Visiting her father was something she needed to do. She knew there was no way out of her situation, and it wasn't the quest that had her on a leash. It was the unknowing of her everlasting life that seemed just as cold and impossible to break as the snow in Coldhaven. It was the impossibility of her being a danger to most because, oddly enough, she was an omen of death—something far worse than a soul eater. They had not yet found what she was, but she knew it wasn't anything good.

"You did ask me to stay away from him. I wonder if you knew something," she said to the air, recalling her last conversation with her father. While forbidding her to go to the ball meant nothing at the time, Seraphine felt as if Leander was somehow aware of something—pertaining to her true self or about Evren Wraithwood.

Shadoweater purred at her side, caressing Seraphine's hand, and she smiled. The cat sith was just like Evren—dangerous looking but somehow tender.

She moved so that her back was fully placed on the grass, her eyes on the darkening sky. A couple of stars were slowly making their appearance.

"I came to say goodbye. I know you had your secrets, and while I won't always like your ways, I believe that things happened as they should have." A crimson tear fell down her cheek, staining the grass red. "Will I ever make peace with the fact that you are gone? Never. You are a part of my soul, and while I stupidly decided to try to numb it all, how could I numb you?"

A few minutes later, she saw it. Right above her, a purple and crimson butterfly battled the wind with her wings.

Seraphine smiled. "I guess you are not completely alone, Dad," she said, standing up. Then, the butterfly settled on her father's grave, quiet and listening. "Perhaps I will see you again," she said to no one specifically.

Snowflakes fell as Seraphine moved toward the Weeping Forest to that infamous entrance to the Otherworld.

Home.

"Ah, little creature, you are back," the sentinel tree said, and Seraphine swore she saw its branches arch in a gesture that one might call appreciation.

Shadoweater started to scratch his long nails on the tree, and Seraphine laughed. "Sorry for that," she said, moving the massive black furball away from the tree. "And yes, I am back, but I won't be returning to this same place for a while. Please don't cry too much. You might rot if there's too much water," she mocked, and the tree laughed.

"Cry for you? I shall not, peculiar creature. But bend for you? Perhaps someday."

She looked at the tree, confused. "What do you mean by—"

"Seren," a voice she knew all too well called out.

Seraphine turned around, Shadoweater positioning himself behind her.

"What are you doing here, Max?"

Evren Wraithwood

Evren found himself holding a damp cloth to his head to ease the headache. He should have listened to Raggart and held himself back. It was almost midnight, and Seraphine was probably on her way back.

Suddenly, the infamous list he had kept for centuries came alive in his mind, and a spark of hope ignited. For the first time, two names had not been scratched off. One would always be a cruel reminder, and the other was a sweet melody of how one could still dream in a realm of nightmares.

Seiren Elaris.

Seraphine Ashcroft.

Two faces of the same coin. *No, they both are the same coin.* Evren couldn't understand how Seraphine was born with those crimson eyes this time. When he had seen her some years ago, he thought it was bizarre but let it go.

They had different eyes, but they were the same. Or maybe not. Evren laughed because no matter how she looked, her soul was always calling to him. Her soul was a song created for him to listen to and admire—so out of reach yet so close.

He had to admit that he liked her crimson eyes more. They seemed more fitting. Seraphine was born an oddity. She always had been in a twisted way, but this time, there seemed to be some meaning behind the change, behind her ability to cross realms and feed on souls.

Evren sighed. Enduring all this must be tough for Seraphine, but she managed to stay kind and fierce. *A deadly combination.*

A sound interrupted his thoughts, and Raggart appeared, out of breath.

"Mr. Wraithwood, she is here but—"

Evren stood up rapidly and moved toward the center of the library. "But what?"

"Something happened."

Seraphine Ashcroft

Max moved so fast that Seraphine found herself trapped in his arms. "Seren, I have been looking for you," he said against her temple. While she used to feel safe with him, she only felt cold this time. *Why is Max here?* After their final conversation, she hoped never to see him again.

Seraphine pulled away, and Max looked exactly the same, his golden hair a cruel match with his eyes. Yet, his expression was anguished and forced—fake. "Look, Max, not sure how you found me, but I have to go—"

"Do not go! Please, there is so much I want to explain," he said, falling to his knees in front of her. "The worst is that I cannot even explain everything."

Seraphine took a step back, closer to the sentinel tree, its branches creaking ominously.

"Just hear me out, Seren, please."

Seraphine looked up at the sky. She had a couple of minutes. She exhaled a long breath and nodded, barely looking at him.

"I-I don't recall getting engaged to anyone, Seren. I'm not even sure I remember half of the year. It feels like a blur. You would honestly think I would do that without telling you?" he said sorrowfully.

Seraphine closed her eyes. He moved closer and took the edge of her cloak, tears in his eyes. "No, I actually would never dare to tell you because the only person I truly wanted, I truly want, is you. I know I sound mad, but you have to believe me, Seren."

Regardless of whether she did or not, there was no return. Seraphine held no regrets or hard feelings toward Max. Actually, she held no feelings for him at all.

She patted his head softly. "I know. I believe you," she muttered, hoping that was enough for him to let go.

"Do you? And yet, you want to go back to that monster?" His voice turned to steel, as though it was someone else speaking.

She tried to pull away, but Max stood up and held her arm tightly, almost hurting her. Before she could protest, he laughed. "Look at this mess, Seraphine. I figured you would want to make things easier, but I guess I was wrong once again."

"What are you talking about?" Seraphine felt something unusual rising from her throat. Max just continued laughing wickedly, freezing her bones.

Seraphine tried to pull away, but Max's hold was stronger than expected, and he looked at her not with anguish but with something similar to disdain.

Suddenly, he smiled, this time taking her gloved hand. "Poor, poor Seren. Always running, hiding." Max pulled her close, his mouth near her ear. "Tell the prince I will be waiting for him in my realm."

Seraphine's heart dropped. "Y-you... know—"

"I know much about you and your dear excuse of a prince," he said bitterly, and when he smiled, she noticed that the gold in his eyes was changing, merging. They turned green, then pitch black, and then finally dark crimson.

Like mine.

Seraphine stumbled at the sight, and she felt Shadoweater cover her, putting distance between her and Max. She could barely breathe. Fearful, she moved closer to the sentinel tree's arched branches.

"Your mother would not want this for you, Seren."

Her eyes widened at that. "What?"

Max closed the distance, unable to touch her with Shadoweater there. "She has a message for you."

Seraphine could barely understand what was happening as the sentinel tree's branches moved, wrapping around her waist.

He narrowed his eyes at the sentinel tree. Seraphine realized he could see the sentinel tree moving, just as he could see or sense the cat sith. All these years, Max had played naive and broken, letting people talk about her, and all this time, he knew. *Everything.* Even worse, it seemed like he was exactly like her.

He moved closer again, kicking Shadoweater with his foot, and Seraphine screamed and lunged for him. Thankfully, the sentinel tree also grabbed the cat sith with its branches. Max just smiled. "Come home."

Those words. They had been the ones Seraphine had heard the woman in her dreams speak.

She wanted to scream at Max, but when she looked for him, he was gone.

"It's time. You must go back and never return here, Seraphine Ashcroft," the sentinel tree warned.

Then, the branches pulled her into the arched entrance, and just like that, the world darkened.

Chapter 31

The Taunting Wolf

My father told me that kisses and fairytales are nothing but a stupid way to trick humans. He is not very nice. Today was my 10th birthday, and he left me behind. If he hated humans so much, why keep playing with them? I don't wish to be a prince; I just want to have fun. I do not hate humans, but I do not care about them at all.

Retrieved from Evren Wraithwood's journal.

Five Days Before the Incident
Evren Wraithwood

The first thing he saw was Seraphine sprawled on the floor, passed out and pale. Right beside her was Shadoweater, who seemed to have an odd wound on his leg, but Raggart was already bandaging it.

Evren slowly took Seraphine in his arms. Her breathing was shallow. His fingers lingered a moment on her cheek, brushing a stray lock of hair away from her face.

"What happened?" he asked Raggart and Shadoweater, his voice tense with worry.

Raggart looked at the cat sith, which moved closer to Evren. Though Shadoweater couldn't speak, as his familiar, he sent small images or captures of memories.

Then, Evren saw it.

He bit his tongue. Evren knew Maxwell seemed familiar the moment they met. He had been too focused on his plan and on Seraphine to realize that Maxwell was actually a monster, just like him. Countless questions surfaced. *If Maxwell was aware of everything, why pretend he was engaged and follow my commands?* He needed to wait for Seraphine to wake up and explain.

With care, Evren took her to their chambers. She seemed unharmed, but he made sure to check every inch of her for any sign of something out of the ordinary. Then, he slowly took off the white cloak and laid her down on his bed, covering her with a quilt.

He sat nearby and watched her, his turmoil intensified with every moment she was asleep.

How had Maxwell been able to trick me so easily? As far as Evren knew, Maxwell was a childhood friend of hers. However, whenever Evren followed Seraphine, she was mostly alone, even as a child.

He met Maxwell a couple of years ago, and that was the first time he saw them together. They seemed close friends, but there had certainly been more at play there.

"Hey," Seraphine crooned, her eyes fluttering open. They met his with a soft, lingering gaze. Evren moved to her so quickly that he almost fell to the floor. She laughed a bit, which relieved Evren.

"Careful there, prince. You almost kissed the floor," she teased.

He smirked, hiding his concern. "Since I promised to behave, I guess the floor is my consolation prize."

Seraphine laughed more, and Evren thanked the Ancients.

"Would you like to talk about what happened?"

"No," she said firmly, then her eyes softened. "Not now. Maybe later. I promise I'll tell you everything."

Evren moved closer and caressed her cheek, his thumb gently tracing her skin. "Is that a deal?"

She smiled. "It is."

"We've made so many deals recently that we might end up tangled for life fulfilling them," he joked.

Her eyes seemed warmer and lighter. Seraphine closed the distance and whispered, "That sounds like a good plan."

His heart stopped for a moment. Evren must have had a surprised expression because she laughed even more.

"Speechless? Well, that is definitely a shocking event coming from you, Evren."

Then, they both laughed shyly and somehow expectant to know more about her change of heart. However, for Evren, she had always been the priority, so he helped her stand for a bath. *Warm water might help, considering the stiffness in her movement.*

Seraphine took her time, and when she reappeared, she went directly to his bed and sat in the corner of it, watching him. She was wearing an excuse of a camisole that he was not sure if he should hide or fill her closet with. As usual, she was wearing thin gloves, hiding those beautiful, delicate fingers of hers. She moved her hand a little and brushed it across her hair nervously. "Can I ask you a favor, prince?"

"For you, Crimson Eyes? Anything."

She looked at his bed. "Can you sleep with me? Just sleep. I-I know my bed is just right there, but I don't—"

He understood and lay down, opening his arms to her. Just like that, she settled in his arms, almost throwing herself at him, which filled his heart with warmth. While they stayed together, Evren told her more stories about his trips, his brothers, oddities about all kinds of creatures, and amazing lands in the Otherworld that he wanted her to see. Evren caressed her hair until she fell asleep. A few minutes later, he did too, a smile on his lips, wondering if the world was giving him a chance back for happiness.

And how long it would last this time.

Evren opened his eyes. Usually, he would see the light from the massive window in the chamber, but this time, he found himself looking directly into a crimson storm of starlight looking right back at him. Seraphine was somehow half on top of him, her warm breath brushing against his skin, her face inches from his. Her eyes widened, as if caught doing something she shouldn't have. He smiled knowingly.

She smiled back and rested her chin on his chest. "You snore. A lot," she spoke, her long lashes flickering seductively.

"I do not," Evren said, still sleepy, but her touch sent shivers down his spine.

Seraphine giggled, the sound like music to his ears, and he wrapped an arm around her, feeling the softness of her body against his. They stayed there in a comfortable, intimate silence, the air thick with unspoken words.

"So, about yesterday," Seraphine said, not making any attempt to move from her current position. Her fingers traced lazy circles on his chest, each touch igniting a fire within him.

He lowered his head a bit and looked at her. "If you want to talk about it, Crimson Eyes, I am all ears. If not, I will understand."

She nodded and asked, "How is Shadoweater?"

"He is fine, just a scratch. He is with Raggart now, but as soon as he is fully healed, he will return to my skin."

"That is so very weird… to have such a bond. I am glad he is fine. He took good care of me."

Then, she cleared her throat. "When I was about to leave the human realm, Max appeared out of nowhere. He seemed strange, and at first, I thought he was just feeling guilty. You did mention that you used him a little once, so I thought nothing of it."

"But then, he changed, Evren. His eyes looked just like mine, and he told me something—something I had heard in a dream. But I am starting to believe there is more than we know about all of this."

Indeed, it was like everything was becoming more twisted with every step they took.

"What did he say?" Evren asked her carefully.

She shifted, her body pressing against his in a way that made his heart race. *I really need to get a hold of myself.*

"He said that my mother wanted me to go home. I had this dream of a woman saying those same words to me. Isn't that strange?" she said, her hair falling on his chest and the side of his face, caressing him like a silken curtain.

This time, he could not suppress a sigh. She giggled again, the sound vibrating through him, and he softly pinched her side, just like she liked to do to him. She giggled even more.

"It is indeed very strange, especially with the timing of everything happening. Seraphine, I am sorry you had to—"

She cut him off, covering his mouth with both hands, looking at him with a softness that made his heart ache. "No, this is not your fault. We will figure it out, Evren. Right now, I wish to focus on the quest and—"

"And?"

She smiled wickedly at him, closing the distance, not a single inch separating their bodies, her mouth on top of his. Like magic, he closed his eyes, feeling her warmth seeping into him.

"And..." He could feel her soft breath on his lips, her scent enveloping him. "I am dying for..."

As if he were enchanted, he repeated, "Dying for what?" He was already lost in her closeness, her cheerfulness, and those small giggles.

She hummed, and then, quick as a storm, she gave him a quick peck on the cheek. "Dying for one of those berry roses." Then, she stood up, laughing, leaving him there, the scent of her fresh on him.

Sweet, cunning fox.

Days later, they traveled again to the forbidden section of the Mystweave Library. Evren leaned back on the couch, watching Seraphine furiously flip through yet another ancient tome. The journey to the forbidden library had yielded nothing but dead ends and frustrations, wearing on her. Her eyes, usually so bright, now glimmered with impatience.

Nearby lay the odd book with the spike, still as mysterious as when they first found it. Seraphine's gaze kept drifting to it, her frustration mounting. She had asked this morning if she could take it to Dorah, but Evren felt like it might endanger all of them, leading Seraphine to be mad at him for about two hours.

She closed the book in her hand with a sharp snap and exhaled loudly.

"We're not finding anything useful. I see nothing more than gibberish about the history of the Underworld. I'd rather eat deadly thorns than keep reading these useless texts," she said.

Evren smiled. "Well, that can be arranged—the food part. I do not have thorns, but there is a certain berry rose that I know you'll delight in," he said playfully.

That sparked her interest. "You have them here? Where are they?" she said, a little too excited.

Evren winked at her. "Of course, I have some here, and they are all yours..." He couldn't keep teasing her. "But only if you give me a kiss. Deal?"

She narrowed her eyes at him, a spark of amusement breaking through her frustration. "A kiss, huh? Is that all it takes to get some food around here? Seems kind of cheap coming from a prince." She purred and moved her hair away from her neck. Today, she was wearing a dark blue dress that was a little too tight on the chest—a distracting view indeed.

He shrugged, still smiling. "That's the deal. A kiss for a meal."

To his surprise, and before he could explain it was a joke, Seraphine slowly straddled him, her knees pressing into the cushions on either side of his legs. Her dress parted in such a way that it was hard for Evren to keep his eyes up front. She leaned in, her breath warm against his lips, and Evren's body locked up, feeling more like prey than ever.

"All right, prince. A kiss it is."

Before he could muster a word, her lips met his, soft and sweet at first. Evren's hand found her waist, pulling her closer as their kiss deepened, feeling the nice curves of her waist and hips and breathing in her scent. The world outside the couch melted away, leaving the two of them lost in the moment.

Evren reveled in the sensation, the softness of her lips, the heat of her body pressed against his. Her kiss became more insistent, her tongue gently parting his lips, exploring, tasting. It was intoxicating, and he didn't want it to end—not now, not ever. He could spend a lifetime in her arms.

"You know," he murmured between kisses. "Your crimson eyes are the most beautiful gems I've ever seen. Not even the prettiest roses, riches, nor rubies can compare."

She laughed softly, her breath mingling with his. "Flattery will get you nowhere, prince." However, she kissed him again, gripping his shirt and pulling him close.

Evren moved her slightly, but Seraphine had other ideas. She pulled him down, guiding him to lie on the sofa with her. His hand roamed her back, feeling the delicate curve of her spine and the warmth of her skin through the thin fabric. Her fingers tangled in his hair, tugging him closer and brushing his cheeks with her delicate, gloved hand. Her touch was electrifying, sending waves of desire coursing through him.

Their kisses grew more passionate, more urgent. Evren's hand slid under her dress, feeling the smoothness of her skin. He ventured higher, fingertips grazing the soft swell of her breasts. Her breath hitched, and Seraphine arched into him. Her touch roamed over his chest, tracing the lines of his body as if memorizing him.

"Maybe we should make this a regular thing, prince," she said, her voice breathy as she kissed a trail down his throat.

Evren sighed. "Considering breaking our little deal?" he said, pulling her hair softly so his lips were now trailing down her neck. "I'd like that very much, Crimson Eyes."

Evren's hand moved around her long legs, gliding up while caressing with soft circle movements, each one venturing higher. He couldn't help but memorize all the little sounds from her. As he was about to suggest they move to a more comfortable position, she winced, pulling back sharply.

"Ow!" she muttered, sucking on her finger to ease the pain. Somewhere between her playfulness, Seraphine had placed her hand on the mystery book with the spike, and now blood welled up on her fingertip.

Evren's eyes widened. He started to rise, using the edge of his shirt to wipe the blood. He was about to tear the tome to pieces, but then he noticed it was beginning to change. The spike, now smeared with Seraphine's blood, seemed to pulse with a strange light. Roses, blood-red and vibrant, began to bloom around the book, their petals shimmering with an eerie glow.

Seraphine followed his gaze, and they both watched, entranced, as the roses spread across its surface, forming intricate patterns. Trembling, she took the book in her hands. The once black and empty pages began to fill with text and illustrations, the title emerging in ornate lettering: *Aurum's Journal.*

Chapter 32

The Bloody Fox

Keys are devilish things,
Forged in steel, if you're fortunate,
Triggered by blood, if you're bold.

In realms of chaos, blood runs thicker than metal,
But blood is also a charm—dangerous,
Addictive.

Retrieved from *Encyclopedia of Ruins & Blood*
by Varian Galehollow, Ch. 13, p. 56.

Seraphine Ashcroft

Seraphine took the book and pushed Evren back onto the couch with a slight huff. Still straddling Evren, she opened the book. It was filled with so many sketches and notes.

She heard Evren laugh. "Wow, not even my kisses get you like that. Should I be concerned?"

"Of course you should. I just found the most interesting thing in this whole place—no, in the whole realm—and I get to read it," she said, excited about the discovery.

Evren pulled himself up while still holding Seraphine. Delicately, he fixed her dress and pulled up the fabric on the front side. The tenderness of his touch made her consider leaving the journal alone for a couple more minutes.

Considered and rejected.

"Aren't you excited about this?" she said, looking at Evren, who was the image of decadence—his shirt half-open and torn, his hair all over the place, and his eyes somehow sleepy.

Oh, I did that.

He cleared his throat and smiled. "Are you asking me if I am thrilled to check the thoughts and secrets of one of the most powerful beings in the world? Without a doubt!"

As Seraphine went to read the first page, Evren cut her off and took the book from her hands. While she wanted to fight, the book disappeared. "I'll transfer the book to our chambers. I think we might want to get comfortable," he said, this time sliding an arm around her legs and carrying her to the pond at the center of the forbidden section.

"I am hungry, so let's have something to eat, and if you behave, I will give you those dazzling berry roses you love so much."

Seraphine let him carry her, and he sat down at the pond's edge, his legs in the water, ready to dive deep with her back to the main library building. "Wasn't the kiss enough to get me one of those?" she purred at him, hugging his neck so their noses were just a breath apart.

"From you?" he said, caressing her nose with his. "It'll never be enough, and I want it all, Crimson Eyes."

Her heart was once again melting and flying. Somehow, after her last visit—an unpleasant one, thanks to Max—to the human realm, she decided to give in to whatever she felt for Evren. For once in her life, she felt cherished, and while she would never admit that to him, she knew he knew.

"We have a lifetime, don't we?" she said, and Evren kissed her one last time before diving deep back into the library.

Seraphine picked one final berry rose from the plate. After a long discussion, she convinced Evren to have supper in their chamber while reading the journal. There was so much insightful information, and she couldn't put it down. Thankfully, Raggart had brought them plenty of food.

Evren was lying on his side, trying to peek at something from the journal. They had been sharing the same bed since she arrived from the human world.

"Don't be like that, Crimson Eyes. I want to read it too." He pouted. She needed to use the memory canvas artifact on him to capture the memory of him making that face.

Seraphine moved so she was comfortable between his arm and neck. "Look here," she said, pointing out one entry in the journal. It was dated a couple of centuries ago, just around the creation of the veil.

"The part about the argument he had with Nemera?"

"No, here: 'I tarried for her days, months even, but she never returned to us. She vowed to find a means of escape from her household, and then we would meet near the Valley of Nightsiths. We envisioned a life together, a family. But alas, she never came back. What a profound sorrow it is to endure existence without my beloved Sorrowspring.'"

Seraphine felt a pang of sadness. "It seems like unrequited love," she muttered.

"Didn't you mention that there was a book showing a peculiar family tree with a descendant of Aurum?" Evren asked, and she nodded.

"He says in that part that whoever it was left them alone. *Them*." Evren paused and then pointed at the last part. Aurum had written as if it was not only him. "And here, I think I know who they are referring to—the Sorrowsprings."

Seraphine looked at him, waiting for an explanation.

He moved closer, their legs brushing, and took a black leaf from his shirt pocket. Seraphine had asked him about his leaves, and he mentioned that those were one of the remaining gifts he could hold before the veil's creation and the curse his father bestowed upon him. He could still use leaves as a conduit for his magic.

Evren eyed her knowingly. "You paid no attention to me when I explained the meanings behind the colors, did you?"

She smiled at him, feeling the warmth of his body so close.

He sighed. "Black leaves are for note-taking." He manipulated the leaf, which started to drop some black ink, and pulled out a paper, moving the leaf without touching it and drawing what seemed like a map. His fingers brushed hers, sending a small jolt through her. "This was the territory before the veil's creation. Each portion was handled mostly by the human realm and the Otherworld, while the Underworld had always remained separate. And here… This area was ruled by the Sorrowspring lineage."

Seraphine marveled at the detail of it. "Those are… keepers of water creatures?"

"Correct. Now, before the veil's creation, the ruler used to have three children: Elowen, Galen, and the youngest one, Lyra Sorrowspring."

"I see. So, you think one of them was Aurum's lover and the one who bore him a child? Wouldn't that be problematic? I mean, is it even possible to be a half-blood from the Underworld and Otherworld?"

He made a face, somehow nostalgic. "I was close to Galen, and I remember Lyra very well. She was always… different. She was prone to destruction and always in trouble."

Was. As if she no longer exists.

"Anyhow, Lyra was sentenced to death. She was imprisoned during the veil's creation, and decades later, I found out about her death. No one knew the reason, but if my reasoning is correct, they probably found out that she was getting closer to Aurum and perhaps that she gave birth to a forbidden being. That might be why Aurum never saw her again. The timeline fits."

"That is so incredibly sad." Seraphine inhaled the words, her hand finding Evren's for a brief squeeze.

"That it is," he said. The paper and the leaf disappeared in flames. He stretched like a cat, and Seraphine noticed Scarlet bouncing from one corner of the room to another. "What if we take a break and continue tomorrow?" He sounded a little tired.

Feeling guilty, Seraphine moved so she was looking at him, their faces inches apart. "I was very pushy today, wasn't I?"

"Of course not. I am—"

She hugged Evren, silencing whatever he was about to say. She felt the steady beat of his heart against her cheek. "Let's sleep. This time, let me tell you embarrassing stories of how I once ended up cursing a cottage in Coldhaven."

He laughed at that. "Ah, that sounds like a very good story."

Seraphine watched him fall asleep and wondered if she was mad for loving these little moments as much as she did. Energy buzzed in her body. She no longer felt forced to help him—she wanted to. She stood out of the bed, quietly enough not to wake up Evren, and took the journal.

Evren Wraithwood

A warm, delicious feeling tugged at his shirt, moving him from side to side. Evren heard the most beautiful sound calling out his name and couldn't help but think about that cunning and sweet crimson creature.

"For Nemera's wing, Evren! Wake up, you smelly wolf!"

He grunted, keeping his eyes closed. "I knew this was too good to be true."

Seraphine pinched his side hard. "Evren, c'mon, this is important. I—"

Evren felt someone hovering over him. With his eyes closed, he hugged and pulled down Seraphine, muttering into her curly head, "Just one more minute."

He opened one eye to find Seraphine standing at the corner of the bed. She was not the one in his arms. Her mouth twitched, barely containing a massive laugh. Beside her was Raggart.

"Well, Evren, I knew we were close, but I have to say, you surprised me with such gentlemanly treatment this time," the curly-haired person he was holding said.

"Should I give you two a moment?" Seraphine teased him, and Evren kicked the ever-loving soul out of the body he had hugged so passionately.

He had made a fool of himself so thoroughly that he thought about covering his face with the bed covers.

The curly man chuckled. Evren looked at him: green eyes dotted with yellow, blond curly hair, and a face full of freckles. *I will never hear the end of this.*

"Ah, do not be shy with me, prince! I am delighted to know I am to your liking."

He heard Seraphine laugh, and just this once, he promised not to kill him.

"What do you want, Theron?"

"What a hard head you are, Ren. You called me! Raggart sent those terribly detailed letters," Theron said, and they both looked at Raggart, knowing the creature had sent mere drawings.

Theron moved while Evren finally decided to step out of his bed. Although he knew Theron would never harm Seraphine, Evren positioned himself in front of her.

"Either way, I've been trying to communicate with you for decades! Where in Nemera's wing have you been these past 26 years? Do you know how many times I tried to send something and—" Theron stopped himself, realizing now might not be the best time to open a discussion, given Seraphine's presence.

Seraphine moved closer to Evren's back and slowly placed her head on his shoulder, smiling. "Ren?" she repeated.

"Yes, that's his nickname, oh mighty Prince Wraithwood," Theron joked. Evren rolled his eyes at him, holding himself back from growling.

Seraphine hummed. "I like that nickname, Prince." Then, she moved to sit on the bed, looking at both men. "This, by far, has been the most interesting morning I've ever had the chance to witness." She giggled, and Evren noted that she was still in her nightgown and gloves.

He lightly covered her with quilts, noticing her pale and tired appearance. "What is going on, Crimson Eyes?"

She looked up at Theron. "I-I read the whole journal while you were asleep," she said, almost apologetically. "At first, I thought I found something, but then I considered it nonsense."

His eyes widened at her diligence.

"I went to your—our chambers as soon as I found that little note in the journal. I thought you might know more about it, but I never got a chance to say anything because your friend was waiting outside your chamber to talk to you."

Theron cleared his throat. "Now, the good thing is that we both have the same information for you."

"What do you mean by that?" Evren said, eyeing them both.

Seraphine moved closer to Evren and took his arm, pulling him to the bed again. "At the end of the journal, Aurum wrote that a being from the Otherworld appeared or found its way into the Underworld. From what I could tell, that creature was cursed by Nemera herself."

Theron continued, "I came across the same information. It seems there was a strong curse on that creature. There are no records of who that was or the curse, but if it came from Nemera, it must have been pretty strong and nasty." He glanced at Seraphine, sensing they needed to talk. Theron was surpassing his surprise at this point, and Evren could not be more thankful.

"For better or worse, the creature sought Aurum in the Underworld—which makes sense since he had ruled his own territory for years, unlike Nemera or Brannon, who are nowhere to be seen. Aurum offered to lift the curse."

"There is no way," Evren said, standing up. "You're telling me that Aurum undid whatever curse was done? Just like that?"

Seraphine sighed. "Not exactly. It seems like Aurum put some kind of trial in place, which the creature did not pass. It ended up dying." Her eyes lowered.

"But it makes sense. Aurum still holds the power of death, destruction, and also transformation. It makes sense that he could somehow kill or undo any kind of magic," Theron finally said.

Evren studied at Theron. "And how did you find out about this?"

For the first time, his friend looked a little ashamed. "I, well… I slept with a kelpie a couple of years ago, and she told me the tale, which sounded odd. So, I asked some sources and then came here after receiving…" He looked at Raggart, who was smiling proudly as if he had done the most amazing thing. "Those strange drawings with no meaning." At that, Raggart's ears moved, and he seemed offended.

What a lovely morning indeed.

Seraphine moved her hand and held Evren's shirt. "This just supports the idea that maybe there is a way out for you."

"And then what? Are you expecting me to go and offer myself to Aurum? There is no open portal to that realm, Crimson Eyes," he said a little too harshly and immediately regretted it.

She released him and somehow made herself small. "I was just trying to help, just like you always do with me. I'm sorry," she said, her voice breaking.

Evren looked at Raggart and Theron, both understanding that he wanted to be alone with her for a moment.

Evren moved to her side, wrapping his arms around her and whispering into her hair, "I am sorry, Crimson Eyes. I just—" He breathed deeply. "I know you want this quest to be over and be free of me, but I am just so content with you here by my side that I—"

"No, that was not why I did it," she interrupted, hugging him closer. He could smell her, a soothing mix of vanilla and roses. "I thought it would be a great start for you to be whole again. I honestly don't want the quest to be over, and don't take me wrong, I wanted it to linger a little longer, but I also didn't want to be selfish."

Evren almost laughed at that. He had been the one who had pulled her into the most terrible situation, yet she was telling him she wished to stay with him.

Even after the quest is over...

"Selfish is a word I would never dare use to describe you, Crimson Eyes. And I am keeping you today, tomorrow, after the quest, and in the afterlife if you allow me to." He lowered his face to look into those beautiful eyes of hers. "I was the chaos in your life. I made your life miserable and tricked you, deceived you. I even made you immortal. But let me make up for that. We have all the time in the world. Not because your life clock is frozen or because of my nature. No. Because with you, I feel like I do not need to rush. I just need you and your giggles. Have I told you how much I want to bottle those and save them?"

Seraphine giggled after that, brushing her nose against his neck, her touch sending shivers down his spine. "I must correct myself. Words do take you everywhere," she said before looking up at him. "You can keep me if I can keep all of you too. Because I am selfish, Evren. I want it all: this library, this room, your smile, you."

If Evren could capture another memory, it would be this one. "So, it is a deal, Crimson Eyes? I keep you, and you keep me?"

She smiled, and he wasn't sure who moved first, but their lips touched. Then, there were no more words, just kisses and caresses and a million promises he intended to fulfill.

Evren felt her fingers tracing patterns on his back, her touch both gentle and possessive. He responded by pulling her even closer, deepening the kiss, savoring every second of their connection.

"I want to spend every moment with you, making you happy," he whispered between kisses, his voice thick with emotion. *This time, things will be fine.*

Chapter 33

The Suspicious Hawk

Primal siths may appear mostly human,
But they are anything but.
Guardians of their realm, they are shapeshifters by nature.

Some transform into fish to remain hidden in the depths,
Others sprout wings to watch over the skies,
And some grow fangs to hunt and roam in the dark.

Retrieved from *Ancient History of The Realms*
by Malvrek W., Ch. 3, p. 23.

Two Days Before the Incident
Seraphine Ashcroft

Looking at them, Theron asked, "Then, what is the plan?" They were in the room that Raggart had transformed into a supper area. Theron took a long sip of wine. Evren was the one she knew to be from a high seat in the realm, and she guessed that Theron was, too, since he almost looked human. He was excessively beautiful, and according to Evren, he was from the Galehollow lineage, the ones that oversaw air creatures.

Seraphine moved closer to Evren, their legs touching, wanting to be close. As if Evren were reading her mind, he put his hand on her leg, making slow circles up and down in a slow, hungry motion.

Evren cast a look at her and then at Raggart. "Even if all this is true, how would we get to the Underworld?"

Theron seemed torn, as if this were all a puzzle. "Ren, you asked me before you were kicked out of this realm to find a way to dispel the curse. I searched for centuries, and this is the closest we've ever been." He moved and opened a bottle of wine. "What if we continue looking for centuries and find nothing? What if this is it, Ren?" He looked at Evren, who tensed and sighed loudly, closing his eyes.

"I just can't risk it for a mere tale with no real proof," he said, moving his fingers a little higher on Seraphine's leg.

Seraphine cleared her throat. "But if we don't risk it, we'll never win. There is a price for everything. That's why we deal and trick. We risk what we have for something greater."

"Or worse," Evren said.

She peered up at him and pinched his side, which was a bad move since he moved his hand higher, and she almost dropped her glass of wine. "We'll never know if we never risk it, will we?"

He smiled at her and kissed her cheek. "Aren't you a smart and very convincing little creature, Crimson Eyes?"

"Oh, this is too cheesy," Theron muttered, turning around to avoid looking at them.

Theron seemed nice, but Seraphine noticed that he couldn't hold her gaze. Perhaps it was her eyes.

"Let's ask Dorah. If anyone knows a way into the Underworld, it's her. And if she agrees that there is no way out, then we can keep looking for clues," she said. This time, she put her hand on Evren's leg, a little too high, and he choked on his wine and coughed.

Raggart, who looked even smaller than before beside Theron, nodded. "That sounds fair."

"I can go with Seraphine and visit... Excuse me." He paused, looking confused. "Who are we visiting?"

"Theodorah Hollowspring," Evren pressed, an evil smile spreading on his mouth.

Theron tensed, his green eyes twisted. He seemed out of place as he moved his hand over his face. "Ren..."

Evren stopped him with his hand. "No, just go there with Seraphine and retrieve any valuable information about ways into the Underworld. Nothing more, Theron. Get over it."

This was the first time she heard Evren sounding so demanding, like a king giving orders. Theron slowly nodded, knowing his place in all this.

While there was something here she was unaware of, she moved out of her seat and kissed Evren's cheek. "Okay, let's get some answers then."

Theron and Seraphine walked outside the Mystweave Library toward the Shadowmarket. The moment was awkwardly silent.

"Do you find me strange?" Seraphine asked, internally cursing herself for not knowing when to keep quiet. Of course, he found her odd. All creatures found humans peculiar, and she wasn't sure she was human either.

Theron looked ahead, expressionless. "No."

Well, that was a sharp answer I could've gone without. Seraphine needed to focus on the plan. *One nightmare at a time.*

Theron cleared his throat. "I mean, not entirely in a bad way, Seiren."

"Seiren?"

He closed his eyes, and she swore that Theron seemed as if he was about to have a breakdown, as if he had said the worst thing in the world.

That name resonated with Seraphine, though, so it must mean something.

"Seraphine, sorry. It's quite a nerve-wracking day for me," he muttered.

It was indeed a nerve-wracking day. They either found answers, or they could be left with more questions and an endless pile of books. Still, Seraphine went back to the name. She had seen that name—it was on the list she had found in Evren's room.

"Seiren was his fiancée."

While the thought of her in the past caused tricky feelings inside her, like spiders crawling and webbing her alive, it now seemed to have the opposite effect. Seraphine felt bad for Evren's dead fiancée. She never got to live a life with him, see the world, or enjoy the dance of the snowflakes during winter.

Theron, massive and agile as he looked, stumbled at that. "How do you know? Did Evren mention something?" he asked, cautious.

"No, I saw her name on a note, and I connected the dots. I mean, you could have just denied it. But I guess you fell for it. Hence, you told me, but no worries, I won't say a word to Evren if you behave." Theron's eyes widened, and she smiled sweetly. "And you must have known her. I guess that your surprised face after mentioning that name was because of that," she said and continued walking.

While Seraphine would like to know more about the topic, the closer they got to Dorah's shop, the more she felt nervous. She wasn't sure she would feel relieved if there was a way into the Underworld.

"Ah, I thought—" Theron moved his hand, looking somehow relieved. "Never mind. Yes, I knew her and—"

She cut him off. "Do not bother. I'd rather have no details. Right now, I need to focus on whatever Dorah might tell us."

She heard a bellowing laugh, loud and almost cracking to the core.

Seraphine arched a brow at Theron. "Why in Brannon's realm are you laughing?"

"Dorah?" He sounded amused and shocked at the same time, his freckles as diverse as his expressions. "You are indeed her friend. How... convenient." Then, his green spring eyes turned cold and hard.

"Sounds like you know her, and you dislike her quite a bit. That is very shallow coming from creatures not based on vanity," Seraphine spat back. Hags were very respected among these parts.

Theron dismissed her comment, and they continued walking, reaching the door to Dorah's shop. Before going through the door, Theron faced her, his eyes shadowed and somehow hesitant. "I am not vain in any regard. Perhaps I should not tell you this, but I proposed to her centuries ago," he admitted, and Seraphine almost choked. High-house members marrying common creatures was unusual.

He sighed. "I do not dislike her. I just don't trust her." Before Seraphine could say anything else, the door opened, and Dorah stood before them. She looked even older, and that realization struck Seraphine. Theron was probably centuries old. Evren too.

Dorah's roses moved, and her eyes widened slightly. "Well, what an unpleasant visit. Weren't you supposed to be the smart one?" the hag said to Theron.

This would be a perfect time for Aurum or Nemera to appear and take my soul so I wouldn't have to be seated between two ex-lovers.

"I would rather eat a kelpie than have you in my presence," Dorah sneered at Theron. As soon as they entered the shop, he started touching potions and other oddities, which seemed to enrage Dorah, who threw a rock at his face.

This led to a heated discussion about how annoying they found each other.

Seraphine wondered if maybe the creatures from this realm were more human than they were told to believe.

"Oh, I am sure you would eat that. Actually, you would probably feast on a bunch of them, you little witch," he spat back, his eyes iridescent green. "You have done worse, which is why you are the way you are now, so do not even turn this into one of your jokes."

That seemed to hit a nerve with Dorah, her eyes narrowing as her sharp nails moved closer to him.

Seraphine pushed Theron behind her quickly. With one gloved hand, she pointed at Theron while looking at Dorah. "Pay no mind to this circus clown. He is only here as my escort. I needed someone strong. I am the brains here," Seraphine said, smiling at Dorah, who ended up laughing.

Theron muttered something she could not place, but it sounded quite frustrated. *Him being a jerk makes sense as to why he's so close to Evren.*

"What goods should I interest you in, Seren?" Dorah asked, moving closer to Seraphine. "Maybe some new gloves? Why are you—"

She smiled. "Another tale for another time, Dorah." She moved closer to her. "I need any information you can give me on possible entrances to the Underworld."

To Seraphine's surprise, Dorah smiled again, her sharp teeth coming alive. For the first time, the bizarre roses in her hair moved and smiled alongside her. "Ah, quite sensitive information. What are you willing to give for that?"

"Anything of value to you, just if the information you have actually leads us to something."

Theron declared, "I will pay the price, I—"

"There is nothing of value that you can give me, Theron," Dorah spat and moved to Seraphine once more, intrigued somehow, excited even. "I will give you a ticket to the Underworld, a map to a door." The hag's eyes dilated.

Seraphine could take whatever could help them, so she nodded, hiding her mixed emotions. There was a way to the Underworld, and this should feel like a win, but it tasted bittersweet.

"And what is the price? Name some options, and I will try to match them. Or we can play a deal's game or perhaps some shadow chess?" Seraphine knew this dance very well and was not afraid of whatever Dorah might ask.

Dorah took an oddly-shaped branch from her pocket. It was barely the size of her hand, and with a soft blow of her breath, it turned into a dazzling bracelet, gold with small rubies in the shape of hearts and butterflies. "I will tell you how to enter the Underworld, but you must wear this on your wrist. You won't be able to take it off," she said and opened a map of the Shadowmarket. "There are multiple ways to enter the Underworld, just like your precious library. You only need to find the portal to take you to the right place." She circled a tree near the Shadowmarket.

"Here," she continued, and Theron and Seraphine seemed skeptical. "Now, as soon as you get there, just take any of the ruby figures from the bracelet."

Seraphine looked at her curiously. "Wait, how did you get your hands on this bracelet? And why haven't you tried to go through the portal yourself? There must be valuable things you can get from the Underworld. What about how we know it's the right place? Or perhaps, telling us what is there—"

"That I shall not do. You asked for a way in. There it is. As for how I got the bracelet, it was a fair trade I did centuries ago. I did try to get to the Underworld, but it did not work for me."

Moving closer to Dorah, Theron intervened, "And how in the world are you so sure we will be allowed? This seems like a useless trick to gain something—"

"You need the right key to move across realms, you idiot," Dorah growled, turning to Seraphine. "Ever wonder why you, little human, are allowed to be here? Why was Evren able to cross just by being with you? The key is not just the bracelet. You need a realm jumper."

Seraphine caught her breath. "You think I am one?"

"Seren, I don't know why you were born with that trait. Perhaps something with your eyes? But if you can jump to the Otherworld, it may be worth trying to see if you are the second key needed to go to the Underworld. I am not certain, but this is all I can offer you."

"If this is not certain, then we won't—" Theron started, but Seraphine held his arm, stopping him.

"We can try, Theron," Seraphine said.

"So, will you wear it and get on your way, or would you rather find another way in?" Dorah asked, a smirk on her old face.

Theron sneered sarcastically, "How in the realms will we know it is the right place? Is there a sign like 'Welcome to the Underworld'?"

"You will know."

"Look, you hag, do not take us as—"

"Deal," Seraphine spoke before she could regret it. It was a risk, but she knew Dorah would never hurt her. *I trust Dorah.*

"Clever indeed," Dorah muttered, snapping the bracelet on Seraphine's wrist.

An electric push pressed on her wrist.

"Safe travels, Seren. Say hi to Aurum from me." With that, the hag winked and waved Seraphine and Theron away from the shop.

Chapter 34

The Playful Fox

Hidden within the realms, the gates to other lands lie veiled,
Once open to creatures of every kind,
Now sealed and concealed from most eyes.
Yet certain eyes may still find these doors.
Will they dare to cross into the unknown,
Or retreat to the familiar yet twisted dangers of the known?

Retrieved from *Golden Tales from the Otherworld*
by Galen Sorrowspring, Ch. 22, p. 93.

One Day Before the Incident

Evren Wraithwood

Seraphine and Theron came from Dorah's with information, and it seemed like they all had different ideas. Theron was against trying this out, and Raggart sided with Theron, suggesting they should check other sources.

"I have an idea," Seraphine said, looking at Raggart and Theron. "An idea I would like to discuss with Evren in my chambers, if that's okay with you both."

Oh, for the Ancients, this sounds like a problem.

They both nodded, and Seraphine moved quickly to their chambers. As soon as they were there, she muttered, "I have a theory." Her voice was filled with excitement and anticipation. Evren expected her to be mad, but she seemed smitten.

She gently pulled Evren down onto the bed, straddling him gracefully. Her dress slid up her thighs, revealing just enough to make his breath hitch. Now, Evren understood why she wanted to discuss this alone with him. She was using all her tools to move him to her side.

"Do you?" Evren rasped, wrapping his hands around her delicate waist and pulling her closer. She nodded and smiled mischievously.

"Would you like to know my theory, prince?" she purred, her voice sweet and melodic, as she brushed her gloved hand around her chest, fingers lingering near the delicate lace of her dress. "Let's make a deal," she said, her eyes locking onto his with a playful glint as she slowly played with the knot there.

Evren gulped. "What is it that you want?" He was captivated. The way her crimson eyes lit up and sparkled was enough to make him forget everything else.

"If you help me unlace this here—" she mentioned, pointing to the upper part of her dress that was tight and left nothing to the imagination. "I will tell you my theory."

Ah, this is all a trick.

However, it was one he would happily fall for.

So, he pulled the knot and unlaced her dress, the upper part falling and pooling at her waist. Her shoulders and neckline were exposed, the fabric no longer hiding her perfect form. When he moved his hand to caress her upper body, Seraphine playfully swatted his hand away.

"No, no. Let's make another deal," she teased, closing the distance between them. "I will tell you the theory and my plan, and if you agree with it, then…"

"Then?"

She licked her lips slowly, moving her head to whisper something in Evren's ear. He gripped the sheets tightly, struggling to maintain control. "You can have me."

"In what sense? You are quite the trickster," he said, caressing her cheek with his nose, inhaling her intoxicating scent.

Fearless as she was, she said, "All. You can have all of me and do as you please for tonight."

"Only tonight?" he asked, his voice a mere whisper.

She hummed and pulled away slightly while Evren fought to keep his eyes from drifting to her exposed skin. "Yes, you are right. I am being unfair to you," she muttered, looking him in the eyes with a smoldering gaze. "Tonight, tomorrow, in the morning, on the desk, in the library, in this bed, in every place, at every moment. For as long as I live and wherever you are. I am yours."

Evren's breathing hitched, and his heart beat so fast that he feared she might hear it. "Deal," he said, pulling her by the waist, his hand moving up and down near her waist, taunting her with feather-light touches. "Tell me your theory and plan, and I shall see if I wish to agree to your generous offer."

Seraphine sighed softly, biting her lip. *Ah, sweet torture.*

"The bracelet's rubies should trigger some kind of door, just like the blood we give to the nightsith roses," she explained, touching the bracelet. Six crafted rubies rested there.

Evren moved his hand down her waist toward her navel and below, making her gasp and move toward his hand without realizing it. This time, she gulped. "So, the bracelet can be used multiple times since just one ruby is enough to open the entrance."

He smiled. "You want us to go first and test it out, don't you? Before actually going." He moved his hand lower, and she whimpered. He loved how responsive she was in every sense.

Seraphine nodded. "Let's check if there is a door, and if there is, let's just leave and keep our research about the Underworld. We cannot go unprepared. I—" Evren touched a very sensitive part of her, and she closed her eyes. "I won't risk you or anyone without confirmation. There are still a lot of books in the forbidden section."

Evren hummed, his fingers gently exploring her while she moved to the rhythm of his hand. "Not sure if I should accept," he teased, knowing she wanted this just as much as he did.

She opened her eyes, her gaze locking onto his with an intensity that made his mind stutter. "What a shame that would be, prince." Slowly, she lowered her own hand, her fingers grazing over her breasts, sending a shiver down his spine. Seraphine continued her descent, tracing her fingertips along her abdomen, feeling the soft curve of her navel until she reached his hand.

With a wicked smile, she moved his hand away. "A shame for you, of course," she said, her voice filled with playful seduction. She then placed her own hand between her legs.

Evren's eyes widened as he watched her. Her fingers moved with a rhythm that made her back arch slightly. He could see every detail, the way her fingers glistened, the soft sounds of her pleasure. Her breath quickened, her moans growing louder as she continued.

For Nemera…

Then, she whispered his name.

"Deal," Evren said, and she smiled knowingly. At that, he pulled Seraphine onto her back and moved to undress her fully and himself.

The world was filled with kisses and touches. Evren kissed her tattoo that bonded them together, the constellations of beauty marks and counted each of them. When he kissed her below the navel, she breathed his name, and he kept whispering hers.

Everything was her, all was her, and she was his, and he—he had always been hers.

Evren kissed his way up, paying special attention to her, kissing her softly. Seraphine arched in a way that made him plan how it would be in the morning, the day after, and during their whole life. Moving together, their bodies were in perfect harmony, and the sensation was overwhelming. Her warmth enveloped him completely.

"You feel incredible, my undoing. You are perfectly made for me," he whispered, savoring every moment.

"Don't stop," she pleaded, her voice a sweet symphony. "Please, don't stop."

He had no intention of stopping. Evren moved with her steadily, their connection deepening with each tender movement. "You're perfect," he said, his lips brushing against her ear. "Absolutely perfect."

"Evren," she cried out, her body trembling.

He felt her tighten around him, her release approaching. "Come with me, Seraphine," he urged softly.

Her release came in a wave, her cries filling the room. Evren followed her into bliss, his own release coming over him as he held her close.

They stayed together, their bodies molded perfectly as one. Her gentle tremors sent shudders through his body, each wave echoing hers. Evren could feel every soft breath, every heartbeat, as they shared this intense, intimate moment.

As they began to come down from their high, Evren buried his face in her neck, breathing deeply. "You are delirium, Crimson Eyes," he said under his breath, pressing a kiss to her damp skin.

She smiled, her fingers gently tracing patterns on his back. "And you're mine," she replied softly, her voice filled with love and contentment.

"Why are you hiding?" Seiren said again, sitting in her usual spot in front of the waterfalls.

He moved slowly, his tail brushing across the bushes, his fur making a soft sound. Seiren looked at him as if he wasn't a wolf.

She looked at him, knowing he was so much more.

Seiren smirked. "Smelly, muddy wolf."

He barked in response.

She laughed, and her eyes lit up. "Oh, is a scary wolf like yourself afraid of a human like me?"

Moving closer to her, he wondered how unafraid she was. *How can a human be so absolutely enchanting and wicked?* Once in front of her, Evren felt her caressing his furred ears, giggling. "Want to hear a tale?

Evren hadn't dreamt about that in decades. He smiled at the tender memory of her.

Seiren.

Seraphine this time.

She was sleeping, her hair a messy halo on the pillow, looking peaceful. The soft rise and fall of her chest with each breath captivated him. Her long lashes cast delicate shadows on her cheeks, fluttering slightly as she dreamed. Evren could watch her for hours, painting her serene form bathed in the gentle morning light filtering through the curtains. He smiled even more after remembering last night. Seraphine moved, and he noticed she was still wearing gloves.

Evren frowned at that. Whatever connected Seraphine to the Underworld wasn't something she should feel the need to hide. He had promised her freedom, and seeing her in gloves felt like seeing her in cuffs. Hopefully, they would find a way to help her control it and rid her of those gloves.

He smiled at that thought and kissed her softly once again. She slowly opened her eyes and smiled at him almost timidly. "Ready for a second round?"

Evren chuckled and held her close. "Always."

There was a third and a fourth round too.

Seraphine Ashcroft

Seraphine stood in the middle of the library, wearing her new crimson cloak. It was late in the afternoon, and she was waiting for Evren. They had decided to try her plan. Theron, Evren, and she would go today to the place Dorah had marked on the map to see if there was indeed a way into the Underworld.

Safe and quick, she wanted to be back to continue her research in the forbidden section. *And on Evren.* There was so much to learn about him. She smiled at that thought and flushed immediately at the memory of last night and this morning.

"I hate lovebirds," Theron said beside her.

She giggled. "So, what happened between you and Dorah?"

"I fell in love with her centuries ago. She was the most beautiful aos sí."

"Well, sorry to break it to you, Theron, but she is a hag," Seraphine said.

He looked at her. "She was an aos sí, but..." Theron looked conflicted. "She did something unforgivable and paid the price with her beauty."

Seraphine was surprised by such a cruel punishment. "And she lost you."

He stayed quiet, and thankfully, Evren arrived in time. He was wearing a black cloak, his face fully hidden. She almost forgot that he was one of the most wanted beings in the realm. "Shall we?"

The group walked for about fifteen minutes until they reached a small forest near the edge of the Shadowmarket, the trees a beautiful blend of yellow and orange.

"She circled the whole thing here," Theron said, annoyed, uncertain of what they were looking for.

Evren wrapped his arm around Seraphine's neck, playfully tugging at her new red cloak while rolling his eyes at Theron.

"Do not be so human, Theron." Seraphine pinched him on his side, and he laughed. "No offense, love," he muttered in her ear.

What a dreamlike word.

She sighed softly and moved Evren's hand off her cloak. "Let's just check the area and see if we find anything out of the ordinary. It can't be that difficult to search this small garden."

They all agreed, each one taking a different route. It was indeed a very colorful forest, small enough that she could sometimes see flickers of Evren and Theron. There was no fear of getting lost here.

Seraphine took her time, marveling at the beauty of the place. The trees were pretty plain, unlike the talking trees near the Shadowmarket.

She hoped Dorah hadn't tricked her into this as revenge for wiping the floor with her while playing shadow chess a couple of days ago.

"*Crimson, Crimson Eyes, come and play, you better hide*," a light voice sang.

Seraphine's spine stiffened.

"*Crimson, Crimson Eyes, come and play, you better try.*"

This time, she followed the voice, which seemed to come from a cluster of trees.

"*Crimson, Crimson Eyes, come and play, you better pray.*"

Where is it coming from? She looked around, her eyes trying to focus on the trees or anything that might give some clue about the source of the song.

"*Crimson, Crimson Eyes, come and play, you better cry.*"

An icy feeling enveloped her as she continued walking. The air seemed colder, and she wrapped herself in the cloak. Then, Seraphine saw a very thin tree with almost no leaves hidden behind massive and wide bushes.

However, this was not a regular tree. The few leaves were crimson red and heart-shaped. It looked like a sentinel tree but fearsome. When she approached the tree, she noticed a face carved into it, unmoving, with a big hollow resembling a mouth with sharp teeth.

This has to be it. Seraphine was relieved that Dorah hadn't tricked them. She looked up and watched one of the leaves. It was crimson red and textured like silk. They just needed to test this out, return home, and continue their research. She turned around, ready to scream for Evren and Theron, but a voice stopped her.

"What an unexpected view. Weren't you dead?" A raspy and dark voice came from the shadow, and with it, a man appeared. His eyes were blue and gray, similar to the ones she had learned to adore, but instead of having white dots like snowflakes, they had dark dots like falling leaves. He was tall with raven-dark hair, dressed in fur, and menacing like a lion.

Like a king.

Seraphine knew who that was without a shadow of a doubt.

King Malvrek.

CHAPTER 35

THE VENGEFUL FOX

Pain wears many colors, blue and black,
Yet it shimmers in the white.
In life's journey, darkened shadows
Turn to a ghostly light.

The purest brightness fades to night,
Pain, sharp as a needle's sting,
Or sweet, like revenge's bite.

Retrieved from *Golden Tales from the Otherworld*
by Galen Sorrowspring, Ch. 33, p. 105.

Day of the Incident
Evren Wraithwood

Once he stumbled upon Evren, Theron muttered angrily, "I even turned into a hawk, but everything looks plain. This is a dead end, Ren."

Evren sighed, looking for Seraphine. "Why are you so moody, Theron? That is so unlike you." He peered behind some bushes, thinking it should be something obvious, but there they were, turning over rocks and hugging the trees as if they were playing hide and seek.

Theron huffed and kicked a tree. "It is painful to see her, Ren."

Ah, it's about Theodorah. Theron had fallen in love with her years ago and was lucky enough to have a supportive family. She was a creature from the Otherworld but far from what was expected for someone like him to fall in love with. Evren could relate to that. They had all been great friends, Theron and Theodorah, closer than most.

"Is it because of how she looks now or because of what she did back then?" Evren was curious. What Theodorah did was an impulsive act of jealousy that ended tragically for all of them, but she also gave him and Seraphine a chance after centuries of suffering.

Theron sighed, looking defeated. "Both? It's just that she could have done the right thing, and you too, Evren… Even if it hurts."

If she had done the right thing, if I hadn't asked for it, Seraphine wouldn't be here. However, she wouldn't have gone through that miserable endless loop of death and chaos she was still unaware of for centuries, either.

"And yes, it pains me to look at her and what she did to her," he finally said, and Evren could understand the mixed feelings.

"Maybe you should talk to her. I think she honestly cares about Seraphine this time. They've become friends, and—"

Screams echoed around them, and without hesitation, they ran toward the source. *Was it Seraphine?* He prayed to the ancients that it was just a mere banshee and not her.

"Here." Theron pulled Evren toward a cluster of trees. There was another scream, but he couldn't tell if it came from Seraphine.

They reached a tall, thin tree with crimson leaves. Before it, a Bánánach—gaunt and ghostly, its hollow eyes burning with malice and its twisted limbs ending in claws sharp enough to tear through shadows—covered Seraphine's mouth. Its very presence seemed to suck the warmth from the air, leaving a chill of fear in its wake. Beside her was Theodorah.

Theron was shocked. "What are you doing here, Theodorah?"

She smiled, but it seemed forced. Somehow, she looked younger. "Didn't you hear my screams?"

Evren tried to approach Seraphine, but the monster pulled out a dark knife. "I wouldn't do that if I were you, prince," a voice behind the tree said. After centuries of disdain and decades in the cold, Evren had thought nothing in this world could make him shiver with fear.

However, seeing Malvrek, his father, holding Seraphine in his grasp once again, made him drown in it.

"Ah, you seem quiet. Things have changed indeed," Malvrek said, stepping out from behind the tree. "Cuff her."

At his command, more guards appeared, dragging Theodorah forward and cuffing her wrists, pushing her to the ground. She hissed at Malvrek, "Monster."

Malvrek laughed. "Monster? If I am a monster, what are you, Theodorah? Once again, you fail to make the right decision out of vanity."

He crouched down and took Theodorah's face in his hand. "Wasn't that the deal? To regain your beauty in exchange for my son?"

As he spoke, Theodorah's features smoothed, her hair became glossy, adorned with colorful roses and leaves, and her eyes turned green again. She was back to her original form.

Theron stepped back as if he had been struck, and Evren couldn't find words. She had misled them again, and they had fallen for it once more.

"How could you, Theodorah?" Theron said, sounding hurt.

Theodorah managed to grab Evren. Guards came to pull her away, but she held her cuffed hands on his cloak. "Evren, listen to me. This was the only way. You must trust me this time," she pleaded.

"The only way? What? To have all of us killed?"

The guards dragged her down, but she pulled herself up. "To save her," she whispered lowly before she kicked the guards. Theron was frozen, like he was seeing a ghost. "Get Lyra's ring and find her again."

Evren summoned his familiars, who jumped onto some guards. "Find who again?" he demanded.

"Seraphine."

"What do you mean by—" Evren started, but a guard punched Theodorah in the head, knocking her out. His head was a swirl of thoughts and emotions, but he needed to focus on the most important thing: Seraphine's safety.

Evren's familiars were tearing guards apart, and Theron slowly blinked back into reality. Evren hoped he would turn into a hawk to escape this, but knowing him, he would not dare to leave Evren alone.

Evren turned to his father. "Let her go. She has no part in this," he said, pointing at Seraphine.

His father laughed. "Ah, but she does. I was surprised when I saw her. Seraphine, is it this time, sweetheart?" Malvrek said, holding Seraphine's face and smiling at her. "How delighted I was when my son killed you."

The monster holding Seraphine's mouth let her go. "What?" she asked, confused and dizzy, likely from being hit. Evren's rage rose.

Malvrek laughed harder. "Ah! What a twist of events. My son didn't tell you?" He looked at Evren. "You, my son, are quite the liar, even to this day," he said almost proudly, and Evren gritted his teeth.

Evren moved toward his father, ready to die fighting him rather than let him harm Seraphine. However, before he could move, he felt a slice on his back. Then, he saw Theron fall, blood on his back. Losing balance, he collapsed beside his friend.

Poison. Evren had been so focused on Seraphine that he missed that the guards encroached on them. *Of course, my father would stoop so low.*

"And so disrespectful," Malvrek continued. "Oh, did you know that my son killed you centuries ago because he wanted to marry you?" He laughed even harder. "What a miserable choice."

Seraphine stood up. "That is nonsense, you monster. *You* killed Seiren, not Evren," she snarled, looking for a way out.

Evren saw her removing her gloves while his father slowly pulled out a sword, a smile on his face. "You wish her to live a couple more minutes? Tell her. Let your lies be your undoing, son."

His father moved the sword closer to her, and Seraphine closed her eyes.

No, no, no.

Evren put a hand on the ground. "Seraphine..." he said, trying to push himself up. "You... He is not entirely lying... You were Seiren. You are... That was your first life."

Seraphine Ashcroft

Seraphine looked at Evren. He was hurt and bleeding. *It can't end like this.* She closed her eyes and tried to concentrate. The idea of killing sickened her, but she could not let anyone hurt him. Evren was hers.

However, time stopped, and her eyes fluttered open. "What do you mean by that?" she asked, her voice cracking. Confusion filled her head and heart. What he was saying was impossible, unbelievable. *It has to be a lie.*

However, the look on Evren's face and the way Theron shut his eyes, trying to avoid what was to come, froze her heart. Then, it all came back. *Evren's knowledge about me. The rooms, the dresses.*

Even after what they shared and what they promised, he had lied. Seraphine let herself be tricked again, be used again.

Evren's eyes blurred with tears. "I... when my father tricked me into killing you, Seiren... he turned you into a fox and asked me to hunt you to get his approval for our marriage," he uttered, his voice breaking. Then, a tear, white as snow, fell from his eyes. "Seraphine, I... did not know you were a fox, and I killed you. I—"

This isn't happening. Seraphine was her own person. She was not the one he had killed. All his desires and love had never been for Seraphine. They had been for a version of her, an obsession with what he wished she could be.

"I even tried to poison myself to end my life. That's why I knew about the frozen heart deal and poison elixirs," he said, crawling on the ground toward her.

Seraphine dropped to her knees, the ground having been swept from underneath her. At that moment, she could not help but ponder all those bizarre dreams, what the crimson woman had said, the signs. *The fear I felt in my dreams had been memories of my past.*

Malvrek looked at her with pity, disdain, and something akin to anger. "It was such an interesting death. What I never expected was to see you again. That I would like to know, son. Don't you want to know, Seraphine?"

She couldn't speak, her mind shattered.

"Crimson Eyes, listen to me. I... was so heartbroken that I asked Theodorah to help me before I was kicked out of the Otherworld when the veil was created. Her mother was a powerful hag, so she had that same type of magic in her. I asked her to bring you back, and—" Evren broke, yet she held his head in her trembling hands. She needed to hear everything. *I want the truth.*

"Keep going, Evren," she muttered in his ear, and he shivered. She did, too, because he was the most dangerous being in the realm. Evren was a wolf, a hunter, her killer. For the first time, she feared him—what he had become and how he manipulated everything for his sake.

Another snow-like tear fell on the ground. "Theodorah hated you centuries ago. I didn't know why, but she did. Yet, she promised to bring you back, and when I was sentenced to the human realm, I had no hopes of seeing you again. Years passed, and I wandered alone in the human realm. But then I saw you! Seraphine, I saw you, a version of you." He cried so hard that she almost felt pity for him. However, pity did not mean much to her anymore. "And I thought I would have my happy ending, but it wasn't like that. You died on your 26th birthday."

Theron, barely breathing, whispered, his hand signaling Theodorah's body, which lay unmoving on the ground, "Theodorah brought you back, Seraphine, but as a curse, a loophole with no end. You will be reborn, your soul never to move on, and you will die on the same day, at the same age."

She could barely breathe, but Evren continued, "I watched you die again and again, sickness, killed, all of them terrible deaths. And yes, every time, you were born in different circumstances, in different places, and in different families. I sometimes could tell you the truth, but in most cases, it was too late. But I always found you and... I tried to figure out a solution, but I was limited to the human realm and poor deals," he said.

Seraphine remembered the list with the names, her names, all her lifetimes, all the times she had lived and died.

She closed her eyes, and a tear fell. The pain Evren had endured after watching her die so many times must've been tremendous, unimaginable. *How much pain have I been enduring for a selfish wish?* He should have let her die. "It is okay," she muttered, moving his raven hair out of his face, taking one last look at him and picturing it on an eternal canvas in her head.

Evren managed to pull his arm up and hold her face. "I... I decided to give a chance to a new plan, to make your life so miserable, to break your heart and world so you could ask me for the frozen heart deal just minutes before your 26th birthday. I did it because I couldn't see you die again, and I wasn't sure it would work, but it did!" He smiled softly, caressing her cheek. "You lived. Your life clock stopped just before the cursed day, and that way, I found a loophole for you. If I had my full essence, I could—"

Seraphine was pulled toward the tree while Evren fell to the ground, guards cuffing him and dragging him far from her.

Malvrek looked at his son in a way that Seraphine could only describe as watching an insect being toyed with for amusement.

"You are a monster," Seraphine said.

"Ah, but so are you, my dear." He motioned to his guards, who carried Evren and Theron away.

Evren kept muttering things, but he seemed to be in a daze. She heard those three words she loved so much, and another tear fell down her cheek, crimson red like her eyes. *Those three words are meant for a memory of what he wanted me to be... not for me.*

"Well, this was certainly fun. Now, I will have the pleasure to kill you. Or torture you. Tell me, Seiren, what do you prefer?" The king said in her ear, and she turned her head, disgusted.

You're going to regret this.

"Seraphine," she sneered at him.

Malvrek looked torn, his smile turning rotten. "What?"

She took a breath. "I am *Seraphine*, not Seiren. Seraphine Ashcroft, you sad excuse of a king." *Remember that name. Remember the name that will one day lead you to your doom.*

At that, she spat at his shoes, and Malvrek slammed her head against the tree. Pain erupted through her, but she stayed on her feet while the king paced between creatures, barking orders, perhaps assuming Seraphine wasn't much of a threat.

"Seren," Dorah muttered from the ground, looking dazzling, even covered in dirt. Seraphine had forgotten she was there—actually, she had forgotten about her the moment Dorah betrayed her. "Take out a ruby."

Seraphine looked toward her wrist at the bracelet. She huffed at Dorah, "I am not naive enough to trust you ever again. You are not my friend. All of this is because of you. You could have let me know."

Dorah flinched. "Please, Seren, this was the only way. They would have killed you and him one way or another. There is so much you do not know, the things I regret. In the past, I…" She gulped and then choked on purple blood from her mouth, her eyes sad. "Please, for once, just... trust me this one time."

Malvrek kicked her. "Wicked monster. Take her too. Alive," he muttered. Seraphine marveled at the chaos—crimson everywhere. Beyond that, she realized she no longer wanted to be the fox of the story. She wasn't a wolf either. She could be something far greater. A smile crept across her face, her mouth dripping crimson, highlighting the devilish gleam in her crimson eyes.

I am tired of it all.

So, she took a leap of faith. Seraphine stepped back slowly, gripping the crimson tree. She watched as heart-shaped leaves fell around her, covering her—guarding her. Near the center of the tree's trunk, she noticed an unusual hole.

No more nightmares.

No more chances.

No more feelings.

"Come, try to kill me. You didn't have the guts the first time," she said to Malvrek, her eyes bright as a rose and sharp as a ruby dagger. She felt the tree moving behind her, and a buzz traversed her.

However, before she could see Malvrek's reaction, she used her nails to pull out a single ruby from the bracelet on her wrist. Guided by instinct, magic, or perhaps something else, she placed it in the hole in the tree that resembled a mouth. Then, she smiled. Somehow, she could feel the tree smiling back at her.

Looking back at the chaos, her smile widened, full of promises and things to come. She might be on a leash with Evren now, but not for too long.

I will see you all drown in fear.

Malvrek stepped back, something akin to fear on his face, as he looked at the tree behind her, which seemed to grow and expand. Its branches were breaking and morphing, a rain of crimson around them.

Moving her hair out of her face, Seraphine winked at him and turned around to the tree, giving her back to the king, the chaos, her heart, and the sweet memories.

The hole in the tree widened, the wood twisting into the shape of fangs. It resembled a massive, gaping mouth, larger than her, filled with the potent scent of roses. This time, she didn't close her eyes, didn't hold her breath, didn't pray for the nightmare to end. This time, she knew the nightmare had just begun—and it was *her*. Seraphine smirked as the tree swallowed her whole.

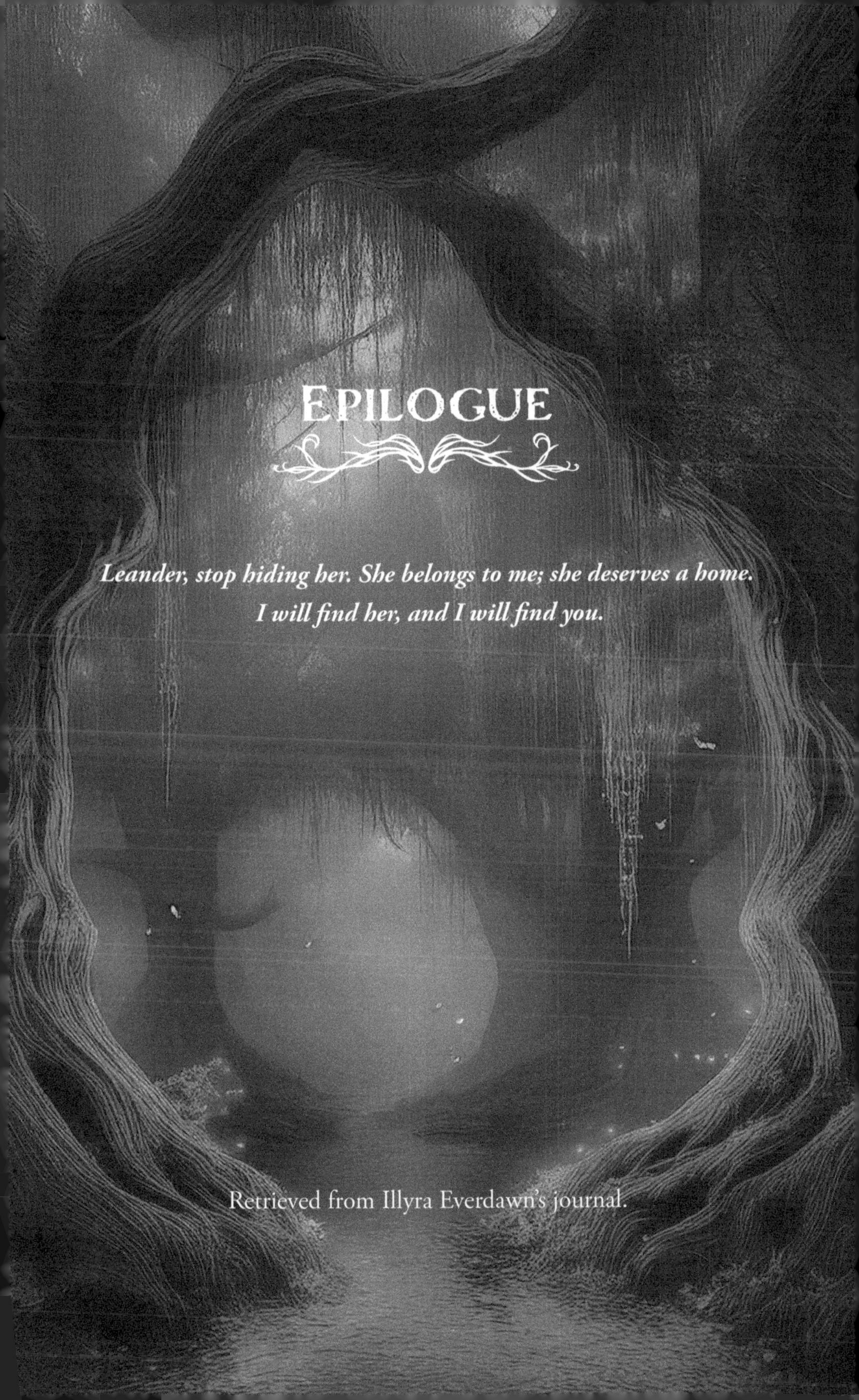

EPILOGUE

Leander, stop hiding her. She belongs to me; she deserves a home. I will find her, and I will find you.

Retrieved from Illyra Everdawn's journal.

Seraphine Ashcroft

Seraphine wasn't sure how much time had passed, but when she opened her eyes, she saw flowers.

Black and red roses cushioned her body, their petals glistening like crimson tears in the dim light. The sky above was a canvas of dark velvet, pierced by a crimson moon that cast a haunting glow over everything. Stars, also tinged red, sparkled like blood droplets suspended in the night.

"I told you that you were making a mistake, Seren," a voice she recognized said. She might've hated the voice, but she would use him anyway.

"Where am I?" she asked, her voice wary, looking at Maxwell Everheart's familiar face as he emerged from the shadows. His eyes, the same shade of crimson as hers, held a glint of amusement. A smile tugged at his lips as he extended his hand toward her.

"Home," he said. She remembered the dreams about being told to come back home. *I guess I am home for now.*

Seraphine smiled sweetly at him, but if she needed to fake it to get what she needed, she would drown in sweetness and naivety.

Taking his hand, she felt an unexpected warmth in his touch. As she stood up, the scent of the roses filled her senses, intoxicating and sweet. Seraphine batted her eyes at Max and pulled him close, whispering purposefully, "Then, let's have fun, shall we?"

Crimson Memories

"Would you?" Evren asked her as they played around in the waterfalls.

"Of course, I would," Seiren said, laughing, and he had never heard something so beautiful.

"You must like me very much," he muttered, watching her enter the waterfalls, a glint in her eyes.

"I do. Even if I am gone, and you are still here, I would rather be born again as a butterfly so I could find a way back to you. Oh, or perhaps a rose so that you can find me." Those words filled his heart with so much emotion.

Nearing her, Evren took her face in his hands. "I would gladly find you. I'll look at every butterfly, every rose, every leaf for you."

Seiren smiled at him, diving deeper into the waterfalls. "Even if I am a thorned rose?"

He nodded. "Thorned, but I bet you'd be the crimsonest and brightest rose in all the realms. All so that I can find you."

END OF THE CRIMSON SNOW

The end is only the beginning. Prepare to plunge into the shadowed crimson waters, where roses bloom in the depths of the Underworld. In 2025, the territory of Crimsonland will claim your heart—and the Crimson Grim Hunter will haunt your soul.

Acknowledgements

There are countless things I could say about this journey, but first and foremost, I must thank the books. The stories that carried me when I was lost, the tales that whispered promises of faraway worlds and adventures, and the endings that stretched beyond my wildest dreams—thank you for being my constant companions. Through the hardest moments of this year, when the weight of it all nearly broke me, these stories helped me rise, and from that brokenness, *The Crimson Snow* was born. It came from my heart, and I can only hope it will one day touch another heart, leaving behind a glimmer of magic.

To my incredible readers, my ARC team, and my street team—you are the stars in the night sky that guided me through the darkest roads. Your belief in this story kept me going when the path seemed impossible. I am endlessly grateful to each of you. In return, I hope to fill your lives with the same magic, wonder, and adventure you've given me. This journey is ours, and I look forward to many more chapters with you by my side.

To my parents, my greatest champions, the ones who first saw the spark in me. You watched as I scribbled songs and stories, your smiles encouraging me when I doubted myself. You gave me my first journal, where the worlds in my mind began to take shape. Thank you for enduring countless nights of listening to me dream aloud about this book. Your unwavering support has been my haven, and this story is as much yours as it is mine.

To Ross, Cami, Sofi, Juli, and Santi—my pillars of strength from the beginning. Cami, you are the closest thing I have to a sister, and this book is for you. Sometimes, the greatest adventures are those filled with the discovery of ourselves. I hope we continue to share our stories through every twist and turn of life.

Lastly, to Seraphine and the Grim Wanderer—yes, I'm thanking my characters! Thank you for letting me tell your story, for leading me through the snow-filled paths of your worlds, and for healing me in ways I never expected. You've given me a gift beyond words. With all its heartaches and triumphs, this journey was worth every moment because of you.

What's to Come

The Crimson Snow is merely the beginning—a single snowflake in the storm about to unfold. For me, this is the gateway to a far greater world, a realm where magic and darkness intertwine and where the line between life and the Underworld blurs. Seraphine's journey is far from over. Prepare to follow her into the depths of the Underworld, where the cold bites deeper and the stakes grow higher. The shadows are stirring, and what lies beneath the surface is more dangerous—and more beautiful—than you can imagine.

As I weave the magic of the second book, I'm eager to hear your thoughts, for your love and support have been the wind beneath my wings. You, my readers, are the reason this world feels so alive, so full of enchantment. While I work on the spells of book two... and perhaps even book three... let's continue this adventure together. The best is yet to come, and I promise, what's waiting in the shadows will be worth the wait.

About the Author

Laura Vega, a passionate storyteller and cat mom of three, has always been captivated by dark fantasy and poetic fiction. Her latest novel, *The Crimson Snow*, takes readers on a mesmerizing journey through Coldhaven, where magic and mystery intertwine. When she's not crafting tales, Laura loves connecting with her readers and sharing bookish adventures.

Check out more about Laura and her books on Goodreads.

Discover *The Crimson Snow* on Goodreads and Amazon.

Milton Keynes UK
Ingram Content Group UK Ltd.
UKHW040829091224
3516UKWH00031B/203

9 789695 692493